YOU CAN
TRUST ME

ALSO BY SOPHIE McKENZIE

Close My Eyes

YOU CAN TRUST ME

SOPHIE McKENZIE

St. Martin's Press
New York

YOU CAN TRUST ME. Copyright © 2014 by Rosefire Ltd. All rights reserved.
Printed in the United States of America. For information, address St. Martin's
Press, 175 Fifth Avenue, New York, N.Y. 10010.

www.stmartins.com

Designed by Omar Chapa

Library of Congress Cataloging-in-Publication Data

McKenzie, Sophie.
    You can trust me : a novel / Sophie McKenzie. — First U.S. edition.
        pages ; cm
    ISBN 978-1-250-03399-4 (hardcover)
    ISBN 978-1-250-03398-7 (e-book)
    I. Title.
    PR6113.C4874Y68 2015
    823'.92—dc23

                                                    2014040747

St. Martin's Press books may be purchased for educational, business,
or promotional use. For information on bulk purchases, please contact the
Macmillan Corporate and Premium Sales Department at 1-800-221-7945,
extension 5442, or write to specialmarkets@macmillan.com.

First Edition: April 2015

10 9 8 7 6 5 4 3 2 1

For Roger, Dana, and Alex—with much love

ACKNOWLEDGMENTS

With grateful thanks to Jessica McCarthy and Philippa Makepeace, who brought Devon to life for me. Also to my editors—Maxine Hitchcock at Simon & Schuster in London and Jennifer Weis at St. Martin's Press in New York—for their invaluable insights and advice.

YOU CAN TRUST ME

It's an impossible choice. How am I supposed to make it?

I think back over the past few weeks and everything that has happened to bring me to this point.

It doesn't matter. *None* of it matters now.

All that counts is this choice.

This impossible choice.

CHAPTER ONE

One month earlier . . .

The text arrives as I'm getting out of the car. I'm so anxious about the evening ahead that I barely register the beep. The setting sun is casting soft swirls of pink and orange across the Exeter skyline, thinning and sharpening the tops of the cathedral towers. The air is warm but I'm shivering, my heart beating hard and loud against my ribs. Will throws me a worried glance. I pull my phone from my bag, wondering vaguely if the text is from the babysitter. But it's Julia's name that flashes up. For a second my anxiety eases a little. Whatever my closest friend has written is sure to be an offering of support, expressed in Julia's customary style: big and bold and full of feeling. But when I open it, the text is short and terse.

PLS CALL, I NEED TO TALK TO YOU.

I know it's an overreaction, but I can't help feeling hurt. Julia knows I'm dreading this dinner. She knows what I'm facing. Or, rather, whom. And yet her text is all about *her.*

Maybe I shouldn't be surprised. Julia has always been a bit self-obsessed. But still, it's not like her to forget about tonight. I close the text. I don't have the time or the inclination to reply right now.

Will puts his arm around my shoulders as we cross the road to the house Leo and Martha moved to just a few months ago. It's a new construction, a sleek white cube that contrasts with the brick town houses on either side.

"Impressive, isn't it?" Will says. He sounds tense. I shoot him a

3

swift glance. The signs of his own nervousness are there in the slight clench of his jaw and the tightness around his eyes. Good. I'm glad he feels anxious too. So he bloody should.

The house is, frankly, amazing. Designed to within an inch of its life and perfectly reflecting the aspirations of Leo Harbury, Will's boss. The door opens as we approach. A young man in a tux with a tray of champagne flutes stands in front of us. I smile and he smiles back.

"Will and Livy Jackson," Will says.

"Please come in." The young man steps back to allow us inside. "Leo and Martha are through there." He points across the hall to a door on the left. "Bathroom and cloakroom to your right."

I follow Will to the door on the left. My heels tap noisily on the mosaic tiles. The décor in the hall is stylish and simple. If the house, with its show of money, reflects Leo Harbury's ebullient personality, then the plain white walls and tasteful furnishings are a testament to the restraining influences of his wife. I catch sight of myself in the gilt-framed mirror on the wall. I went to the hairdresser today, but I should have gone yesterday; my hair, carefully blow-dried into a feathery pale brown bob, looks too "done." I might as well be carrying a sign saying WOMAN MAKING AN EFFORT. I smile again, in spite of myself, at this Julia-ism and turn slightly, checking out my Hobbs cocktail dress. It's nice enough, but it looks like what it is: a High Street purchase rather than a designer one. Normally this wouldn't even occur to me. Leo and Martha Harbury are not snobs, and though Martha is bound to be dressed to the nines in something floaty and elegant she will also say how nice I look, with one of her warm smiles. I tell myself to get a grip. It's too late now to do anything about what I'm wearing.

Will is watching me, chewing on his lip. Despite the gray hair at his temples, he looks young—younger than I, though in fact he's two years older—and handsome in his dark suit. I finger the platinum necklace he gave me last year for our thirteenth wedding anniversary. It feels hot against my skin, though the air in the hallway is still and cool.

Will and I reach the door on the left. Sounds of the party float toward us: the low hum of chatter, the dip and soar of violins in the background music, the clink of glasses.

"You okay, Liv?" Will asks.

I nod, though both of us know it's a lie. Will takes my hand but I pull it away. Which probably isn't fair. Will feels terrible that we are here, under these circumstances.

It's still his fault.

"I'm sorry," he starts, but I hold up my hand. I don't want to hear any more apologies. Especially not tonight.

I've had six years of apologies. None of them turned back the clock. None of them took away the pain.

And none of them is going to prevent me from having to meet Catrina in the next few minutes.

"Tell me how many people are going to be here again?" I say. My voice sounds strained to my ears.

"Twenty or so, I think." Will makes a face. "Paul and Becky, of course, other people from the office, plus a few clients and agents we're working with in Switzerland and Germany, their partners, maybe some people from the States. . . ." He trails off.

Catrina's unspoken name fills the space between us. I wipe my clammy palms down my dress. Leo and Martha's "kitchen supper for friends and colleagues" is an annual event, though this is our first visit to their new house. Of course, "kitchen suppers" is a misnomer that fails to hint at the style and formality of the actual events. Leo is a successful businessman who started his media and marketing company thirty years ago and has built it into a big, local success story.

"Ready?" Will reaches out for the door handle.

My phone rings. I fumble to retrieve it from my bag. The name on the screen is JULIA.

"Who's that?" Will asks.

"Just Julia." I switch the call off, then my entire phone. If there's a problem at home, the babysitter can call Will. I can't deal with Julia. Not now, anyway. I can't even think straight. I glance sideways

5

at Will again. He looks terrified, his hand still on the doorknob. With a miserable stab of jealousy, I wonder how he's feeling about seeing Catrina again. She worked with Will briefly, before being sent to Paris to direct Leo's French operation. I try to recall the girl from the picture on the Harbury Media Web site: a delicate-featured blonde with a snub nose, perfect makeup, and a seductive smile. Or did I imagine the smile?

"Liv?" Will is looking at me. Someone inside the room beyond laughs. "I'm so sorry about this," he whispers.

I nod without looking at him directly. I want to turn around and shout at him that sorry isn't any good. It won't give me the absence of fear, the peace of mind I want. He and Catrina took those things away from me six years ago with their months of stolen afternoons. Will was infatuated with her. He always denied it was love, but I could see the obsession in his eyes. And back then, I hated her with a raw fury—for blundering into my marriage, for risking my family life, for threatening to tear to pieces the fabric that held up my children's world.

I've never hated anyone so much in my life.

Well, maybe one other person.

Will leans across and kisses my cheek. "You look beautiful."

I shake my head. It's not that I think he's deliberately lying, but after nearly fourteen years of marriage, you kind of stop seeing each other, so I can't help but think he's overcompensating, trying to be nice. Anyway, whatever he's trying to do, it's too late. Flattery won't get either of us through tonight.

"You do," Will insists, smoothing away a stray strand of hair from my cheek.

"Come on."

With a nod, Will reaches out again and opens the door. The room beyond is full of people, but I can still see that it's as beautifully designed as the rest of the house: with a cluster of leather couches, some funky low tables, and simple cream curtains at the windows. Pieces of modern art are dotted around the walls. Will holds my hand as we walk across the room. I'm all eyes, looking everywhere for Catrina.

The room is full of people, surely more than the twenty or so Will suggested would be here. I can see Leo by the window, holding court. He strides over to the drinks table, still speaking, with that classic swagger of his. I look around the room. No sign of any blondes, at least none under fifty.

I look up at Will, my eyebrows raised. He shakes his head.

I blow out my breath. Catrina isn't here. Yet.

A couple standing nearby advances toward us, bright smiles on their faces. They look about the same age as Leo and Martha, early sixties.

"Good to see you, Will. Last time was that conference in Basel, wasn't it?" The man has a Texas accent. He shakes Will's hand enthusiastically, then turns to me to introduce his wife.

She continues to smile as Will introduces me back. She is wearing what can only be described as a gown—it's pink and trails in soft, silk folds onto the floor. I look down at my cocktail dress, a black knee-length sheath with a lacy overlay. I can't decide whether it's too young for me or too unstructured for my figure. I've put on twelve pounds since Zack was born.

Will and the two Texans are deep in conversation now. Another young man in a tux comes by with a tray of drinks. I take a glass of white wine. It's delicious, dry, and smooth, with a distinct hint of gooseberry. The small talk around me continues. I smile and nod, though I'm not listening. All I can think about is Catrina. She's younger than I am and doesn't have children, as far as I know. I'm certain she will be sexy and skinny—as well as successful. She's been based in Paris for almost six years now, and is still Harbury Media's youngest-ever director. When I told Julia that a few days ago, she'd rolled her eyes. "Brace yourself, Liv," she'd said. "Worst-case scenario—she's picked up a wardrobe of French couture, a grooming regime to die for, and a Parisian sneer."

Thinking of Julia, I'm half-inclined to make my excuses and slip out to the bathroom to return her call after all—I don't care, right now, that she's maybe been a bit selfish tonight; I need to talk to my best friend—but before I can utter a word, Martha and Leo are here.

Leo beams and pumps Will's hand, giving him a mighty slap on the back.

"Good to see you, sir," he says in that mock posh accent he often affects in public situations. Both Martha and Will insist that Leo is privately a lot less confident than he appears in company, but he always manages to unsettle me. There's something overbearing about his presence, something unnerving about his piercing gaze. "How's the promotion sitting with you?"

This is a reference to the fact that Leo recently added deputy managing director to Will's job as planning director. It's a recognition of Will's talent and his hard work, and brings with it a little more money and a lot more stress.

"It's sitting very nicely, thanks," Will says with a slight blush.

Leo winks at me, his gaze straying briefly to the neckline of my dress. I fidget from side to side. It's not that I think Leo is perving after me; he's never even flirted openly. But there's a restless quality about him—you never quite know *what* he's thinking.

"Livy." Martha draws me toward her, planting a soft kiss on my cheek. "You look lovely. How are the kids?"

I smile, grateful for her warmth, all thoughts of calling Julia quickly forgotten. Martha never fails to ask after Hannah and Zack. She is childless herself and often says with a lighthearted smile that if she'd had a daughter, she'd have wanted her to be like me.

"The kids are good," I say. "Hannah's getting all hormonal, but Zack's still Zack. Your new place is lovely, by the way."

"Glad you like it." Martha says. A frown creases her forehead. "But Hannah surely can't be that old," she says.

"Afraid so. She'll be thirteen in October." I fish Will's phone out of his pocket and show Martha the screen saver: a photo of Hannah and Zack looking suntanned in shorts and T-shirts from our Easter holiday in Spain. As Martha coos with an almost grandmotherly pride over the children, Paul and Becky wander up. It's good to see them, not just because we haven't hooked up in ages, but also because of our long-standing connection.

Paul and I met studying History at university, though we didn't really become good friends until after uni, when Paul took a job at Harbury Media and introduced me to Will, who already worked there. Paul met Becky soon after that, and for a while, the four of us spent a lot of time socializing together.

"Zack looks so cute," Becky gushes. "Just adorable."

I smile once more, resisting the temptation to launch into an anecdote. Paul and Becky don't have kids, and I'm painfully aware that their interest, unlike Martha's genuine delight in my children, stretches only so far. As if to prove my point, Becky turns away from the phone and whispers something in Paul's ear.

I watch them. They are both aging well: Paul all slim and suited with slicked-back hair, and Becky elegant in a blue cocktail dress. I've known Paul such a long time that I often forget Leo is his dad—a product of Leo's first, never-talked-about marriage. It must be weird, working for your own father, but Paul seems happy enough.

I hand Will back his phone. A moment later, Leo steers him away to talk to Werner Heine, a client from Germany.

I catch Martha's eye.

She offers another smile, this one resigned. "They never stop working, do they?"

I smile ruefully back. Paul and Becky are still chatting away to each other, not listening to us.

Martha moves closer to me, lowering her voice. "I'm so sorry about Catrina," she says. "Leo invited her without thinking—then it was too late. I found out only a few days ago." She rolls her eyes. "Men, honestly."

I nod, my face burning. So she knows. I've never talked about the affair with Martha—or with anyone aside from Julia. I know Martha is just being her usual, kind self, but it's hard not to feel humiliated.

Martha squeezes my shoulder, clearly concerned. Embarrassed, I glance around the room again. A lot of the people here work in Leo's office with him and Will. How many of *them* know? Will told me he'd never said anything to anyone at work about his affair. I guess I was stupid to think that meant no one had noticed. Or that gossip wouldn't start and spread.

"I love what you've done with this room," Becky says to Martha, who gives my shoulder another squeeze, then falls back into hostess mode.

As Martha and Becky begin a detailed conversation about Farrow & Ball color choices, Paul catches my eye. Unlike Leo, he has a long, narrow face with no trace of his father's square, fleshy features except perhaps around the mouth.

"How are you, Livy?" he asks.

"Fine," I lie.

"Did I hear you saying Hannah's getting all 'moody teenager'?"

Encouraged by his interest, I dive into my latest story about Hannah requesting a leg-waxing appointment "when she hasn't even started her period." Paul looks slightly embarrassed at this mention, and I silently rebuke myself. He's always been a tad fastidious. I remember him very politely insisting that Hannah's diaper should be placed directly in their outside trash can on our first visit after she was born. The request was fair enough, of course, but it kind of signaled the start of our mutual retreat from the friendship the four of us had enjoyed up until then. Over the past few years, our visits to each other's homes have dwindled, though we still meet every few months for dinner or drinks out in Exeter.

Becky joins in the conversation again as Paul explains how they're having their house—a rambling Victorian mansion in Topsham—remodeled over the summer. Becky is a maths teacher at the local private school, petite and strikingly attractive, with a mane of glossy dark hair swept up in an elaborate bun and eyes as dark and sparkly as her husband's. Paul, of course, works for Harbury Media, though as the company's account director with special responsibility for digital marketing, he is one step lower down the pecking order than Will. Paul has a charming line in self-deprecation, stopping short of false modesty but insisting that his work, though challenging, is dull and that his wife is the one with the brains. On this occasion he is complimenting Becky on her understanding of the structural work being done to their house.

"She totally keeps the builders on their toes, he says, looking at his wife admiringly. "Brains *and* beauty."

She blushes and kisses him on the cheek. Instinctively, I glance around for Will. Paul and Becky got married the same year as Will and I did, though they seem blissfully happy, while Will and I managed only seven years before his affair. We've almost been married as many years since, but the second half has been harder. Right now it's hard not to feel envious of a couple who are so obviously still in love.

I ask Becky whether she's looking forward to the end of term, coming up in the next couple of weeks, and the planned renovations to her and Paul's house.

"God, yes," she says, "but mainly because we're moving out and letting the builders get on with it until September."

"Where are you going to stay?" My eyes flit across the room to where Will is chatting with some of his work colleagues. I don't know all the women in the group he's talking to, but I'm certain none of them is Catrina.

Becky launches into a description of her parents' place in Spain, where she is heading the day after term ends.

"Of course I'll miss Paul," she says, giving her husband an affectionate smile.

"And I'll miss you." Paul turns to me and grimaces. "Thanks to work, I won't be able to join her for ages"

"Over a month." Becky kisses his cheek. "Aw, sweetie."

I stare at them, trying to dispel the envy I'm feeling at the ease of their intimacy. Even in the good days, Will and I were never one of those couples who finish each other's sentences.

"So where will you stay before you fly out to Becky?" I ask Paul.

"One of my mum's places," Paul explains. "She owns a few houses in the area."

I nod. I know very little about Paul's mother. As a teenager, he had a falling out with her—and with his stepfather, whom he'd loathed.

I'm aware they're in touch, but it's obvious Paul isn't close to his mum, even now. Neither Leo nor Martha ever mention her, though I do know that Leo's marriage to his first wife ended when Paul was very young, long before meeting Martha. Paul has never seemed bitter about that, maintaining with a wry smile that if he'd been married to his mother, he'd have left her too.

We carry on talking and drinking for a few more minutes. Leo and Martha's cat, Snowflake, a beautiful white Persian with blue eyes, stalks by, drawing many admiring glances. Will comes over and he and Paul start chatting about motorbikes, the shared passion that sparked their original friendship. Paul has, apparently, just bought a new Ducati. Will's eyes widen as Paul tells him the exact model. I know he would love a bike himself. Will sold his last motorcycle when Hannah was a baby so that we could buy a new car, and his own bike-riding days are now long behind him.

Becky is still talking about Spain—Andalucía, to be precise—and the hikes she and Paul enjoyed on their last holiday there. By now, there's a fixed smile on my face. It's not just the display of wedded bliss I'm having to witness, that's making me feel uncomfortable but also the fact that I'm all too aware Catrina will be here soon. If she isn't already.

After a few more moments, Martha says she has to check on the food and slides away to the kitchen. Becky follows her. Paul and Will are still talking about bikes. so I gaze around the room. This is hell. My glass is empty. I've knocked it back far too fast. The waiter wanders over with another tray of wine and champagne. I take a drink and press the cool, damp glass against my cheek as Leo strolls over.

"Hey, Dad." Paul gives his father a pat on the back. "Good party—the clients are loving it.

Leo acknowledges the compliment with a small smile. I notice—not for the first time—that Will shrinks into himself a little in his boss's presence, as if attempting to adopt a more deferential air. I wonder if Leo realizes that.

Another few minutes pass. More guests arrive. I find my eyes constantly drawn to the door, watching and waiting. Leo spots me looking and touches my arm. There's nothing inappropriate about his touch, yet his hand feels too heavy on my skin.

"We really appreciate you coming, Livy," he says in an uncharacteristically gentle voice.

I can feel my cheeks reddening. He knows about Catrina too. I glance around. Paul is watching me while listening to Will describe some classic motorbike he saw yesterday. Does he know as well? Does Becky?

For a few sickening moments, I wonder how *much* they know. Catrina had been working in the office for a while. Probably all the guys fancied her. Probably Will thought he was the luckiest man in the firm when their eyes met over the photocopier or however the whole sleazy business began.

Leo's hand is still on my arm. I shift slightly away from him and he removes it at last. As he turns to Paul, I close my eyes, remembering the days of obsessive worrying and imagining. How did it start? How many times? How good was the sex? When and how and where was I lied to?

And through all the fights that followed the confession I forced from my husband's lips: Will's terror that I would leave him. His insistence that it had been a moment of madness—well, two months of moments. That I was the love of his life. That our home and our children and our life together were his whole world.

I forgave him—and I tried to forget. But over the past six years, the memory of the affair retains its power to corrode my trust, like acid or rust. It's ironic: when I was younger, before it happened, I imagined an affair would be a nuclear explosion in my marriage, obliterating it. The reality has turned out to be more like a nail bomb, leaving shards and fragments in unexpected places. Less annihilation, more attrition—though possibly just as fatal.

I open my eyes. Both Paul and Leo are watching the door. Simultaneously, their gaze switches back to me. I look over to the door myself. Oh God. It's her. She's shorter and curvier than I was expecting, in a clingy blue dress. Her face is smiling and open, but she is attractive rather than pretty. Certainly not beautiful. I stare at her.

I've spent so long imagining a lingerie-toting supermodel that it's hard to accept the ordinary-looking girl I see in front of me. One thing's for sure—she is young. Her skin is plump and fresh, her eyes sparkling.

I realize I'm still staring and look away. Will presses his hand into the small of my back. *I'm here.*

I don't look him in the eye. Can't. I feel flushed and exposed. I wish I weren't here. I wish I were anywhere else. At home, reading Zack a story or listening to Hannah argue for the millionth time how everyone else in her class has an iPhone.

Will is talking now, some detail about work with Leo and another colleague. I stare down at the beautiful parquet flooring and notice that the polish on my right big toe has chipped. And then I feel Will stiffen beside me. Instinctively, I know that this means Catrina must have come over. I look up. Freeze. She's standing in front of us, that blue dress hugging her curves, a pair of elegant drop earrings glittering in the lamplight. She extends her hand to Will, and he has to take his palm from my back to shake. She is as groomed and polished as Julia predicted, but utterly without the Parisian sneer.

"Will, it's been ages," she says with a smile. She has a Yorkshire accent. I'm taken aback. I wasn't expecting this . . . this mix of down-to-earth friendliness and sophisticated glamour.

She turns to me. "Laura, is it?"

"Livy."

We stare at each other. Beside me, I feel the tension radiating off Will.

"Oh, I'm so sorry." She is young, but her nose is slightly blobby and her eyes set too wide apart. There's an appealing vulnerability in her manner, but she's no femme fatale.

Still, I'm certain the mistake with my name was deliberate. Which surely means she cares. She *still* cares. I look anxiously at Will. Does he care back?

I watch him talk to Catrina, trying to read the body language between them. He is reserved and awkward. Is that because of her? Or just the situation? Catrina is all surface poise, but her unhappy eyes give her away. Will's hand is back on my spine, pressing my dress against my damp skin.

"Please excuse us," Will is saying. "There are so many people I want my wife to meet."

He steers me away. I catch a glimpse of Catrina watching us.

"Livy." Will leans into me as we cross the room. "Are you okay?"

I say nothing. I'm trying to process the fact that Catrina still wants him. Perhaps I imagined that. I look around again. She is still watching us. She looks desperately miserable.

"You do know how much I love you, don't you?" Will's voice is an urgent whisper in my ear.

I turn and face him properly. I see no desire for Catrina in his face. Only concern for me. For the first time since we left the house, I relax a little. I've met her now. And Will doesn't want her. It was all a long time ago. Over. At least as far as he's concerned.

"I think she still likes you," I say with yet another forced smile, searching his face.

Will shakes his head. "No," he says. "It wouldn't matter even if she did." He lowers his voice. "It's only you, Livy—you know that, don't you?"

His eyes plead with me. I nod as Martha appears at the end of the room to announce that dinner is ready.

The next hour passes in a blur. Martha has tactfully sat Catrina at the opposite end of the table from Will and me. I can see her chatting with Paul and Becky.

Dinner itself is delicious and served by more men in tuxedos who glide silently around the room, ferrying silver platters of Greek salad, then lamb noisette to each guest.

Dessert is a selection of mini mousses and tarts. Then we have coffee. The evening is drawing to a close—Leo and Martha's dinners are never late affairs; Leo is famous for rising early, even crediting his business success to the hours he puts in *before* the working day begins—and I've almost forgotten how humiliated I felt earlier, when Leo pitches up again. His cheeks are flushed and he carries with him the vague scent of cigar smoke.

"Crisis in Geneva," he growls. "It's bloody Henri again."

Will, who hasn't left my side all through dinner, frowns. "What does he want now?"

Leo explains. Lucas Henri, as I already know, is Harbury Media's biggest client. He owns a high-tech company based in Switzerland that supplies electronics goods to several outlets across the South West. Will hates him with a passion. Everyone at Harbury hates him, as far as I can tell. "He's got all the worst qualities of a client," I remember Will telling me once. "He never knows what he wants, only that you haven't provided it. He micromanages. And he's always trying to slip extra jobs into the workload when they're not in the original agreement." Tonight, it seems, someone has messed up on the dates for a hugely expensive marketing campaign, and Henri is panicking.

"He's threatening to pull his entire operation." Leo sighs. "I need you out there with me, Will. Right now."

Will shoots me an apologetic look.

"It's fine," I say. I'm used to these last-minute business trips. It's one of the penalties of being married to someone who speaks fluent French and German. Catrina must speak great French too if she works in Paris. A spike of jealousy pierces me.

"The distributor has a charter leaving just before midnight," Leo goes on. His earlier, jovial air is completely gone. He's stern and focused, all business mode. Will stiffens and straightens beside me in response. "Go home, pack an overnight."

"I guess *I'll* be going home too, then." I mean it to sound light and funny, but the words have an edge. I shouldn't let my housewife status get to me, but surrounded as I am by strong, successful women like Becky and Julia, it's hard sometimes not to feel sidelined.

Leo looks at me, his gaze softening. "Sorry, Livy, but I need my best man on the job." He pats my arm. Again, his hand feels too heavy, too insistent somehow. "Don't worry, it's Geneva, not Paris, just me and Will."

Oh God, he must think that I'm worried Catrina might be traveling with them. My cheeks burn, but Leo doesn't notice.

He has turned to Will again. "The girls are e-mailing you your ticket right now. Nothing else to be done." And with that, he strides off.

Will opens his mouth, then shuts it again. I can tell he doesn't know what to say and that he's worried this will be the last straw after everything he's put me through tonight. It's funny. Will is valued at work for soothing neurotic clients in three languages, but he's tongue-tied around his emotions with me. Not to mention hopeless when it comes to anything practical like putting up shelves or mending the garden fence.

"I'm sorry," he stammers at last.

"It's okay." I smile. At least now we get away from Catrina. "Everyone'll be leaving soon anyway."

We say good-bye to Martha. Catrina looks up from her conversation with Paul to wave at us both. I nod in response. Then we head home.

I breathe a sigh of relief as we get in the car. Will's phone rings immediately. It's Leo again, with an update on the situation in Geneva, which appears to be getting worse by the minute. I stare out of the window as we drive the short distance back to Heavitree. I know these streets so well. I grew up in Bath but came to university in Exeter twenty years ago. I haven't lived anywhere else since. Usually the lack of adventure in my past doesn't bother me, but right now it feels like yet another way in which my life and experiences are limited. Certainly I'm more limited than Will, who comes from London—and had already spent a year in France and Germany when I met him—and Catrina with her undoubtedly chic Parisian existence.

Will switches off his phone with a sigh, then asks if I'm all right. I reply rather curtly that I'm fine, then feel guilty for being short with him. After all, he has done everything tonight that he possibly could to reassure me.

As we walk up to the front door, I take his hand. "Hey."

Will turns to face me, a worried frown on his forehead. I reach up to kiss him, letting my lips linger on his mouth. He responds by pulling me into a hug.

17

"Oh, Livy." His breath is hot against my ear. There is so much feeling in his voice—relief and desire and love—that I suddenly feel stupid for having doubted him.

"Hey," I say again, drawing back and holding his face between my hands. "Everything's fine. Don't worry."

Will smiles; then we let ourselves into the house. The kids are both in bed and asleep. While Will disappears upstairs to pack a bag, I pay Bethany, our babysitter from along the road, then go to give him a hand. There's a small kerfuffle over the exact location of his laptop, which turns out to be lurking underneath Hannah's in a corner of the living room. And then he's off in a taxi to the airport. Miraculously, the children have slept through his entire departure and the house is suddenly, oddly silent. I watch TV, then take a long bath. It's only as I'm getting ready for bed that I remember Julia's earlier text and the call I didn't answer. I switch on my phone. She's left a voice mail asking me to ring her. The message says it's important, so I send a text asking if she's still up. There's no reply, and as it's well past eleven now, I send a second text saying I'm sorry I missed her and that although Will has had to go away, the kids and I will see her for lunch tomorrow as planned.

I sleep soundly, far better than I did the night before, when the dinner was still ahead of me. I awake with a jolt to Zack bouncing onto the bed, tousle-haired and smelling of sleep and chocolate; there's a telltale smear around his mouth.

He dives under the covers and throws his arms around my neck. "Mummy," he croons in my ear, his hands in tight fists, pulling me toward him. "There was three *Ben 10*s in a row."

I snuggle him close, feeling the familiar rush of love that Zack brings out in me. At seven, he is getting leaner, no longer a chubby-limbed little boy, but his huge appetite for physical affection shows no sign of diminishing, thank goodness.

"When are we going over to Julia's?" says Hannah, speaking from the door.

If there is a more scathing tone of voice in the world than the one a twelve-year-old girl can put into the most anodyne query to her mother, I have yet to hear it.

I glance over the top of Zack's head. Hannah is leaning against the doorframe, her blond hair snaking down her back. She is on the verge of puberty—narrow-hipped, long-legged like a colt, and with small buds of breasts. With her pale skin and gray eyes, she looks more like Kara every day. I soak her up as the memories wash over me: Kara as a little girl, giggling with mischief; Kara wide-eyed as she described her first student party; Kara weeping when our dog was sick and had to be put down—

Kara dead.

I shiver. I never actually saw her body, but sometimes I imagine her stone-colored eyes as they must have been in death: cold and hard and empty.

"Mum?" Hannah's tone is impatient. "What *time*?"

I shake off my morbid thoughts and glance at the clock by the bed. It's almost ten. No wonder Zack's been eating chocolate. I can't remember the last time I slept this late.

"Are you hungry, baby boy?" I ask.

Zack nods, nuzzling into my neck and planting a huge slobbery kiss on my right earlobe.

"I'm right *here*." Now Hannah sounds injured. I look over.

Oh God, she's welling up.

"We'll go to Julia's at eleven," I say, trying to smile in the face of Hannah's volatile emotions.

"Fine." She flounces off.

I sigh, then reach for my phone. My call goes to Julia's voice mail, so I leave a message saying we'll see her soon. Julia still hasn't responded to the text I sent late last night. Thinking about it, I realize she's probably still in bed. Whom did she say she was seeing at the moment? Some younger man. He was fair-haired, "my Dirty Blond," she'd confided with relish. I can't recall his actual name—or even if Julia had gotten around to telling it to me yet.

I bribe Zack up and off me with the promise of a bacon sandwich. I make one for myself too, but Hannah refuses to eat.

"I'll have something at Julia's," she says.

I shake my head. It's pointless to argue. Julia will have provided food—there'll be nibbles from her local deli, along with huge gin and tonics for me and her, followed by something super-sophisticated for lunch, with no quarter given to the idea of a kids' menu. "Quail eggs before chicken nuggets," she always says, refusing to make any allowance even during Zack's long year of eating only sausages.

Over lunch, Julia and I will drink Pouilly-Fuissé wine, her favorite, and there'll be a jug of proper lemonade for the kids. Julia will slip two cubes of ice and a slice of lemon into Hannah's glass to emulate our earlier G&Ts.

"A glamour drink," she will say with a smile and a wink. "To get you ready for the big time, Hans."

She's always had a special relationship with Hannah. In many ways, they're alike—brittle and egocentric but capable of genuine warmth too. I know the fact that Hannah looks like Kara has always haunted Julia as well as me. After all, it was my sister's death—and our impotent fury against her killer—that brought Julia and me together.

Hannah is dressed and ready to leave by ten thirty—she's in skinny jeans and a silk vest of mine that is both too old and too big for her. I am too busy bribing Zack to get dressed to say anything either about that or the eyeliner she's applied rather heavily. She adores Julia as much as Julia adores her. I understand why she wants to look good. Julia brings out that side of me as well.

Once Zack is ready, I hurry into my own tea dress and sandals. Julia is never late herself and hates unpunctuality in her guests. It seems odd that she hasn't replied either to my call or my text, but I don't give it much thought as we pull up in the sunshine outside her apartment.

And then she doesn't answer the door.

I frown. I've never known Julia—a self-confessed control freak—to miss one of our Sunday lunch dates or, indeed, be late for any arrangement. For all the force and flamboyance of her personality, Julia is one of the most considerate people I've ever met: well-mannered to a fault and as openly grateful for the stability my friendship offers as she is needful of constant change and stimulation in other areas of her life.

The two of us grew close after Kara's death. Before then, Julia was really my sister's friend. Unmarried and childless herself, Julia couldn't be more different from me. But she is godmother to my eldest child, and the first person I turned to when I found out about Will's affair.

"Oh, honeypie," I remember her saying with a weary sigh, "Didn't Momma tell you never to put all your eggs in one bastard?"

She's always quoting Dorothy Parker—I gave Julia a collection of the author's sayings for her most recent, thirty-sixth birthday. Once we've settled the kids in front of a DVD, I know she'll be full of questions and opinions about Catrina and how the dinner party went.

I ring the doorbell again. Still no reply.

"But she's *always* here when we come," Hannah says.

She's right: Julia would never let my kids down by forgetting the date. I check my phone again. No message. For the first time, Julia's text about needing to talk sends a shiver down my spine.

"What are we going to do, Mum?" Hannah asks anxiously.

Zack, sensing the atmosphere has changed, shuffles closer to me.

"Maybe the intercom's not working." I take out my keys. The spares to Julia's building and apartment hang on my old leather key ring, just as my keys dangle from her silver Tiffany fob. I open the building's front door.

Once inside, the kids race up the stairs to Julia's second-floor apartment. They hammer on Julia's front door, but there's still no reply. I join them, starting to wish I'd turned around and left when we were downstairs, but I can't stop now. Worry pricks the hairs at the nape of my neck. Where is she?

I open the door and we walk inside. I feel like I'm intruding, despite the key. The kids, suddenly quiet, hang back. Maybe they sense something in the air. It's all too fast for me to be sure. And then we're in the living room and Julia's lying there on the sofa. And she could be asleep but I know that she's not.

A long second passes before I let out my breath and the knowledge slams into my brain.

Julia. My best friend. Is dead.

HARRY

I see a pattern, but my imagination cannot picture the maker of that pattern. I see a clock, but I cannot envision the clockmaker.

—Einstein

There's only one thing that counts: honesty. And I promise faithfully that I will never lie to you. So, no lies. And no false modesty either. I'm going to be straight about who I am and what I do.

Let's start with myth number one: that I am a psychopath. That word comes with so much baggage but really it just means "suffering soul." Isn't that beautiful? How could anyone fail to be moved by the idea of a mind in torment? But slap a pseudoscientific label on the bitch, and suddenly it sounds ponderous and medical, certainly in need of medication.

Whatever, it's a false diagnosis, based on fear and misunderstanding. Because, and here's my thesis, we are all psychopaths under the skin. For whose soul doesn't suffer? Life is suffering. That's not me, that's the Buddha. And who could argue? Still, I much prefer the old term "psychopath" to the more modern "sociopath." Sociopath is one of those bits of nonsense jargon—like "cadence" and "granularity"—that I hear at work all the time.

Apologies, I'm getting ahead of myself. Let me begin at the beginning and explain how my so-called psychopathy started. No names, no pack drill, obviously. But you should know that I had a relatively comfortable early childhood. Sorry to disappoint expectations, but there it is. My parents were perfectly normal. I wasn't beaten or sexually abused or neglected. I had food to eat, a bed to sleep in, and clean clothes every day. A middle-class psychopath. Ha! In your face, analytical psychologists.

23

Then Harry came to live with us.

I can see what you're thinking: Harry. Probably an uncle or a lodger. Harry: Abuser. Groomer. Pederast.

No. Harry was our cat. Black and very, very furry. A rescue cat. An interesting cat. Quite possibly a psychopath himself. Certainly sly and narcissistic and without a conscience. I don't think Harry cared about the mice he killed. He lived to find them, catch them, and watch them suffer. Harry was cruel and I had no interest in cruelty. But I was curious about Harry. He had a long bushy tail—on the surface, all fluffy fur that shed on every piece of furniture we owned—but underneath the fur, his tail was like thick wire. Harry's tail obsessed me. It was not what it seemed, much like Harry himself. Soft yet hard. Strong yet weak. There one minute, whipped out of the way the next.

I'm sure Freud would have loved my preadolescent obsession with this phallus substitute. But, as so often with Freud, his analysis would have been off by the limits of his own understanding. You see, my interest in Harry's tail wasn't pseudosexual. No. It grew out of the startling discovery I'd made that one thing could in fact be two things. Once this occurred to me, of course, I saw the reality repeated everywhere. For instance, there was nice Mummy, who gave me chocolate cookies, and nasty Mummy, who got cross when I made crumbs. And so on . . .

I kept looking at Harry and thinking about his tail, and one day I knew that I wanted to see how he would react if I took a bit of the tail away. I found a notepad and wrote scientiffik experiment *on the front. Well, I was young. Then inside the notepad, I wrote down the day and made two columns: one to say what I did, the other to say how Harry reacted.*

| **Monday** | Got sharpest knife from wooden holder in kitchen. Put Harry under arm. Went to bottom of garden. Chopped bit of tail at end. | Harry made a lot of noise and tried to scratch me. I let him go. |

(continued)

Wednesday	Sharpened knife using sharpener in drawer. Put Harry under arm. Went to bottom of garden. Chopped more of tail. Half a centimeter. I measured.	Harry wriggled and made noise before and during the chopping this time.
Friday	Did the same.	Harry can't run now. Why? I didn't cut his leg.
Monday	Did the same.	Harry same. Tail same. Harry fell over. Looked it up. Tail helps balance. Mum found Harry by door. Saw tail. Thinks it was door that cut tail. (Stupid.)
Tuesday	Harry at VET. Vet says Harry's tail infected.	Harry ill.
Thursday		Harry dead.

There you have it—my first experiment. The first, but not the last.

Not by any means.

Of course, Harry was my last animal and my last male. Soon after Harry, I reached puberty, and my thoughts turned to girls. A development that Freud himself would acknowledge was normal.

I say "girls" but really there was only one girl who mattered.

And her legacy has been my life.

CHAPTER TWO

Somehow my legs carry me over to the sofa. There's a smell of stale urine in the air. I stare down at Julia. Her eyes are closed, and one arm is folded over her chest. She looks peaceful. She's dressed in sweatpants and a ribbed cotton top. Classic Julia-wear for a girls-only night in. Her dark red hair, starting to fade from the fiery glory of her twenties, falls over her face in messy strands. There's a bottle of Jack Daniel's on the coffee table. An empty glass. I notice each item in turn. I'm aware of Hannah and Zack beside me. They're peering down at Julia too. For a second, I hope against hope that this is a game, that any moment, she's going to open her eyes and say, "Boo!"

"Is she asleep, Mummy?" Zack asks.

"I'm not sure," I say.

But I am. I don't know what gives it away—maybe the paleness of her face or the stiffness of that arm across the chest. I look down. There's a stain on the front of her sweats where her muscles have relaxed and she has wet herself.

"Why does it smell of pee?" Zack clutches my leg.

"Mum?" Hannah's voice quavers. Now she's drawing closer as well.

I have to act. I have to do something. I must protect my children. These thoughts run through my head as I reach out and touch Julia's cheek. It's cold. I run my fingers up her temple, brushing the hair off her forehead. Her skin—her whole being—is rigid. Unnatural.

I start shaking. How can this have happened? How can Julia be dead? She's thirty-six, only two years younger than I am.

"Mummy?" Hannah suddenly sounds as young as Zack.

I draw my hand away from Julia's face. Time seems to have slowed down. I'm still trembling. I can't think. Inside I'm screaming, but I don't make a sound.

"Mum?" Hannah's voice, sharp and terrified, forces me into action.

I draw my phone from my bag. I dial 999. Surreal, this is surreal.

"Emergency services. Which service do you require?"

"Ambulance."

Hannah gasps beside me. Zack leans more heavily against my leg.

The woman on the other end of the phone asks me what has happened. It's like she's speaking to me through a long tunnel.

"We came to see my friend." I give Julia's name and address, feeling numb. "I think she's . . . she's . . . She's not conscious." I can't bring myself to say it. "My children are here, with me." I pray the 999 woman will understand.

She does. Her voice is soothing but firm. "Is Julia breathing?" she asks.

"I don't think so." My voice is a hoarse whisper. I feel lost. I've never been this close to a body before—neither Dad nor Mum had wanted me to see Kara's. Yet it is obvious Julia is dead. There is no doubt in my mind, but I can't say the words. It feels like too huge a truth to own.

A few more questions. The 999 woman says an ambulance is on its way and asks if there is any evidence of a struggle, if the front door lock was broken.

"No," I say. This hasn't occurred to me. "There's just a drink."

As I speak, Hannah reaches for the glass.

"Don't touch that," I snap.

Hannah snatches her hand back. She starts crying. The 999 woman tells me to take my children into another room. She tells me again that an ambulance is on its way. She tells me to stay on the line. But I need both hands to deal with Zack, whose arms are clamped around my waist as if he'll fall over if he lets go.

I lead the children out of the room. We go into Julia's bedroom. This is Hannah's favorite place in the whole world. Normally, she would wander around, trailing her fingers over the huge vanity table overflowing with Julia's jewelry and cosmetics, but today we huddle together on the bed.

I put my arms round their shoulders. "Julia has had an accident," I say. I still can't form the words.

"Is she dead?" Zack peers up at me, his huge blue eyes round with shock.

How dare my children be put through this. Fury fills me for the second time in twelve hours. And yet here, there is no Catrina. Here, there is no one to blame.

I nod. "I'm sorry, baby." I pull him closer. Hannah too. She is still weeping, the tears falling unchecked down her cheeks, splashing onto Julia's blue silk comforter. The bed is made. Unslept in. I register this with the same sense of detachment that I'd abstractly noticed the Jack Daniel's.

A few minutes later, the intercom buzzes. I get up. Zack stays with me as I walk into the living room to let the paramedics in. All at once, the atmosphere changes. The paramedics—an older man and a younger woman—are unfazed by what they see. It takes them just a few seconds to process what I am only just beginning to absorb, that Julia has been dead for hours.

Now they are more concerned with the three of us. The woman ushers Zack and me back into the bedroom, where Hannah is huddled at the far edge of Julia's bed. The paramedic sits us down and talks quietly to the children. She offers sympathy for the shock we have experienced.

Zack is more fascinated than upset now. "Is she really gone, not waking up? Why did she pee herself?"

Hannah sits in silence, chewing on a strand of hair. Normally, I would tell her to take the hair out of her mouth. Right now, I can barely formulate the thought. At this point, the male paramedic beckons me back to the living room. We stand in the doorway. I can see Julia's legs from the knees down. Her sweatpants are rolled halfway up her calves. Her toenails are painted silver. The same shade she put on Hannah's nails on our last visit.

"The police are on their way." He speaks with a strong Northern accent. His voice is soothing. "They'll want to take a statement."

"Police?" I stare at him.

The man nods. "It's procedure in a . . . when there's a suspicious death."

My mouth is dry.

"How old was your friend?"

"Thirty-six. She was my sister's best friend. I've known her since my sister . . ." I trail off.

"Well, thirty-six is very young to die so suddenly if, as you say, she was in good health?"

"As far as I know . . ." Could there be something Julia hasn't told me? My mind lurches back to the text she sent last night just as Will and I arrived at the Harburys' house.

PLS CALL. I NEED TO TALK TO YOU.

"There are no signs of a struggle or a break-in, but the police will want to know if you or the children have touched or moved anything."

I shake my head. Was Julia's text a cry for help?

A few minutes later, and the police arrive. Suddenly Julia's small, chic apartment is full of people. Men and women in white coats and hairnets examine the living room. A policewoman in uniform speaks to me and I repeat what I told the paramedic.

"Is there anyone you'd like us to call for you?" She gives me a kindly smile.

"Will." I want my husband. Here. Now. I don't care that he's in Geneva.

The policewoman takes my phone as a plainclothes officer arrives. He is obviously someone senior. Everyone busies themselves as he walks in. He strides over, all purposeful. Despite his graying hair, he doesn't look much older than me.

"Mrs. Jackson, I'm Detective Inspector Norris." He asks me more questions. He's mostly looking for information about Julia's life. Did she have a partner? Any known allergies or medical conditions? Did she drink heavily? Take drugs? Any recent life events like losing a job or a relationship breakup? What about family?

I answer as best I can, but it feels like I'm wading through mud as I speak. I tell him about Julia's family and her job as a freelance journalist . . . that she's never been married . . . that she had mentioned seeing someone new recently but I didn't know his name . . . that she has lived here for over ten years . . . that nothing out of the ordinary had happened in her life recently . . . that she liked to drink Jack Daniel's, but I rarely saw her drunk—and definitely no drugs.

As I speak, Julia's acerbic voice rings in my ear. *Drugs? You have to be kidding, honeypie. Have you seen Keith Richards's skin?*

I stop. Tears well up. I can't believe that she's gone. I can't believe I won't ever hear that voice again.

"Why are you asking all this?"

Detective Inspector Norris clears his throat. "We need to work out what happened." He pauses. "Were you aware if your friend had any suicidal thoughts?"

I stare at him. "No." I'm emphatic. "No way. Not Julia."

I follow Norris's gaze to the Jack Daniel's and the empty glass. "She wasn't . . . she didn't . . ."

Julia's text flashes into my mind again: PLS CALL. I NEED TO TALK TO YOU.

I tell DI Norris. He nods. "The postmortem will give us more information."

I glance over at the bed, where Zack is snuggled up against a young, pretty uniformed officer. Hannah is still hunched in the corner, twisting her hair around her finger. Her eyeliner is streaked across her cheeks. I hate to see her so distraught. It's ironic. When Hannah was little, I was crucifyingly overprotective, unwilling even to let her out of my sight, yet I never imagined I would have to protect her from anything like what she has seen today.

I look back at DI Norris. "My children—"

He pats my arm. "I'll find an officer to take you home."

As he walks away, the female officer returns with my phone in his hand. "Your husband."

I take the phone. "Will?"

"What the hell has happened? They're saying Julia's *dead*?"

Will's outraged disbelief mirrors my own feelings so precisely that I can't speak. Background noise fills the silence. People are chatting and laughing behind him.

"Liv?"

"I don't know," I gasp. "Yes, I mean. She's . . . gone. I just don't know why . . . how . . . When will you be back?"

"Um . . ." Will hesitates. "Not sure. Leo's here. I'll explain the situation. It's a nightmare here, the client's being completely unreasonable."

The voices in the room behind him rise. There are two: Leo and a woman. The woman has a Yorkshire twang.

I suck in my breath, shocked. "Is *she* there?"

"What? Who?" Will knows whom I mean. I can hear it in his voice. He sighs. "Leo made her come. It was an order. He decided *after* we left the party. I didn't know until we all met at the airport." Will lowers his voice. "Liv, please. Catrina being here had nothing to do with me."

I look over at the sofa. Two women dressed head to toe in white forensic gear are examining Julia's fingernails. I gulp, my thoughts suddenly clear.

Julia is gone.

Catrina is irrelevant.

"I know," I say into the phone. "Just get back as soon as you can."

Will tells me he loves me; then we say good-bye. As promised, a man in uniform takes us home. The children are in a terrible state. Zack is clingy and Hannah won't stop weeping. The police officer asks if there is anyone who could come over to help me. He gives me a card with a telephone number and a small brochure.

"Call this if you remember anything or if you want help or advice on dealing with what's happened. For you or the children." He reels off the names of various support groups and counseling options. "They're all in the brochure."

I take very little of this in. At home, the house feels cold, though it's a warm day. I glance at the kitchen clock and am staggered to

31

find it is not yet 1 P.M. It feels like an entire day has passed since we entered Julia's flat. Years since Will left for Geneva last night after the dinner party.

Julia is dead.

It still hasn't sunk in. I make beans on toast, moving around the kitchen on autopilot. Zack eats. Hannah refuses and disappears to her room. Zack follows me around the kitchen as I empty the dishwasher and put on a load of laundry. I don't know what to do or where to go.

I gave the police officer Julia's mother's name earlier. She calls in tears, unable to focus. I hear guilt in her voice. She and Julia rarely spoke. Julia called her "the Martyr" because of her name, Joanie. As in Joan of Arc.

"I can't believe it," Joanie says over and over again. "How can this have happened?"

I don't know what to tell her. She says she's on her way to Exeter from Bridport, where she lives. She'll be staying with Robbie, Julia's twin brother. A few minutes after Joanie hangs up, Robbie himself rings. We used to all hang out together a lot when we were younger. In fact, a million years ago, Robbie and I went on a date. It was a disaster, him being two years younger and overwhelmed with his crush. I felt guilty for not being interested and tried to let him down as gently as possible. Julia never said, but I think she was relieved we didn't end up an item.

Robbie sounds bewildered, demanding details of how I'd found her. I deal with him as best I can, but there's a tension between us on the phone. The awkwardness isn't just because of that long ago date. Robbie and Julia weren't close. Despite being twins, they never really got along. Julia was always a bit too wild for the rest of her family and rather looked down on Robbie, who got a trainee job in hotel management for an Exeter-based hotel chain while she was at uni. He worked his way up through the ranks to become conference and banqueting manager, but other than a few work trips abroad to other hotels in the same chain, his life remained as unglamorous as Julia's was full of adventure.

Robbie rings off, sounding as shell-shocked as he was at the start
of the call. I put down my phone and notice that the light is beginning to fade from the day. Hannah still hasn't reappeared, so I go
upstairs and try to talk to her but she shouts at me and slams her
door. I bite back my anger and console myself by watching *Toy Story*
with Zack, even managing to laugh along with him when Buzz insists he can fly. I run him a bath and hold his hand as he falls asleep.

Will calls again. His voice is soft and sympathetic. He is full of
concern for me and the kids. He will be on an early flight home tomorrow evening. I cry down the phone, a mix of misery and relief
that he is there, a solid presence unchanging among the chaos. Before I can mention her, Will says he's sorry that Catrina is with him
on the business trip and repeats that he had no part in the arrangements and that the two of them have barely exchanged two words
since they arrived.

I reassure him that I believe him, that it doesn't matter anyway,
that Julia's sudden death has put everything in perspective. Will
sounds deeply relieved and my heart fills with affection for him. I
have met Catrina now. It's done—and so comprehensively overshad-
owed by what has happened to Julia that any lingering doubts in my
mind about the affair have been laid, at last, to rest. Will and I say
we love each other and ring off. I'm exhausted. I haven't eaten all day.
I heat some soup and take a bowl to Hannah. This time she eats and
she cries and I hold her and for a few minutes I feel like we are sharing our grief. But I am holding back my own tears and when Hannah realizes she accuses me of not caring and this is so far from the
truth and my heart is so wrung out and exhausted and I am so devastated as the pain of losing Julia settles inside me that I turn on
her and shout that she is selfish.

Hannah screams at me to get out of her room and I go and I run
to our bedroom and hurl myself on our bed as if I were twelve too,
not thirty-eight and a married mother of two, and then I reach for
the phone and call my own mother, who is shocked like everyone else.
And she says the words I've been failing to face since this morning.

"Oh my darling, it's like Kara all over again."

Immediately I'm back in my third year at university. My dorm room. The knock on the door. The two policemen with serious faces. "Please come with us—there's been a terrible incident." And time passing, Mum and Dad arriving, then Kara's freshman tutor; us all gathered with pale faces in the waiting room. Then Dad going to identify the body and Mum's low moan breaking the silence as he walked back to us, his mouth trembling.

Kara was viciously attacked one cold February night in her first year at university as she walked along the canal back to her student housing. They think her murderer attacked her as she passed under a bridge. He raped her with a knife, then stabbed her in the stomach. She bled to death on the footpath. Her killer was never found.

I feel sick. I get off the phone and go to check on Hannah. She's asleep. With her face in repose, she looks even more like Kara. As a child, my sister was sunny-natured and smart. Everyone loved her. Her death was a terrible violation, a gash that tore right through the mundanity of our small, suburban lives. It killed my father. That's what Mum and I believe, anyway. Dad couldn't bear that he hadn't protected her: his sense of failure destroyed him. I look at Hannah, her makeup still streaked and her hair over her face, and I know I would feel exactly the same.

But it wasn't like that with Julia. Mum is wrong about that. Unlike Kara, Julia has died peacefully, presumably from an unknown medical condition. At least it looks that way.

I fall asleep, trying to focus on that one thread of comfort. I hold on to it the next day when I let the children stay home from school and that evening when Will returns and hugs me as I cry. I hold on to it the day after, when Julia's mother calls me with endless inquiries about her daughter's life, her resentment that they had hardly spoken for years simmering under every question. And I hold on to it the day after that, when Martha drops by, full of gentle concern, and at the school gates, when the other mothers ask me what happened—news having somehow spread.

But then Thursday comes and, with it, the first piece of news from the postmortem. Julia's mother calls to tell me. She sounds angry but resigned.

Julia's body contained lethal doses of Nembutal as well as three times the legal driving limit of alcohol.

"We have to face it, Livy," she says. "Julia killed herself."

The words are too brutal. The idea is impossible.

"No," I say. "Julia would never—"

"The postmortem is clear. There was nothing else wrong with her."

"But—"

"Livy, this isn't helpful." Julia's mother is cold and hard. "The police found evidence on her computer of Web sites she'd visited going back two months, plus a brochure about Nembutal on her desk."

"But . . . but all that was for an article she was researching on suicides in the fashion industry. She told me about it," I explain. "Some young girl killed herself, and Julia was looking into a connection with the fashion industry using skinny models."

I suck in my breath, remembering Julia shaking her head as she told me about the pressures on some of the models she had spoken to.

They all think they're too fat, she'd said wearily. *They skip breakfast, lunch is black coffee and a cigarette, then it's a paper tissue for dinner. They're worse than dancers. . . .*

"No article was ever published," Joanie insists. "No one commissioned her to write one."

"I know," I say. "She was just interested."

"Exactly."

There's a long silence. I rack my brains, trying to work out how I can convince Joanie there is no way Julia would have killed herself.

Then Joanie clears her throat. "She left a note, Livy."

My mind reels. Julia left a suicide note? No, that goes against everything I've ever known about her. "What does it say?"

"Please, Livy." Julia's mother's voice, then her words, cut me like a knife. "It was addressed to me . . . well, to the family. It's private."

What is she saying? I am . . . was . . . Julia's best friend. "Please." My voice breaks. I can't bear the thought that Julia left a note I can't read. "I need to know, to understand."

"It was on the open screen, on her computer. The police found it. It just says . . . 'To my family. I'm sorry, I can't go on. Please make no fuss, no flowers, no religious service. Just remember me kindly. I love you. Julia.' It's very short. There's no reason given." Now Julia's mother sounds hurt. Her voice trembles. "This is very hard for me."

"I know, I'm sorry." I speak the words, but inside I'm raging. I don't believe this . . . *can't* believe this. There is no way Julia would write such a note. . . . Make no fuss. Indeed—she *lived* for drama; no way she wouldn't have spoken to me.

And then I remember her missed call and the text she sent:

PLS CALL. I NEED TO TALK TO YOU.

She tried to speak to me. And I ignored her.

"I'll let you know the details of the funeral," Joanie continues briskly. "It would be helpful if you could e-mail me a list of friends, colleagues, people we should invite."

"I can help contacting people too," I offer.

"Thank you, but we can manage. I'm with Robbie and Wendy."

My breath catches in my throat. Irrationally, I feel hurt. And on Julia's behalf too. She would hate to think of her brother and sister-in-law organizing anything connected with her.

"Please, I'd like to help—"

"That's very kind of you, but we have everything under control. It will be a nondenominational service, in line with Julia's wishes about not having a religious service. "So . . . the West Devon funeral parlor, we're thinking." Julia's mother sniffs. "Anyway, please send me that list of friends and colleagues when you have a moment."

In a daze I take down her e-mail address; then I say good-bye.

An hour passes. The sun blazes outside but I sit at the kitchen table, staring into space. Images of Julia parade through my head—fierce, proud, funny. I think of my traumatized children. Julia loved them. She loved me. If she'd felt down, I would have known. But she was happy and enjoying her work. She was into her new guy, her Dirty Blond. She *loved* her life.

I shake my head. It can't be true. I won't accept it. There must have been something else, some other factor. I become obsessive in my search for more information. I call all the numbers the police officer gave me. The police confirm the coroner's verdict of suicide. Julia died between 10 P.M. and midnight. I can't stop thinking how hectic that evening had been, then how quiet the house seemed after Will left for the airport and how I'd gone to bed thinking it was too late to call Julia back. If only I had ignored convention, as I'm sure Julia herself would have done.

I call the editors of the interior decorating, beauty, and fashion magazines for which Julia freelanced. I call the bloggers and journalists I met through her. I call the two ex-boyfriends of hers with whom I'm still in touch. And I speak endlessly to Will, who listens patiently as I rant that Julia wasn't capable of killing herself, and then weep in his arms.

All these people agree that it is shocking—then they sigh and say that it's hard, but that we must accept it. They hint, to greater and lesser degrees, that I'm refusing to face the truth only because I feel guilty. Which, they say, I shouldn't. Some tell me directly that it isn't my fault. I want to shout at them that I know. That this isn't the point. Julia's death is not about me.

Mum and Will both tentatively suggest I'm letting Kara's death all those years ago influence me. "But there is no killer here, just a deeply unhappy woman who fooled us all, who put a brave face on things," Will says, his sympathetic tone belying the fact that he, like everyone else, thinks I'm completely mistaken.

And so, another week passes, the body is released, the funeral draws near, and Julia's story is rewritten. She was not really happy and full of life, but secretive and depressed. I hear many mentions of the therapist she saw for several years in her twenties, after Kara died. Likewise, there are frequent references to Julia's numerous "evenings in with Jack."

"But when she said that, it was meant lightly, ironically," I tell people.

They purse their lips and talk about solitary drinking and quote stats on whisky and suicide.

I grow tired of the conversations. I withdraw, watching my children closely. Zack, in that amazing way young children do, is bouncing back—I can see his memories of Julia fading already. Hannah is withdrawn at home, but her teachers say she is behaving normally at school.

Life slips back into its old groove: I ferry the kids around, shop for groceries, and pay bills. And yet, even as everything remains the same, it is all different. I notice a woman in Jackie O sunglasses and a green jacket coming out of the Waitrose supermarket on Gladstone Road. She looks so much like Julia that I actually follow her for a few steps until she turns a corner and I see the hook nose of her profile and the youthful tilt of her chin and I realize that it isn't Julia after all. On instinct, I take out my phone to call and tell Julia my mistake. And then I remember. I stand in the street, my shopping heavy in my hands. I can almost hear her caustic cackle: *I'd lay off the happy pills, Liv,* she'd say. Or: *Earth to housewife: Get a grip.*

Every day there is something new I want to tell her: the picture Zack draws of a car that—if squinted at from a particular angle—looks bizarrely like one she used to drive, or the actress I see in some drama who reminds me of an old mutual friend. I try to tell Will instead, but the memories aren't his, and anyway, he is preoccupied with work and exhausted when he gets home at night.

And so it is that the two of us talk less and less about Julia, even as I miss her more and more, while through it all, the options turn over in my mind.

Not sickness. Not suicide.

Gradually, silently, the only other alternative seeps like a poison into my mind, shifting everything known and unknown.

No one takes Nembutal by accident. It's not even legal without a prescription, and Julia's medical records confirm that she certainly wasn't prescribed it. Her death wasn't an accident, and it wasn't her choice.

Which leaves only one remaining explanation: Someone else took Julia's life and made it look like she'd killed herself.

CHAPTER THREE

Will takes the day off work so he can go with me to the funeral. He doesn't think the children should attend. I agree with this when it comes to Zack, who continues to take Julia's death in his stride and expresses all his feelings in the form of questions: *What happens when you die? Is it just your heart stops? When your heart stops, can your brain think? Where will the Julia bit that isn't her body go? Was it like lying down on the sofa and going to sleep? What would it have felt like? Could it happen to me? Could it happen to you and Daddy?*

I answer his questions as best I can, trying to strike a balance between honesty and reassurance. Sometimes people do get suddenly ill, I explain, but usually only when they are very old and their own children are grown up. It hasn't occurred to Zack that Julia might have taken her own life—that such a possibility might even exist. I can't see how his understanding or his grieving will be helped by going to Julia's funeral.

That is not the case with Hannah. She asks point-blank what the police have told me about Julia's death. I hedge a little but cave in under Hannah's persistence. One look at the horror in her eyes and I regret my honesty. Hannah, unlike Zack, already knows that suicide is possible. But she has no greater resources for understanding how Julia might have killed herself than I do. I tell her that no matter what the police and the coroner and everyone else thinks, I don't believe the suicide verdict. However, Hannah is swayed by the weight of all the authority figures ranged against me, including that of her own father. She cries in her room, one minute pulling me to her, the next pushing me away. She refuses to talk. Will tries. So does my mum. But Hannah doesn't speak. I recognize the hurt that bleeds from her eyes. She knows she was special to Julia, and she is asking my own questions: *How could Julia take herself away from us? Why weren't we enough? How could she do this to us?*

I ask those questions every day and I'm still coming up with the same, single, simple answer: Julia would *never* have killed herself. If nothing else, she would never have let herself be found by my children. She knew we were coming over. Our Sunday lunches were a regular arrangement on weekends when Julia was at home, and we'd confirmed this latest one only two days before. I remember the conversation:

I'd called to check what time she wanted us to arrive. She'd sounded distracted, her tone uncharacteristically tense and anxious. I'd asked if she was okay and she'd said she was fine, just preoccupied with work. Then she said something that had sounded strange, a vague reference to "looking into something." She'd mentioned her new man too, Dirty Blond. Was he connected to the thing she was investigating? I'm struggling to remember the exact flow of the conversation.

Suppose she found out something about him . . . something she didn't like? She was far more secretive about Dirty Blond's real name than usual. Why was that? Is the man married? This thought circles my head. It seems unlikely Julia would have had an affair. In all the years I knew her, she never once slept with a married man. Not knowingly, at least. Perhaps she found out he was married just before she died? Was that what her text on Saturday night was about?

PLS CALL. I NEED TO TALK TO YOU.

It eats away at me.

Julia passed away on a Saturday night, so why wasn't she with Dirty Blond then? Why hasn't he come forward since her death? Was there a fight? There's no way Julia would have killed herself over a man—*best treated as pets, men, bless them*—but maybe she found out he was married, or something else equally abhorrent to her, and finished it. Dirty Blond might have turned nasty. But then why no signs of a struggle? My mind flashes to Julia lying peacefully on her sofa. It crucifies me to think how much she would have hated being discovered as she was—her sweatpants soiled, her hair a mess.

I suggest to Hannah that she might want to go to the funeral to say good-bye to Julia, but she shakes her head.

"It'll all be grown-ups there, Mum," she says. "I want to say good-bye just me and her."

I promise to take her to Julia's favorite spot, overlooking the sea along the coast at Bolt Head. She told the kids she liked it because of the kites that so often flew there. She confessed to me it was also where she had met several handsome, well-heeled men whom she'd taken home for fast, furious sex. Hannah agrees to the kite trip, but I can see that it's small consolation. I press on, telling her how we'll sit on the cliff looking out to sea and drink those mock G&Ts Julia used to make for her.

"But it won't be the same," Hannah says in a small, lost voice. And of course, she is right.

Will is annoyed that Hannah knows about the suicide verdict—he would rather have kept the whole thing from her. We argue about it on Sunday, after which he remains tight-lipped for several hours. Hurt, I keep my distance. We thaw out by the time the kids are in bed, chatting about our holiday plans for later in the summer as we eat takeout together. This is typical of the way we make up, letting issues and tensions slide away rather than working them through. I've always liked the fact that we rarely argue, but today I'm aware that this is yet another occasion on which not talking means nothing under the surface has really been resolved.

The following morning we're dressing for the funeral when Mum phones from Bath full of flu. Despite her temperature and sore throat, she is still determined to drive to Exeter for the service. It takes me a while to talk her out of it. Mum was always fond of Julia, just as Julia always had a soft spot for her, for both my parents.

"They're my home away from home, Liv," she once said. "You've no idea how lucky you are."

So, in the end, it's just Will and me. We travel to the mortuary in a companionable silence. I'm lost in my own thoughts, running over the short eulogy that Joanie invited me to deliver at the funeral. After being left out of all the arrangements, at least I'll have a chance to talk about Julia, to remind people what she was really like, but as the moment approaches the responsibility is weighing heavily. Will and I arrive half an hour early. The service isn't until eleven, but Julia's mother and brother are already standing outside with Wendy. After several dry, sunny weeks, the weather today is humid, the sky leaden with dark clouds.

Robbie sees me and smiles. He looks nothing like his sister, his jowly face and balding head making him seem far older than thirty-six. Julia always enjoyed being mistaken for the younger sibling, teasing her twin for looking "ancient" before his time—taunts that never failed to get a rise out of Robbie.

Despite the fact that he lets his hair grow too long at the back, presumably to compensate for its loss on top—Robbie is actually better-looking now than he was at any point in his twenties. Certainly than when we went on that disastrous date all those years ago when his skin was covered with acne. Will maintains that Robbie still has a crush on me. He is beaming at me now, dropping his cigarette as Will and I walk over.

I glance at the glowing stub on the ground. Julia and I used to smoke too. I struggled to give up the year I married Will. Julia carried on cheerfully smoking until her thirty-third birthday when, for reasons she never really explained, she just decided to stop on the spot. As far as I know, she let go of her pack-a-day habit without any difficulty—becoming evangelically anti-smoking within the week. I never saw her with a cigarette again.

Joanie offers us a miserable grimace as we walk up, but Robbie leans over and kisses me warmly, then shakes Will's hand. Wendy, a gym instructor with a hard body and a face to match, just scowls. She looks as toned and severe as ever, in a long, fitted black skirt and boxy gray jacket. The masculine style of her dress is reinforced by her pinched face and sharp chin-length peroxide bob. Julia couldn't stand her. *Hitler in a blond wig,* she used to say with a scathing chuckle.

"How are you guys?" Robbie asks.

"Okay. How are you holding up, all of you?"

"We're hanging in there," Robbie says.

I look at Joanie. She shakes her head, not meeting my eyes. Wendy pats her arm. I shuffle from side to side, feeling uncomfortable. Robbie opens his mouth, clearly keen to chat, but Will gets there first.

"We're so sorry," he says. "We'll see you inside. Come on, Liv."

He takes my hand and we head toward Paul, Becky, and Martha, who have just arrived and are standing on the other side of the parking lot. Over the next fifteen minutes or so, the area outside the funeral home fills slowly, mostly with people I don't recognize. A smattering of Julia's other friends and colleagues come over to talk in low voices. All of them have shocked, solemn faces.

Another five minutes pass; then everyone goes inside. For some reason, Wendy—who said nothing to either of us in the parking lot—heads straight over as we're standing in the aisle.

"Livy." Her bony fingers clutch at my arm like claws. The people on either side of her melt away. "I should have said outside, thanks so much for coming."

What? I bristle. I can feel Will beside me stiffening too. Who is bloody Wendy to be welcoming me to Julia's funeral? After they fell out, she and Julia met only three or four times, mostly at the few family functions Julia was unable to extricate herself from.

"Hi, Wendy." I hesitate, indicating the room. "It's great there are so many people here."

"Family." Wendy offers me a thin smile. "Julia had thirty-three cousins, you know."

I did know. It was one of the many differences between us—Julia, estranged from her massive extended family; and me, an only child after Kara's death, tied tightly to my parents and, now, to my mother alone.

Wendy clears her throat. "Everyone's here to support Julia's mother, of course." She shakes her head. "So selfish of Julia. Typical, really, to be attention-seeking even in death."

My mouth drops open.

"That's too harsh," Will says emphatically. I feel his hand squeezing my shoulder, and my heart swells with gratitude. "We don't know what was going on with Julia . . . why she would have—"

"*If* she would have," I correct him.

Wendy offers up a contemptuous sniff. "Perhaps she wasn't as close to us all as we thought she was."

This dig is clearly directed at me. I want to defend myself and Julia—to tell Wendy that we told each other *everything.* But I know it isn't true. I *did* let Julia down. I didn't call her back. I didn't know what was on her mind that night.

I wasn't there when she died.

The music starts up and Wendy wanders away. The funeral parlor is almost full. Trying to put the pointed remarks of Julia's sister-in-law out of my mind, I turn to the row behind and speak to some of her journalist friends. At least these people genuinely care that she is gone. The fashion writers are dressed in snappy black dresses with shiny white gold jewelry and designer handbags on their arms. Most of the others are in summer coats and high-heeled sandals. Plenty look shell-shocked, but I get the same line from all of them:

I had no idea she was depressed and drinking heavily. Did you?

She wasn't those things! I want to yell at them. But it's no good. Even those people who are clearly devastated that Julia is gone still believe she took her own life. I am the only doubter.

It's a big relief when Paul, Becky, and Martha slip into the seats beside us. Paul met Julia through me, when we were all at uni. They even slept together once, though neither of them were ever interested in taking things any further and I'm not sure if Becky even knows their history. During the period when Will and I spent a lot of time socializing with Paul and Becky, Julia was often around—though we hadn't all hung out together for a long time. In contrast, Martha met Julia only a few times and is here, I know, simply to support me.

All three of them are as shocked as everyone else that she is dead.

"I wish I'd known her better," Becky says softly. "But she was always quite private. A lovely person, though. Full of life. You'd never have any idea . . ."

I bite my lip.

44

Paul frowns. "I'm so sorry, Liv. This must be so hard for you."

I smile gratefully at him. He sighs.

"Leo wanted to be here too, you know that, don't you?" Martha says.

Paul nods. "That's right, but it's hard with both me and Will out of the office. He sends his love, though."

"Absolutely," Martha adds.

"That's kind," I say, not really listening. It is nice of Leo to think about Julia's funeral at all. After all, like Martha, he met her only a few times. And it's lovely of Martha, Paul, and Becky to have made the effort to come. Still, what does it matter who turns up to this funeral, if Julia's memory is so badly served by it?

Wendy, Robbie, and Joanie emerge from the waiting room and take their seats at the front of the room. The first two rows are reserved for FAMILY ONLY. I see this and feel like crying, even as I tell myself I'm being petty to care.

What matters is Julia. And yet being sidelined because I wasn't related to her by blood is heartbreaking. "I'm so glad Hannah isn't here," I whisper in Will's ear. "She would be crushed."

He nods.

Everyone is sitting down now. I'm at the end of a row, so it'll be easy for me to stand and speak. A few butterflies flit around my stomach. At least I'm involved. My name is here on the order of service, toward the end, after Wendy reads a poem and Robbie offers a short eulogy for his sister's life. I can just imagine Julia's verdict on this: *That dickweasel doesn't* know *anything about my life.* Still, that's where I come in, to fill in the gaps.

The service is going to feature two pieces of music—a song by one of those pop-classic Italian tenors I know Julia would have hated, and *Air on a G String* at the conclusion. Lovely, but not a piece of music I ever heard Julia listen to. Joanie walks past me as I think this. She's leaning heavily on Robbie's arm, her face pale and drawn. I sigh, feeling guilty. Maybe *Air on a G String* means something to them.

The only G-strings in my life get played with in bed, honeypie. I can almost hear Julia's ironic drawl as the chatter in the funeral home dies down and Joanie, Robbie, and Wendy take their seats right at the front. And then the coffin is brought in. My breath catches in my throat to see it—to think that Julia's body is inside is both surreal and horrific. I'm so angry. This funeral shouldn't be happening. She shouldn't be dead. This is all so wrong.

A man from the crematorium leads the service, then invites Wendy to speak. She actually reads her poem well, her harsh voice carrying clearly across the room. There are a few mournful sniffs after the Italian tenor sings. Then Robbie stands. He scowls as he talks. At first I think he's just self-conscious about his grief; then I realize he's resentful. It's not apparent in what he's saying—all anodyne stuff about Julia being clever and successful as a freelance journalist—but in his tone of voice. He is furious with her. Wendy's earlier words drift back into my head.

So typically selfish of Julia to be attention-seeking, even in death.

Robbie is communicating the same, angry sentiment with every adjective. I can't believe it. He tells no anecdotes and recounts no instances of Julia's warmth or generosity. He speaks for less than three minutes outlining Julia's career and making a snide connection between her "many trips away from home" and her dislike of commitment in her romantic relationships. As he sits, it occurs to me that though he hasn't mentioned how Julia died, her suicide is all around us.

The funeral director calls my name. The weight of serving Julia's memory feels heavy on my shoulders. My legs tremble as I walk to the front of the room and take my place beside the coffin.

I gaze out over the faces. Some are in tears. They all think she killed herself, and somehow I have to make them realize she didn't.

The paper trembles in my hand. I take a deep breath and fix my gaze on Will. He smiles encouragingly. I have written down what I want to say about Julia, but now that I'm here, the words I've prepared seem hopelessly inadequate so I don't look at them, letting my feelings well up instead.

"It's hard to believe Julia is gone, when she was always so very much here," I say. "People talk about people being full of life and energy, but Julia really was. She was the funniest person I ever met." I pause. There's a story I wanted to tell, but I'm blanking on it, now that I'm in front of everyone.

"Sometimes being witty got Julia into trouble, but she hated meanness as much as she hated people being late." There are a few nods here. Julia's impatience with unpunctuality was well known—she once walked out of an interview with a top designer because he'd kept her waiting while he took a phone call. "So . . . Julia had strong opinions." I hesitate. This isn't what I want to say. "What I mean is, Julia was my best friend. We talked. All the time. She told me everything." My voice cracks. "She wanted to talk to me the night she died, but I wasn't there. . . ." I gaze out over the mourners. Nearly everyone is looking at me. Most of the faces I see are full of sorrow and sympathy. I catch Becky's eye. She smiles at me. Paul squeezes her hand and smiles gently too. On his other side, Martha wipes away a tear and gives me a supportive nod.

Encouraged, I carry on. "What I'm trying to say is that Julia was generous—with her time, with her money, and with her love. She was brittle and acerbic and she didn't suffer fools, but she was also wise and kind and *fun*. We met when we were at college, so I've known her since she was eighteen, and she was always full of energy. Of course, she had down days, but she had such an appetite for life. Her work as a journalist, clothes and handbags . . . she loved those . . . and her home, her flat . . . Most of all, she was loyal to her friends. We talked about getting older together. How, if we ended up alone, we'd live in a flat together with a couple of smelly cats. And she adored my children. . . ." My voice cracks again, and tears well up. "There's just no way she would have done . . . what they think she did . . . it's . . . it must have been something else . . ." My voice is choked. I can't get the words out. The people in the mortuary swim blurrily before my eyes. Most are looking concerned, glancing at each other. Embarrassed.

And then Will is at my side. My knees buckle and I lean against him, letting him lead me back to my seat. There's a hushed silence. I catch sight of Wendy and Joanie and Robbie as I pass the front row. They are watching me with pity—and, in Wendy's case, contempt.

A terrible grief swells inside me. I have convinced no one. If Julia were here and the situations were reversed, she would have found the words to tell the world I could never have killed myself. But I have failed to make anyone see the truth. I have failed Julia. Tears stream down my face. Those we pass avert their eyes, unwilling to witness the rawness of my pain. Will stops as we reach our seats. I glance to the back of the room. People are standing behind the last row of seats, packed in on either side of the exit. All of them are watching me, not quite meeting my eyes.

All except one. He is tall and ruggedly handsome in a dark suit. Even before I clock the giveaway shaggy blond hair and the fact that he's clearly a few years younger than most of the other guests, I know instinctively that this is Julia's Dirty Blond.

Our eyes lock on to each other. His burn with fury. His whole body radiates it. As I stare at him, he tears his gaze away and leaves the funeral parlor. Will presses me into my seat. I feel flushed. Will doesn't seem to have noticed the man.

He leans over, his hand on mine, whispering in my ear. "Are you okay, Livy?"

I nod, wiping my eyes. The undertaker offers us the chance to take a minute's silence to pray or to reflect on our time with Julia. Then *Air on a G String* begins and the curtains in front of the coffin close. I look around again, but the blond young man has definitely gone.

Before I know it, the service is over and everyone is leaving the mortuary. Will puts his arm around my shoulders and leads me outside. The air out here is fresher than before, the sun fighting to emerge from behind the clouds.

Julia's family avoids me, but several people do come over: friends and colleagues of Julia and both the ex-boyfriends. Martha, Paul, and Becky are particularly sweet. They offer me sympathy and hugs and reassurance that I didn't let Julia down in any way. I hate that this is how my supposed eulogy has come across—a plea for exoneration. None of the mourners here allow for the possibility I might have been right about Julia's death. I ask a few if they know the name of the blond guy who was standing by the exit, but no one does. That furious look he gave me stays in my mind's eye, sending anxious shivers down my back.

What was he so angry about? *Does* he know something about her death?

I try to explain my suspicions to Will, but he won't listen. He thinks I'm wrong about Julia—that my perspective is skewed by guilt and grief. He also points out that I am only guessing that the man at the service at the funeral was Julia's Dirty Blond.

"The state you were in, you could easily have imagined the angry look," he suggests.

"I didn't imagine it," I say, stung.

"Okay, if he really was involved with Julia, why didn't he introduce himself to anyone, Liv?" Will asks quite reasonably.

I don't have any answers. I look around as the crowd thins out, people heading to the hotel where Joanie has organized a small-scale wake. There's definitely no sign of Dirty Blond here.

Will and I give a couple of Julia's journalist friends a lift to the hotel. The talk is light and polite, with only passing mentions of Julia. It's ironic that someone with so much personality should have so little influence over her own funeral. I feel heavy and alone with my grief and my misery continues at the hotel, which is nondescript: beige and modern, the sort of place Julia would have hated. There are a few complimentary bottles of wine, which disappear fast, leaving only tea and coffee—and the cash bar. The room is hot. Soon, all the men have taken off their jackets, which only adds to the informal, lighthearted atmosphere of the wake. Most of Julia's journalist friends have disappeared. I see a couple of girls I recognize from uni in a corner, but they are engrossed in their conversation and don't notice me.

I speak to Paul and Becky for a while. They are concerned and attentive, almost making me cry with their kindness. After a while it emerges that Becky's teaching term has just ended—the private schools always break up before the public ones—and she is leaving for Spain the next day. On hearing this news, I insist the pair of them head home so she can pack and they can spend a last evening together, and after some reluctance, they go, taking Martha with them.

Alone for the first time since the service ended, I look around the room. Will is over by the window, talking to Robbie and Wendy. After the pitying looks they gave me in the mortuary, and Wendy's words about Julia's selfishness, I can't bring myself to join them. As I watch, Will's phone rings—I recognize the ringtone, one Hannah downloaded for him, coming from the pocket of his jacket, which is slung over the chair beside me. I glance across the room. Will is still deep in conversation. He hasn't heard his mobile. I fish it out of his jacket pocket, still ringing.

It's Leo.

"Hi," I answer.

"Livy? So sorry to bother you while you're at the funeral." Leo doesn't sound like he means the apology. His tone is self-important and overly insistent, much like his hand on my arm the other day.

I clear my throat. "It's fine, we're nearly finished." And, indeed, the room is emptying fast.

"Awful about Julia. I only met her a few times, of course, but she was so full of life." I sigh. Leo isn't unintelligent, but he's falling back on the same inadequate platitudes as the rest of us. "How, er, how was the funeral itself?"

"It was okay," I said. My voice fills with tears. "Actually, it wasn't okay at all."

"I know." Leo's voice fills with sympathy. He sounds genuine this time. "I'm glad Martha and Paul were there for me, to pay my respects."

"Thanks." I sniff. "Sorry. Did you want Will?"

"I'm afraid so—it's one of the French accounts. Is he nearby?"

I head over to Will and hand him his phone. I don't want to stay and chat with Robbie and Wendy, so I make an excuse and retreat to the bathroom. I look around for Dirty Blond as I cross the room. But he still hasn't arrived. Clearly he isn't going to.

The anxiety I felt before settles into a knot in my chest. Dirty Blond knows something about how Julia really died. I am sure of it. And now I'm not only miserable that Julia is gone. I'm scared too.

GEORGINA

And God said: "This is the sign of the covenant which I make between me and you."

Genesis 9:12

This will amuse you.

Before I met the One, there was Georgina. She was our babysitter when I was twelve or so—and thought, of course, that I was too old to need a babysitter. I tolerated Georgina because she was pretty, or at least appeared so to me then.

It was summer—and my mother was having a party to celebrate our moving to a new house in the area. Naturally my father was not there, but Georgina was. I remember she arrived at the party in a daringly short skirt. Her hair was in braids, and her full lips were coated in a bright red lipstick, giving her the veneer, at least, of adult sophistication. Most of the men at the party—husbands of friends of my mothers—couldn't keep their eyes off her. But Georgina was my property. It didn't occur to me that she was eight years older that I was—not to mention five inches taller. I had never been kissed, and I decided, in that moment, that I wanted Georgina to kiss me and that nothing was going to stand in my way.

It was hot, a textbook summer's afternoon, complete with blue skies and the perfect amount of breeze. The adults were standing in the garden, sipping wine and beer, smoking, chatting. It was all very boring and suburban. Georgina herself was busy flirting, the little tramp, enjoying the attention of all those older men. I told her I needed to speak to her around the side of the house. Reluctantly, she followed me.

We stood between the rough brick of the kitchen wall and the lilac wisteria that trailed down the rickety wooden fence that divided my house from its neighbor.

"What is it?" Georgina asked, her tone impatient.

"Kiss me," I said, looking up at her. The sun was catching the fine hairs above her top lip and making her long fair braids shine like gold.

Georgina laughed. "Puh-leese," she said. She bent down and pecked me on the cheek. "See ya, kiddo." She turned away, clearly intending to head back to the party.

I was outraged. That was not the kiss—or the attitude—I had been looking for. I grabbed her wrist, twisting the skin as she tried to pull away.

"Stop it," she snapped.

"No." I stared at her, full of confidence. "Kiss me. Or I'll tell Mum you stole her necklace."

"What are you talking about?" Georgina frowned. "What necklace?"

The item in question—a bequest from my late grandmother—was in fact in my own pocket. Using the cover of the party, I had just taken it myself and I was looking forward to selling it next time I found myself in the center of town where I could pass unquestioned and anonymous. I can't remember now what I wanted to buy with the money, but it wasn't the first or the last time I took small items from my family and friends. Strangely, though the objects themselves were invariably missed, I was never suspected as the thief. Too good at covering my tracks, even then.

Georgina was still frowning. I repeated my threat.

"You won't tell your mum any such thing," she said, and despite her words, I could hear a slight uncertainty in her voice.

I twisted the skin on her wrist, harder than before. "I swear," I said, "that I will."

She hesitated. "Go on, then, you stupid little creep, but she won't believe you."

I released her and she marched off, back to the party. I filled with contempt. How dare she doubt me?

A few minutes later I crept up beside my mother and informed her that I had just seen Georgina taking the necklace from the jewelry box in her bedroom. Mum took Georgina into the kitchen, where Georgina denied everything. Her attempt to put the blame for the accusation on me was some-what undermined when Mum demanded to see her pockets—into which I had, of course, slipped the necklace as I made my threat.

Mum was shocked and upset. So, naturally, was Georgina. I watched from the kitchen door, enjoying the spectacle.

Georgina left the house with Mum threatening to call her father as soon as the party was over and tell him what she had stolen. This was a heavy threat, because it was well known that Georgina's father was a drunk and a bully. I caught up with Georgina halfway along the road, insisting that if she would only kiss me after all, I would tell Mum the whole thing had been a prank.

Georgina angrily agreed. She pulled me behind the nearest buddleia bush and proceeded to kiss me. Properly. With tongues and everything. I had never experienced anything like it. After about ten seconds, she pulled away, leaving me inflamed with excitement.

"Okay?" she snarled.

I pointed to her chest. "Show me them too," I said.

Georgina protested.

I insisted. "Or my mum tells your dad."

Georgina hesitated, then unbuttoned her shirt. Less angry now, her face was red and her fingers were trembling. One of the little plastic buttons popped off. I picked it up, took a good look at Georgina's breasts, then asked her to raise her skirt.

Again, she hesitated, then hitched it up. I peered at the tops of her skinny legs, at the triangle of blue cotton.

"Down," I ordered.

She wriggled the pants halfway down her legs, turning her face away from me. I took my time examining what she had revealed, enjoying her shame as much as her body. After a while I told her she could go.

As she readjusted her clothing, she looked me in the eye. "So you'll tell your mum the necklace thing was a joke, yeah?"

I turned and walked away, rubbing the plastic button from her shirt be-tween my fingers.

She called after me. "Please?"

A smile crept across my lips.

I returned to the party. No one had noticed my short absence. I had, to be sure, lost out financially today, but I'd gained something far more precious.

Did I tell my mother the truth?

What do you think?

A few hours later Mum made her phone call and a few days after that I saw Georgina in the street with a black eye and a few days after that we got a new babysitter named Kim.

CHAPTER FOUR

After the wake, Will drops me at home, then drives into the office to deal with whatever Leo needed doing on the French account. He seems distracted as he says good-bye, and it flashes through my head that he may be about to speak to Catrina, who, after all, works out of the Paris office. The old fears flicker inside me. Could seeing her again have reignited his desire for her after all?

No, that's ridiculous. There is nothing in Will's behavior that justifies my thinking that. I put on a wash and tell myself not to be stupid.

Mum calls as I'm hanging out the wet clothes. She sounds terrible, all croaky and snuffling. She keeps saying how sorry she is for missing the funeral, for not being there to support me. I can hear in her voice that she's not wildly impressed that Will has gone back to work this afternoon, and immediately I leap to his defense.

"It's hard when you're not family," I insist. The way I was sidelined at the funeral by Joanie and Robbie springs into my head. "Leo was actually very sweet, but Will's too senior to take off the whole day. He's deputy MD now as well as planning director, remember?"

Mum falls silent. I wonder if her memories are taking her back to my sister's funeral eighteen years ago. It was so different from Julia's, I hadn't really thought about it earlier, but now the recollections fill my mind. Whereas Joanie made use of a nondenominational mortuary and requested no flowers, as per Julia's supposed suicide note, the church near Mum and Dad's was awash with blooms of every description. In a terrible parody of a wedding, flowers filled the side aisles with sweet scents—not just the lily of the valley and roses that decorated the church, but also hundreds of bouquets laid inside and outside the church by the friends and neighbors who had gathered in force to support us. The press was there too. Plenty of people were moved, I suppose, by Kara's death—and by her youth and her beauty.

At Kara's funeral, everyone cried. Girls her own age and their boyfriends, all red-eyed and weeping and clutching each other for comfort. And the parents: her friends' parents and my parents' friends. They approached Mum and Dad with horror in their eyes.

"Impossible to take it in."

"Such a lovely girl."

"The worst nightmare."

Dad fielded them all with his customary tact. I'm not sure Mum even heard them. She stood at his side, nodding and murmuring, but her eyes were dead. I knew both my parents were hurting, but back then, full of my own grief and without children of my own, I had no concept of the depth of their pain. I'm not sure I can really imagine it now. Or perhaps I just don't want to.

Mum dissolves into a coughing fit, then asks what the weather's like with us.

"Mild," I say. "A bit sticky, but okay."

We both fall silent. It's funny, you'd think Kara's death and then Dad's would have brought us together, but each bereavement just seems to show us more distinctly how separate we are. Kara was Mum's favorite. Her baby. While I was a classic older sister, forging ahead at school, working hard in all my classes and diligently practicing the piano every night, Kara skipped and dreamed through her childhood. She rarely sat still for more than a few minutes yet had phenomenal focus and an excellent memory. She effortlessly got better grades than I did despite giving the appearance of doing very little work. She was a talented artist too, spending much of her free time on sketches of the actors and pop idols she romanticized and adored.

Kara and Julia were both stunningly attractive, but apart from their pale skin, they were complete opposites in both looks and personalities. Mum once said that it was as if a butterfly and a tiger had decided to become friends. She liked Julia, though. I think both my parents hoped that Julia's street smarts would protect naïve, gentle Kara from the big bad world she had entered by leaving home and going to college. I was always closer to Dad, who in his quiet, solid way felt like the backbone of the family, my go-to parent for comfort and advice.

I say good-bye to Mum and wander restlessly around the house. My mind flickers back to the funeral and the angry face of the blond man.

A hefty dose of Nembutal, a note, and the coroner's verdict may stack up on one side of the argument for suicide, but that furious look on Dirty Blond's face adds up to a powerful counterargument. I think back to Julia's text.

PLS CALL. I NEED TO TALK TO YOU.

Suppose she and Dirty Blond had fought that Saturday? My theory about him being married and Julia finding out and dumping him isn't the only possible scenario. Julia had lots of boyfriends, and despite that rule about never sleeping with married men, she was rarely exclusive. Even the few ex-boyfriends I did meet over the years lasted only three or four months. She'd told me about Dirty Blond only a few weeks ago and didn't seem inclined to introduce him. Maybe he minded being kept at arm's length. Plenty of her former lovers had.

If they'd fought and Julia was heading for an evening in alone, that would explain her text to me *and* that she'd had a couple of drinks. But what if Dirty Blond had come back later in the evening? Julia would have let him in—that would definitely explain the lack of evidence of forced entry—perhaps hoping another conversation would heal the rift. Julia was five-six and slender. She told me Dirty Blond was tall and muscular, and indeed, the man I saw at the funeral was over six foot. I'd previously wondered why there were no signs of a struggle, but how hard would it have been for such a strong, young man to force her to take the Nembutal? Or maybe he just slipped the drug into her Jack Daniel's?

I check the time again. Julia's flat is only a few minutes out of my way to Zack's school. I usually walk to pick him up, but if I drive, I should have at least forty-five minutes to see if I can find something the police have missed.

I grab my keys and set off.

The air feels damp and heavy as I get out of my Mini. The car was bought at Julia's suggestion and in the teeth of Will's opposition. He thought it was too small to be our family vehicle—his own Rover comes courtesy of Harbury Media—and wanted me to get a station wagon for ferrying the kids around town. As I shut the Mini's shiny, scarlet doors, I remember Julia oohing and aahing over its curves. *Such an icon, Livy,* she'd said admiringly.

Did I buy it because I knew she'd be impressed? Or because at some level I was aspiring to Julia's own, streamlined existence? Either way— and I hate to admit it—Will was right about it being too small for family life.

Outside Julia's front door, my hands tremble as I fit my key in the lock. The last time I stood here, I had no idea that Julia was dead. Now, the image of her body on the sofa is seared into my brain. *It's not there now,* I tell myself. *Her body is gone. Burned.* As I open the door, I wonder for the first time what Joanie will do with the ashes. No one has, so far, mentioned this, at least not in my hearing. Neither, now that I come to think of it, has there been any talk of a will. It would be unlike Julia not to have made one. A self-confessed con- trol freak, she carefully filed all her paper invoices and bills in color- coded folders, reflecting—she once told me—the more extensive files on her computer.

Julia's flat is eerily quiet. It feels somehow stale and anonymous, like a hotel room, but maybe that's just because it hasn't been lived in for over a week. I glance at the photos lining the hall corridor— from a holiday Julia and I took to Africa the year after Kara died. I had met Will just a few months previously and bored Julia insane by talking about him at every opportunity. She tried to get me to flirt with the guys we encountered on the trip, but I refused. It wasn't just loyalty to Will. I was always useless at talking to people I didn't know. Julia, on the other hand, was a born flirt. Even back then, when she was only nineteen, she had a uncanny knack for zoning in on the alpha male of any group and catching his eye. Of course, it helped that she was strikingly beautiful. Not in the same fragile, elegant way that Kara was; Julia's features weren't regular or doll-like, but her eyes danced when she talked, her laugh was a throaty and sensual cackle and she looked like she'd be the best fun you'd ever have in bed.

"That girl practically sweats sex," I remember one of her ex-boyfriends saying admiringly.

None of that is reflected in Julia's choice of photos from that African trip, which hang on the wall: a series of shots of the various animals we came close to—monkeys, a pair of giraffes, and my favorite, a baby elephant.

Into Julia's living room and I hold my breath. I don't want to look, but of course my eyes go straight to the sofa, where the dark stain lingers on the seat. My heart is beating fast as I look away, around the bookshelves and across to the table and chairs that are, as always, positioned under the window.

Wait. Where's the art? Julia had a couple of pieces—nothing valuable, just some abstract stuff she liked. I don't know the names of the artists. The walls are bare—also missing is the flat-screen TV that used to stand in the corner of the room.

I head into Julia's bedroom. Her jewelry lies scattered across the dressing table. There's so much here, I can't tell if any of the more expensive pieces are missing. There's certainly no sign of the diamond and emerald ring she was given by one of her wealthier former lovers. Alan Rutherford was a widower who doted on Julia. The ring wasn't the only extravagant gift he presented her with. He died a couple of years after they broke up, and much to Julia's astonishment, he left her his seaside cottage in Lympstone, which they had, apparently, visited occasionally on weekends. Julia immediately began supplementing her income by renting it out. What will happen to it now?

Wondering about both the ring and the cottage, I stroll into the spare room, which Julia used as an office. I gasp. Her computer is gone, leaving a large square gap surrounded by papers in the center of her desk. The sun shines on the wooden surface, highlighting the layer of dust at the edges of the gap.

I grip the back of the chair, suddenly panicked. Who has taken all this stuff? The police? Why would they bother? They've already accepted the suicide verdict.

I whip out my phone, intending to call Joanie. Then I remember that I am, effectively, intruding here and that it's still only a few hours since Joanie buried her only daughter.

I put my phone away. There are no signs of a break-in. Joanie herself has probably removed the missing items. Perhaps she felt they would be safer away from an unoccupied flat.

I still don't like it, but there's nothing I can do. And I'm here to look for evidence that Julia didn't kill herself. That's the priority.

I go back into Julia's bedroom and sit down on the bed where Zack, Hannah, and I huddled just two weeks ago. It feels like a million years have passed since then. Without access to Julia's phone, which I already know Joanie has with her, or her computer, I'm not sure what to look for. A diary? Julia was never one to pour out her soul on the page, but she definitely kept an appointments book. She always refused to use the calendar on her phone and computer, buying instead an annual Moleskine diary. *It's a journalist rite of passage, Liv, a way of channeling Hemingway without the dead bulls. . . .*

I rummage in Julia's bedside drawers. I feel voyeuristic looking here, though I know what I'll find—nail file, hand cream, paperbacks, cigarettes (she kept them for guests), condoms (ditto), and pens and Post-it notes. No sign of her diary. She always kept that in whichever handbag she was using at the time. *A girl can't have too many bags. Or shoes. Or orgasms.* I wander over to the large fitted wardrobe and slide open the door. Julia's dresses and tops hang from a rail. On impulse, I grab a handful of Prada silk shirt and hold it to my face, hoping for a scent of her. But all I can smell is the faint whiff of chemicals. I sigh. Trust Julia to be on top of her dry cleaning. Shoes and boots line the second section, with skirts and pants hanging from the rod above. I rummage through the final, shelved section, my fingers stroking the soft, delicate lingerie that Julia loved to buy. I hold up a pair of black silk panties, then a lacy basque. I remember Hannah wide-eyed when Julia showed her a recent purchase: a blue bra and panties in soft satin with a thin cream trim. Julia had grinned at Hannah's awe. *Beautiful underwear, honeypie, will always be your greatest gift to yourself after financial independence and an inquiring mind.* Hannah had nodded solemnly, as if Julia were offering her the keys to adult life.

Perhaps she was. It's funny, but I never resented how much Hannah looked up to Julia. I was always grateful that, having lost her aunt, my daughter at least had a godmother who adored her.

The huge bottom shelf is full of handbags. Small and large, High Street and designer, they're testament to Julia's lifelong search for *that one, perfect bag to go with every occasion.*

Stupidly, my eyes fill with tears as it strikes me she will now never achieve her ambition.

For God's sake, Livy, get a grip, I mutter under my breath. Handbags are the least of it.

I root around for a bit. Julia's Kelly bag isn't here. Neither is her vintage Chanel clutch nor her tiny Versace shoulder purse. I open the bags I saw Julia use most frequently. The third I pick up is one of Julia's recent High Street purchases. I hadn't thought it was anything special myself, but Julia was ecstatic when she found it—*total Prada knockoff, Liv,* she'd told me as proudly as if she'd designed the thing herself.

The diary is lurking in the inside pocket. My throat is dry as I take it out. This, suddenly, feels like I'm touching her life in a way that the clothes and bags do not.

I flick back through the pages to the week Julia died. Our Sunday lunch is logged in her bold, firm hand, but apart from a few work meetings, most of the week to either side appears empty. The Thursday two days before her death is marked: *A.H. 9pm.* I wonder for a moment who A.H. is, then turn to the week after her death. It's blank, apart from a dental appointment.

My heart sinks. I'd so hoped for some clue to her state of mind here, but there's nothing. In fact, the absence of appointments surely serves to support the verdict of suicide.

I turn the page again, to the current week. I stare at today's date. It's empty. How bizarre to think that Julia might have flicked over this page, never dreaming it would be the date of her own funeral. I shiver and move on. Tomorrow night, Tuesday, contains the following entry:

SHANNON, 10:30 PM, ACES HIGH

I stare at the words. Aces High is a singles bar in Torquay that Julia once described as a *lean-meat market, full of skinny, trashy women and classless men. . . .*

Why would she be going to meet someone there? Julia hated bars like that as much as she disliked Torquay itself. And who is Shannon? I'm certain Julia doesn't have a friend with that name. I'm intrigued and encouraged. Because this, more than the work or dental appointments, suggests that Julia was looking into the future before she died. Maybe I'm clutching at straws, but it feels like fate that I've found this. It's something to hang on to at least.

Something to help me act.

It takes me most of the following twenty-four hours to face up to what that action needs to be: I have to go to Aces High and meet Shannon myself. Of course, she probably won't be there. Chances are she will already know Julia is dead. But I have to try.

I put off telling Will—I know he'll come up with all sorts of logical reasons why I shouldn't go to a meeting arranged between a stranger and a dead person. Put like that, it does sound crazy, and yet whoever Shannon is, he or she may know what it was Julia wanted to talk to me about. Or even something relevant about how she died.

I troll through the guest list for the funeral, which Joanie e-mailed me last week. There's no one with the name Shannon. I call Joanie herself, hoping to check that there aren't any other friends or family members I don't know about—as well as to ask about all the stuff missing from Julia's flat—but she doesn't answer her phone. This isn't a surprise. Julia often complained that her mother screened all calls.

Joanie certainly has a reason not to want to speak to people at the moment. She's probably still with Robbie and Wendy anyway.

It makes no difference. I'm going. I'm going to Aces High to honor Julia's arrangement to meet Shannon. If no one is there, then I'll have lost nothing except a couple hours of my time.

And Will's approval, of course.

As the day wears on, I get more and more nervous—and less and less in the mood to tell Will what I'm planning. I could phone him at work, but I don't. He doesn't get in until almost eight. I could—maybe should—say something straightaway. But I hesitate. He's tired and grouchy and I decide to wait until he's had a chance to take the edge off his mood with a glass of wine and a bowl of pasta.

I've already eaten with the kids, so Will takes a spoon and scarfs the remaining Bolognese out of the saucepan as he slumps in front of the TV. Apart from a good night to the kids, he has barely spoken since he got in. I read Zack a story, then turn out his light and head downstairs. I mean to tell Will now. I really do. But he's in the middle of some History Channel documentary on the D-Day landings and has such an *I'm zoning out, please don't disturb me* look on his face that, again, I can't face telling him.

I tidy up in the kitchen, then check on Zack. He is already asleep, snuffling peacefully into his duvet. I nag Hannah out of her bedroom and into the bathroom to clean her teeth. She protests, as usual, at her school night bedtime of 9 P.M. with lights out at 9:30. I make sure she's in bed and reading, then go into my own room and put on some makeup. I'm not dressing up—jeans and sandals will do fine—but I don't want to look totally out of place, so I select a silky top and fuss over earrings for a bit. I go back to Hannah and insist she switches out the light. She claims she's not tired and she wants to finish the chapter she's reading. Clever middle-class kids who know how much their parents value books miss no tricks. I give in and wait a few minutes. Of course, she still hasn't finished by nine forty-five, but it's starting to feel like this could be a long, drawn-out battle, so I insist and flick off the wall light as she's still looking at the page.

She swears at me. Normally I would take issue. Or fetch Will to back me up. Today I ignore her. To reach Torquay by ten thirty, I'm going to have to leave in the next fifteen minutes or so, and I'm already anticipating a spat with Will. I can't get into one with my daughter as well.

For a moment I feel an overwhelming resentment that I'm so often left to be the bad guy with Hannah—that Will tends to abdicate responsibility for bedtimes unless I call on him in a crisis. I remind myself this was the deal we made when Zack was born. I would give up my junior family law job, which barely covered Hannah's child care fee as it was, while Will would bring in the big bucks and leave the kids to me during the week.

Being a homemaker's a job too, Julia had said wryly at the time. *Just one without status, remuneration, or opportunities for promotion.*

I start to head downstairs then, suddenly self-conscious about turning up at a night club underdressed, I go back to my bedroom and change out of the flat sandals and into my open-toed Lanvin wedges. Julia found them in a sale and, knowing they would fit me perfectly, bought them as a birthday gift last year. I peek around Hannah's door. For all her protests at not being tired, she is already asleep, the book she was reading still defiantly in her hand. Sleeping is when Hannah looks most like Kara, and the sight of her still body sends that image of Kara's lifeless eyes into my head again. I shiver, unable to stop myself touching Hannah's arm for reassurance that her skin is warm. I remove the book and ease her under the covers. I smooth her fine, silky hair off her face and pull the duvet up over her shoulders. Over the years, I might have become less neurotic and overprotective, but if I'm honest, seeing her safe and asleep is the only time I feel truly secure.

With a sigh, I turn away and head downstairs. I need to leave. Now.

"Will?" I stand in the living room door for several long seconds before Will tears himself away from whatever program he is now watching to glance irritably at me. He does a double take when he sees how dressed up I am.

"Liv?" he says. "What's going on?"

"I have to go out."

"What?"

"Hopefully I'll just be a couple of hours."

Will looks so bewildered, I feel terrible, but his shock makes it even harder to explain what I'm doing. I turn and head for the front door.

Will follows me. "What the hell are you talking about? *Where* are you going? It's almost ten o'clock, for God's sake."

I reach the front door. "Julia had a . . . meeting with someone called Shannon for ten thirty P.M. tonight," I said. "I found it in her diary. I'm going to be there for when this Shannon turns up." I open the door.

"Are you crazy?" Will strides over. "Why the hell do you want to do that?" He stands right beside me. "Whoever it is won't be there, anyway. They'll know Julia is dead."

"Not necessarily," I say. "And if they don't know, I can tell them."

"But it's *late,* Liv." Will's eyes are wild with shock. He gesticulates behind him, indicating the kids upstairs . . . the whole house. "You won't be back for ages. It's *mad.*"

"No, it's not," I say. "Anyway, you're often out late yourself."

"That's *work*. It's different." Will snaps, "You shouldn't go alone, anyway. Not to a club. This 'Shannon' could be anyone. It's not safe."

"For God's sake. I'm thirty-eight," I say. "And you can't come. You've got to stay with the kids. They're both asleep. They won't even know I'm gone."

Will gapes at me, now completely at a loss for words.

"It'll be fine," I say.

"No, Livy." He finds his voice as I open the door. "This is crazy. You're becoming fixated on Julia's death. It's affecting Hannah."

"What?" I stare at him. Where the hell did that come from?

"It's the truth." Will levels his gaze at me. I used to find that dark, intense gaze of his sexy. Now I'm just infuriated.

"I'm not fixated, and Hannah's just at a difficult age. Plus she's upset about Julia, which is perfectly natural."

"It's more than that."

"I don't think—"

"She's quieter than she used to be. Introverted. She hardly ever smiles. Her confidence is shot to pieces."

"What?" I don't recognize the picture he's painting. "That's ridiculous. Hannah's just starting to go through puberty. It's . . . it's more hormonal than anything."

"I'm not going to argue about it." Will rolls his eyes. "The point is, you can't just walk out at a minute's notice."

"Why not? You do it all the time." Properly furious now, I stomp away from the house and wrench open the Mini.

Will calls my cell phone before I've even driven to the end of the road, but I don't pick up and he doesn't leave a message. I'm seething over what he's said. For a start, he is totally wrong about Hannah. She's just acting out a lot at the moment. Julia's death hasn't made a big difference to that. And what colossal nerve, telling me I can't just walk away from the house when he does exactly the same thing whenever work demands it. Look at how he went to Geneva the other night.

I calm down as I drive through Exeter. The streets are virtually empty. It's weird to be going out this late and without Will. Once I did it all the time. Now I actually feel a little nervous—and not just because I'm about to meet a stranger.

Is it marriage and motherhood that have drained all my confidence?

Or is it just that I miss Julia?

I did go out a lot in my early twenties, but most of the time Julia was with me, steering a clear passage through all social waters, drawing me effortlessly along in her wake.

There's a queue at the next set of lights. As I wait for the red to turn green, I gaze at the Asian couple huddled in a doorway, poring over a phone together. They look so young, so hopeful, their lives in front of them. I lean my head against the car window, watching them as rain trickles down the glass.

My life is already almost half over, and I don't feel as if I've properly begun it yet. Apart from the children, what have I really achieved?

Undergraduate honors in History and a few dull years in a law office don't add up to much. Once I dreamed of being an academic with a tenured professorship: authoring important papers, giving talks at glamorous conferences, and guiding graduates through MAs and PhDs, then going home to my handsome, loving husband and brood of bonny babies. I'd successfully juggle it all, and eager students like the girl I once was would look at me with admiration in their eyes, seeing me as a role model and an inspiration.

I reach Torquay and stop to let a group of young women in short skirts above bare, mottled legs cross the road ahead. It starts raining very lightly, but the girls don't seem to notice. A few moments later they have giggled and tottered their way past me, leaving empty sidewalks gleaming under the streetlamps.

The music is deafening. That's my first thought. The second is how long it has been since I set foot inside a nightclub. Aces High is designed in the shape of a diamond, with several themed rooms set around a large, square glass bar. It took less time than I was expecting to get here, so it's barely 10:20 P.M., and the whole club is practically empty. The bouncers and the girl in her ACES HIGH T-shirt stamped my hand without a second glance, but now I feel everyone is looking at me. The group of men at the glass bar certainly are. But then they're checking out everyone.

I wander out of the bar area and into the first themed room, feeling horribly self-conscious. Diamond Room is glittery, with high, tiny tables for standing around, and lit with artificial candles. It's empty. I pass through an arch into Club Room. It's gloomy and musty-smelling, all fake-wood paneling and black leather chairs. Like Diamond, it's completely deserted. I walk on, into Heart Room. Unlike the previous two spaces, Heart at least looks comfortable. Three or four pink sofas are arranged around a heart-shaped coffee table. Three young women with high heels and bare midriffs are giggling over a mobile phone. Two men stand at the door, watching them. No one gives me a second glance.

I check the time. Ten twenty-five. I walk into Spade Room. The walls are dark purple and hang with chains and masks. A long whip snakes down from the ceiling, into the corner of the room. There are no proper seats, just functional black-matted slabs on chrome bases. They look like torture tables. All very Red Room of Pain. I feel stupidly embarrassed. Two men are sitting in opposite corners. They both stare at me. I decide neither can possibly be Shannon and scurry away, back out to the light and bustle of the main bar. This is starting to fill up,—plenty of singles dotted between the groups—but a number of stools are still available. I perch on one at the far end, which gives a good view of the whole bar. At least out here, where it's busy, I feel less noticeable. I look around. Julia's phrase for the bar—*lean-meat market*—comes to mind. All the women are over-made up and underdressed, and some of them—the older ones, mostly— are also giving off an air of desperation that belies the grim smiles fixed to their faces. As for the men, they're as predatory and cold-eyed as they are unattractive. To me, at least. The muscular barman wanders over and I order a white wine—I'm driving, but one drink is fine; I need it to steady my nerves. The barman brings it over and lays it down on a small white circular napkin. He doesn't look at me. I drink the wine. More people arrive at the bar. Most of the girls are in pairs or groups. They are all dressed to the nines in low-cut tops and thigh-skimming skirts. They cast excited glances around them. Some of the men are in groups—hunting packs. Others pace the perimeter of the bar—lone wolves.

I shake myself. I'm being far too cynical. This is just mating and dating at its most naked and obvious. Of course the people here are looking at each other hopefully—it's a singles bar.

It's ten forty. Surely Shannon must be here by now? I'm cursing myself for not realizing that a bar was a hopeless place in which to identify a total stranger. Does that mean Julia had met Shannon before? What I don't understand is why she ever agreed to come here. She hated places like this. At least she always told me she did. I sip my wine, overwhelmed by the sense that I'm being watched. I look up. A middle-aged man across the bar is staring at me. I look away quickly. The last thing I need is to be propositioned.

The fear of getting hit on spurs me into action. Shannon clearly isn't going to arrive with a name badge hanging around his or her neck. And I've come too far to give up this easily. I hold up my glass and wave at the bartender. A minute later, he appears in front of me.

"Another wine?" he asks. He has undone the entire front of his shirt, and I can't help but stare at his six-pack as he speaks.

"Er, no, thanks!" I have to shout to be heard over the music— something tuneless with a heavy bass thump. "I was just wondering if you know anyone who comes here called Shannon?"

To my amazement, the barman nods. "Sure." He jerks his thumb across the bar to where a round-faced, curly-haired young woman is sitting on a stool, legs neatly crossed.

As the bartender wanders away, I watch her, my heart drumming against my throat. *This* is Shannon. She's dressed less provocatively than most of the girls here. Her dress is skintight, but it comes down to her knees and there's no cleavage on show. As I watch, one man after another approaches her. Shannon flicks her gaze toward them for just a second, smiles, then mutters something. In the space of thirty seconds, she's fended off three of them.

Well, whoever she is, I'm impressed. I ease myself off my stool and walk around the bar toward her. There's no seat next to her, so I stand. Now that I'm closer, I can see she's really pretty in a soft, baby doll–type way. Big blue gray eyes and long, highlighted hair in soft curls.

"Are you Shannon?" I say. I'm gripping my wineglass tightly.

She nods, her eyes wary. "Yes," she says. "Why?"

"What's your secret?" I ask, affecting a casual laugh. "For getting rid of the guys."

She stares at me curiously. I guess it is a strange question to be asking in a singles bar. "I tell them the bartender's my boyfriend," she says. "He's not really, just a mate. He's actually gay."

I follow her gaze over to the muscular bartender. A beat passes. I take a deep breath. "You're here to meet Julia Dryden, aren't you?"

Shannon says nothing, but her eyes betray her recognition of Julia's name.

"I'm Julia's friend. I saw your name in her diary," I gabble on. "I had to meet you, to find out—"

Shannon frowns. "Julia's not coming?" she says.

I bite my lip. So she doesn't know. Which means I have to tell her. And it's still hard to say the words, to face the truth. "Julia died," I explain. The music blares out around me. Shannon's eyes widen. "She died two weeks ago. Please, I have to know what . . . why she was meeting you?"

Shannon looks horrified. She gets off her stool. "What happened to her?" she demands. "Who are you?"

I sense the people on either side of us staring, but I'm intent on stopping Shannon from backing away. I reach out for her arm, desperate. "I'm Livy Jackson. I was a good friend of Julia's. Please—"

"No." Shannon wrenches her arm away. She takes a step back. "Why are you here?"

"I just want to find out why Julia was talking to you." I'm close to tears now.

There is fear in Shannon's eyes. "How did you know about me meeting Julia?"

"I told you, I saw it in her diary."

"I can't speak to you."

"Why? Please, I—"

But Shannon has turned and is already weaving her way through the crowd. Considering her vertiginous heels, she's remarkably fast. I hurry after her. She rushes through Club Room. I'm right behind. There's a fire door I hadn't noticed before, in the corner. Shannon presses the bar. Darts outside. I race after her, but as I reach the fire door myself, a large hand slams it shut.

It's the barman.

"Sorry, madam," he says with fake politeness, "but you don't seem to have paid for your drink."

Shit. I look down. I'm still carrying the glass of white wine in my hand. I set it down and fumble in my bag for my purse. I fish out a ten-pound note and shove it at the barkeep. He stands aside to let me leave. I rush past, through the entrance lobby and outside.

The air is cool on my face. I'm in a backstreet opposite the high walls of a multilevel parking garage. An empty plastic bag drifts along the tarmac. There's no sign of Shannon. I head for the brightly lit end of the cul-de-sac, where it opens onto the main road. It's dark and more than a little spooky, but I don't notice. I'm only intent on finding Shannon. I'm halfway along the alley, running toward the traffic noise and the light.

And then a figure appears at the end of the cul-de-sac, cutting me off from the road.

I stop dead. The light from the streetlamps beyond cast a halo around his fair hair. He is tall and young and his eyes are fixed on me. He walks toward me, and I see his face more clearly.

It's the man from the funeral. The man I assumed was Julia's Dirty Blond.

I look around, hoping to spot some kind of escape route . . . some open door . . . an exit. . . .

But there's nowhere to run.

CHAPTER FIVE

I'm frozen to the spot, consumed with fear. The seconds I stand in the deserted cul-de-sac seem to stretch into hours, the dark shadows around me suck out my breath. The man—his eyes glinting with fury—walks toward me. Even as my heart thumps I am telling myself to run. But there's no way past him. No time.

He stands in front of me, his forehead creased with a frown. With a jolt, I realize that his expression is actually more confused than angry.

"You're Livy, aren't you?" he says. "At the funeral . . . you said you didn't think Julia killed herself?"

I stare at him, startled by the sudden intimacy of his words.

"That's right." Several questions start to form in my head, but I'm still too scared to focus properly. And then the man's shoulders release and I see just how much tension he was holding in them before. He extends his arm. "I'm sorry," he says. "I should have spoken to you at the funeral, but it was all so . . ." He hesitates. "I'm Damian Burton. I was . . . a friend of Julia's. A *good* friend . . ."

"Her boyfriend?" My hammering heart ratchets down a notch.

Damian nods. "I wasn't sure how much she'd said about me . . . if anything."

"I only knew a nickname."

He raises his eyebrows. "You mean Dirty Blond?" he says with a smile. Close up, in the lamplight, I can see he is even more handsome than I'd thought from my brief glance at the funeral, with a strong, square chin; smooth, even features; and hazel eyes. My fear eases further. This man was Julia's lover. I still don't understand why he is here, but he doesn't feel like a threat anymore. And then I remind myself that there's no way I can know that for sure. A nice smile and an attractive face can mask unutterable evil.

"It's a play on my initials," Damian says. "D.B.—Dirty Blond."

"Very Julia," I say.

"Yes."

A gust of wind blows along the alley, rustling the litter that's escaping from the scattered garbage bags and sending the stink of rotting vegetables into the air.

"Why are you here?" I ask. "How did you know *I* was here?"

"I've been coming here since Julia died, every couple of evenings," Damian says. "I walked in and saw you with that blond girl. Someone spoke to me and when I looked round, you'd disappeared, so I came out the front. Saw the blond girl going up the road and thought maybe you'd come out with her, through the fire door, which you obviously had." He pauses.

I wait for him to go on. This man clearly isn't intent on harming me—at least, not here and not now. But what's he doing at this singles bar—if it's not for the obvious reason? And what is it that he wants to say to me?

"Julia's funeral was awful, wasn't it?" he says softly.

I look up, surprised. There's real pain in his eyes.

"It was all wrong. Nothing of her," Damian goes on. "That horrible brother . . . I'd never met him, but she used to call him 'that dickweasel.' "

I nod. Julia did often refer to Robbie like that.

". . . and she'd have hated the music and the flowers," Damian goes on. "And everyone making out she was some kind of sad victim. It was like there was a script and everyone was forcing Julia to fit in with it."

He's reflecting my own thoughts so accurately, I can't quite take it in.

"The only bit that made sense to me was when you were talking," Damian says. "I mean, Julia had told me about you, of course, but when I saw you, it was obvious how much you loved her, how *real* your friendship was. . . ." He trails off.

"Julia talked to you about me?"

"Of course. She was so proud of you. And Hannah and Zack." He stops talking for a second to acknowledge my surprise that he knows my children's names, then clears his throat. "She said you'd had the courage to make a commitment to—to Will, is it?—and stick with the relationship through all the ups and downs of married life. And she adored your kids. Said she'd always been too scared to even think about being a mum."

"Too scared?" It's hard to imagine Julia being scared of anything. "She always said she didn't *want* children of her own."

"She did say that," Damian agrees. "But there was more to it than just not being an earth mother. . . ."

This is surreal. Damian sounds like he really knew Julia. *Understood* her. "How long were you . . . ?"

"Together?" Damian sighs. "Six months or so." He looks like he wants to say something else, then falls silent again.

Six months? My suspicions rear up again. That *surely* isn't possible. Julia never went out with people that long.

Damian looks up. "Julia told me once that the 'no kids' thing was because she was scared of . . . of loving anyone that much, of taking that risk."

Another gust of wind sends litter swirling about our feet. My eyes fix on a burger wrapper, and I'm transported to the first time I met Julia, a few weeks or so after she and Kara became friends. They were both at the start of their first year at uni, and giddy with the excitement of living away from home for the first time. I was at the beginning of my junior year—jaded from a breakup with a boyfriend and long bored with the reality of having to sort out my own rent and shopping and washing. I remember the pair of them eating burgers as they got dressed up for Halloween. Kara was wearing tiny shorts and a basque, with dark, heavy makeup. She looked—to my eyes—ridiculous and disturbing, like a small child playing at being a whore. Julia was carrying off a similar look with much greater conviction—her hair teased into a wild frame around her head, the slight slant of her eyes accentuated with kohl and wearing a short leather skirt over ripped tights. I'd turned up, unexpected, at Kara's student house and was fussing over her, trying to make her at least put a proper shirt over the basque. Kara, as always, submitted to my bossing in silence—I knew she'd put the shirt on to shut me up, then take it off again once she was out of sight—but Julia soon lost patience.

"You really put the mother in *smother*, Livy," she'd drawled. "Go and have your own children and leave Kara alone."

I resented her then and over the next few months, especially when she spent the whole of the subsequent Christmas break in Bath with Kara and our parents. I tried to be generous about that—after all, it was sad that Julia felt so cut off from her own family—but despite Julia's charm, it was hard to have our normal traditions infiltrated. It was only after Kara's death that she and I became friends, when all our earlier differences seemed so petty and unimportant. Because the irony was that the night she was raped and murdered, Kara had been wearing jeans and tennis shoes—nothing provocative at all. I'm still not sure whether that meant Julia was right not to worry or whether I was wrong to knock Kara's confidence by trying to change the way she dressed.

"Livy?" Damian's been speaking, and I haven't heard a word. I look at him properly. "Would you like a drink?" He indicates Aces High. "I don't mean that place. There's a much nicer pub just up the road."

"Sure." We walk to the Lamb and Flag, an old-fashioned pub with ropy furnishings and a big pool table out the back. I'm surprised Damian considers it nicer than Aces High. There's nothing fancy or designed about it, and Damian looks too young and too stylish for such a place. His hair glints in the harsh overhead lights: an attractive mix of browns and yellows. I've known women who pay good money to acquire hair like that, but Damian's looks entirely natural. I wait while he buys a couple of mineral waters—he's driving too—and we take our drinks over to a quiet corner table.

"What do you do?" I ask as we sit down.

"I'm a graphic designer," he says. "That's how I met Julia—on a shoot for a magazine I'd been working for. I was going out with the model. Then Julia turned up. . . ."

I smile to myself at the thought of Julia's sex appeal being powerful enough to prize a highly attractive younger man away from a woman paid for how she looks.

"So you're not married, then?" I say, remembering my previous suspicions.

"No." Damian frowns. "Of course not. Julia wouldn't have come near me if I was."

There's a pause. "You still haven't explained why you wanted to speak to me," I say.

"Okay." Damian takes a big breath. "The reason I'm . . . Well, it's that I don't believe Julia killed herself either."

Something releases inside me, a sense that I'm not alone. To my surprise, emotion rolls up in a wave from my guts and I have to press my lips together to stop myself from crying.

"I know from what you said at the funeral that you don't think she did it," Damian goes on. "But . . . the thing is . . . do you have a specific reason for thinking that? Or is it just that you knew her so well that you just can't believe it?"

I set down my glass. "Mostly the latter," I admit. "Except, well, she texted me the evening she died. She said she really wanted to talk to me. Everyone else seems to see that as a cry for help, but—"

"But she *did* want to talk to you," Damian interrupts. "I *know* she did. We had a fight about it—that's why I wasn't with her that night. . . ." He pauses, his eyes filling with pain at the memory. He swigs his drink. "Julia had something important to tell you. I . . . I asked her what it was, but she refused to say. She said she had to talk to you first, before she could tell anyone else. She was so bloody loyal. . . ." He shakes his head.

Relief and gratitude whirl inside me.. All this is validation of the terrible and lonely thoughts I've been living with for over two weeks. Until this moment, I hadn't realized how hard it has been to carry

77

alone the burden of my belief that Julia *didn't* kill herself. That someone else took her life. And yet, my suspicions rear up again. How do I know Julia didn't want to talk to me about Damian himself? Can I really be sure that Damian is telling me the truth and not simply what I want to hear?

"What about the suicide note?" I ask.

Damian rolls his eyes. "I heard. 'I can't go on . . . please make no fuss . . . .' Yeah, right. Julia wouldn't have written that in a million years."

"I know."

"And it was found, open, on her computer screen, so no handwriting, no signature. Which basically means whoever killed her could have written it as she was dying."

I nod, hanging on every word. I want so much to believe what Damian is saying, tears prick at my eyes. "I'm sorry, but I wasn't expecting this. I wasn't expecting you."

Damian raises his eyebrows. "Funny. Julia said exactly the same thing to me once." His eyes bore into me. He is powerful and masculine in that open, confident way Julia always went for. Not me. I've always preferred my men quiet and brooding. I wriggle on my seat. "Do you know what Julia wanted to talk to me about?"

Damian holds my gaze. "It was to do with Kara," he says.

"My *sister*?" I frown. "What do you mean?"

Damian hesitates.

"*Tell* me. What do you know?"

Damian sits forward. "I know that Kara was murdered eighteen years ago. I know that you and Julia became friends after her death. I know the murderer was never caught."

I stare at him, surprised again that Julia has told him all this. Except for our conversations about Hannah and Kara looking alike, Julia and I hadn't talked properly about my sister for years. We mentioned her, of course, but it was Mum and Dad whom I turned to on all the anniversaries: the Christmases and the midsummer birthdays that left Kara eternally youthful while the rest of us aged. Julia used to try to talk about Kara more, but all her memories revolved around their shared life at uni, the boys and the parties. I didn't really recognize the Kara Julia knew, the young woman my little sister was trying to become.

"I'm sorry I didn't come and see you before." Damian sits back. "I've just been in shock since . . . Julia. I didn't know whether it was right to—"

"*What* did Julia want to tell me about Kara?"

Damian rubs his forehead. "Okay, I don't know how to say this, because I know Julia never told you anything about it. . . ."

"Go on."

"She told me that she felt guilty that she hadn't protected Kara . . . that night. In particular, that she didn't go home with her. She carried the guilt with her all the time. *Always*."

I'm seriously surprised now. I remember Julia expressing remorse eighteen years ago that she had stayed at their friend's house, leaving Kara to find her way home alone. But everyone told her what had happened to Kara wasn't her fault, and I suppose I'd assumed that, in the end, she believed us. In fact, I thought *I* was the guilty one. I was Kara's big sister. I should have been there to keep her safe.

"*Always* felt guilty?" I say. Surely Damian's exaggerating.

"Yes, *always. Intensely*. She said it was her fault Kara was even at the party, that she'd not wanted to go, that Julia had made her. Then Kara wanted to go home and she asked Julia to leave with her, but Julia was having a good time. There was some guy she liked. . . ." He takes another gulp of water. His glass leaves a wet ring on the cracked wooden table and he smooths out the stain with his hand. "I know she didn't tell you, but she never forgave herself for not being there for your sister and she never stopped trying to find out who killed her. Every week, she spent hours tracking down leads. Sometimes she even went to different places, following clues."

"No." I can't believe it.

"It's true." Damian leans forward, insistent. "It's why she stayed in Exeter after uni. She could have a gotten a job in Bristol or London—maybe worked for a big-name fashion mag, but she settled for Exeter and the chance to follow leads whenever she could."

I stare at him. I'm so used to seeing my own life as curtailed and Julia's as one big glamorous adventure, that it's hard to think of her existence as in any way constrained. And yet it does make sense of Julia's many short trips away from home. She was always haring off to seminars and conferences, or so she said. Sometimes she gave me details of the people and places she had visited, but other times she was strangely vague. I always took her at her word that her days away had been too boring to relate: *Please, Liv,* she would say, *I already had to live it once.*

Could she really have been following up leads on Kara's death? I can't imagine what on earth she could possibly have discovered.

"But the police effectively stopped looking sixteen years ago. They said there was nothing to go on. No witnesses. No DNA."

"I know." Damian shrugs. "But Julia couldn't let it go."

I sit back, absorbing this. "I can't believe Julia kept all this from me."

"She didn't talk to you, because she didn't want to raise your hopes," Damian says. "It was private. I came across the files by accident, though I think by then she wanted to tell someone. But the night she died, it was different. She needed to talk to you." He takes a deep breath. "She was going to tell you that she knew who he was . . . that she'd found him."

My blood turns to ice. *"Him?"*

Damian nods, the light catching the green in his hazel eyes. *"Him,"* he says. "Kara's killer."

KARA

To do all that one is able to do, is to be a man; to do all that one would
like to do, is to be a god.

—Napoléon Bonaparte

My childhood was, as I have explained, a normal one. Ah, nostalgia, that
"land of lost content," those happy memories of that other country, where they
do things differently. Blah, blah, blah. I've never been one to idealize the past.
Suffice it to say, I experienced all the usual developmental stages, coming early
to the realization that my mother and father, albeit in very different ways,
were both deeply flawed human beings.

I found the first few teenage years a difficult time, but once I had filled out
a little and come to terms with the inevitable changes to my body, I settled into
an easy groove at school. The work wasn't hard and I had friends enough,
when I wanted them.

I look back now on my teens as a time of experimentation and discovery.
Of course, it was a different era back then, but the hormones were the same
and it took me a while to work out how to deal with girls. There were several
who stick in the mind:

Kerry-Ann from Scotland, with her zits and straggling hair, was the first
girl I had sex with. She gave up her virginity—gratefully and pathetically—in
a bus shelter overlooking the sea. Then came slutty Samantha, and then, a
while later, Melissa, with whom I went out for a few weeks—and who at-
tempted suicide soon after. I learned a lot from these girls—I found out that
being clean, open, and smiling was usually enough to win them over and that
what little allure they held for me soon passed. I enjoyed female company. I

81

still do. But none of these girls had anything special to offer me. I liked pursu-
ing them but bored of them quickly.

All that changed with Kara.

We met at a bar one autumn night. Years had passed since the girls I
named earlier, and my adult life had so far proved a massive disappoint-
ment. Despite an easy flow of lovers, I had never experienced any emotion
akin to actual love. But that night, when I walked into the bar and saw Kara, it
was as if all the other people in the room evaporated, like mist swirling around
a beautiful work of art.

Kara was an angel, the picture of innocence. Slim with long legs and small
breasts, she looked fresh and demure, certainly compared to most of the other
girls in the bar, with their heavy makeup and slutty clothes. Kara's hair was
tied off her face in a ponytail that hung like a sleek, blond whip halfway down
her back. She wore a short black dress and flat black shoes. Nothing reveal-
ing, nothing ostentatious.

Reader, I wanted her. I planned my attack. She was surrounded by other
students, so I picked my moment, waiting until she went to the ladies' alone
and then happening to pass by on the way to the cigarette machine. No one
saw as I asked her how she was getting on at uni, insisting that if she found
anything in Exeter confusing or overwhelming, she could talk to me about
it . . . that I knew the city well and would only be too happy to help. Blah blah
blah. Except I meant it.

Kara offered me a shy smile and I asked her more questions: about her
home life, her hopes and dreams. We didn't talk for long, and frankly, I re-
member none of her answers, just the smooth perfection of her sweet face and
the promise of her scent. She seemed younger than the girls she was with and
yet an old soul too.

I was desperate to have her. But Kara was shy, unwilling, chaste. One of the
reasons I have evaded detection for so many years is that I leave no "tell," no
signature. I chose my methods to suit the moment, the bird in the hand, so to
speak. (The other main reason is that I am phenomenally careful.) And so
there is no pattern to my actions, but there is a purpose . . . and that purpose
was formed that night with Kara and all she stood for. Even then, I knew that

Vonnegut—or whoever the guy was he took the line from—was right when he said the saddest words were "it might have been."

Because despite every secret attempt I made to win her over, she only ever saw me as a friend. And so time passed. Time stretched out in front of me, a deathly horizon. Objective time. Subjective time worn, as Barnes says (and I paraphrase) on the inside of the wrist, close to the pulse. Eternities passed. I was waiting for inspiration. I see that now. Of course, I was learning, studying too. But in limbo, sleepwalking, treading water. Not truly alive.

Until that night in February. I had followed her many times before and did so again that evening. I was alone, naturally, while Kara—my shy bird, happiest to flutter in company—was at a party. Music blared from the first-floor windows as I waited. And waited, biding my time "like patience on a monument." Ha! "Was this not love indeed?"

To my amazed delight, Kara emerged alone from the party shortly after 1 A.M. I followed her along the road. She wore jeans and a jacket and was looking around nervously as she scurried along. I waited until she was past the surveillance camera, then rushed over, exclaiming at the coincidence of her being here, and she smiled, all shy and trusting, looking up at me with those big doe eyes of hers. Kara wasn't like most of the young girls I saw around town, who talked about sex in a loud, crude, and unpleasant way. My poor Kara was surely mortified by whores like that. I knew, though she had of course never said, that she was a virgin.

This was my chance. I was prepared. The tools were already in my bag: my knife, my plastic coat, my gloves and mask. It had to be tonight. And fate had thrown me a helping hand in terms of our location. We were right by the canal—a quicker route home than the one Kara had been going to take, but perfectly safe now that she was with me. The steps were nearby and I led her straight down to the canal towpath, thereby missing the next street camera as I had missed the last. The nearest bridge was just a few meters away. The thrill of anticipation throbbed through me. It was going to happen.

We wandered along the towpath, by the dark water, gazing out over the shimmering ripples. I kept close to the wall, in the shadows. I could have taken her there, but I knew I had to wait for the bridge. One scream—and this was my first time, remember, I had not yet mastered the art of how to grip a throat so there is no room for either air or words—would have brought all sorts running.

When I think of Kara now, it is as she looked then, in jeans and sneakers, gazing out over the canal as she walked, the breeze lifting her soft blond hair with invisible fingers. I wanted that hair in my fist. So badly. As we strolled along the path, my excitement mounted. I look back now and feel nostalgic for the purity of my intent that first time. All of me focused on all of her. I listened to her soft pad along the damp stone, to the canal water lapping at the banks, smelling the tarnish of the stale depths. I kept my distance, hidden in the shadows, until we reached the bridge. All shadow. For a moment I couldn't see. I glanced around. The world was silent. Deserted. I ran over, swift and soft. The plastic casing was already over my shoes, no risk of footprints. A flash of her blond hair as she turned toward me. In the silence, I heard her draw breath. An excited gasp. She knew I would come for her.

Then I took my knife. "Your first time," I murmured, sweet, in her ear. "And mine." I could see in her eyes that Kara wanted me, but did not know how to express this. She was a goddess, a virgin queen.

She had to die, because it was simply impossible to imagine her living. Not in our real world, where lives are "nasty, brutish, and short." But she lives on in my mind. It is true that when the pupil is ready, the teacher arrives. Kara was my teacher. She changed everything. Made me the man I am.

After it was done, I turned to leave, and the glint of metal caught my eye. An old-fashioned locket around her neck. I took it and added it to my bag. Then I left, knowing at last my life's purpose. Since that night, I have never felt the life of "quiet desperation" I know that most men endure. For there is nothing hidden that shall not be revealed, and my work on earth is to know a person's darkest shame and have them face it in their final, glorious moments.

With Kara, I came of age. She was the touchstone for all that followed. My guiding light, to see me safely home.

CHAPTER SIX

Julia knew who killed Kara?

No way. I'm instantly suspicious again. And angry.

I stare at Damian. He's watching me intently. "I don't believe you," I say, my fury building as I speak. "Julia wouldn't have persisted in a pointless, one-woman investigation for eighteen years. And she would certainly have told me if she had." I stand up. "She would also have told me if . . . if she had feelings for you. She didn't say any of it."

"I know." Damian's forehead creases in a deep frown. "I know this is out of the blue, but—"

"How come I've never met you?" I say, drawing back and crossing my arms. "If you and Julia were so serious, why didn't she say something? You're not even in her diary."

"You don't put people you see almost every day in your diary," Damian says. "Anyway, Julia didn't want to admit how she felt—not even to herself." For a second his face relaxes into a crooked, sexy grin. He seems so . . . I struggle to think of the right word. Authentic. Confident. It's hard to disbelieve him. He leans forward, his expression beseeching. "I knew Julia. Better than anyone. I *saw* her. All the fears she hid away, all the little insecurities. And practical stuff too—how she liked to drink Pouilly-Fuissé and Jack Daniel's and how her favorite place was Bolt Head, looking out to sea. I know I probably sound delusional, but the truth is that Julia tried to stop seeing me several times. Every time, after a few days, she called. And I always knew she would."

I study his face, the intelligence in his eyes. I can certainly see the attraction. His light, thoughtful manner complementing Julia's sharp wit beautifully.

"Okay . . . never mind you and her." There's clearly no way I can prove how long Damian and Julia were together or how strongly she felt about him. But the stuff about Kara—that's surely nonsense. "If Julia really thought she'd found out who killed Kara, how come she didn't go to the police?"

"She was going to—as soon as she'd told you. *With* you," Damian explains. "But then she was killed, so—"

"So why didn't *you* go to the police?"

"I did. That is, the police were in her flat when I went round the evening after she . . . after it happened. I'd been too angry to call before but . . . but I wanted to make up, so I went in person." Damian closes his eyes, and a shadow passes over his face as he remembers. "The place was packed. They'd taken her body away, but there were police swarming all over everything. That was how I found out. . . ." He shudders, then opens his eyes. "I knew it wasn't, it *couldn't* be suicide, though that was clearly what the cops thought. But to me it was obvious: Julia had found out who Kara's killer was and the killer had murdered her to keep her quiet. I told the police everything I knew, but I guess I sounded mad, especially when they couldn't find anything to back up what I was saying. In fact, I think me telling them Julia thought she had identified the killer after so many years just made them more convinced she was . . . troubled . . . a bit delusional . . . just like they interpreted the text she sent you about 'needing to talk' as a cry for help—"

"Wait." I hold up my glass to stop him saying any more. I can't believe any of this is true. And yet, why would Damian make it up? "If Julia really carried on an investigation, she must have had files . . . records. I've been in her flat a million times. I never saw anything like that."

"Of course she did." Damian runs his hand through his hair. "She had maps and paperwork from the coroner and copies of all the police records—God knows how she got hold of half the stuff. I think there was some police guy she had wrapped round her little finger at one point, wasn't there?"

I nod. The policeman Damian's referring to is the man who gave Julia the diamond and emerald ring missing from her flat and who left her the cottage in Lympstone when he died. He was a chief inspector, way older than Julia's usual lovers; I never met him. At the time, so many years after Kara had died, the connection with her murder didn't occur to me, but Alan Rutherford was a local guy who must have had access to all sorts of files.

What did occur to me, hearing about his obvious devotion to Julia, was whether a steady, older ex-cop wasn't just what she needed. My guts coil into a sickening knot as I remember that Julia dumped him a few weeks after his retirement, saying he was getting too keen. I can't help but wonder now if, once he'd left the force, his usefulness had come to an end. By the time he died, a few years later, I'm certain Julia had virtually forgotten all about him—the terms of his will certainly came as a big shock. "His name was Alan Rutherford."

"Right, so Julia used him to get all sorts of information. And she added to it herself. She kept everything hidden in that trunk at the end of her bed. She covered it up with old clothes, things she never wore."

I know the trunk he's talking about. I've sat on it a million times. When Julia was a student, she would routinely show me some of the more outrageous items she kept inside it, but that was a long, long time ago. I haven't seen the contents of the trunk for years; I have no idea if Damian is telling the truth.

"So what happened to all this stuff, all the records?"

"That's the point. It wasn't there when I went round on the Sunday evening, when the police searched her flat after she died."

The knot in my guts twists again.

"I think whoever killed her—whoever came round and made her take the Nembutal," Damian goes on. "I think they deleted everything about Kara on the computer and took all the notebooks and paper records. That's why the police couldn't find anything."

I stare at him. Is he really serious?

"There's more," Damian persists. "Whoever it was must have known she had research on her computer about suicide. All they had to do was leave the Nembutal brochure on her desk to reinforce what was already on the Mac."

My blood feels like ice in my veins. "But that means she must—"

"—must have known the person who killed her," Damian says grimly. "I know. Which explains why there were no signs of a struggle. Julia must have let whoever it was into the flat; then, after they killed her, they must have taken the paperwork, deleted the electronic files on Kara, and added that suicide note to her computer. "

"How do you know all the Kara information *was* destroyed . . . deleted?"

"Partly from the police, partly from Julia's mother." Damian sighs. "I told the detective—DI Norris, his name was—to look on her computer and in the trunk." Damian groans. "Of course, I was in shock and when Norris said there was no sign of any files, I didn't know what to do." He sighs. "The police were nice enough—they took my details, said I'd be questioned later. I gave a statement, but I'm not even sure they believed I was a serious boyfriend. It didn't help that Julia had told literally no one my name, just 'Dirty Blond.' Anyway, I've heard nothing from the police since the suicide verdict." He pauses, frowning. "Not that it's surprising they didn't take any notice of me. They wouldn't believe *anything* I said."

"What do you mean?" I ask.

"Nothing." Damian says. "Just that in their eyes I was simply her latest squeeze, nobody significant."

I turn the conversation back to his mention of Julia's mother. "You said before, you'd talked to Joanie as well as the police? What did she say?"

"Nothing helpful." Damian grimaces. "The police gave her Julia's computer after they examined it. They'd told her what I'd said, about all the missing files. She dismissed it out of hand. Then, when I called her, she said the same to me—that there was nothing about Kara's death on the computer or in any of Julia's papers, but I don't even know if she looked properly—"

"I think Joanie might have taken stuff from Julia's flat," I say. "Jewelry, pictures, even a couple of handbags. . . ."

"Probably." Damian sighs. "She won't talk to me now. I *told* her Julia had a whole folder on Kara, that if I could just get someone to look properly—more than the police would have done—there'll still be info stored on the hard drive, but Julia's mother refused to let me take the computer. She's just accepted that Julia was odd, therefore unstable, therefore suicidal. Just like everyone else."

I open and shut my mouth without speaking. I can't take in what he's saying. It's impossible. Surely, it's impossible? There's a tight feeling across my chest. I don't know whether it's the idea of Julia acting for so long outside my knowledge, or the thought that she might have found out who murdered my sister all those years ago. I look closely at Damian. What did Julia really feel about him?

Damian meets my gaze. His lips glisten from his drink, soft in the lamplight. "I loved Julia and she loved me," he says quietly, as if reading my thoughts. "She hated how vulnerable her feelings made her, she fought herself over it. That's why she refused to tell anyone about me, but it's true, look." He takes out his phone and scrolls through to a picture. He turns the phone so I can see the screen. It's a photograph of the two of them together. Damian is handsome in a thin sweater, his eyes sparkling straight at the camera, which he is clearly holding. Julia sits beside him, her face turned toward his. She is radiant . . . smiling . . . her eyes full of what I can only describe as adoration. I'm transfixed. I've never seen her look like that. Damian presses the dot in the center of the screen, and the picture comes to life. Julia is laughing, watching Damian's face. He carries on facing the camera, sexy as hell as he stares into the lens. But it's Julia I can't take my eyes off. She looks so soft, *so* in love. With a jolt, I remember the cold rigidity of her face in death. A sob twists in my guts. I look away.

"I'm sorry," Damian breathes. His voice breaks. "I know how difficult it is to see . . . her . . ." He trails off.

A million emotions around my head. This is a Julia I did not know: her heart in Damian's hands and apparently so consumed with guilt over my sister's death that she spent the second half of her life trying to find Kara's killer.

"I asked her to marry me just a week before she died." Damian's voice swells with emotion.

My mouth gapes with shock as Damian meets my gaze. "She said yes," he goes on, his lips trembling slightly.

"But . . ." I can't believe it. *Surely* he is making this up. "But Julia said *nothing*," I splutter.

"I know." Damian sighs. "I know it must sound mad to you, but we'd planned to buy a ring at the end of the month . . . that was when she was going to tell everyone."

I gaze out the window. The street is busy, a group of shrieking girls rushes past. The lights of Aces High glimmer along the road.

"Why did you say you kept going back to the club?" I ask.

"Because Julia went there two nights before she was killed." Damian finishes his beer and sets it firmly on the table. "When we met later, she was all . . . agitated. I pushed her to tell me where she'd been. You can imagine what it sounded like, when she said she'd been to a singles bar and she wouldn't say why. . . ."

I gasp, remembering the initials A.H. from Julia's diary entry two days before her death. I hadn't seen the connection before, but perhaps A.H. stood for Aces High. I stare at Damian. This is the first real evidence I have that he is telling the truth. "Go on," I say.

"So I let it go, but the next day, Friday, Julia went out again and this time she wouldn't say *anything* about where she'd been. I saw her that evening. I was so pissed off that she was refusing to tell me what she'd been doing. I mean, she'd agreed to marry me less than seven days before, so it felt like she was totally pulling away. But Julia kept saying she couldn't say anything, so I stormed out. Then we spoke the next day, Saturday, in the early evening. That's when she finally admitted she'd found out who Kara's killer was, that she had to speak to you."

"And you argued again?" I ask.

He nods, shamefaced. "I didn't understand why she couldn't tell me what she'd found out." He groans. "I can see now that I overreacted, but it was *so* frustrating. Julia just kept saying that she had to speak to you before she did anything else. I thought she was exaggerating, to push me away, like she had done before." He gives a miserable shrug. "I was an idiot. But I was fed up of her putting up barriers between us. She was already insisting we waited to tell people we were getting married. . . . I said she had to trust me or everything we'd ever said to each other—including our being engaged—meant nothing."

"Did she mention anyone called Shannon?"

"Not that I remember. No, I'm sure she didn't. Why?"

"Shannon was the girl you saw me talking to in Aces High." I explain about the entries in Julia's diary and her planned meeting with Shannon tonight. As I talk, a shiver scrapes down my spine. Is it possible Julia thought there was some connection between Shannon, Aces High, and Kara's killer? I can't imagine what it could be, but if Julia did go to Aces High two nights before she died, and if her behavior really changed from that point on, then there was *surely* some sort of link?

"Maybe the link is the place, not Shannon," I suggest. "After all, Shannon would only have been a kid when Kara died."

"Mmm, except kids can still see and hear stuff," Damian says with a frown. "Perhaps Shannon witnessed something to do with Kara's murder. Whatever it was, we need to find her." He takes a long pull of his beer.

"The bartender at Aces High knew who she was," I say. "Maybe he has a surname or a phone number?"

We head back to Aces High, but the barman refuses to give out any information about Shannon. After all tonight's revelations, it's a frustrating dead end. As we walk out onto the sidewalk, I check the time on my phone. It's nearly midnight, far later than I'd thought, and my mobile, which I switched to silent hours ago, is registering a missed call from Will. I chew my lip, feeling guilty.

We stroll to my car. My head is spinning, I feel, almost overloaded with information, and yet I'm also wired, full of purpose. Just before I drive off, Damian and I swap phone numbers and agree to speak again tomorrow, to work out what to do next.

At home, the house is in darkness, save for a light in the upstairs front room. Our bedroom, where poor Will must be waiting up.

I find him sitting up in bed, his laptop balanced on his knees. "Good time out clubbing?" he asks sarcastically.

I wince, irritation and guilt twisting inside me. "Don't, please." I sit down beside him and start telling him how Shannon ran away when I approached her and how I talked with Damian.

"He's Julia's Dirty Blond," I explain. "I think she liked him more than she let on."

Will raises an eyebrow. "That doesn't sound like Julia."

I don't really want to go through the whole conversation, but I also feel somehow that I owe Will an explanation, so I tell him everything Damian and I discussed and then look up, expecting to see shock on Will's face. Instead I see skepticism.

"What is it?"

He shrugs.

"Don't you believe Julia found Kara's killer?"

Will makes a face. "I believe she *wanted* to, but I don't see how she could have when the whole Devon and Cornwall police force failed to eighteen years ago."

"But what about all the stuff that Damian said was missing from her flat when he went round the evening after she died? All the papers on Kara gone and the computer wiped clean of information?"

Will falls silent.

I head for the bathroom and brush my teeth. I have to see Joanie. I have to ask her about the stuff missing from Julia's flat—plus get a look at Julia's computer too. Damian agreed that Joanie probably took the valuables. Maybe she took the paperwork as well. I can examine it. I knew Julia and Kara better than anyone. I should be able to spot references . . . notes or clues that maybe wouldn't mean anything to other people.

I walk back into the bedroom. Will has set his laptop on the chest of drawers. He is leaning back against his pillow, hands behind his head. His eyes follow me as I cross the room to my side of the bed.

"The police didn't find anything suspicious in the flat, did they?" he asks. "Nothing on the computer, no papers?"

"That's right—like I said, the killer took or deleted everything." I get in beside him. Will is still looking at me, his face serious.

"What?"

He takes a deep breath. "Livy, I'm not trying to undermine you here. I understand this is really important to you. But I think you're overlooking something."

"What's that?"

"You only have Damian's word that Julia *had* found out who Kara's killer was or that there *were* any papers or information on the computer. The police obviously didn't take him seriously. Why should you?"

A shiver snakes down my back as I remember what Damian said about the police not believing anything he said. What did he mean by that? *Why* wouldn't they? Was it really just because they didn't take his relationship with Julia seriously?

I know Will is right to be suspicious. But I don't want to hear it. I turn pointedly away from him and pull the duvet over my shoulders. Will turns out the light with a sigh.

I close my eyes, but it takes a long time before I fall asleep.

CHAPTER SEVEN

"Mum, Zack's eaten all the Kashi. *Again.*"

Hannah's whine shakes me from my reverie. Will may have dismissed Damian's claims out of hand, but I need to know for sure. I'm still determined to persuade Joanie to let me look at Julia's papers and get on Julia's computer. However, from our encounter at the funeral, I'm not hopeful that Joanie will even listen to my suspicions, let alone let me act on them.

"There's another pack in the cupboard," I say absently, glancing over at the kitchen table, where my children are sitting at either end, each indulging in their own particular style of breakfasting. Will, of course, left for work long before they were up.

Zack sits in front of a huge blue bowl of cereal, slopping milk over the side as he wolfs it down, intent on finishing and getting on with the next thing. Hannah, on the other hand, languishes over two seats, like a Victorian lady on a fainting couch. Her makeup and several mirrors are positioned around her own, as yet empty, bowl and she touches each item with trailing, delicate fingers.

"Why do *I* have to get it?" She looks up at me, pouting. "It's not fair. You make me do everything."

"For goodness' sake." I'm in no mood to argue with her. We've already had one fight this morning over the state of her room. I stomp past her chair, pull out the fresh pack of cereal, and run my finger under the flap. I'm not concentrating, and the cardboard catches the skin. It smarts, a thin line of red oozing up from the cut. I wince, then feel irritated at myself for being so clumsy.

Zack finishes his cereal in two massive mouthfuls. He stands up and carries his bowl to the sink, using both hands as I've taught him. I put the new box down beside Hannah's place and she snatches it up angrily. Having deposited his bowl, Zack turns and flies up the stairs. I know he's going to brush his teeth, that he will come down in a minute and bare them for me with an out-breath to show they are "minty fresh"; then he will put on his shoes and give me a big hug. Sometimes it seems to me that while my son fits effortlessly into the running of the house, my daughter exists purely to throw wrenches in the works. This is one way in which she is most unlike my sister, who specialized in a more passive kind of resistance.

Right now, Hannah is casting me evil looks as she pours cereal into her bowl. One eye is made up—a job she does beautifully, with soft peach eye shadow and just a lick of mascara. I don't like her wearing makeup to school at twelve years old, but the rules allow for a minimal, natural look, and if I don't see what she puts on at home, I'm fully aware she will be applying cosmetics at school. Anyway, the makeup is slight, and like Kara before her, Hannah has a knack for the visual. I worry more that, like Kara, she is unhealthily obsessed with her appearance and often—though she tries to hide it—attempts to skip meals.

"Kashi is *so* disgusting," she says, her voice dripping with contempt.

"You wanted some five minutes ago. And it's organic," I argue.

Hannah fixes me with a hard stare. I know full well she's capable of turning a disagreement over cereal into World War III, so I speedily change tack. "How about oatmeal, then?" I try to keep my temper by focusing on her long, skinny fingers as they trail anxiously over various pimple-cream options. She is still such a child, whether she knows it or not.

"I *hate* oatmeal," she snarls.

Shaking my head, I leave the room.

My palms are sweating as Julia's mother, her tone characteristically brisk, answers my call later that morning. I pretend that I have an

95

appointment with an old friend in the Bridport area and would love to drop by on my way. Joanie agrees, though I can tell from her tone that she's not exactly thrilled at the prospect of my visit.

It's a pleasant drive through the Devon and Dorset countryside. At this time of year, with the sun shining and the fields lush and green, the whole area is at its best. As the traffic slows for a stretch near Lyme Regis, I remember coming to a conference for work at a hotel near here many years ago. I didn't know it at the time, but it was actually the high point of my working life. My boss valued me, wanted to fast-track me after I'd won an essay competition, and yet I was torn between the legal career that potentially lay ahead and my long-desired ambition to move back into academia. I glowed with confidence—as testified by the three men who, separately, tried to chat me up over the weekend. I turned each one down with a smile. Will had just proposed, and we were planning on buying a house in Exeter and doing it up. Life seemed full of possibilities, my work and home existences in perfect balance with each other.

As I turn off the A35, it occurs to me that my life shrank when I got married. Ironic, I think, that in giving up my maiden name, Small, I started down a track to a narrower, more limited life.

I park outside Joanie's large detached home. It always amazes me that Julia grew up here. There is nothing of her wild, city persona in either the 1930s house or the quiet, leafy street in which it's situated. It's a big place for Joanie on her own, but she has always refused to consider moving, even after Julia's father died of cancer a couple of years ago and the bills started to mount up. Julia was dismissive of her mum's reluctance to move on, sneering that Joanie was too set in her ways to consider it. I wondered at the time if the story was really that simple. Julia used to insist that her mother had been born with a "gene for martyrdom" and would go to her grave complaining that the world was against her, but then Julia had hardly spent any time with either parent since she went off to uni—so how would she really know anything about Joanie's state of mind?

I straighten my skirt as I walk over to the neatly manicured front lawn. A warm breeze ruffles my hair. Two black trash cans stand on either side of the gate, like plastic sentinels. My heart thumps as I ring the front doorbell. Joanie answers promptly.

"Hi." I offer up a smile.

"Hello." Joanie doesn't respond in kind. Her voice is cold, and for a moment, I actually wonder if she's going to invite me inside. She's dressed in a cotton blouse and what my own mother would describe as slacks. Her hair is neatly styled, with no signs of any gray roots. Her skin is remarkably smooth and her figure still trim. I look deep into her face. There's nothing of Julia about her, except, perhaps, in the shape of her eyes and nose.

"Come in," she says at last.

"Thank you. It's kind of you to see me." I smile again, trying to ingratiate myself. Joanie purses her lips. There are lines around her mouth, a legacy from her two-packs-a-day smoking habit.

"I'm going out later, for lunch," Joanie says, opening the door. "But I can offer you a cup of tea."

I'm about to reassure her that I'm not intending to stay for long, when Robbie looms into view. I'm so startled to see him that I actually gasp.

Joanie emits an exasperated *tut*, though whether this is directed at me for being thrown by his presence or at Robbie for leaping about like an overgrown puppy is hard to tell.

"Hi, Livy—God, it's *fantastic* to see you," Robbie gushes.

"Er, you too," I say, feeling my cheeks burn.

"Mum said you might pop by," Robbie goes on, sailing past his mother to plant two huge kisses on either side of my face. "What brings you to Bridport? I came up to see Mum yesterday. I've taken a few days off from the hotel. If I'd known you were coming, I'd have offered you a lift."

He bustles me past Joanie and into the living room while I repeat my "old friend in the neighborhood" cover story. A quick look around the furnishings, all rather stiff and formal, reminds me of how much older than my own mother Joanie is. Almost a different generation. The lawn through the French windows is mown in careful stripes. A charred patch in the corner—presumably from a recent bonfire, though it's an odd time of year to be having one—makes a sharp contrast with the manicured rose beds. Unlike our overgrown garden at home, there's not a weed in sight.

"Would you like a cup of tea? Coffee?" Robbie hovers over me as I sit at one end of the couch.

Joanie perches on the armchair opposite. Up close, I can see the strain in her eyes.

"Nothing, thanks."

Robbie nods and takes the seat beside me. He's sitting too close. I shift away. *Back off, Dickweasel.* That's what Julia would say.

But I am not Julia.

"How's Wendy?" I ask.

"She's fine," Robbie says, smoothing his fingers through the hair that creeps over his shirt collar at the back of his neck. I wonder idly why he can't see that keeping it long at the back just accentuates how bald he's going on top. "Wendy's at home right now with the kids. I've been helping Mum go through some of Julia's things."

"That must be hard." I hesitate. "Er, perhaps I could help?"

"No need." Joanie purses her lips. "We're actually rather busy," she says pointedly.

"Right." I gulp. I'm clearly going to have to be more direct, though Joanie certainly isn't making it easy. "I'm sorry to barge in on you. I . . . I've been so upset about Julia. I *am* so upset—"

"We *all* are." Joanie speaks with feeling.

"Of course." I pause. "The thing is, there are some things—unanswered questions, really—that have been puzzling me."

Joanie raises her eyebrows. I can feel Robbie's presence, still too close. He is watching me intently. I have a sudden flashback to the day I met him. He didn't go to university himself but came to Exeter on a regular basis—mostly, as far as I could see, to muscle in on Julia's social life. We met one evening when he was out with Julia and Kara. I didn't take to him much on that first occasion; he seemed nervous around his own sister—who teased him mercilessly—and strangely overawed by mine. And he didn't know how to talk to me, veering between shyness and swagger. For a while I wondered if he might be secretly gay—he seemed so uncomfortable around women. It strikes me now that, with a mother like Joanie, it would have been surprising if he'd behaved any other way.

"Unanswered questions?" Joanie's voice is like steel. "Is this related to your . . . your outburst at the funeral?"

"Sort of." I launch into my prepared story, explaining how Shannon ran away from me when I met her in Aces High. Not wanting to reveal that I found the details of her meeting with Julia in a diary in Julia's flat, I say vaguely that Julia had mentioned she was planning to see Shannon and that it was important for some reason. "Shannon was waiting at the bar. She didn't know Julia was dead, and, when I told her, she looked terrified."

"That must have been terribly upsetting for you," Robbie says. His voice is overly sympathetic.

I nod, not wanting to meet his gaze. A black cat wanders in through the open door as Joanie stares at me. I stroke her back, then watch as the cat slinks across the carpet and rubs herself against Joanie's legs.

Joanie gives the cat a pat and I remember Julia telling me how Joanie *showed way more affection to her bloody pets than to us when we were growing up . . . always a cat on the go, never dogs, they need* real *love.*

"So Julia told you that she was planning to see this girl, but not *why* she was meeting her?" Joanie raises an eyebrow, and for a second I get a glimpse of Julia: coolly sardonic and nobody's fool.

Beside me, Robbie sits back. He's still watching me intently. His gaze is unsettling. Between his overt interest and Joanie's naked contempt, I'm rapidly losing my handle on our conversation.

"Like I say, there are unanswered questions," I press on. "I know Damian—Julia's boyfriend—has been in touch and he's also, er, concerned. He believes Julia was investigating something from—"

"Stop." Joanie raises her hand, palm toward me. "Livy, I've always liked you. I know you and Julia were good friends. But you're presuming too much." She hesitates, lowering her hand. "In fact, I'm sorry about this, but I have to ask you something."

"No, Mum." Robbie sits forward, suddenly anxious.

"What is it?" I press my lips together. My emotions right now feel so turbulent, I could just as easily shout as weep—possibly both.

"I need to ask you if you've been to Julia's flat since . . . that terrible day? . . ."

My cheeks burn. What was it that gave my illicit visit away? I look into Joanie's cold, judgmental eyes, and a shudder runs through my body. I see no warmth and no concern, just hostility. No wonder Julia described her mother as an emotional vampire.

"Livy?"

I clear my throat. "I did go back, just the once. I had keys, you know, Julia and I kept each other's keys."

Joanie nods. "Ah, I thought that must be the case. Which means these must be *yours*." She fishes in her handbag and hands me my own spare keys, presumably taken from Julia's silver Tiffany fob.

"Yes, er, thank you."

"I'd like Julia's set back now, please."

My fingers tremble as I remove Julia's keys from my key ring. Just like at the funeral, I feel as if I'm losing her in some small yet significant way. I hand the keys over.

"So what did you take?" Joanie's question is so direct, I almost gasp a second time.

"What? *Nothing.*"

Joanie purses her lips. It's obvious she doesn't believe me. Then I remember how Julia's computer and TV and a few pictures, vintage bags, and bits of jewelry were missing.

"I didn't take anything," I insist. "The TV and her Mac and things in her bedroom . . . they were already gone when I got there. I . . . I thought *you* took them."

"That's right, we did." Robbie smiles, clearly trying to ease the tension. "Mum and I took away some of the more valuable items as soon as the police allowed us."

Joanie raises an irritated eyebrow. "Obviously we did that for security reasons. Julia left no will, you see, but the more significant pieces of jewelry were itemized on her insurance."

"No will?" Is she serious? I can't believe organized, efficient Julia didn't make a will. Okay, so she had no dependents, no pressing reason to make sure her affairs were in order, but Julia would have considered it messy not to tie up any loose ends. She owned two properties, after all—not to mention all the designer outfits and the jewelry.

"We checked all the expensive things," Joanie goes on. "Everything is accounted for except one item: a diamond and emerald ring valued at just over eight thousand pounds." She glares at me with cold eyes. "I would have had no objection to you taking a memento or two, but that really wasn't acceptable."

My jaw drops. Joanie thinks *I stole* the ring?

I glance at Robbie. He is looking away, unable to meet my eyes. *My dickweasel brother is* such *a coward.* Julia's voice sounds in my head. Robbie might still like me, but clearly not enough to defend me to his mother.

"I didn't . . . I *wouldn't* . . . ," I stammer.

Silence.

A memory shoots through me, hard and painful as a spear. There was missing jewelry when Kara died too, a silver locket that Julia had bought her as a Christmas present from a market. It was a pretty little thing, worth far more than Julia had paid for it, with a curly *K* inscribed on the front. Kara had loved it. I remember her showing off the gift. Kara had put a picture of herself and Julia inside the locket—smiling heads from some photo booth. Kara had been delighted and wore it around her neck constantly. It was discovered missing after her death. Julia insisted Kara had been wearing it the night she died. If that was true, then either her killer took it, presumably for its cash value or, more likely, it was ripped off and fell into the canal when he dragged her under the bridge. Either way, the locket never turned up. And now Julia's ring has disappeared. Is that coincidence? Or is it a sign of something more sinister?

I glance up at Joanie. She's still watching me, hooded eyes icy and aloof. Robbie is watching me too. He mouths the words *I'm sorry* at me. At least he doesn't think I'm a thief.

"I didn't take Julia's ring," I say.

Joanie tilts her head skeptically to one side. "I do understand that

Julia meant a lot to you, Livy. As I say, if you had asked me directly for a keepsake, I would happily have given—"

"I *didn't* take it. I didn't take *anything* and I don't *want* anything." A lump lodges in my throat. Emotions swirl about my head, the injustice of Joanie's accusation but also the pressing thought that an expensive ring might give a new slant to Julia's death. "Suppose whoever killed Julia took the ring?" I blurt out.

"For goodness' sake."

"Livy, don't," Robbie adds.

"Please, I just want the truth about her death. "

"The truth?" Joanie snaps. "The truth is that Julia was willful and selfish. She saw a therapist for several years in her twenties—as you know—and while she hadn't done so recently, she was still unstable."

"No," I protest. It's true that Julia saw a therapist after leaving university for a year or so. She didn't speak much about the experience, though she told me it had helped her come to terms with Kara's death.

"I'm sorry, Livy, but it's the truth," Robbie says.

"Quite." Joanie sits back, clenching her hands over the arms of her chair. Her knuckles are white, her jaw rigid.

"No," I repeat.

"Enough, Livy," Joanie insists. "I understand that you're upset and I know that Damian is upset too. I think you both feel guilty that you weren't enough to stop Julia from killing herself. God knows, I do. But we all have to be strong. We have to accept reality, not indulge in fantastical conjectures."

"I think there's more to it than th—"

"I said stop." Joanie raises her voice. She stands up and paces across the room to look out through the French windows. "This is hard enough, Livy. I'm really disappointed that you are denying taking that ring."

I turn to Robbie helplessly.

"We're not accusing you," he says.

"Yes, you *are.*"

"Yes, we are," Joanie snaps. "As far as I can work out, no one else had keys to the flat. Damian didn't. None of her other friends. Just you. And there was no break-in, so . . ."

I don't know what to say to convince her I'm not the thief. "Perhaps if you let me look on Julia's computer or in her papers, I'll be able to find something that helps prove what I'm saying."

Joanie turns to look at me. Her eyes are like chips of ice. She points to the burnt patch of ground outside. "We destroyed the papers. The computer too. It had little resale value, and Robbie felt it would only upset me to have it here in the house."

I stare from her to Robbie, too shocked to speak. Robbie nods, confirming his mother's words. He looks uncomfortable.

"You *burned* her papers?"

Joanie nods.

"And her *computer*?"

"Yes, well, the hard drive, anyway. There was nothing important on it, a few work articles, old invoices, that sort of thing. It seemed more secure than just throwing it away. Same with all the paperwork."

"But they could have been important." I'm on my feet, facing her now. "There could have been stuff that meant something to Julia in there. . . ." Maybe information about meeting Shannon and the identity of Kara's killer. I don't say that last thought out loud.

Joanie shakes her head. "I think we've talked about this enough, Livy. Thank you for the keys to Julia's flat. I'll be handing them over to the estate agent next week. I don't think there's—"

"Estate agent?"

"Yes, we're selling the apartment as soon as all the legal forms are sorted. And that cottage of hers in Lympstone. It shouldn't take too long. As I was saying, I think it's probably best if you leave now."

A hollow feeling swells inside me that has nothing to do with Kara's death years ago or the idea that Julia might have met a violent end herself. It's the terrible sense that just as her story was rewritten to make her a victim, now Julia's entire past is being wiped out. Soon I will be left with no tangible trace of my best friend. And there's nothing I can do about it.

"You're putting the flat on the market next week?" I whisper.

Joanie offers a curt nod. She walks to the living room door. She's wearing proper shoes indoors, I notice, with mid heels. In a daze, I let myself be shown out of the house. Robbie, who hasn't spoken since his mother mentioned burning Julia's things, gives me a big hug while Joanie opens the front door.

"See you soon," he whispers, his breath hot against my ear, his voice too low for Joanie to catch. For a second I want to snap at him, Julia-style, for not defending me better to his mother, but of course I don't. Instead I turn to Joanie, feeling more dazed. She pecks me on the cheek—her lips are cold and hard—and I stumble down the front path toward my car.

I look back as I reach the sidewalk, but Joanie has already shut the door. I take a deep breath, tears pricking at my eyes. Joanie's wheelie bins stare accusingly at me. The things of Julia's that Joanie and Robbie have burned must be inside these trash bins. My pulse suddenly races. I glance up at the house again. There's no sign of either of them.

Without stopping to think, I flip open the first trash can. The stench of cat pee, presumably from a litter tray, is overpowering, but underneath I catch the scent of burnt paper. I reach in and take out two white garbage bags. Leaving them on the sidewalk, I turn to the second barrel. This one contains a single large black bag. And a definite burnt smell. I whip it out, then carry all three bags to my car. I shove them on the backseat, then get in quickly. A final glance back at the house, but neither Joanie nor Robbie are looking out.

I start the engine and maneuver the car onto the road. As I drive away, I imagine the shocked look on Julia's face if she could see me now: *Livy Small does it all,* she'd say, her eyes wide with wonder. *Housewife. Mother. Thief.*

CHAPTER EIGHT

It's almost time to pick Zack up from school, and Damian and I are still sifting through Joanie's junk in my back garden.

I called Damian on my way home. Whatever his motives, there was no one else I could turn to, and as I expected, he was eager to help. If he was shocked at my theft of Joanie's trash bags, he didn't show it, just got straight down to examining their contents, looking for anything that might lead us to Julia's investigation into Kara's killer. An hour and a half in, and we've still found nothing.

It's painstaking work—after a dry, sunny start, it has turned into one of those horrid overcast, humid summer days, and we're both filthy and sweating. Damian takes a break for a cigarette. It's the second he's smoked since he got here. I'm surprised. Since giving up the vice herself, Julia was vehemently anti-smoking. None of her previous boyfriends would have dared light up in her presence. I point this out to Damian. He grins and tells me they argued about it. I get the impression Damian won the argument, and that Julia loved him standing up to her. A welcome breeze dances across our faces as we talk, sharing our reminiscences. Damian laughs—a huge, warm belly laugh—when I tell him how Julia bought the kids a board game they'd wanted last Christmas, but forgot it needed batteries. After a long look at Zack's disappointed face and a quick and fruitless search of her kitchen drawers, Julia's eyes had lit up. "She said she knew where there were some," I explain. "So I followed her into her bedroom and found her removing the double As from her vibrator."

105

"Only Julia." Damian shakes his head, still grinning, though I can hear the sense of loss in his voice.

I smile back. I am warming to him more and more. He speaks of Julia with such affection, and again, I feel comforted, no longer so alone with my grief.

I gaze back at the contents of the three trash bags that now litter our overgrown lawn. Most of it is ashes. I watch the curls and wisps tumbling over the grass and think of Julia. Morbid, I know, but I completely forgot to ask Joanie what she is planning to do with Julia's ashes. Will I even be invited to be part of whatever she decides?

My thoughts drift to the only other comparable ceremony I have ever been part of. Julia herself wasn't there when we scattered Kara's ashes the autumn after her death. Mum and Dad wanted it to be just the three of us. It didn't occur to me at the time that Julia might have felt left out by our decision. It hurts that I can now neither find out, nor make it up to her.

We'd picked the Botanical Gardens, near our house in Bath. I walked between my parents, our arms linked as we reminisced about previous, happier visits. We'd gone there often while Kara and I were growing up. I used to love exploring the nooks and crannies of the rock garden while Kara—who always carried life more lightly than I did—ran about on the grass and exclaimed at how pretty the flame-colored maple trees were.

We scattered Kara's ashes in the Great Dell. Mum kept looking around, worried because ash-scattering wasn't officially allowed. Dad was irritated by her anxiety, her need to follow the rules. He used to be a conventional, rule-following kind of man himself, but the rules hadn't saved his beautiful, beloved girl, and her loss left him unanchored, his worldview as shattered as his heart. I can still see him now, face creased with pain, refusing to allow himself the release of the tears shed freely by Mum and me.

I shake myself. This isn't the time to indulge in reminiscences. For one thing, I'm going to have to get Zack in a moment. For another, I need to focus on how I'm going to explain the mess on the grass to Will.

Damian has stubbed out his cigarette and is poring over the small pile of items that survived the bonfire. So far, all we've found apart from some food waste, are various bits of metal, plastic, and charred cardboard.

"I feel like paparazzi," I say with a sigh.

Damian looks up. There's a dark smear across his cheek and ash in his hair. He really is ridiculously handsome.

"Anything?" I ask.

He kneels back on the grass. "Does it seem strange to you that Joanie and Robbie *burned* everything?" he asks. "It's just so . . . *final*."

I shrug. "I guess. Joanie said having Julia's things around was too upsetting, once she'd stopped accusing me of being a thief."

"Is that how *you* feel? That seeing Julia's stuff is upsetting? I mean, even if it was, then wouldn't you pack it away somewhere you didn't have to look at it, not destroy it all two weeks after she dies?"

A gust of wind blows more ash across the grass. I push my hair out of my eyes. "What are you saying? There wasn't any information about Kara on the computer anyway—the police examined it before they let Joanie and Robbie take it."

"Maybe there was something else." He holds up a crispy fragment of hard drive. "Look at this. I'm just saying it's odd."

I check the time again. Only five more minutes, then I'm really going to have to leave to get Zack. I squat down beside Damian and finger the edge of one of Julia's Moleskine notebooks. Its contents have been destroyed completely, just a scrap of the leather binding surviving. As I lift it up, I notice the edge of a business card with a row of tiny red hearts along the bottom underneath. I pick up the card. Each heart is slightly different. The first is whole, the second has an arrow through it, the third a zigzag separating the two halves for a broken heart; then the pattern begins again. It looks like a logo.

The top part of the business card is burnt away, only the surname WALKER remains, and part of the first name:

. . . NNON WALKER

My heart skips a beat as I stare at the name. Could this be *Shannon's* business card? I shove it under Damian's nose.

"What do you think?"

He looks up at me. "Shannon *Walker*?" he says. "The same Shannon Julia was due to meet at Aces High last night?"

"It's got to be," I say. "Which means Julia must have met her before, in order to have this card."

Damian nods. "Julia went to Aces High two days before she died. Maybe she met Shannon then."

"Maybe it was Shannon who told her who Kara's killer was."

We stare at each other. "Let's Google 'Shannon Walker' now," Damian suggests.

I check the time again. "I can't." I make a face. "I have to pick up Zack."

"Okay, I'll do it," Damian says. The wind whips a strand of hair across his face. He brushes it back, hesitating before he speaks again. "Shall I wait here until you get back? Or would you rather I left?"

For a moment I'm not sure what to say. It feels like a risk to leave Damain alone in the house. Apart from anything else, what if Will comes home unexpectedly? On the other hand, Damian seems so genuinely in love with Julia, I can't believe he meant her—or, by association, me—any harm. That look of pain in his eyes couldn't, surely, be faked.

"I know Julia didn't let you meet her friends, but did she meet any of *yours*?" I ask.

Damian shakes his head.

Despite all my misgivings, my heart goes out to him. How awful to have no one to share such a huge loss with. Even if Will and the other people who knew Julia don't agree with my beliefs about her death, at least they can share some of my pain at losing her.

"Why don't you wait in the house?" I suggest. "You can use my laptop to do the search."

I set off in the car to get Zack, leaving Damian at the kitchen table with instructions to help himself to tea and coffee.

I'm distracted on the way to school, nearly running a red light. A couple of the other mums chat idly at the school gates. The end of term is next week, and the traditional summer fair is coming up on

Saturday. Megan Matthews from the PTA committee is making a last-minute attempt to organize people to bring cakes and other edibles, as well as organize shifts to man the many stalls.

I agree distractedly to provide a batch of chocolate brownies and stand back, watching Megan flit around, a pen tucked behind her ear. She's not carrying a clipboard, but she might as well be. Like me, Megan used to work for a law firm. Of course, I left over twelve years ago, when I was pregnant with Hannah, and was only ever a lowly junior solicitor. Megan didn't give up work until her third child was born last year, and she was a high-flying commercial lawyer. I'd say, from the looks of it, she misses her job.

Zack appears at his classroom door. He looks around for me, his face breaking into a huge smile as he spies me at the gate. He charges across the playground and hurls himself at me, hugging me fiercely.

"Today I did a wonder goal at break," he boasts. "I got past six players and there was a one-two, then I got the volley and put it in the back of the net."

"Hey, brilliant," I say, hugging him back. I have only the vaguest idea what he's talking about. It always amazes me how eloquent Zack becomes when he's talking about football—he struggles to retell any other kind of anecdote.

As I put my key in our front door fifteen minutes later, I have a terrible premonition that I'll find the house empty, burgled, certainly our computers gone. After all, how much do I really know about Damian?

But he's still there, hunched over my laptop at the kitchen table. He stands up to say hello to Zack, who breezes past, barely noticing him. I settle Zack in front of the TV, then go back to Damian.

"What did you find?" I ask.

"Quite a few Shannon Walkers, but no one who obviously fits with the girl in the Aces High bar," he says. "It's hard to tell on places like Facebook or Tumblr, there are so many people with the same name." He pauses. "Do you have a scanner? If we copy and paste the row-of-hearts logo online, maybe we'll find a match for it."

"Sure, er, how do we do that?"

"Easy." Damian gives me a wink.

I give Zack a juice carton and promise I'll make him a sandwich in a minute; then I take Damian upstairs to Will's office. The printer/scanner is set on a shelf above Will's computer. I switch the machine on, and it whirrs into life.

Five minutes pass. Damian scans the logo and fiddles expertly with the picture online, posting it on some kind of image-based search engine I had no idea even existed. A match pops up immediately: Honey Hearts.

"What on earth is that?" I ask.

"No idea." Damian clicks on the link. A Web site flashes up. It's gray on pink, with the repeated rows of hearts across the top, just above the menu. I peer over Damian's shoulder and read the home page:

Relationships are built on trust. But what happens when that trust is broken? Here at Honey Hearts, we understand just how hard it is to live with anxiety—and our mission is to help you understand the truth, so that you can move on, secure either in renewed trust for your partner, or with the knowledge you need. We help you to make all-important decisions that will enable you to live your life to the fullest.

Our service is open to people of all genders and any sexual orientation. Our fully trained professional Honeys will test your loved one and report back with complete discretion. Is your partner a Trust-Staker or a Heart-Breaker?

With Honey Hearts, you'll know for sure.

"It's a honey trap agency." I pull the spare chair over and sit down beside Damian, feeling confused. "I've heard of them, but . . ."

Damian looks round. There's a deep crease in the center of his forehead. "Why would Julia . . . ?" He trails off.

I shake my head. "Let's see if we can find Shannon on the site."

The home page menu offers links to *Rates, About Us, Contact,* and

Honeys for Hire. The address given is in Exmouth, about half an hour's drive from here.

Damian clicks through to the *Honeys for Hire* page. It outlines the parameters of the Honey Trap Service, how users can "match" their partners to a man or woman they are likely to be attracted to. It stresses throughout that the women never take things beyond a conversation and act in an entirely discreet, professional way throughout.

I'm fascinated. It never occurred to me six years ago that I could hire an investigator to tail Will. Such a dramatic course of action would have felt far too Hollywood. I thought about following him myself, though. I gaze at the picture of the kids by the computer, remembering how small they were at the time, how unaware of how close our family came to being torn apart.

My suspicions started early one morning when Will arrived home after claiming to have pulled an all-nighter at work. I didn't think anything of it when he'd checked in the evening before; he often worked very late. But there was something furtive in his manner the following morning—and he smelled different too, as if he'd washed using a new, heavily perfumed soap.

I hinted around the subject for most of the rest of the day and then, stung by Will's irritation at my persistence, finally asked straight-out if he'd slept with someone. Will denied it indignantly. In fact, he carried on denying the affair for the next two weeks. He said I was being paranoid and I started to think it was true. His letting me think that is what has always hurt the most. After that first night away, he made sure he came home on time, but still something felt wrong and twice he wasn't in when I called the office after failing to reach him on his mobile. For thirteen days I almost went insane, full of suspicions that he dismissed and derided. Until the Thursday of the following week, when he received a text and went into the next room to read it. Later, while he showered, I sneaked a look at his mobile. With trembling fingers I found Catrina's message—WISH YOU WERE INSIDE ME RIGHT NOW—and a whole conversation between the two of them going back almost two months: explicit and obsessive and like a knife to my heart.

Damian clicks through to the *Gallery* link now, and the sound brings me back to the present. Here are twenty or so pictures: women, mostly, though also a few men. I scan them quickly. Is Shannon here? The Honeys come in all shapes and sizes: from blondes with huge cleavages to slim, athletic brunettes. They are all extremely pretty, though in very different ways, and all, bar one or two, clearly under thirty.

"There." Damian points to a blonde in the middle of the selection.

I peer more closely. It's Shannon, without a doubt, the same big blue eyes and wavy, highlighted hair.

"Disgusting," Damian says with a hiss.

I look at Shannon again. She is dressed more discreetly than most of the other girls, curvaceous in her T-shirt and jeans, but not revealing much skin. Just like at Aces High. "She doesn't look *that* trashy," I say.

"I don't mean *her*," Damian says. His voice is terse. "I mean the whole thing. Hiring girls to entrap men. It's wrong. You're just asking for trouble if you send a pretty girl after your average guy. And what does it prove, anyway?"

I stare at him, shocked by his response. And then I think I understand. "D'you think Julia hired her to . . . to, er, approach *you*?"

"No," he snaps. "At least, that girl"—he points at Shannon—"she *didn't* approach me. There must be some other reason for Julia meeting up with her. I can't see what yet, but—"

"Maybe she wanted Shannon to entrap the man she thought killed Kara?"

Damian nods. "I guess that's possible, but why? Why not confront him herself? Or go to the police? And how does involving some random girl help, anyway? What was she supposed to find out?"

"I don't know. I don't get it."

"I don't get it either." Damian indicates the screen. "But then, like I said, I don't get *any* of it."

I shrug. "I do. Not why Julia hired Shannon, but I can totally see why a wife who's been cheated on would want to be sure her husband wasn't going to do it again."

"Where's the trust in that?"

"Well, maybe he destroyed the trust first." My words come out with more force than I intend. My cheeks burn hot.

Damian clearly senses he's touched a nerve. I suddenly remember all the details Julia shared with him. It's highly likely she told him about Will's affair too. My face reddens further.

Damian touches my arm. "I'm sorry, it just seems wrong to me. At least we've found Shannon Walker. So what now? How are we going to speak to her?"

I look back at the screen. The answer is obvious. "I'm going to have to contact Honey Hearts," I say. "I'm going to have to pretend to hire Shannon myself—I can't see another way of finding out what Julia wanted her to do."

I make the call late the next morning, when the house is empty. The phone rings three times before a woman answers.

"Honey Hearts, Talullah speaking. How may I help?"

I take a deep breath. "I'd like to make an appointment. I'm interested in . . ." I hesitate, not knowing how to put it.

"In our service?" Talullah says matter-of-factly. "Of course, let me take some details."

I give her my maiden name, Small, so there's no link with my married name, Jackson, which I've been using for most of my adult life.

"And you suspect your partner of a possible infidelity?"

"Er, yes."

"My sympathies," Talullah says, brisk but kind. "I'll set up a meeting for you with Alexa Carling. She's our account director."

"Okay."

Talullah and I exchange a few more practical details; then I hang up and slump into a chair. Will's suit jacket from yesterday lies in front of me on the coffee table. He has no idea I'm planning to visit Honey Hearts. After his reaction to my visit to Aces High—and his skeptical response to Damian's claims that Julia had discovered the identity of Kara's killer—I don't feel inclined to confide in him. Anyway, once I'd deleted Damian's scan, there seemed no point in explaining that he'd ever been in the house. Zack barely noticed him, and Damian was gone before Hannah got back. If I'd told Will about Damian being here, I would have had to explain my visit to Joanie and the "theft" of the garbage bags, not to mention the discovery that Shannon Walker works at Honey Hearts. I told the kids some trash had spilled in the garden and made a game out of clearing up the debris. Hannah sniffed at getting involved at first, of course, then became competitive, sweeping up her ashes into a pile with great gusto. It was easy not to talk when Will arrived home at eight thirty. He was tired and irritable, barely able to make the effort to ask after my day and not really listening to my vague reply.

My appointment at Honey Hearts is made for Monday morning. I call Damian and tell him what I've done. He sounds as troubled as he did yesterday. He must be wondering, though he denied it, if Julia had been using a Honey Hearts girl to entrap *him*. What that could possibly have had to do with finding Kara's killer, I can't imagine. Anyway, this version of events would be totally uncharacteristic of Julia. Surely, if she suspected Damian of being unfaithful, she would have confronted him, as she'd urged me to confront Will all those years ago when I told her I thought he was having an affair.

I can't believe how in just a few days, my life has been turned on its head, that my thoughts no longer revolve around school pickups and laundry but seduction and murder. Even so, the weekend passes slowly. Will takes Zack to his Saturday morning football game. This used to be a time when Hannah and I would do stuff together—arts and crafts when she was little, more recently baking cakes or shopping in town. Now Hannah wants to do none of those things with me. How has she grown up so quickly? She isn't even a teenager yet. I expected she would pull away, but not this fast or this soon. We have yet another argument over her room, which is messy now on an epic scale. Hannah hates me going in there, but I insist I have to pick up the mugs and bowls and that she needs to sort out her laundry or I refuse to wash any more clothes. As I shove a pile of clean sweaters into a drawer, my eye is drawn to a flash of fake leopard skin. It's a padded bra, made from cheap nylon. I gasp as I take it out and find a matching thong underneath. Both items have the price tags still in place. I am horrified. When did she buy these? When on earth was she planning on wearing them? Does she realize what kind of signals such cheap, vulgar underwear sends out? I try to stay calm, but soon I'm shrieking these questions at Hannah, frustrated beyond endurance with her sulky, tearful refusal to acknowledge she is too young to dress up like this.

We both grow hysterical, and I leave her bedroom trembling with fear and fury. My instincts are to call Will, but I know he will just tell me this is normal adolescent behavior, that Hannah is simply "trying on being a woman" for size.

I call Mum instead.

"I'd get it if she just wanted nice underwear—she used to love looking at Julia's lingerie," I wail down the phone, "but these things—"

"Isn't it just part of growing up?" Mum asks gently. "You wanted a bra when you were twelve, and you didn't really need one."

"It's not that she wants to grow up that gets me," I sigh. "It's that the clothes she's picked are so completely inappropriate."

Mum sighs too, then points out that on Hannah's pocket money, a scrap of cheap nylon is all she'd be able to afford and asserts, quite rightly, that the real villains in this scenario are the manufacturers and shops selling trashy lingerie for little girls.

After a while I calm down and seek Hannah out again, determined to try to explain my point of view with less emotion. I find her curled up on the sofa, watching some kind of pop channel. It's like the underwear situation all over again. I hate the fact that the young women on the screen are so sexualized, gyrating about in bikinis, and try to explain why. Hannah looks at me with scorn in her eyes, as I attempt to impress upon her that a woman's identity, and validation, should never come from her body alone.

"Shut *up*, Mum!" she snaps, her voice oozing with contempt. "We already do all that stuff in health class."

Feeling myself on the verge of tears once again, I chew her out for telling me to shut up, then turn off the TV. She rounds on me, and another argument ensues. Apparently I am out of touch and fascistic in my parenting. All the other girls have cool mothers. And iPhones. She hates me. She can't wait to leave home.

Battered and bruised, and with no idea how to handle her, I retreat to the kitchen to make the brownies for Zack's school fair this afternoon. I am angry and upset as I fling the butter and chocolate into a bowl. I hear the door slam upstairs. I want to go up and try to find the little girl, the sweet, loving daughter I know is inside her, but I'm scared. Scared of her hurtful rejection and scared of my own turbulent feelings. No one in my life has ever pushed my buttons like Hannah does.

I talk to Will when he gets back, asking if he thinks I'm too lenient, or maybe that I've been overprotective, as I used to be when Hannah was little.

He shakes his head wearily. "She's just acting out," he says. "I know she pushes it, but you mustn't take it so personally."

I shake my head. Will doesn't understand, not really. He and Hannah still get on well. Not that they spend much time together. He is so tired and preoccupied during the week that it's only on weekends that he really has time for either child. Zack is happy, in his straightforward way, if they play football together and if Will watches his matches. Hannah routinely asks Will for help with her homework on the weekend, help that he always gives immediately and that I suspect she doesn't always really need. Afterwards, the pair of them can often be found snuggled up on the sofa watching documentaries that I'm certain she isn't in the slightest bit interested in.

Later, the four of us go to Zack's school fair—Hannah sulking the whole time at being forced to demean herself with a return to her primary school. She's utterly delightful to her old teachers, then vile to me once we're alone again. Will drives us to Shaldon afterwards, but the sun is out and there are too many people on the beach. Living within thirty minutes of the sea has its drawbacks: We're so used to having the coast to ourselves half the year, it's hard to share it during the summer months.

In the end, I'm relieved to get home. I miss Julia terribly on weekends like this. She was always around for a coffee and a chat. I would tell her Hannah was being difficult, and she would laugh that sardonic chuckle of hers, and say something like: *Oooh, mother of pubescent girl in taken-for-granted shock!*

I chat with both Mum and Martha while the kids are watching TV. Later that evening, Will and I go for a drink with Paul. He's on his own, now that Becky has left for her parents' in Spain. Paul says he misses her dreadfully, but he's settled for the summer into the place of his mother's, keeping busy at work and managing to Skype with his wife every night. I envy the way his eyes light up when he talks about Becky. It's lovely how much he still craves her company, how lost he clearly feels without her. We order a bottle of wine, and Will and Paul hunker down to an in-depth conversation about Paul's new Ducati motorbike and the pros and cons of some Harley-Davidson.

My self-pitying mood deepens as it occurs to me that Will and I have talked about nothing other than mundane domestic arrangements for days. We used to have shared interests—music and movies and even browsing antique shops—when we were younger, before the kids. But somehow those have all faded away now.

As Will chats with Paul, I'm reminded of how attractive he still is, especially at moments like this, his face animated and his voice full of enthusiasm. It strikes me that it's Paul who's bringing out this side of him—that I haven't seen Will like this when it's just the two of us, not for years.

I'm heading to the bathroom a few minutes later when Damian texts to check that I'm still okay about visiting Honey Hearts—and with our plan for getting information. I reply, reassuring him that I'm prepared to do what's needed, then fall to wondering about him again. I just know so little about his life. I pull up the browser on my phone and search his name.

Nothing appears. That is, the name Damian Burton shows up on Facebook, Twitter, and Tumblr, but I can't find any profiles that seem remotely connected to the person I've met. I try again, refining my search to target Exeter and his graphic designer job. Still nothing. That's odd, isn't it? I try my own name. It takes four pages of results before I find a reference to myself on Facebook, but then I don't have a job or any kind of professional identity. I search for Will, then Julia and Paul. Each of them, in turn, can be found online through their work within a few seconds.

So why is there no trace of Damian Burton at all?

HAYLEY

Whatever your heart clings to and confides in, that is really your God.
— Martin Luther

And so time passed. I felt sure, now, after Kara, that I was capable of far more than I had ever supposed. A heady feeling, that, to glimpse my potential. I suppose I existed in a liminal state for a while, letting this new awareness seep through me.

Kara stayed uppermost in my mind for a long time. Of course, I was linked to her personally—and witness to Livy's and Julia's grief on many occasions. But what concerned me more was that my life—both working and private—had hit something of a slump. I felt stuck . . . not that there was anything wrong, more that nothing, yet, seemed quite right. After the triumph of Kara, this was a comedown.

And so life's petty pace crept on. And on. Over the years, I developed a love of rich tea biscuits, strong black tea, and single malt scotch—the peaty variety. More important, I learned just how limited and blinkered the state authorities truly are. Can you believe that the case to find Kara's murderer, so frenetic and impassioned in the first few months, was allowed to fade and quietly die, like an old dog in the corner of a cold kitchen? The police, it costs me something to acknowledge, were not worthy of me. How very disappointing.

So . . . I lived, I worked, I played. I indulged in short, casual affairs. There were easy triumphs and small successes. It was simple to keep my real interests secret, even from my wife. Too simple. And very, very tedious; "weary, stale, flat, and unprofitable" indeed. Anyway, before long, I felt the itch burn

119

inside me again. Soon after, came Hayley. I met her on one of my business trips abroad. She approached me in a hotel bar because she heard my accent and thought, as a fellow Englander, I might offer temporary protection from the attentions of two men at a nearby table as she stood, waiting for her husband to finish checking in. He had sent her to buy a drink, but the bar, like the reception desk, was overrun and understaffed, and Hayley—not the sharpest knife in the drawer—was frightened by the boisterous drunks and assumed someone who shared her accent might actually care about what happened to her. At least that's what I thought when I saw the look of panic on her face. Later, I understood her anxiety was more worry about displeasing hubby than fear of the drunks. As I said, the bar was crowded and it was virtually impossible to get served. I was finishing off my Laphroaig and intending to head back to my own hotel. Still, something drew me to Hayley. She had the defeated slump of a woman well past her prime. It was there in the sag of her skin and the curve of her back and the cluster of three tiny liver spots on the back of her right hand. She was dressed in a gray silk dress with matching shoes—stylish even for the hotel we were in, with its ornate chandeliers and mahogany furniture. The straps of the dress were thin and shiny against the tan of her shoulders. I felt myself staring as one strap slipped down her arm, nestling against the pashmina she had drawn around herself.

"Here," I said with a smile. "Let me help." I reached out and touched the skin under the strap. I kept my eyes on Hayley as I slid the strap up to her shoulder. Hayley responded with a tiny movement, somewhere between a flinch and a shiver. I took my finger away, clocking the bruise at the top of her arm and the desperation in her eyes. And I knew then that I had to have her.

We talked a little more. I stood too close, knowing she was interested. In the two minutes that followed, I also learned that Hayley was eager for love, like a kicked puppy, and that her husband hit her. Not that she told me these things but it was there, in that hunch of her shoulders and the prayer of her eyes. And it was confirmed when her foul husband finally found her in the bar. He was short and ugly and balding with a large paunch. He threw me a dismissive glance as he strutted over, demanding to know where his drink was.

I melted away as Hayley began to stammer her explanations. I kept eye contact from across the room for a while, then let the crowd swallow me up.

The next morning found me outside their hotel, waiting. At 8:36 A.M., the husband left, besuited and with a briefcase swinging from his arm. Just over an hour later, Hayley appeared, peering tentatively out onto the street. She was neatly and smartly dressed in dark jeans and a red cotton shirt. I followed her cautious walk to the local designer shops, waiting for her to reappear from a boutique store, then contriving to bump into her. Her face radiated with a smile when she saw me. So easy. I took her for a coffee. Within half an hour, she was pouring her heart out. How her husband liked rough sex. She didn't go into details, of course, but my imagination supplied what her blushing explanations avoided. She told me how angry he got when she tried to resist and how hurt she felt that he didn't seem to care about her.

I leaned forward and let my lips brush her cheek. "If you were mine," I whispered, "I would make it my life's ambition to satisfy you." She wriggled in her seat, self-conscious, as she flushed with pleasure.

Easy. Easy. Easy.

We arranged to meet later to take the tram into the countryside. I wore a baseball cap pulled low over my face. I saw Hayley blink as she clocked it. I explained that I knew it wasn't very stylish but that my daughter had bought it for me before she died of leukemia. That I wore the cap for sentimental reasons. Hayley was openmouthed as I gave her my sob story. I left no detail unmentioned: the compassion of the nurses, the agony of the chemotherapy, the unutterable pain of seeing your child die. Hayley hung on every word. I almost believed the story myself by the end. Ha!

Off the tram and into the country. The conversation flowed. How my daughter's death had led to the breakdown of my marriage. How since then, there had been no one ... no company ... no sex. I smiled shyly at this, then ventured: "Though what I really miss is being held in someone's arms ... that intimacy. . . ." Hayley was all over me before we reached the woodland I'd been heading for. But I held back until we were in the depths of the copse, where the earth was still damp. Hayley held up her face to be kissed, offering herself. So I took her and tasted her and slid the belt from her jeans and unbuttoned her shirt. As Hayley took a bottle of wine from her straw basket, I put on my gloves and my mask; then I took her belt and wound it around my fists.

She turned and saw me, and her final sound was an irritating moan of

121

defeat. Afterwards, I cleaned the serrated blade of my knife, then gathered all Hayley's clothes and put everything of both hers and mine in my bag. Her stupid husband was ultimately convicted of the murder. The old bruises on her arms and back brought him down, along with the weakness of his own alibi.

I followed the case from afar. The lack of crime scene evidence baffled the local police. As always, I left no traces of my DNA and I had disposed of everything Hayley and I had brought with us—all our clothes and the picnic things, everything—in the trash heap near the tram stop, buried deep under other debris. If the police had done their job properly, they would have found this, of course. I've learned over time that I can leave all manner of clues with little worry that I will be traced through them. I don't expect you to understand, but risks like this make the whole enterprise more exciting.

I kept just one thing, the buckle from Hayley's belt. It intrigued me: a snake design woven through a circle, with the prong for a long, vicious fang. A perfect companion to Kara's locket.

I record Hayley, rather than others at the time because she showed me that although there was life after Kara, in my heart I still sought a bigger, deeper challenge for my "vessel grim and daring."

And, soon, my chance came.

CHAPTER NINE

The Honey Hearts office is on the second floor of an ugly, concrete office building in the center of Exmouth. Damian meets me in a café along the street to go over our plan one last time. I want to ask him why his name doesn't show up online, but I'm too nervous about what I'm about to do to have the conversation right now. I could well need Damian's help in the next half hour; I can't risk him stalking off because I've been snooping. I resolve to confront him as soon as I'm done at Honey Hearts; then I head for my 10 A.M. appointment. My heart is thumping as the receptionist buzzes me through the door into an unprepossessing reception area. The Honey Hearts logo runs along the edge of the front desk and around the walls. A huge vase of orange and yellow gerbera sits on the table. Otherwise, the room is municipal and beige, with bland, abstract modern prints hanging on the walls. The receptionist would be pretty, if her face weren't hidden under masses of makeup. She's very sweet, though, offering me a cup of tea while I wait and patting me kindly on the shoulder when she takes my coat.

I fill out a form, a written version of the basic questions I was asked on the phone, again using my full first name, Olivia, and my maiden name, Small. After a few minutes, a slim, groomed woman I'd guess is in her late fifties appears. She is dressed in a business suit, with high spiky heels. Her face is suspiciously wrinkle-free, but the skin on her neck is creased and a little saggy. She's the sort of woman Julia used to declare, sotto voce, had *the whiff of a Madonna video about her.*

"Olivia?" She holds out her hand and I shake it. "I'm Alexa Carling. Please come through."

She leads me into another bland beige office. The window overlooks a courtyard with plant pots. Pink roses adorn the desk. I could be in a bank, or a lawyer's office.

"Please call me Alexa," the woman says with a polite smile.

This wasn't what I expected at all. I'd imagined something either much seedier or far more glamorous.

Alexa offers me a glass of water from the jug on her desk, then indicates the sofa opposite. We sit down at either end, and Alexa examines the form I've just filled in. She looks up with another smile. "How are you feeling?"

I'm taken aback by the question. "Er, I'm okay," I stammer.

"Good." Alexa says, "A lot of people feel guilty once they're actually here. They start worrying about what they're doing, now that this incredibly brave step they've taken is a reality, rather than just a vague idea."

I nod.

Alexa leans forward and fixes me with her steel blue eyes. "I'm here to tell you to stop worrying. You're not alone and you're not going mad. You've got suspicions and we're here to find out whether they're correct or not."

I fidget uncomfortably in my chair. Alexa's words are too close to home. I remind myself this is the point. I should be able to pull off this visit precisely because I understand what fearing an infidelity feels like—and why someone might want to entrap their partner.

"So, er, how exactly does this . . . the honey trap thing, actually work?"

Alexa clears her throat. "Well, first step is you tell me about your relationship, a few details on you and your partner, your circumstances, jobs, home life. That's so I can build up a profile of the pair of you. Then we discuss what, precisely, you want to know. What you are suspicious of. After that, it's simply a case of finding a girl we think he might be tempted to go for. I have some portfolios—" Alexa indicates a shelf of folders to her right. The row below is full of ring binders of files labeled CLIENTS, alphabetized in groups. My eyes rest for a second on the *A–D* set. *D* for Julia Dryden. Would that be where the details about her hiring Shannon are stored?

I turn back to Alexa. "And then . . . ?"

"Then you tell us where to find the man and we send the chosen girl to see how he responds to a little flirting. Our girls wear a wire, so you'll be able to hear the whole conversation afterwards. And she'll take a friend for backup and security. We are very responsible, Olivia. All our Honeys are fully trained. Discretion is the priority. Their aim is, on first encounter, to find out if they can whether the man has been unfaithful before and to see if he asks for their number in order to set up a date. Before you get our full report, we wait to see if the date actually happens, if the man goes through with it. You meet with the designated Honey twice: once before her first meeting with your man and once after her second. Do you see?"

I nod. If Julia was using Shannon as her designated Honey, that makes sense of the two meetings I'm aware of from the diary. The first to set up the entrapment, and the second, which Julia missed, when Shannon was due to report back. That's if Julia *was* using Shannon in that way.

I *have* to find out.

"Good." Alexa sits back, her manicured hands folded in her lap. "I think it's time for you to tell me about your partner, then, if you wouldn't mind?"

I dive into my story about a husband who I suspect may be having a second affair. The irony pricks at me as I speak. I don't give Will's name as I talk, but I do tell our actual story . . . the one from six years ago, when he didn't come home until morning, smelling of that different soap. I almost forget the real reason I'm here as the tears well into my eyes and I relive the confusion I felt; how what truly hurt was Will's willingness to leave me in an agony of doubt.

"That all turned out to be true, and now it feels like it's happening again." I wipe my eyes. "I'm *sure* he's lying. I just can't prove it."

Alexa considers me for a moment. "Most likely he's put himself in a situation where he feels cornered by his own actions. There's no way out now without pain for somebody, and he's trying to avoid that." She sighs. "He's like a rat in a trap."

I take a deep breath; I have to pull myself together. The story I give Alexa doesn't matter. What counts is making it convincing enough to lead to a meeting with Shannon Walker so I can ask her straight out whom Julia asked her to entrap. And why.

Alexa takes notes on a clipboard as I speak. I'd envisaged a sophisticated operation, but Honey Hearts is fairly low-tech, still operating a mostly paper-based system. It's all depressingly mundane.

Alexa listens sympathetically to my story. She asks for a few details: about what my husband does for a living, any hobbies and interests, and about his sexual history. Again, I keep as close to the truth as possible.

"We met in our early twenties, so not masses of exes."

"What about socializing? Is he more likely to meet people for a coffee in a café? Or a beer in the pub?" Alexa pauses. "It helps to know, so that we make sure our Honey gives out the right signals when she goes to meet him."

I nod, thinking it through. Again, it's simpler to stick to the truth. "Definitely not a coffee," I say. "He only really likes tea. He doesn't drink that much: a glass of red wine or a single malt, though he usually goes to the pub after work on Fridays for a couple of drinks."

"Hobbies?"

"He likes motorbikes, though he hasn't actually had one for years." I trail off, thinking of the mountain of classic bike mags in our garage, then of Will's long conversation with Paul in the pub the other day. I used to like photography in the same way. Before I had the children, Will and I went on long walks so I could take pictures of the moors and the cliffs by the sea. I used to own a Hasselblad. Now I rarely even take photos on my phone unless they're of the kids. There never seems to be time for anything else, I give myself a shake. "He works long hours, so there's not much time for other hobbies."

Alexa nods as I speak, listening intently and making notes. She points out, when I say I don't have a photo right now, that I'll need to bring one to my meeting with the Honey I choose. At last she reaches for the two large portfolios on the shelf.

"So what would you say your husband's 'type' is?" She sets the first portfolio down on her lap.

"Blond," I say emphatically.

"Ah." Alexa raises her eyebrows in an expression that says very clearly, *how predictable*.

I visualize Shannon.

"I think he'd go for someone blond, but not overtly tarty. More baby doll–looking, you know, big blue eyes . . . innocent smile, that sort of thing. And young, not *too* young, though. Maybe mid-twenties."

Alexa flicks through one of the portfolios, her thumb keeping her place as she marks out ten or so pages. She hands me the book.

"These are all our regular blondes under thirty," she says.

My mouth is dry as I scan the pages. The girls here have a similar look: attractive but not intimidatingly beautiful, with good figures and inviting smiles. None of them is Shannon.

My palms are sweating as I close the portfolio and rest my hand on top.

"Some of these might work," I acknowledge. "But none of them are as good as the girl I saw on your site before I made the appointment. She looks just like this ex of his that I know he still fancies."

"Okay." Alexa's eyes rest on mine for a second longer than is necessary. Has she seen through me? My stomach clenches with anxiety.

"Show me the girl." Alexa leads me to the computer on her desk and leans over, clicking quickly through to the *Gallery* page.

I run my finger down the portraits, pretending I can't find her at first; then I point to the photo of Shannon.

"Her," I say. "She'd be perfect for him. You know, he says he looks but he doesn't touch, but—"

"But we all know how easily one thing can lead to another." Alexa sighs. "I'm afraid this is an old picture. This particular girl no longer works for us."

I stare at her. How can Shannon not work here? She went to Aces High to meet Julia less than a week ago. . . .

"No longer works for you?" I affect a laugh. "Has she moved to another agency, then?"

"Not at all." Alexa bristles slightly. "No, I'm afraid she just didn't show up for an appointment last Wednesday, and we have a zero tolerance policy on punctuality.

My heart skips a beat. I saw Shannon myself on Tuesday evening. Was it meeting me—and the news of Julia's death—that made her stay away from work?

"Did you sack her?" I ask, hoping Alexa will give me some clue as to Shannon's state of mind.

"Not at first," she says. "I tried her twice, but she didn't answer her phone. Then I left a message telling her she was fired. I haven't heard anything back. Very unprofessional, I know, but there you are."

I stare at her. "And that's it?"

Alexa shrugs. "My best guess is that she's upped and moved on. It happens sometimes—the girls are young."

I stare at Shannon's picture on the computer screen as another possibility worms its way into my head. What if Shannon didn't leave of her own accord?

What if someone killed her too?

"Olivia?"

I look up. Alexa is gazing at me curiously.

"I was suggesting an alternative girl—Brooke," she says, pointing to a Honey from the same row as Shannon on the on-screen gallery. She enlarges Brooke's picture so I can see her properly. Another twenty-something, sparkly-eyed blonde, though her expression lacks the coy tease of Shannon's.

I think fast. My mind is still reeling from the fact that Shannon is missing, that all my efforts to invesigate have come to what looks like a dead end. Then I rouse myself. I can't accept that. Not yet. There must be some way of finding out if Julia set Shannon to entrap someone, who it was and why. I glance over at the Honey Hearts case files on Alexa Carling's shelves.

"I wonder if I could just use the ladies' while I have a think about all this," I say.

Alexa sits back in her chair. "Of course, take all the time you need." The frown is still on her face, and I realize she is worried that I am getting cold feet, that if I walk out of the office, so does my money.

"It's just such a big decision," I explain as I head for the door.

"I know it is," Alexa says with warmth. "But I've been where you are Livy. I'm happily single now, but both my husbands cheated on me. It was devastating. With my first husband, I had no idea anything was wrong until the day he walked out on us. And with the second, it was worse—he left me and the children with nothing." She sighs. "Knowledge is power, Olivia. I have to tell you that it's very, very rare for any of our clients to regret hiring our Honeys, whatever they find out. You see, if your partner doesn't respond, you get the reassurance you are hoping for. If he does, you have proof instead suspicions."

I nod, then scuttle along the corridor to the ladies' room. As soon as I'm safely inside a cubicle, I text Damian, as arranged. I take my time in the bathroom, psyching myself up for what I am going to have to do next. I just make it back to Alexa's office, when the commotion in reception begins. Alexa's face reddens as Damian's voice—full of indignant fury—fills the air.

"How *dare* you send one of your slags to try to get me into bed, preying on my wife, winding her up to think I'm seeing other women. You should all be in jail."

"Please, sir, calm down," the receptionist pleads. "I'm sure there's just been a misunderstanding."

I glance at Alexa. She's listening intently to the conversation.

"I demand to see the person my wife spoke to. Alexa Carling. Where is she? Get her out here now?" Damian shouts.

"I'm afraid Mrs. Carling is in a meeting, sir. Perhaps if you gave me your name, I—?"

"I'm not giving you *anything*!" Damian yells. "Get her out of the meeting!"

Alexa meets my eyes, her expression at once concerned and apologetic. "I'm sorry, Olivia," she says. "This has *never* happened before."

"It's fine," I say, my heart racing. "Go. I'll wait here."

Alexa scurries away and I dart over to the shelf with the case files. I pick out *A–D*. If Julia did hire Shannon, I can't imagine she'd have used her real name, Dryden, but I don't know where else to start. The cases are divided by colored plastic sheets with the clients' names at the top, followed by a copy of the form they are asked to fill out on arrival, plus the sheets clearly compiled by Alexa during the face-to-face meeting. There are pictures of and notes from the Honeys themselves and then, at the end, detail on the men under surveillance alongside written reports of the encounters between them and, in some cases, numbered references to recordings that are, presumably, stored elsewhere.

I flick from back to front, through the *D*s. A selection of Honeys flash before my eyes: pretty girls with sparkling eyes. I turn from DURSLEY to DENHAM. I turn the page back. No Dryden. My heart sinks—so Julia didn't use her real name. It's not surprising, but it leaves me feeling hopeless. Outside in reception, I can hear Damian still shouting, then Alexa's cool, quiet voice as she tries in vain to calm him down. He's very convincing.

I look back at the file in my hand. I don't know what else to do, so I keep turning the pages. Past DERBY to DAWSON to DAVIS. Some, but not all, pages are stamped with the letter *P*. What does that mean?

Suddenly I spot Shannon, her photo tacked on to the front of a case file. I look to the top of the page. The client's name is Julia D'Arc. I can't help but smile at this. Was Julia using part of her made-up name for her mother as her own cover name? I scan hurriedly down the page, noticing as I do that it hasn't been stamped with a *P*, like some of the others.

Outside, Damian is still yelling. Alexa is threatening to call the police if he doesn't leave. I don't have much time. My finger sticks to the page as I read, my brain tripping over the notes in my haste. Julia is reporting concerns in a long-term relationship, a man she is involved with whom she suspects of having an affair. This *has* to be a cover. Which means it must *surely* be related in some way to Kara's killer.

My finger traces to the bottom of the page, where the name of the man under investigation hits me like a punch. I suck in my breath, shocked beyond words.

Because the man Julia hired Shannon to entrap is my husband.

CHAPTER TEN

I reel back, away from the page. For a few seconds, the room seems to spin around me. Outside, Damian is still kicking up a terrible racket. Alexa Carling's voice is raised too as she tries to calm him down.

I peer back at the file. Will's name is there in black-and-white at the bottom of the page:

SUBJECT FOR INVESTIGATION: WILL JACKSON.

It's him. It's undeniably him. I run my finger to the top of the next page, trying to take in what Julia has said about him, but I get only as far as the first line:

SUBJECT IS DESCRIBED AS OUTGOING AND CONFIDENT,
A PROFESSIONAL MAN WITH A REPUTATION FOR—

A door slams outside. I suddenly realize the shouting coming from reception has stopped. Footsteps *clip-clop* along the corridor toward me. Alexa Carling must be coming back. I close the file and shove it back on its shelf. Then I scurry back to the sofa, sitting down just as Alexa walks into the room.

"I'm so sorry about that," she says smoothly. "Now, are we going with Brooke?"

I shake my head. "I'm sorry," I stammer. "I really need more time to think about this."

"Of course, but—"

"It's a big decision." I get up. Somehow my shaking legs carry me to the door. I just about remember to turn around and thank Alexa for her time. I register she looks perplexed, and a little frustrated. And then I'm out of there. Along the corridor, past reception and down, out onto the street. I glance along the road. Damian will be waiting for me in the café down the street, but I can't face him just yet. I turn and walk in the opposite direction, thoughts swirling about my head.

As I pace along the sidewalk, it starts to rain. Soft drops patter onto my head and down my neck. People around me scuttle for shelter in shop doorways. I keep walking, trying to make sense of what I've just seen. Julia hired a woman to attempt to seduce my husband. Why would she have done such a thing? The notes made no mention of his being married, but did say she had been with him for a long time.

That can't be true, can it? Julia was with Damian. She couldn't have been seeing Will. She would never have done that to me. *Will* wouldn't have done it. Would he? My husband and my best friend. Images flash into my head. I feel sick. Panic rises inside me. If Julia and Will betrayed me with each other, then nothing is safe. Nothing is certain. I turn a corner and stop walking. I force myself to take a deep breath. I need to think it through calmly, rationally. I huddle in a doorway, wipe the rain from my face, and turn the possibilities over in my mind.

The first and most obvious reason for Julia hiring a girl to entrap Will is that she *was* having an affair with him—and suspected him of cheating on both of us. I can't believe this is true. Julia would *never* have betrayed our friendship like that, and despite the sudden waves of doubt that sometimes wash over me, when I stop and think it through, I'm certain Will has been faithful since his affair with Catrina all those years ago. Plus, I saw Will and Julia together a million times, and not *once* did I ever sense any kind of frisson between them.

It is far more likely, knowing Julia's fierce sense of loyalty, that

133

she thought Will was seeing someone else and wanted to find out more before she confronted him about it, or told me directly. I sigh. This may be more likely, yet it still seems improbable. Even if Julia had believed Will was having an affair and wanted to find out more, why not simply follow him herself? Even hiring a private investigator would surely make more sense than the elaborate contrivance of a Honey from Honey Hearts?

Which brings me to the third and, ultimately, most horrifying possibility: Could Julia have suspected Will of some involvement in Kara's death? She was clearly convinced that Shannon held the key to the truth, and adamant that she had to speak to me before going to the police. I thought before that this was because I was Kara's sister, but now I'm wondering if it was so she could warn me. I think of Hannah and Zack, and my blood chills in my veins. They are Will's children as well as mine.

No, there is absolutely no way that Will was involved in my sister's murder. And surely no way that Julia could have believed he was.

My mind slides back, over the years, to the day we met, but it's impossible to disentangle my meeting with Will with the way Julia and I had become friends. It seems so long ago now, a jumble of events all merged together, punctuated by a few single, searing memories.

Kara died during February, and I stumbled through the last few weeks of that spring term of my final year in a daze. Looking back, I have no idea what I did with my time, but it certainly didn't involve writing essays or preparing for exams. I remember lying curled up on the sofa of my rented house, staring into space for hours, my housemates tiptoeing around me. Back then, there was a wall between me and the rest of the world of people who didn't have to live with the reality of a murdered sister. I barely ate, though people whose names I can no longer remember placed food in front of me. I scarcely registered when the TV was switched on and turned off again. I crept from the sofa to bed and then back again, letting life drift around me. I stayed like that for over a month, rousing myself only to visit my parents. It was on one such trip home that I discovered they had invited Julia to spend the Easter holiday with us. I remember feeling a flicker of annoyance at the intrusion, then resigning myself to her arrival. What did it really matter? What did anything matter anymore? Kara was gone, her life, beauty, and innocence destroyed, and I had not protected her.

Julia breathed life into me, into all of us. She came into our home and tended to my parents with tiny, sensitive touches, placing my dad's paper by his armchair, helping my mother chop vegetables in the kitchen. Her hard edges softened by grief, I think she was simply trying to offer practical help, but it ended up being so much more than that. As if Julia were holding a rope to a new life without Kara to which we knew we had to make our way. She knocked on my bedroom door on the morning of the second day of her visit and told me gently but firmly that I needed to do more to help my parents. I was silent at first, turning my head to the wall, but Julia persisted and eventually I turned on her, shouting at her to "fuck off" and mind her own business. Julia stood her ground, bearing my rage for as long as she could, then started shouting too. I don't remember what we said, but I was hoarse by the time I yelled that I missed Kara, that I hated the world for taking her away, that I was so angry she was gone. The terrible pain of it consumed me; my legs buckled and I collapsed on the floor in tears. There was silence, and I thought Julia had gone. Then I looked up and she was sitting on the floor herself, leaning against the wall watching me, and I saw my own agony reflected in her eyes.

I always thought that Julia saved me after Kara's death, but maybe we saved each other. We certainly spent the rest of my final year almost exclusively in each other's company. After that Easter break, I managed to get back to my studies and somehow made it through my final exams. Thanks to my hard work on earlier units and with the help of a note from my tutor, I ended up with a respectable 2:1 in History.

Julia and I went on holiday together that August. A tiny apartment with kitchenette in Ibiza. That week away was the first time I realized the magnetic effect Julia had on men. She slept with several guys on the holiday—men she met while we were at clubs, with whom she had sex immediately. Shockingly fast, it seemed to me, on beaches, in parking lots, under trees. I got used to her sudden disappearances from the dance floor but learned to trust that she would always be back by dawn, ready to walk home with me. It was never spoken out loud, but I knew she wouldn't leave me to return to our apartment alone. Not after Kara.

I came home, clear about my future for the first time. I battled my way onto a conversion law course back in Exeter, and though I was similar in age to most of the other students, I felt much older than everyone around me. Julia returned for her second year at university, and though we were based in completely different parts of the city now, we still talked all the time and made the effort to get together as often as we could.

I met Will a couple of months later, through Paul. He and I hadn't seen much of each other since our uni course ended, but we'd arranged to meet for a pre-Christmas drink that December. Paul had just taken up a junior position at Harbury Media, working for his dad. Naturally enough, several of his colleagues were in the pub too, including Will, who had already been working at Harbury for just over a year.

Will was twenty-four at the time, two and a half years older than me and radiating a smooth, easy confidence. I remember being impressed by his sharp suit and piercing blue eyes as he offered to buy me a drink. I tried to brush him off, but he persisted. He chatted away with the other Harbury staff, but whenever I looked up, he caught my eye. I remember—and it makes me laugh to think of it so many comfortable, married years later—that he seemed dangerous and sexy to me then, oozing charisma, with his hair slicked back and something brooding about his expression.

I said no when he asked me out that first evening. Other men might have slunk off, chastened, but Will just asked me what I was hiding from.

"Nothing," I said.

He shook his head and told me that he could see the sadness behind my eyes and that he wasn't going to let my fears put him off.

Maybe it was a line, but I was lonely and it felt good to have some-one see beyond my brittle social smile for once. I agreed to a date the following weekend, and as we ate seafood and drank white wine, he asked about my family and I slowly, agonizingly, told him about Kara.

I think back, searching my memory for any signs Will already knew my story. He remembered the murder from earlier in the year, but not Kara's name. He expressed horror and offered sympathy, so that tears pricked at my eyes. I tried to hold them back, but Will took my hand.

"Cry," he said. "I don't think you've grieved in all the ways yet."

I knew what he meant. I'd cried with Mum and with Julia and on my own. But even after all these months, I hadn't spoken of Kara to anyone who didn't already know what had happened to her. I hadn't told her story, my story, to a stranger; I hadn't grieved in *that* way yet.

"I should have looked after her," I sobbed. "She was still a child."

"Hey." Will squeezed my hand. "It wasn't your fault." And then he smiled gently. "So who looks after you?"

I cried some more, then went to the ladies' where I realized how blotchy-cheeked and red-eyed I looked. My heart gave a weird skip. After all, if this cool, sharp-suited marketing guy was interested in me, despite my tears and messy face, then maybe I had more going for myself than I'd thought.

Back at the table, Will didn't dwell on Kara's death. He showed no morbid interest, just concern for me. He told me later he'd started to fall in love with me that night, seeing how much I loved my sister, how much I was capable of bearing and of feeling. And yet, he never—I'm certain of it—defined me by my sister's death in the way so many of my university friends had.

So, Julia might have saved me by sharing my grief, but Will saved me by seeing past it.

It is entirely impossible that he is my sister's killer. Or that Julia—who liked and respected him—could have thought so.

I turn and retrace my steps, heading for the café where Damian is waiting. It's still raining and I am soaked, my jacket clinging to my back and my hair wet around my cheeks. Damian is sitting at a table by the café window, looking out. He stands as I enter, his face wreathed with anxiety.

"Are you okay?"

"No."

He looks at me, expectant. I hesitate for a moment; then I sit down opposite him and tell him everything I found out at Honey Hearts.

Damian listens with shocked eyes. He is clearly as baffled as I am that Will is the man Julia set Shannon to entrap.

"Julia never once mentioned that she thought he was unfaithful to you—quite the opposite. She was always so impressed at the way the two of you made your marriage work after . . . after that one time. . . ."

I raise my eyebrows, a blush of defensive humiliation rising in my cheeks. So he *does* know about the affair. "Julia told you about that?"

Damian nods. He looks embarrassed. "She said it was a long time ago and that Will seemed like a different person afterwards—more *grown-up,* I think she said." He pauses. "She liked him as a friend, she said he was a good dad, a good fit for you."

For some reason, hearing Julia's opinion of my marriage from someone she clearly trusted calms me like nothing else so far has. I remember that although she was angry with Will over his affair, she never once suggested I leave him. *He's made a mistake and he's sorry, Liv,* she said. *He deserves a second chance. We all do.* I smile, remembering how she'd paused, her eyes sparkling, before adding: *I'd make him pay, though. Some decent diamonds and a holiday to the Caribbean, at the very least.*

It's still raining outside, and the café is dark and depressing. Damian gazes at me, his forehead creased with deep lines.

I sit back and sigh. "So . . . if Julia didn't hire Shannon to go after Will because she thought he was unfaithful, then why hire her at all?"

Damian looks away. My heart shrinks. I don't want to think about what Damian suspects Will might be capable of.

"I need to talk to him," I say firmly. "Find out if Shannon really did approach him. What she said."

Damian looks up. "We should try to track down Shannon too, find out what Julia said to her. Were there any contact details on the form you saw?"

"Not for Shannon, not that I noticed."

"What about the date Julia went to Honey Hearts? Was that on the form?"

"I don't think so." I'm less sure about this. The truth is that I hadn't looked for a date. "There wasn't much time and—"

"It's fine. We know it must have been before she met Shannon in person at Aces High—it doesn't particularly matter when it was." Damian thinks for a second. "Wait a minute, didn't you say they take someone with them to meetings? A friend, as backup?"

I shake my head. "That's when the agent goes to meet the guy. There are basically five steps: One, the client goes to Honey Hearts and sets up the whole thing. Two, the client is assigned an agent and *they* meet—that was Julia meeting Shannon two days before she died. Three, the agent seeks out the guy, and then possibly four, they set up and go on a 'date' together. Five, the agent reports back to the client—that was the meeting in Aces High that I went to, the one I saw coming up in Julia's diary."

"So we don't know if this girl, Shannon, ever did go to entrap your husband."

"She *must* have. Why else would she have turned up for that second meeting? She was there to report back to Julia." My breath catches in my throat as I realize the implications of this. Shannon Walker *must* have approached Will. What did she say? How did Will respond?

"We don't know any of this for sure," Damian says. "Just as we've got no idea how to find Shannon."

I sigh. "All the more reason why I *have* to talk to Will."

"That's not going to be easy," Damian mutters.

He's right. For the first time since I saw Shannon at Aces High, I regret how much I've kept from Will. If I'd told him I was going to

Honey Hearts in the first place, then this latest development might not come as such a shock. As it is . . .

Damian and I say good-bye, promising to speak again tomorrow, when I've had a chance to talk to Will. I go home in a daze realizing only after I've left that I have completely forgotten, again, to ask Damian why he has no online presence. I'm distracted for the rest of the afternoon, barely listening to Zack's eager chatter about his football game at break time. I feel guilty I'm so preoccupied—and only too aware of how quickly this time when Zack wants to tell me all about his day will pass.

As if to prove the point, when Hannah arrives home an hour later, she stomps straight to her room without even saying hello. I follow her up the stairs, trying to hold my temper in check. I peer around the door, smiling, to ask how she is, but Hannah explodes before I can get the words out.

"What do you want? Why are you *always* following me everywhere?"

"I'm not." I grip the doorframe, trying hard not to lose it. "I just wanted—"

"I will tidy up on the weekend!" she yells. "God, Mum, school is so stressy, and now you're being really mean."

"For goodness' sake, Hannah. I was just going to ask if you want a drink or a snack," I snap.

"Well, I don't."

"There's no need to be so rude."

"*You're* the one being rude. You're the one in my room. I don't want you in here."

"You know what, Hannah? I don't want to be here either." I march back downstairs and sit at the kitchen table, my head in my hands, shaking with rage and hurt.

A single tear trickles down my cheek. I wipe it away. Will's right, I am taking Hannah's acting out too personally, but it's hard to have lost my little girl as well as my best friend. If Julia were here, she would cheer me up with a smart, pithy observation and that dirty laugh of hers. The fact that she isn't here and will never be here again makes everything ten times worse.

Zack wanders in and, sensing my sadness, offers me comfort the only way he knows how, burying his head in my stomach and wrapping his arms tightly around my hips. I let him play *Angry Birds* while I make tea. Hannah slouches in fifteen minutes after I call her, then has the nerve to complain that her shepherd's pie is cold. Both children light up when Will arrives home, earlier than usual, at six thirty. He hugs Zack, pecks at Hannah's forehead, then plants a kiss on my lips.

"You're in a good mood." I try to smile at him, but all I can see is his name on the Honey Hearts form.

"The Henri account settled down at last," he says with a grin.

"That took a long time," I say, trying to work out how on earth to begin the conversation I need to have.

Will sighs. "I know. Bloody ages." He pauses, and when he speaks again I can hear the pride in his voice. "The client said some nice things about me, actually. And Leo thanked me in front of the whole team, whatever that's worth." He laughs, but I know how much Leo's praise means to him.

"Well done." I reach up and kiss him on the cheek. Zack is already tugging at his arm, wanting to show him his *Angry Birds* score. Will and I can talk later, after the kids are in bed. I murmur something about sorting out dinner for the two of us, then give him a hug, breathing in the familiar scent of his suit jacket: wool and aftershave and a lingering aroma of office.

See? I tell myself. *No strange-smelling soap. Everything's going to be fine.*

It turns into a good evening—at least the early part of it is. As usual, Hannah's mood lightens dramatically around her father, while Will seems particularly relaxed tonight. It just goes to show how important his mood is to the overall atmosphere in the house. Those nights where he gets in grumpy and tired lay a pall over everything.

My chance to talk comes after Hannah disappears up to her room at nine o'clock. Will has spent most of his time since dinner trying to match Zack's *Angry Birds* score on his phone, while intermittently reading a report on his laptop and sipping at a whiskey.

As I join him in the living room, he puts both gadgets down with a sigh. "Can you imagine how humiliating it is being beaten at something by your seven-year-old son?"

I laugh, then close the door gently. "Can I talk to you?"

Will swings his legs off the sofa and sits up, an expression of concern on his face. "Sure, what's up?"

I take the chair opposite him and lean forward. My heart beats fast as I launch in, explaining that Damian and I decided to try to trace Shannon Walker.

"You didn't tell me that," Will says, his eyes darkening.

"I knew you'd think it was me being obsessive or whatever, but seriously, Will, there's something really suspicious going on." I carry on, the words tumbling out of me as I explain that Damian and I tracked Shannon down to Honey Hearts, then going on to confess that I visited the place this morning.

"You did *what*?"

"I sneaked a look at Julia's file," I explain.

"I can't believe you'd do that."

"Well, I did. And I found something out. Julia hired Shannon Walker—that was the connection between them."

"Come on, Liv." Will shakes his head. "That doesn't sound like Julia. Not her style."

"I know." I gulp. "That's the thing . . . I don't think she was testing her own boyfriend. Damian, Dirty Blond. He said he didn't recognize Shannon and . . . anyway, it wasn't his name in her file."

Will frowns. I watch him intently. There's no guilt, no acknowledgment of what I'm saying . . . of where I'm going. I can't believe he knows.

"So . . . what are you telling me, Liv. I don't understand?"

I take a deep breath. "I don't understand either, but I have to ask you about it. You see, the man Julia put on her form she wanted to entrap—was you."

Will stares at me blankly. "Me?"

I nod.

"You think Julia suspected me of being unfaithful?" His eyes bore into me. "What . . . with you? With *her*?" He pauses, his expression hard and cold. "Well?"

I squirm in my seat. "She might have thought something like that, I guess, but no I don't seriously—"

"Oh, good," he snaps, his voice dripping with sarcasm. "Just so long as you trust me."

I hesitate. "Please don't be angry, Will. It's not my fault your name was in that file."

"Fuck off, Livy."

I gasp. Will hardly ever swears—and certainly not at me. He looks up. His fists are clenched, the vein in his neck throbbing.

"So what do you expect me to say?" he asks.

"This . . . Shannon." I shiver, he looks so angry. "She was blond and blue-eyed. Pretty. Mid-twenties, I'd say."

Will raises his eyebrows. "Are you asking if she came onto me? Is that it? You think I slept with some tramp from some sleazy agency?"

"No." Tears spring to my eyes at the fury in his voice. "No, of course I don't think you slept with her. I'm just trying to work out what Julia was doing. I think it might be connected to her trying to find out about Kara's killer. There are just a lot of things that don't add up. Julia's mother is convinced one of Julia's rings is missing. In fact, she thinks I took it. And then there's the fact that though the police searched Julia's apartment and her computer, they didn't find any of her files about Kara. I think Shannon knows something."

Will spreads his arms wide in a gesture of disbelief. "You only have this Damian's word that there *were* any files. Jesus." Will's voice rises. "And it's outrageous to suggest I slept with—"

"I'm *not* accusing you of sleeping with her," I insist. "I'm not even suggesting that you reacted in any particular way. I'm just trying to make sense of why Julia hired her. Surely you can understand why I have to ask?"

Will stands and paces over to the TV. His fists are still clenched. He turns and fixes me with a furious glare. "I have absolutely no idea why Julia put my name on her form, but what really makes me mad is you jumping to conclusions about what it *means*. Maybe it was a *joke*. Maybe it wasn't Julia. Maybe it was some other guy called Will Jackson. Don't you see? If you go looking for problems, you find them."

"But—"

"How can you even *consider* I might have been with anyone else? God, haven't the past six years since . . . haven't they meant *anything*?"

"I'm not saying that." My voice cracks. "I just—"

"Well, the answer is I haven't seen this *Shannon* girl, or anyone else." He pauses. "And as for this nonsense about Kara. It's getting ridiculous. Whatever you say, you *are* obsessed with this idea Julia was murdered. Meanwhile, you're living the rest of your life without noticing what's going on around you."

"Not noticing what?"

"Well, quite apart from the effect on Hannah, there's us. We haven't had sex in weeks. Not since before Julia died."

My mouth gapes. Will's right, though it hadn't occurred to me. I don't know what to say to him. My mind flashes back to the first time we made love properly. Not the first attempt. *That* was a disaster, thanks to me being so self-conscious and unwilling to lose control that I stopped him halfway through and ran away. No, I'm thinking of the following evening, when Will, to my astonishment, pursued me home even more determinedly than he had the night before and spent hours talking me into bed, then touching me until, for the first time in my life, I let go for long enough to have an orgasm.

"I . . . I . . . ," I stammer. Sex is so little a part of my thinking these days, even before Julia's death, it is slightly shocking to realize that I can't actually remember the last time Will and I made love—or the last time it crossed my mind that I might like to. I want to talk to him about this, but as I struggle to find the words, Will makes a dismissive gesture with his hand.

"Forget it," he says.

I stare at him. This is what we always do: circle a problem with hints and snipes, but never tackle it head-on. I open my mouth again, about to insist we should talk about what he's said, but before I can speak, Will is off again.

"The point is, you have to trust me. And you have to accept what happened to Julia. You have to move on. Julia killed herself. Under all that sass and wit, she was sad and lonely." He lowers his voice, the words firing like bullets from his mouth. "You know the real truth, Livy, is that you weren't enough to save Julia. Neither was this Dirty Blond of hers who's been egging you on."

"He's not egging me on, for God's sake." Anger boils inside me, all thoughts of talking about our sex life forgotten. "And it's not fair of you to say I don't trust you. I'm just—"

"Then why did you assume this Shannon person had tried to seduce me and I hadn't told you?" Will hisses. The vein at his temple bulges. His fists are clenched. I can't remember the last time he was this furious.

"I didn't," I say. "That is, I didn't mean to. I trust you, it's—"

"Yeah?" Will snorts. "You know I've done everything I can to prove to you that I'm faithful. Years of living with the guilt of your suspicions and never *ever* being able to complain because it was all my fault in the first place."

I suck in my breath, overwhelmed by the force of his words.

"Saint fucking Livy, but you know what? All your good deeds weren't enough to stop Julia from killing herself, because she wasn't who you thought she was. I think *that's* what really gets you. *That's* why you can't accept Julia killed herself. Because you can't stand how imperfect it makes you feel." He storms out of the room.

I sink into my chair, hurt to the core. Why is he being so vicious? Was I really so out of order to ask him about something that mystifies me as much as him? Surely his reaction is overkill?

Righteous indignation is one of the three infallible signs of guilt, I remember Julia saying once, a twinkle in her eye. *Along with being too nice and begging.*

I sit, raw and hurting. I hear Will stomping up the stairs. I leave him for ten minutes . . . fifteen . . . then I go up, hoping we can talk again and sort things out. But Will has retreated to Zack's room and is lying on the upper bunk, his eyes firmly shut. I whisper his name, but he doesn't respond. I back away, then peer around Hannah's door. She's fallen asleep with her headphones on. I take them off and pull the covers over her. Then I creep into my own room. I'm completely exhausted, yet totally wired. I curl up on the bed and watch the seconds tick away. With every beat of the clock, the pain of Will's harsh words drills into me. Hours pass and I lie there, unhappy and humiliated. I want, so badly, to call Julia and tell her what has happened. She was never quick to judge and always able to make me laugh even in the depths of despair.

The knowledge that I can't hurts beyond tears. I have never felt so alone in my life. In the end, I guess I fall asleep at around two. When I wake, with Zack bouncing on the bed beside me, it takes only a couple of seconds to work out that Will has already left for the office, and the rest of the house is in disarray. Neither child is dressed and we have to leave the house in five minutes in order for me to drop them both at school in time.

I shout at Hannah to get ready, while helping Zack button his shirt. I shove croissants in their hands and bundle them into the car. Hannah is, at least, willing to be bundled, though she grumbles like mad that her croissant is stale, that she wanted to wash her hair, and that I'm a useless mother for not waking her at the proper time. I ignore this as best I can. I know she hates being late, a failure to comply with school rules that inevitably results in a detention. I concentrate on delivering her to school before the eight thirty deadline. We make it with a minute to spare. Then it's on to Zack's school. He holds my hand as we walk into his classroom. Next year—coming up all too soon—parents will be asked to leave children in the playground rather than taking them to their classrooms. The thought brings a lump to my throat. Will's fury is like a weight around my neck. After his anger and Hannah's disdain, the prospect of losing Zack's affectionate need for me is devastating.

I hold back my tears as I drive home, but later—once I'm safely behind closed doors—I let myself bawl. Then I make myself a cup of coffee and blow my nose. I have to pull myself together. Hannah will grow out of her antipathy to me, and Will will calm down.

As I'm thinking all this, the doorbell rings. I run my fingers under my eyes and check my reflection in the hall mirror as I pass. I look okay, if a little red-eyed. Anyway, it'll only be the postman. I open the door. To my astonishment, Martha is standing on the doorstep.

"Hi, Livy." Her eyes are strained, belying the characteristically warm smile on her lips.

"Martha? What are you—? Hey, come in." I smile back.

Martha shakes her head, and gestures to the car parked on the curbside. The sun is shining, glancing bright off its windows, but I can just about make out Paul sitting in the driver's seat. He catches me looking and winds down his window.

"Hi, Livy! All right?" He waves.

"Good, thanks." I wave back, then turn to Martha. "What's going on?"

"Paul's taking me to the Apple Store at Princesshay to get a new computer," Martha explains. "Then we're meeting Leo for lunch, then I'm straight off after that on the train to spend a few days with my mother in Scotland. . . ." She gabbles all this as I stare at her anxious face, feeling more and more bemused.

"I don't—"

"I just had to see you before I went away," Martha carries on. "I promised Leo I wouldn't, but it's not right to leave you in the dark. I think if it were me, I'd want someone to say something. And . . . and anyway, you know how much you mean to me, Livy." She fidgets from side to side.

I reach for her arm. This is Martha as I've never seen her, conflicted and distressed. "Martha, I don't understand. What is it?" I ask. "Leave me 'in the dark' about what? Look, why don't you come in so—?"

"No." Martha fishes in her handbag and pulls out a silk scarf. She shoves it into my hand. "Take this—I told Paul it was yours so we could stop off here on the way to the computer shop. I also told him I'd only be a minute. . . ." She glances around at the car.

"You made an excuse to come here?" I raise my eyebrows.

Martha takes a deep breath. "It's Will," she says in hushed, fearful tones. "Leo and I blame ourselves because of that damn party we had—and the stupid business trip to Geneva."

My chest tightens. I know what she's going to say, and all the old fears surge up, like acid in my lungs.

"I'm so sorry to be the one to tell you, but Leo let it slip last night and I've been agonizing over whether to say something ever since." She hesitates, and the deep burn of humiliation consumes me.

"Go on," I say.

"Will slept with that awful woman again when Leo sent them to Geneva. God, Livy, I'm so sorry." Martha's forehead creases with frown lines, her eyes intent on my face.

I lean against the front door's frame, clutching the silk scarf in my hand, feeling sick. So Will did it after all. Despite all his protestations, all his claims, all his indignation . . . he went and slept with Catrina again.

My head spins. No. *No.* It *can't* be true. Leo must have misunderstood what he saw. Or maybe he mistook Will for someone else.

"What exactly did Leo say?" I ask.

Martha shifts from one foot to the other. "Not much more than what I've told you already. He . . . he said he saw Will kissing her goodbye, sneaking out of her room at five A.M. or so."

The image sears itself on my mind's eye. I can't bear it. Martha looks over her shoulder at Paul, still waiting in the car. He is peering through the window, watching us both.

"Are you all right, Livy?" Martha reaches for my hand, but I pull away. It's irrational, but I hate her for telling me. My husband has cheated on me, and I am the last to know. Worse, it's with the same woman he betrayed me with before. That can't be discounted as a momentary lapse. And he has lied to me. If about this, then about how many more affairs?

"Oh, Livy." Martha's voice is heavy with compassion and remorse. "I did do the right thing in saying something, didn't I?"

It takes a monumental effort to look up and meet her gaze. It's not fair to shoot the messenger. Martha is only doing what she thinks is right.

"Of course. I'm grateful." The words rasp out; my throat is dry.

Martha makes a noise somewhere between a sigh and a groan. "Look, I'll stay. Never mind Leo. I'll tell Paul there's been a change of plan and—"

"No." I take a deep breath. "I'm fine." My mind flickers back to Julia's Honey Hearts file and Will's name on her report sheet. She must have known he was being unfaithful, either with Catrina or someone else. *That's* why she wanted to talk to me. It had nothing at all to do with Kara's death. This thought fills me with a strange mix of despair and relief.

"Are you sure you're okay?" Martha asks anxiously.

I nod. She still wants absolution, to be told it's all right that she has brought me this terrible truth. "I'm fine, really." I take her hand and give it a squeeze. "I appreciate you coming here—it can't have been easy."

Martha squeezes my hand back, but I barely notice the touch. Will had sex with Catrina the day the children and I found Julia dead in her flat. The same day that I cried down the phone and he said he couldn't get back until the following evening. Selfish bastard. Bile rises in my throat. A terrible, coruscating fury.

"It's okay, I'm fine," I repeat, releasing Martha's hand. "Go on, don't get into trouble with Leo."

Martha gives me a long, unhappy look. "Are you sure you don't want me to stay?"

I take a deep breath, holding in my anger. "Of course, go on, go. And thank you."

Martha backs away. I watch her walk to the front gate. She turns and waves. I wave back. Then she gets into the car next to Paul and I shut the front door.

I cross the hall in a daze. Everything I thought was true is a lie. Julia's death and Damian's claims and Shannon Walker's absence fade to background noise. All I can think about is Will and his lies. The rage inside me builds. He has made a fool of me. I took him back

149

because his regret and his love seemed so sincere. But, in fact, I have been an idiot. It's all been a con. He has probably been shagging anyone and everyone for the whole of the past six years.

I stop pacing, letting the thoughts tumble through my head. Julia found out. Which means there must be proof for me to find too. Because I'm certain now it isn't just Catrina.

And I have to know: the who, the what, and the when. All of it. I refuse to live in doubt like I did last time. Yesterday, even after I found out that Julia had put Will on her form, I wouldn't have dreamed of going through his things, but right now, I have no choice. I have to know what he's hiding from me.

I start in the downstairs cupboard. It's been mild, and Will has hardly worn a coat for weeks. There's nothing in any of his pockets except a chewing gum wrapper. I move upstairs and go through all his suits. I spot the one he wore the night he traveled to Geneva and pat it down. I'm half expecting to discover a telephone number, scrawled in lipstick on a napkin, but there's nothing so clichéd, nothing at all, in fact. Of course not. Will would keep a number in his phone, or on his computer.

I go upstairs and switch on the main house computer. Both Will and Hannah have their own laptops, so I'm not expecting much, but it's the only bit of technology I have access to, Will having taken both his phone and his laptop to work.

I check over the machine's history—which is mostly Zack playing a Lego computer game—then rummage through the shelves and desk. I find nothing apart from Will's old work stuff. Sighing, I sit back in my chair. This is hopeless. If Will has been seeing someone, the evidence will be on his phone, as it was before, or on his clothes.

I get up and go into the bathroom. We had it redecorated last year, after my first preference—to construct a new master bath off my and Will's bedroom—proved too expensive. It's a large room, light and airy, but cluttered up with Hannah's neon-bright bottles of toiletries that range across the window ledge. At least all the plastic toys and balls that Zack has now grown out of but which still regularly get tipped inside the tub are inside the net at the end of the bath.

I head over to the laundry basket and start pulling out clothes. Two of Hannah's school shirts are on top of the pile, immediately followed by a pair of her jeans and an assortment of her simple white cotton knickers—a far cry from the leopard-skin nylon panties she chose for herself. It crosses my mind that perhaps I should buy her a bra in the same white cotton. She doesn't need one, but after finding that padded thing in her bedroom, it's clear that she wants one. It doesn't really matter whether she's bothered about keeping up with the other girls in her class or whether she's just impatient to have breasts. I shouldn't dismiss her anxieties. Mum was right—I obsessed about the same thing myself at her age.

I examine the jeans—they are barely worn, just like the three cotton tops of hers that I remove next from the basket. I shake my head. How can Hannah possibly have gotten through all these clothes since I last did a wash two days ago? She must have worn each item for about three hours.

I delve deeper into the basket, past Zack's pajamas and my own underwear, to the trousers Will wore on Sunday. I pat the pockets carefully, then examine the shirt that lies at the very bottom of the pile.

Nothing.

Frustrated, I turn to the towels that litter the bathroom floor. I had assumed they'd just fallen from their rails in this morning's scramble, but all four are damp and creased. Considering she was in here for less than ten minutes this morning, Hannah has outdone herself. I sniff the towels—two at least smell too sour to leave. Gritting my teeth, I chuck them into the laundry basket, pile everything else on top and take the whole lot downstairs.

I load the washing machine on autopilot. My mobile rings. It's Julia's brother, Robbie. I can't cope with him right now, so I turn the phone off without answering. Damian will ring soon as well, to discuss how we are going to track Shannon Walker down. It suddenly seems so unimportant. Whatever Shannon tells me when I catch up with her, it won't make me feel any worse than I do right now. Part of me just wants to walk out of the house—to leave Will. But what about our children? Can I do that to them? Anyway, it's more important to face Will down, to force him to confess before I take any definite action.

His angry words last night circle my head. How dare he say I'm deluding myself over Julia when he has been fooling me himself for goodness knows how many years? How dare he make me feel guilty for asking about that Honey Hearts form?

How dare he put me through all this? Again.

I reach inside the cupboard next to the washing machine, but the box of soap powder tablets is empty. Muttering under my breath, I stomp out to the utility room to fetch another pack. The door through to the garage is next to the shelf with the spare washing stuff. It's the only other place in the house where Will might keep confidential information. He's the only one who ever goes in there, to clean the car or add to his massive collection of classic motorbike mags, which I refuse to allow to clutter up the house.

I set the washing machine going, then head out to the garage. I'm not sure exactly what I'm looking for—maybe a perfume-infused shirt, shoved out of sight on a top shelf, or perhaps a gift buried under all the car-wash gear, ready to give to Catrina. Images of them together flash through my mind. All I can see is her face, tipped back in ecstasy and Will, intent on her, full of desire. Jealousy and hate course through me, as powerful as the life force in my veins.

I walk down the side of the garage, methodically pulling all the magazines on the three sets of shelves away from the wall, a section at a time. Nothing lurks behind or between them. I vaguely wonder if my old, once-prized Hasselblad is stashed out here somewhere. Who am I kidding? Even if I could lay my hands on it, I've got no idea what I would want to take pictures of—other than the kids, of course. It's another reminder of how my life has shrunk since I got married. I grit my teeth. I have sacrificed *so* much for Will, for our family.

I turn my attention to the shelves opposite where Will keeps the stuff he uses to wash and polish our car, as well as several piles of unexamined DIY brochures he downloaded back when he had vague plans to build a garden shed. Will is useless at practical stuff. He can just about change a plug or a fuse. The truth is that he's always ea-ger to start a project, but loses interest long before it's over. It strikes me that this is a perfect metaphor for his attitude to our marriage.

I pull out the contents of each shelf in turn and examine every-thing carefully. There's nothing incriminating. I kneel down and peer under the bench that runs along the wall opposite the shelves. It's empty, apart from some boots. One pair—blue plastic with a picture of Thomas the Tank Engine—stand neatly upright under the bench. I draw them out. Zack grew out of these years ago. Behind the boots is Will's toolbox. He asked for it a couple of Christmases ago and, just as with the garden shed brochures, it looks as fresh as the day he unwrapped it. I open it up. Nails and screws, still in their plastic wrappings, meet my eye. I pick out the hammer and the screwdriver in turn, then finger the coil of copper wiring beside the tape mea-sure. Something glints back at me.

My guts tighten into a knot as I take out what is lying beside the wire coil. Here, in my palm, is Julia's missing diamond and emerald ring.

CHAPTER ELEVEN

I sit on the dusty garage floor, staring at the ring. There's no doubting what it is. Julia wore this almost every day. I know its tiny clusters of diamonds set around the oval emerald almost as well as the detail of my own engagement ring.

This is the ring that Joanie accused me of stealing. What the hell is it doing hidden in Will's toolbox in our garage? My mind races, trying to piece together all the separate elements:

- Julia hired an agent from Honey Hearts to entrap Will.
- Will slept with Catrina and, if Catrina, then probably others.
- Will has Julia's ring.

But why? How? Did he *steal* it? Why would he have done that? *When* could he have done it?

I think back to the night Julia died. The coroner's report said the actual death occurred between 10 P.M. and midnight, and that Julia must have drunk the Nembutal about thirty minutes before dying of respiratory failure. We were at the Harburys until shortly before ten. Will came home with me, then set straight off to the airport. I don't exactly know when he got there, but his flight was just before midnight. Would he have had time to stop off at Julia's flat and slip a fatal dose of Nembutal into her whiskey?

It's ridiculous. Unthinkable. Insane. I think these words, yet the ring, hard and bright in my hand, tells me that anything is possible.

I make it back to the kitchen and sink into a chair at the table. What if Will and Julia were having an affair? Or what if Julia found out Will was having one with someone else?

Maybe he found out that she knew about it.

Maybe she confronted him directly.

Maybe she threatened to tell me about his infidelity.

Could Will have killed her to keep her quiet?

Could he have killed Kara too?

No.

There's no way Will is capable of either murder. He is totally non-violent. He has never come near hitting me or even smacking our children. He traps spiders under a glass and tips them outside the window rather than harm them, for goodness' sake.

And yet the ring is here. Who else could have hidden it in Will's toolbox? Who could have taken it from Julia's flat? Apart from myself, only Joanie and Robbie had access. And no one apart from Will and I *ever* come into the garage.

My phone rings. It's Damian. I say hello in a kind of trance, but he doesn't seem to notice, asking eagerly what Will has said about meeting Shannon Walker.

I pull myself together. Before I talk to Damian about anything, I *have* to find out more about him. My mistrust levels are spiking anyway, and I need to know what lies behind his complete lack of a presence online.

"I've been meaning to ask . . . ," I say. "I Googled your name and I couldn't find *any* reference to you, not on social media and not as a graphic designer, either. If you have a job, it should be there."

On the other end of the line, Damian is silent. After several long seconds, he finally speaks. "There's a reason for that, Livy."

"Go on."

"I will explain," Damian says slowly, "but it's complicated. . . . I'd rather tell you face-to-face. Because you're right, it is odd. But there's a good reason. *Honestly.*"

I take a deep breath. "I'm sorry, but if you want me to trust you, then you need to tell me now."

"Okay." Another silence. "I use a different name at work," he says. "I'm Damian Chambers there, it's called Gramercy Designs. You can check it out."

"Okay . . ." I'm unsure how to respond. Why didn't he mention all this before? "Did Julia know?"

"Yes," he says. "She knew everything about me. Honestly, Livy, I will explain properly. The whole thing. There are good reasons, I promise."

He sounds so sincere that my anger fades. "Maybe Shannon had a good reason for leaving Honey Hearts too," I say more gently.

"Maybe, but I doubt it." Damian tells me about a friend of his who he thinks will be able to trace Shannon's unlisted phone number and address.

As he speaks, my thoughts turn back to Will. There is no good reason for *his* lies.

"I'm going to ask Gaz to take a look at that scrap of hard drive we found on Julia's computer as well," Damian goes on.

"Right," I say, my mind still on Will. "Good."

"Livy?" Damian says, his voice full of anxiety. "You sound really weird. Look, I promise I'll explain all the name-changing stuff when I see you. It's nothing sinister, nothing to do with finding Julia's killer."

"It's not you." Humiliation rises inside me again, a bitter taste in my throat. "It's *nothing*."

"Come on," he says gently. "I can hear there's something wrong. What have you found out? Did you talk to Will?"

I hesitate. "It's hard. . . ." I trail off, unable to speak my shame out loud.

"Okay, wait there." Damian says firmly, "I'm coming over."

I try, feebly, to protest but Damian won't listen. He hangs up and I sit, staring at the kitchen table. I can't seem to form a coherent thought; a jumble of confused images and ideas zoom around my head; *Catrina with Will. Julia with Will. Shannon with Will.*

It's too much to take in.

I rouse myself sufficiently to do a search on Damian Chambers, and sure enough, there he is . . . a senior designer at Gramercy Designs, just like he said. Time passes. I have no idea how long I'm sitting there. Then the bell rings and I somehow drag myself across the hall to open the door. Damian strides inside.

"What is it, Livy? What's happened?" There is genuine concern on his face.

I turn away. I still don't want to admit what Will has done out loud, to make it real.

Damian pulls me to him, wrapping his arms around me. His hand rubs my back. I submit to the hug, too numb even to feel startled by the intimacy.

Then he draws back and looks into my eyes. "Talk to me," he says.

A sob swells in my throat. "It's Will," I say. I don't mean to tell Damian everything, but once I've started, I can't stop. It all pours out of me: how Will has renewed his affair with Catrina, how he has denied it, how I have found Julia's ring—and how I don't know what to do with the vortex of deep, dark fears and suspicions whirling around in my head.

Damian is shocked and confused by turns. He repeats his belief that Julia was not having a relationship with Will, but so what? It seems more and more likely to me that Julia must have found out Will was cheating on me with Catrina and hired Shannon from Honey Hearts to get proof.

Damian agrees. "It's really the only explanation that makes sense," he says thoughtfully. "It explains why Julia went to Honey Hearts and hired Shannon. I'm guessing that before Shannon had a chance to approach him, Will found out Julia was investigating him. He probably went round to her flat to confront her, then . . ." He hesitates.

"No," I say firmly, sensing where his thoughts are going. "No *way.*"

"Come on, Livy," Damian says with a sigh. "It makes sense, especially now that you've found that ring. I don't expect Will actually intended to kill her in cold blood, just to frighten her, maybe, into keeping quiet."

"What, and he just happened to have a lethal dose of Nembutal in his back pocket?"

"I don't know." Damian fixes me with his gaze. "But when you take everything into consideration . . . I mean, Will goes abroad on business sometimes, doesn't he? He went to Geneva the night Julia died, you said."

"Yes, but—"

"Well, maybe all this stuff has been going on for longer than we thought. Maybe Will got the Nembutal from one of his previous business trips. I looked it up after Julia died. It's not that hard to get hold of online or in lots of places outside the UK."

"*No.*" I have to stop this now. "You're just desperate to believe Julia didn't kill herself. You're twisting everything to fit that because you feel guilty and—"

"I'm not twisting anything!" Damian's voice rises. "*You* found Will's name on the Honey Hearts file. *You* found Julia's ring in his toolbox."

We glare at each other. I'm reminded again of how little I know about him, of the facts he has kept from me.

"Why did you change your name?" I ask. "You said you'd tell me once we were face-to-face."

Damian looks at me for a long moment, then gazes across at the bottle of wine, half-drunk and recorked, that stands on the kitchen counter.

"I couldn't do that," he says.

"Do what?"

"Leave the bottle half drunk." He meets my gaze, then takes a deep, shaky breath. "I'm an alcoholic, an addict. It's been five years and three months since my last drink, since I was using."

I stare at him. Shame and pride burn equally in his eyes.

"So . . . so . . . Burton . . . ," he says. "I started using the name when I was first in recovery, after Richard Burton, you know, the actor?"

I nod.

"It was just a game. I still kept my real name for work and tax and all that stuff. My shrink says I did it to avoid intimacy. I don't know. I used it in social situations, with people I didn't know."

"Including Julia?"

"Especially Julia. I was so damn nervous when I met her, though I told her the truth after the first couple of dates. . . ." He trails off. "Look, I'm sorry I didn't tell you from the outset, but I knew if she'd said anything about me, it would be as Damian Burton, DB . . . Dirty Blond, remember? It was easiest not to have to explain the whole eff-ing story on top of everything else I had to tell you."

"Okay." I study him carefully. His explanation makes sense, but how can I really be sure that he's telling the truth? And if he's lying about this, he could be lying about anything.

We carry on talking, our conversation going round and round in circles. It feels surreal.

"The only thing that doesn't fit with Julia suspecting Will of an affair, is that she told me she'd found out who Kara's killer was," Da-mian says eventually. "Either the two things are totally unconnected or—" He stops, but I can hear the thought he is holding back from voicing: *Or Julia believed Will killed Kara and was planning on getting Shan-non from Honey Hearts to somehow make him confess.*

I shudder. Damian gets up and fills the kettle.

"I'm so sorry about all this, Livy." His face softens into a sad smile.

I sip the tea he makes. It's weak but not too milky, just how I like it—as we sit in silence, both lost in our own thoughts. After a while, I come around to the only possible next step. I clear my throat. "I'm going to speak to Will again when he gets in." I check the time. It's just past 2:30 P.M. I can't believe how much of the day has already passed.

"Then I'm going to stay," Damian says firmly. "You don't know how he's going to react when you confront him about the ring."

I gulp, remembering what had sent me into the garage in the first place. "The trouble is it's all mixed up with him seeing Catrina again, and I *can't* tell Will that Martha told me about that. It will get her into trouble with her own husband."

159

"He'll probably confess—to the affair, at least," Damian says, sitting back in his chair. "Most people don't like the burden of guilt, they want to ease their conscience. I did, the one time I cheated. My girlfriend at college. She heard from a friend I had a one-night stand. It was actually a relief to come clean."

I purse my lips. I can't believe Will is going to confess or feel remotely relieved. He will most likely deny everything, and other than Julia's ring and his name on the Honey Hearts form, I have no tangible proof of either an affair or any secret contact with Julia.

"What happened with your girlfriend?"

"She dumped me," Damian says with a sigh.

We talk a little more. I tell Damian he doesn't need to stay, but again he insists. I'm grateful for his desire to make sure I'm okay, but the more time passes, the harder it becomes to talk to him.

I'm in such a miserable daze that I'm genuinely staggered when Zack rushes out of school later, clutching a large pile of colorful paintings and explaining, with a big grin, that they've been allowed to bring all their pictures home today, as the school lets out for summer tomorrow. Which means Hannah's term finishes the day after.

My heart sinks. I love my children too much to wish them a front-row seat as Will and I fall apart. Hannah gets home, her usual surly self, and goes straight up to her room, barely acknowledging me. She does, at least, smile nicely at Damian, whom I introduce as a friend of Julia's.

An hour or so later, I leave Damian downstairs and go upstairs to the bathroom. Feeling raw, I almost break down at the sight of our bedroom—at the bed where Zack was conceived, at Will's jeans splayed on the carpet, and at the photos of our wedding on the window ledge. My phone rings. Robbie again. I ignore the call. This time Robbie leaves a voice mail—a plaintive request "for a chat" when I have a moment. There's no way I'm up to that. Fresh tears leak out of my eyes as I sink down onto the bed. I have never felt so alone in my life.

A moment later, I hear raised voices coming from downstairs.

"Sorry, but who are you?" It's Will. He sounds tired and irritated—and wary. "Where's Livy?"

Damian says something from the living room. I can't hear what. Then there are footsteps on the stairs. Next thing, Will is at the bedroom door, frowning.

"What's going on?" he demands.

Damian has followed him up the stairs, Zack at his side. The two men stare at each other. Actually, "glare" would be a better word. Damian's expression is openly hostile.

"Will, this is Damian, Julia's friend," I say quickly. "Damian, this is my husband, Will." I cast Damian a look of appeal. "Would you wait downstairs, with Zack, please?"

Damian throws me a look that quite clearly tells me to shout if I need him, then retreats, taking a grumbling Zack back downstairs.

Will shakes his head. "What's going on? Why is that man here? I want a shower and—"

"I know about Catrina." The words blurt out of me, unplanned. "Is she why you want a shower?"

"What?" Will stares at me. His expression darkens. "For God's sake, Liv, what are you going on about now?"

I stand up and cross the room to the window. It's muggy and overcast outside, making the early evening far darker than it would normally be.

"We need to talk."

"No fucking kidding," Will snaps. He slumps onto the bed. "Will you please explain what is happening?"

I walk over to him. Julia's ring is hot against my clammy palm. I unclench my fist and hold it out to him.

"I found this in the garage," I say.

Will stares at me as if I've gone mad. "What is it?"

"It's Julia's," I say, watching him intently. "I mentioned it before. Julia's mother thinks I stole it."

"What was it doing in our garage?" Will looks genuinely bemused.

For a second I falter; then I remember the Honey Hearts form with the name Will Jackson—and Martha's agonized face as she told me about Will and Catrina.

I take a deep breath. "That's what I was hoping you would tell me."

"*Me?*" He sits up straighter in his chair, his eyes registering first confusion, then horror. "You think *I* took it?"

I sit down next to him and place the ring on the bed between us. "I don't know what to think," I say. "Firstly, I find out Julia hired a woman from a honey trap agency to try to seduce you."

"*That* again?" Will shakes his head in disbelief.

"Secondly," I press on, "I discover Julia's missing ring in our garage, which you are the only person ever to use."

Will folds his arms, indignant, defensive.

"And thirdly." My voice cracks. "Thirdly I found out for sure that you and Catrina were . . . were together on that trip to Geneva."

Will's eyes widen. "Found out? *How?* What the hell are you saying? How could you 'find out' something that didn't happen?"

"I can't tell you, it doesn't matter." My heart thumps painfully against my ribs. "Are you denying it, then?"

"I refuse to dignify that question with an answer," Will's snaps. "None of this makes sense, Livy. *Not. One. Bit.* It's like you're forcing the dots to join up but they don't make a picture." He pauses. "You're being paranoid. It's just like when you got all overprotective about Hannah when she was little—you've got obsessed and it's making you completely irrational."

What? Is he kidding? I back away from him. "Don't deny Catrina. You did that before and—"

"I didn't fucking sleep with her!" Will's voice rises to a yell.

I stare at him, my whole body shaking. "I don't believe you."

A beat passes as we look at each other.

"Right." Will snatches Julia's ring off the bed. "Are you sure *you* didn't take this, like Joanie said?" he asks nastily.

"Of course n—"

"If this ring is Julia's, then it belongs to her mother now." Will strides to the door. "I'll get it couriered round to Robbie from work tomorrow."

"Will, please—"

He holds up his hand, palm out, to stop me speaking. "I can't cope with this, Livy. Work is stressful. I don't need this bullshit when I come home. I understand you are upset about Julia, but this is too much. Accusing me of sleeping with Catrina, and—" He holds up Julia's ring. "—accusing me of stealing this. You'll be accusing me of Julia's murder next."

I keep my gaze on his eyes, which fill with horror as he clocks my expression.

"Oh, Jesus," he says in disgust. "I don't fucking believe it." He takes a step outside the room. "I'm going to check into a hotel," he says. "Give you a chance to think about what the hell you're doing." He jerks his thumb toward the stairs. "And why that asshole is here."

"Good. That's good." My words shoot out of me, full of hate and anger: "Maybe you'll take a bit of time to think too, about everything you've blown apart for a cheap shag."

Will storms downstairs. I hurry after him and catch a glimpse of Hannah, openmouthed in her bedroom door. Zack is nowhere to be seen, but Damian is in the hall, his hands clenched into fists.

"That man is not staying here, Liv," Will orders.

Damian draws himself up. It flashes through my head that, as far as he is concerned, all the evidence points to Will as Julia's killer.

"I'll be fine," I say quickly to Damian. "You can leave when Will goes."

Will stomps past me into the kitchen to fetch his jacket and briefcase. He returns to the hall and crosses to the front door.

"Daddy?" Hannah's shaky voice sounds from upstairs.

Will and I look up together.

"Everything's fine, Hanabana," Will says. "I just have to go away for work."

Zack zooms out of nowhere, hurling himself at Will's knees. Will picks him up and hugs him, but his eyes are still on Hannah. She nods, but I can tell she's only pretending to believe what Will has just said. A deep sense of shame fills me.

Will sets Zack down. He says good-bye, then looks meaningfully at Damian. Damian gives me a glance.

"It's okay. Go," I say.

And then he follows Will out the front door. Suddenly the house is quiet. Zack drifts away, into the living room. He's used to his father's sudden absences and clearly hasn't registered the tension—or, if he has, doesn't know what to make of it. I turn to Hannah. She's looking at me in disgust. I open my mouth to defend myself, to tell her the truth about her precious father; then I shut it again. She is only twelve. It wouldn't be fair.

"Dad'll be back soon," I say reassuringly, though I don't know if that is true. Or if, indeed, I want him to come back.

Hannah just stares at me for a second, then goes back into her room and slams the door. I wander into the kitchen and start, absently, getting tea ready. As I put the pasta into the boiling water, I decide that once both kids' terms end, I'll take them to my mum's for a few days. It will give us all a bit of respite—and me a chance to think about my marriage.

Damian texts to check I'm okay. I really think he is worried Will might have doubled back to kill me. Through gritted teeth, I reassure Damian that though my husband may be a lying, cheating ass, he is not a murderer.

Damian doesn't respond to this, but sends another text to say he's got his "geek" friend Gaz trying to trace Shannon and that he'll keep me posted.

It's not enough. I need answers *now*. Where is Shannon? What has happened to her? A shiver snakes down my spine as I imagine Julia's killer tracking her down. I tell myself I'm overreacting, that there could be a million explanations for Shannon's departure from Honey Hearts. And yet I can't stop worrying. I feed the kids, then go online and search for reports of missing persons, of mysterious deaths.

It's depressing work—a sad litany of runaways and down-and-outers. There are only two truly unexplained deaths from the past

164

week. A girl was stabbed to death in Bristol a few days ago, but she's younger than Shannon; another fell to her death from a high-rise balcony, but she's older, in her late thirties. There's nothing that can possibly be linked to Shannon.

Trying to put Julia's death, Shannon's disappearance, and my bust-up with Will out of my head, I call Mum. Her bout of flu has cleared up and she's delighted at the prospect of having the kids for a long weekend. I promise to drive them over as soon as Hannah gets out on Thursday. Zack is thrilled. He loves Mum's house with its big garden, huge-screen TV, and endless supply of chocolate cookies. Hannah is predictably furious, though to my relief, she doesn't mention the row she witnessed earlier; I'm hopeful she didn't actually overhear the specifics of what Will and I said.

"But I'm going out with my friends after school on the last day," she wails. "It's a *tradition*."

"How can it be a tradition?" I scoff. "You're at the end of your first year, you haven't had time to build up any end of term traditions."

"*Great.*" Hannah slouches off into the corner and slumps down into a sulk.

I contemplate saying something myself, about how spending a few days with *her* doesn't exactly fill me with joy; then I remind myself that I'm the adult in the relationship, that Hannah has the equivalent of a degree in winding me up and that the situation will only get worse if I react.

The next day passes in miserable isolation. Martha calls from her holiday to check I'm okay. Damian does the same. Will rings to speak to the children. I try to talk to him, but he flies off the handle again when I ask if he's still seeing Catrina.

Why won't he admit it? Surely he knows the truth will come out eventually, as it did before.

In the end, I call Paul. He works in the same office as Will every day. I can't believe he hasn't sensed the affair with Catrina starting up again. Indeed, it's possible that Leo—or even Will himself—has told him about it. However, once I'm actually on the line I can't bring myself to ask directly what he knows, instead mumbling a vague and incoherent question about whether Will has seemed "different" recently.

Paul is too tactful to ask straight-out if I mean an affair.

"Will's been a bit stressed with work," he muses thoughtfully. "I suppose now that you mention it, he has seemed a bit distracted for the past few weeks since that trip to Geneva." He pauses. "Livy, are you guys having problems? Is there anything I can do?"

So neither Will nor Leo have told him what they know. That doesn't really surprise me, but I'm hardly reassured by his reference to Will's being "preoccupied" since the very trip that reunited him with Catrina. I can't bring myself to tell Paul the whole, humiliating truth of the matter, so I say I'm fine and get off the phone. I spend the rest of the evening slumped on the sofa, trying to numb the pain with a combination of red wine and trash TV.

In contrast to the dark misery inside my head, Thursday dawns bright and sunny. Zack, of course, got out yesterday, but he's up and hugely excited to be allowed to go with me as I drop Hannah at school, still wearing his pajamas. Back at home, I pack a bag for the three of us. We don't need much—I keep quite a few old clothes in Mum's spare room wardrobe, while Hannah has already made a careful selection of outfits in a separate case.

Zack and I make some cookies to take to Mum's, then pick Hannah up and drive to Bath. The traffic is terrible and it takes over two hours to get there. We eat supper around Mum's kitchen table, then spend the evening watching TV. Mum clearly senses something is wrong, but she doesn't pry and I don't volunteer any information.

I used to talk to her a lot, before Kara died. We argued, but we also shared our feelings and our worries. Now we talk only about superficial stuff. I might tell her about problems with the kids—as I did over Hannah's leopard-skin lingerie—but nothing really personal . . . certainly nothing about my relationship with Will.

I lie back on the sofa after the kids are in bed, watching Mum snooze in her armchair across the room and wondering when we stopped confiding in each other. Maybe it was after Dad died. Maybe we were both suddenly aware that the other person was all we had left and we didn't want to risk being intimate in case it led to a fight. I don't know. I can't really make sense of it. Perhaps I don't really want to. I like things with Mum being easy and stable. Despite the memories of Dad and Kara that the house holds for me, I always find it comforting to be back here. Mum hasn't changed her style of décor since we were kids, so the house is as cluttered with her willow pattern display china as it always was. Even the squashy sofas in the living room sport homemade scatter cushions from the 1980s that I remember Mum sewing from designs in *Good Housekeeping*.

Will calls at about 8 P.M. to speak to the kids. I go on the phone for politeness' sake but, again, he is cold and distant. "Any plans tonight?" I say lightly.

"Just the usual drinking and whoring," he snaps back.

And that's that.

Damian rings me first thing the next morning. He says his friend has dug up Shannon's address and cell number at last, but that the number has been discontinued, so he hasn't been able to speak to her or even leave a message.

"She lives in Torquay," Damian says. "Not that far from Aces High. I'm going to go there now."

It takes only a moment for me to get him to agree to wait until I can join him. I leave a note for Mum—the whole house is still asleep—telling her I've just remembered a dentist appointment that I have to rush home for, but that I'll be back later this afternoon. It's a pretty lame excuse, but it's all I can think of in the time available.

As I set off, I find myself driving along the same route Kara and I used to walk to school. I feel the familiar stab of guilt at the memory of my many efforts to ditch my dreamy little sister, too old to be cute and too young to be cool—at least as far as the girls in my class that I wanted to impress were concerned.

I drive back to Exeter at top speed, knocking nearly half an hour off yesterday's travel time. Once home, I park and get out of the car. I spot Damian instantly, standing beside a smoky blue convertible a few meters down the road. It's a classic Mercedes—from the late '80s, I'd say—with a large, square trunk. Sunshine glints off the metalwork, and Damian, leaning against the door in his aviator sunglasses, jeans, and black shirt looks for all the world like a model. I can't help but stare at the handsome picture he makes, his hair falling in blond waves around his face as he concentrates on pulling a cigarette from its pack. Several passing women clearly think so too, checking him out as I walk over. Damian, still busy with his cigarette, doesn't notice either them or me.

"Nice car," I say.

He looks up and grins. The smile lights up his face, making him look even more attractive. Without warning, I feel my whole body respond. I flush, shocked at the desire suddenly pulsing through me. Where the hell did *that* come from? "Yeah." He wrinkles his nose. "High maintenance, though."

He opens the passenger door and I slide inside, feeling flustered. Trying to collect myself, I focus on the car's interior. The seats are made of leather, with a gleaming walnut finish on the dashboard. I've hardly ever ridden in a car like this. Since Will gave up his last motorbike, he has bought only sensible modern vehicles, like Fords or Toyotas.

I click the seat belt into place and turn to Damian. "So where exactly are we going?"

"Central Torquay." He props his shades on his head and pulls out. The car—and, of course, Damian inside it—attract several admiring glances as we drive along.

"I bet Julia loved this," I muse.

"My car?" Damian offers me a wistful smile. "She did. She loved beautiful things."

Including you. I don't say the words, but I can't help but think them.

It's a hot day, and after my long, sticky drive on the highway, it feels good to be driving with the top down and the wind in my hair. We reach Torquay, where Damian pulls up outside an unprepossessing block of apartments near the seafront. Brick-built and modern, their only distinguishing feature is the green paint used on the railings of every balcony. I look up. There are four floors with what looks like two flats on each one.

"Shannon is on the third," Damian says looking over. "You ready?"

I nod, but the truth is that I'm terrified; in a minute I might get a definite answer to why Julia sent Shannon to entrap Will.

My earlier desire is subsumed by anxiety as I follow Damian up the stairs to the third floor. The flats are marked 3A and 3B. Damian stands outside flat 3B and presses the doorbell. We wait in silence, the only sound that of the traffic outside. There's no reply.

"Guess she's still not home," I say.

Damian takes a long, flat-tipped, brass pin out of his pocket and inserts it in the lock. "Here goes."

"You're going to break in?"

"How else are we going to get inside?" Damian takes a pair of latex gloves from his pocket and pulls them on. As he hands me a second pair, he raises his eyebrows. "Do you want me to stop?"

I hesitate, but only for a moment. After all, anything could have happened to Shannon. And I need answers.

"No." I take the gloves and step back, giving him room.

Damian closes his eyes, moving the pin this way and that. I watch him, wondering how on earth he knows how to pick a lock. He might have confessed to being a recovering alcoholic, but there is clearly still a lot that he *hasn't* told me. His remark from when we first met about the police not believing anything he said echoes in my head.

A noise from the ground floor, below, chases such thoughts away. I tiptoe along the corridor and peer down the stairs, my heart racing. A young couple is heading our way. I rush back to Damian. Sweat shines on his forehead.

"Nearly there," he whispers.

"Hurry."

As I speak, the lock gives and the door opens with a *pop*.

Damian gives me a triumphant smile, then pushes at the handle. The door opens fully, onto a narrow, cream-walled hallway.

"Come on." He walks inside.

I'm suddenly aware of the magnitude of what we're doing, breaking into someone's home like this. But as I hesitate again, unable to cross the threshold, I hear the young couple laughing, their footsteps on the stairs. My heart leaps into my throat; I can't be found here with the door open.

And so fear of discovery overrides fear of breaking the law, and, still holding my latex gloves, I follow Damian into Shannon's apartment.

ANNALISE

God has given you one face, and you make yourself another.
—William Shakespeare, Hamlet

Ah, Annalise. She was special. Not in herself, of course. Unlike my Kara, she possessed neither innocence nor beauty. But Annalise was special as a challenge to me. She set me firmly along the path I am still on today, toward the man I am destined to be.

I enjoyed a string of encounters after my dealings with Hayley. Much of my time was devoted to keeping these private. My wife is not a stupid woman, and I made sure I still gave her attention. Despite what you might think, you see, I love women. I love the way they look, the way they feel.

Most of all, I love to watch them surrender. But that's another story.

So, back to Annalise. I thought for a while that she herself might be the truly "great challenge" I had been waiting for since Kara. She was certainly clever, with an Oxford degree and a high-powered job. However, her academic and business smarts belied a neurotic insecurity the extent of which I would never have guessed when we first met. That meeting took place in a conference room at her offices. Annalise was a potential client considering whether to use us or not. I was bored during the meeting, as I so often am at work, and she drew herself to my attention with her sparky support for my presentation. She spoke well, articulate and pertinent throughout, and as she tossed her mane of sleek blond hair to make her final point, I felt the familiar twitch in my gut . . . the itch in my fingers. I knew it was deliciously high-risk. Thanks to our business dealings, there were links between us I was not going to be able to hide, let alone avoid. Still, if anything, that merely heightened my excitement.

171

I talked to Annalise briefly after the meeting, indicating my gratitude for her support and my admiration for the persuasive and intelligent way she had expressed it. As I'd suspected, Annalise showed no inclination to fall for my flattery, simply nodding and walking away.

My interest now piqued further, I asked around and found out, through a series of casual inquiries, that Annalise was famous for turning down men. All to the better, I decided. It was easy enough to contact her by e-mail. . . . Another risk to leave a trail, but after Hayley, I was supremely confident that I could face down any problems. My first three e-mails—charming, witty and light in tone—solicited polite but dismissive responses. So I upped my efforts. I knew where Annalise worked, of course, so one day I headed over there. I waited for her outside her office. I pretended to be delighted to bump into her, explaining in brilliantly self-conscious style that I was here again for business reasons. Annalise gave me a skeptical look, just as I'd intended, and I confessed that in fact I was really here (and this was my genius stroke) in order to woo one of her colleagues, a young piece of fluff who acted as PA to the managing director. This Annalise did believe. I could see her attitude to me changing. It was another high-risk tactic from me, but I was sure it was the right one with a woman like her. As long as she thought I was easy to acquire, I would hold no value. Once she believed I had no interest in her, I was confident she would shift her perspective. And I was right. "Hope, blossoming within my heart," I was repaid with first her interest then, soon, her adoration.

I still played it carefully, making sure that, on this occasion, none of my colleagues knew about the affair. Even once I was sure she was hooked, I took my time reeling her in. Two months after we met, at the end of our third date, we made love for the first time.

After that, everything changed. Over the following three months, Annalise gradually lost all the fire she had displayed in that first meeting and showed her true colors, mostly as an insufferable talker. On and on she would go, about how she felt, how I felt, what we both thought and had done and should do. It took all my reserves of discipline not to kill her on the spot.

The final straw came when she threatened to tell my wife about our affair—talking and talking endlessly about how we felt and how we were meant to be together, all the surface confidence melting away, leaving a puddle of whey-faced, red-eyed insecurity. Ugh.

Unfortunately I couldn't kill her straightaway, tempting though it was now to be rid of her. It took me three weeks from leaving her to make sure all ties were cut, that no trace of the contact between us remained. This was a thrilling time as I lived with the huge risk she would go to my wife or someone else. She knew—or knew of—so many people that I did. All I had on my side was my knowledge that Annalise would feel humiliated if our affair was made public. I took two weeks to plan our final meeting, my shining hour. I had everything covered: from the alibi I engineered to the way I contrived to destroy or avoid all records of our final encounter from mobile phone logs to security camera.

I used acid. An entirely fresh and, may I say, hugely satisfying MO for me. I cleared up and left her apartment, taking a tiny gilt brooch as a memento. I knew the police would interview me. It was no secret we had been seeing each other from her old phone records and the witness statements, but my alibi held and I was able to convince the police that our relationship had never gone beyond friendship and that we hadn't in fact spoken in the final month before her death. This was the closest I ever came to discovery, even though the police eliminated me from their investigation early on. But I was confident I would prevail. And I did.

As I always have.

And always will.

CHAPTER TWELVE

Shannon's flat is nothing like I'd expected. From the short time I spent with her at Aces High, plus my long-held prejudice against Torquay, I'd imagined her home would be tacky, but now that I'm here, I feel ashamed of my snobbery. Because Shannon's flat is beautiful. It's small, but every piece of furniture is simple and stylish. Not High Street style either, but expensive designer pieces—at least I'm assuming they are. Damian, clearly more knowledgeable than I about such things, is openmouthed as he wanders around the living room.

"Oh my God, that's a Flap Diamond sofa," he says in hushed tones. "And an Eames chair."

I stand in the middle of the room, struggling to pull on the latex gloves he gave me. Damian yanked his on with a snap in about two seconds. Surely only a doctor or a thief would find it *that* easy? Frowning, I head to the cupboards below a row of shelves elegantly decorated with simple glass ornaments. The flat is as uncluttered as it is beautiful. There aren't many storage places.

"How would a honey trap agent be able to afford all this?" I ask.

"Maybe she had a second job," Damian says, bending over the glass table in front of the sofa.

"Or a sugar daddy," I mutter, opening the first of the two cupboards. Inside is a row of glass vases and a neat pile of *Vogue* and *Harper's Bazaar* magazines. I check the second, which is virtually empty, then head over to the balcony, turn the key that's in the lock and step outside. There's a great view over the communal gardens. A tiny patch of blue sea sparkles above the distant rooftops.

"Let's see if there's anything useful anywhere else," Damian suggests.

We start combing the flat. There's not much to go on. The kitchen merely yields an impressive collection of high-quality appliances, mostly unused, a cupboard full of deli specials like pickled okra and wasabi mushrooms with only a block of Parmigiano-Reggiano in the fridge and three bottles of flavored vodka in the freezer. Damian is rifling through the cutlery drawer at top speed, making surprisingly little noise as he rummages through the forks and the spoons.

"You broke in here like a pro," I say, peering into a cupboard full of tumblers.

Damian shrugs, shutting the drawer.

"What's the deal with the lock-picking?" I ask. "I mean, where did you learn how to do that?"

"Just something I picked up at college," Damian says, not meeting my gaze.

"But—"

"Livy, this isn't the time. . . . We shouldn't stay here any longer than we have to."

"Okay," I agree reluctantly. Part of me wants to push him further but he's right—the sooner we get out of here, the better.

We head into Shannon's bedroom, where Damian studies the contents of the wardrobe, running his gloved fingers over the long row of tops and dresses. "She's got *everything*," he says in an awed voice. "Prada, Westwood, Versace . . ."

I think back to the way Shannon was dressed when I met her—and in the pic on the Aces High Web site. Her clothes were tight, but never slutty, in contrast to the look of most of the other girls. I glance down at the shoes at the bottom of the huge wardrobe. There are three long rows. I spot at least five with Louboutin's distinctive red soles.

"Wow," I say. "All this stuff must be worth thousands."

Damian nods. "Maybe she got money from blackmailing someone? Maybe if Julia told her about your husband, she was trying to get money off *him*?"

175

I stare at him. His cheeks are flushed, his eyes shining.

"No." I insist, angry at Damian's eagerness to make everything fit his theory that Will is the murderer. After all, what does that say about his opinion of me, for choosing Will as my husband? "Anyway, Will and I . . . we don't have that sort of money."

"Right," Damian says, his face falling.

I bite my lip, reminding myself Damian's desperation is simply a consequence of his desire to find out who killed Julia.

Which, in turn, is a consequence of how badly he is hurting.

"Maybe Shannon is just good at making money," I suggest. "For all we know, she could be a financial trader or a talented amateur at predicting the stock markets. Come on, let's look for a laptop or a phone, something that might tell us where she is now."

"Doesn't feel like anyone's been in here for days," Damian murmurs as he ransacks the top drawer of the dressing table, empty save a few old copies of *Heat* magazine.

I shake my head, remembering the last time I explored a bedroom: Julia's flat, even after Joanie's removal of the more expensive items, had been bursting with personal bits and pieces.

"Or else she never really lived here."

Damian throws back the silky bedcover. The sheets beneath are rumpled. He presses his face into one of the pillows.

"Perfume," he says, looking up. "I think she lived here."

"So where did she go?" I gaze down at the dressing table in the corner. The surface is clear, apart from a few half-empty body lotions, some tea light holders, and a row of glass perfume bottles. There's a box that looks like it might have contained jewelry, but all that's left inside is a single hoop earring.

I sink into the chair in front of the dressing table with a sigh and pull open the top drawer. Two tubes of hand creams, a pack of tarot cards, a cigarette lighter, and a handful of change meet my eyes. I reach to the back of the drawer and find a pack of tea lights. I glance over at Damian. He is holding up a silk nightgown. It is long, black, and made for someone far smaller than I am. Despite the lace over the bust area and thin spaghetti straps, it manages to look sexy rather than trampy.

"Beautiful," I murmur.

"Stella McCartney," Damian says reverentially. He places the nightgown back inside the covers and remakes the bed.

"You're well brought up," I say with a smile.

He grins back. "Fierce mum and two older sisters."

I glance out the window—a dull view over the street at the front of the building.

"So what have we found?" Damian asks.

I take stock. "We know she's neat and clean. There's no dust to speak of, so she can't have been gone long, but she still cleared out her fridge before she left."

"Or she left instructions for someone else to."

"You mean you think she might be in league with someone else?"

"Actually, I meant that she might have a cleaner," Damian says with a wry smile. He looks around. "What's missing, that you'd expect to find in someone's home, a girl's home?"

I follow his gaze. "No photos, no jewelry, nothing personal," I say.

"Exactly." He nods. "It's like she's packed up all the most important stuff and just left."

I look down at the bedside table beside me. It's made of cherrywood to match the one on the other side of the bed and sports a simple glass lamp and a notepad with a chunky black pen to the side.

I pick up the notepad and switch on the lamp. The imprint of a single word is visible under the light.

"Look." I tilt the notepad so the indentation falls into shadow.

"What does it say?" Damian asks.

"Magalan," I read.

Damian wrinkles his nose. "What does that mean? Is it a name?"

I frown. The word sounds familiar, but I can't quite recall from where. I close my eyes, trying to remember. It's something Julia once said. I'm certain of it.

From the other end of the flat, the front door creaks open. A footstep sounds in the hall.

I spring up, off the bed. Damian stiffens as the footsteps move toward us. I drop the notepad on the floor. There's no time to run, nowhere to hide.

A split second later, the bedroom door opens.

A young man in glasses and a grubby sweater stands in the doorway. He's holding an document envelope in his hands.

"Er, Livy Jackson?" he says.

I stare at him, the surrealism of the situation hitting me like a fist. "How do you know my name?" I stammer.

He gives an awkward, lopsided shrug. "A man asked me to give you this," he says, holding up the envelope.

Damian strides over. "What man?" he says, grabbing the messenger by the arm. "How did he know Livy would be here?"

The messenger backs away, his eyes widening. "I didn't see him," he says quickly. "The guy just called me, said he was a mate of a mate."

"Which mate?" I ask.

The man shrugs, then offers me the envelope again. I take it. There's something solid and ridged inside it. My name is printed on the front in large, black type.

"What exactly did this man tell you to do?" Damian asks.

"He said I was to go to the trash can outside this apartment, pick up an envelope, come here, and give it to you—then when I went back down, there'd be fifty quid under the same barrel, waiting for me."

The messenger turns away.

"Wait." As Damian speaks, I tear open the envelope. Inside is a sheet of white paper to which four large colored wooden letters from a child's puzzle have been stuck. They spell out a single word:
STOP

What does that mean?

I meet Damian's eye as the horrifying truth dawns on me. If whoever sent this knew I was here, they must also know why, which means this has to be a message from Julia's killer, an order to stop investigating her death.

"How did he know I was here?" The thought slips out of me as a whisper.

Damian shakes his head.

I sit down on the bed, my legs like jelly. I peer more closely at the colored wooden letters. They look familiar. The *S* is decorated with a snake; the *O* is an orange with a red felt-tip mark across the top.

With a jolt, I realize they are pieces from an old puzzle of Hannah and Zack's.

"Hey!" Damian is striding across the room after the messenger, who is disappearing out the door. "Come back."

The two men vanish along the corridor.

I sit, staring at the letters. Whoever delivered these to me has almost certainly been in my house. He knows who I am and where I live and where my children's old jigsaw puzzles are stored. My heart thuds, hard and painful, in my chest.

Shouts sound outside. I can hear Damian yelling and swearing. I rush to the window. Damian is on the street. There's no sign of the messenger. I look straight down, and the yard three floors below seems to rear up at me. I experience a single sickening moment of vertigo; then I'm aware of Damian stomping back to the house.

My skin prickles with fear as I hurry along the corridor and out of Shannon's flat. I pull the front door shut behind me and head for the stairs.

The killer knows who I am. He knows where I live. He has been near my children.

These terrifying thoughts tumble over each other inside my head as I hurry down the stairs. I meet Damian on the second-floor landing.

As we speed down to the ground floor, he talks at me, his voice rushed and breathless. "There was fifty pounds under the bin, just like the guy said. I asked him again about . . . about the man . . . how he knew him, whether he had an accent. But the guy just ran off."

I nod. My legs still feel shaky and I can't concentrate properly on what he's saying. I can barely breathe, I'm so scared. I hold up the paper with the *STOP* letters.

"These are from an old puzzle of Zack's," I explain.

"Jesus." Damian grabs my arm and pulls me toward his car. "Listen, Livy, I'm betting the fifty pounds was put under that bin *after* the messenger found the envelope and brought it in to us."

I stare at him in horror. "You mean whoever left the message and the money was *here*. Could still *be* here, *watching* us."

"Yes," Damian says tersely. "Come on."

He unlocks the car as we approach. I fumble with the door as he rushes around and leaps in the other side. I slam the door shut and look up and down the street. There's no sign of anyone outside, just a couple of kids playing by a front gate. Their cheerful yells somehow make the horror in my own head even worse.

Damian revs the engine. A moment later we're zooming away. Damian's hands grip the steering wheel; his shoulders hunch forward. I glance at the speedometer. We're already doing almost sixty.

Damian takes the first turnoff without signaling. A car honks at him.

"Slow down," I say. I twist around, looking behind us. The road is empty.

Damian drives on, possessed.

"Slow down, there's no one following us," I insist, my hand on his arm.

With a shudder, Damian releases his tight hold on the wheel and slows the car. He signals for the next intersection, and slows further to take the corner. I sit back. I realize I'm holding my breath and take in a deep lungful of air. My whole body trembles as Damian drives on. Neither of us speaks for several minutes.

At last Damian pulls over. He removes a pack of cigarettes from his shirt pocket and lights up. "Oh my God." He takes a long, full drag on the cigarette. "Who the hell sent that guy?"

"Whoever it was knows me," I say, the full weight of what that means dawning. "He killed Julia and he wants me to back off and if I don't, he will come after me and . . . and . . ." I point to the piece of paper with the colored wooden letters, unable to put into words my fear that this man may hurt not only me but also my children.

"Okay." Damian blows out his breath. "Okay, let's think rationally about this." He pauses. "Do you have any idea who could have sent that, who he is?"

"No, of course not," I say.

Damian meets my gaze. "Do you think—? Is there any chance it could have been Will?"

"No." I stare at him. "No way."

"How can you be so sure? He has more access to your kids' things than anyone else."

I press my hands together, trying to find the words to explain. "Will might have had an affair—a whole string of them," I say slowly, "but he couldn't have killed Julia. Or anyone. And he would never hurt me."

Damian looks at me. I can see the questions my denial leaves unanswered tumbling through his head:

What about finding Julia's stolen ring in Will's toolbox?

What about Shannon Walker being hired by Julia to entrap him?

What about all Will's lies?

There's a long pause. The air around us is suddenly stifling.

"It wasn't Will," I insist stubbornly.

Damian still looks skeptical.

"Seriously," I go on.

"Okay, so what do we do now?" Damian asks.

I look around, my skin crawling with fear. Are we in danger right now? On this quiet, leafy street, that seems impossible. Thank goodness the kids are at Mum's.

I hold up the piece of paper with the *STOP* letters. "Being sent this means we must be getting close to the truth about Julia's death, don't you think?"

"Yes." Damian takes a deep breath. "So, like I said, what do you want to do?"

"We could tell the police," I say.

Damian frowns. "What? That someone sent you a few pieces from an old jigsaw puzzle?"

"A puzzle from my own house."

"It doesn't mean whoever sent it killed Julia." Damian pauses. "What we really need is to find Shannon. She's the key to all this. . . . She can tell us what Julia found out . . . why Will's name was on the Honey Hearts form . . . give us something more concrete . . ."

"We have only one clue," I say. "That word she wrote down by her bed: Magalan."

"Have you remembered where you heard it before?"

"It was something Julia said. I can't remember exactly what. . . ." I hesitate, unsure.

"Maybe it's a surname?" Damian suggests. "How about an ex-lover? Or . . . Christ, d'you think it could be the name of the person who killed her?" His eyes are strained and anxious. He's clutching at straws. Again.

"I don't know." I run my mind over the names I'm aware of from Julia's past: the two exes at the funeral—Charlie Framley and Tom Harrison—then further back to the men I only ever heard about. There was a Simon, a Marty, two Sams, and a Jonny, plus Alan Rutherford the policeman . . . *Alan.*

I close my eyes, feeling the full heat of the sun against my eyelids. I feel faint. I can hear Julia's voice in my head.

So he only left me the bloody thing in his will, she'd said. *Even though it's named after himself and his wife.*

My eyes snap open, and for a second, the sunlight blinds me.

"Magalan is the name of her place in Lympstone. The one the police guy left her, Alan Rutherford."

"Magalan is a house?"

"Yes. The name's a mix of his and his late wife's names: Maggie and Alan."

Damian makes a face. "Really?"

"Yeah, Julia thought that was weird too." I smile, remembering Julia's bewilderment at why a pair of grown-ups would choose to name their home in this way. I thought it was sweet, but then that was the year before Will's affair, when I was heavily into my pregnancy with Zack and blissfully happy with my handsome, loving husband and my sweet-natured, affectionate little girl.

"Livy?"

I turn to Damian. "What?"

"I was asking if you've ever been there, this Magalan place?"

I nod. "Once or twice years ago, but then Julia decided to rent it out to make some extra cash."

Damian nods. "She mentioned it to me too, but we never went there."

"So why would Shannon be writing down the name of the house?"

"Julia must have told her about it," Damian says. "D'you know where it is, exactly?"

"Yes." I check my watch. It's only just after eleven. We can easily drive to Lympstone and then back to Exeter before I make my return journey to Mum and the kids.

"Shall we?" Damian raises his eyebrows.

I nod and he starts the engine.

We don't speak much for the next few minutes. Damian drives fast with dance music blaring from his surround-sound speakers. He asks if I'd prefer silence, or if I'd rather choose what we listen to from the selection on his MP3 Player. I tell him I'm happy with whatever he picks.

And I am.

It's crazy, but driving with the sun on my face and the furious bass of Damian's music pulsing through my body, I feel in some kind of limbo, away from everything real: the messenger in Shannon's flat, Will's affair, and my fears about Julia.

The feeling ends as soon as we approach Lympstone. Damian turns off the music so I can direct him to Julia's cottage, which is half a mile or so outside the village. It's another beautiful July day: dry and sunny, but as we pull up along the road from the little sea-front terrace, I shiver. Will Shannon be here? Or have we come on a wild goose chase? I get out of the car and stretch my limbs. Damian's sports car might look amazing, but it's actually not that comfortable.

Damian walks along the sunlit sidewalk to Julia's cottage. The name, MAGALAN, is painted in fading blue over the front door. The front garden is a riot of color and bloom, yet the overall effect is contained. Someone has worked this garden hard; it takes a lot of effort to make wildflowers look so good without letting them overrun the place. Julia must have paid a gardener to do it, she certainly didn't have green fingers herself.

I kill all plants, Liv, she used to say. *I'm the Angel of Death for foliage.*

"Pretty," Damian says.

I peer in through the window. The cottage is smaller than I remember. The front door opens straight into the living room which is dark and cool, set with the plain, simple furniture Julia loved, plus some flowery cushions as a sop to the chintzy quality of the house itself. The kitchen lies beyond and I know from memory there's a tiny backyard leading directly onto the beach out back. There's no sign of anyone inside.

I ring the doorbell. Its musical chime echoes through the house beyond. Nobody comes to the door.

I sigh. "Looks like it's empty."

"Bloody hell." Damian sounds as despairing as I feel.

A click sounds behind us. I spin around.

She's there, at the garden gate. Shannon Walker. Two grocery bags are in her hand and a look of utter shock is on her face.

"What are you doing here?" She takes a step away from us.

"Wait."

"Please."

Damian and I speak at once.

Shannon eyes us warily. She's wearing jeans and a tight T-shirt with silver Chanel earrings. Her blond hair is tied back in a ponytail. "You were in Aces High that night," she says. "You both were."

"That's right," I say quickly. "I went because you had a meeting with Julia. She was my friend." I glance at Damian. "*Our* friend."

"How did you find me?" Shannon asks.

I hesitate, not wanting to admit we broke into her flat and snooped around for clues.

"I told you, I was Julia's friend. I remember Alan Rutherford—"

I point to the MAGALAN sign above the front door. "—the guy who left this place to her."

Shannon keeps her eyes fixed on me. I sense that she's weighing up the situation, trying to decide whether or not to trust us.

"Did Julia tell you to come here?" I ask.

"Do you know who killed her?" Damian blurts out.

He's tense, all repressed energy and powerful presence. Shannon casts a wary look at him, then back to me.

"You said your name was Livy Jackson, right?"

I nod. "Did Julia tell you about me?" I think of Will's name on the Honey Hearts form. "She asked you to go after my . . . Will Jackson, that was the man she told you to . . . speak to, wasn't it?"

Shannon frowns; then she walks toward us through the gate and up the little path. She's in high-heeled sandals that pat softly along the brick. "That guy, your husband, Will Jackson . . . he was just a cover," she says. "The whole Honey Hearts thing was a cover."

Confusion swirls inside my head.

"What do you mean?" I ask.

"Exactly what I say." Shannon reaches the front door and I stand back to let her pass. "Julia just pretended to hire me."

"Why?" Damian demands.

Shannon shrugs. She fishes in her Vuitton handbag and draws out a set of keys.

"How come you're staying here?" I ask.

"Julia told me she was having it painted between renters, and where the spare key was. She said if anything happened to her, if she didn't make it to our second meeting, I should come here and tell no one. That's what I did, straight after I saw you in Aces High."

"Why did Julia think something might happen to her?" Damian asks.

Shannon's gaze flickers over him. I watch her appraise him, taking in the strong lines of his face and his black shirt. My heart is in my mouth.

"Because of me," Shannon says. "Because of what I told her."

CHAPTER THIRTEEN

"You better both come in," Shannon says.

I'm numb as I follow her and Damian through the front door and into the living room. She seems to be saying that Will and the whole Honey Hearts entrapment was some kind of ruse. But to what end?

"Just give me a second." Shannon puts her keys on the side table, then takes her shopping into the kitchen. She sets the bags on the floor beside a pair of sneakers.

Damian goes after her. I look around the living room. The shelves on one wall are empty and sanded down. A pot of paint and two large bottles of mineral spirits stand on the floor beside them ready for the repainting job. The shelves on the opposite side of the room sparkle with fresh cream paint. So does the dresser in the corner, I recognize it from my childhood home. Mum was having a clear out—years ago—and she let Julia take some of the furniture. I'd forgotten this was here. I wander over and run my hand over the wood. I'm not prepared for the unframed photo that's lying flat on the middle shelf. It's of Julia and Kara, laughing, their arms wrapped around each other. Kara is wearing the locket Julia gave her, the one that went missing when she died. God, they look so young. And so beautiful.

A lump lodges itself in my throat as I pick up the photo.

"That's your sister, isn't it?" Shannon asks.

I turn around. She and Damian are standing behind me.

I nod, not trusting myself to speak.

Damian looks at the picture. "Is that Julia when she was a teenager? She never showed me any photos." His voice is hushed.

"It must have been taken just before Kara died," I say, trying to keep my own voice steady.

"Julia gave me the photo when she met me," Shannon explains. "She wanted to show me Kara. She told me how she was murdered. And . . . and she wanted to show me Kara's locket."

"I don't understand," I stammer. "Why did Julia want you to see the locket?" My head is still spinning. What on earth does Honey Hearts have to do with this? Why did Julia pretend to hire Shannon? What was Will a "cover" for?

Shannon frowns. "Kara's locket was how she found me," she says.

"Sorry." I clear my throat, my mind spinning. "I still don't understand."

I can feel the tension radiating off Damian in waves. "Please," he says. "Tell us what Julia said to you."

"She said the locket was taken when Kara was murdered. She gave me the photo as . . . as proof."

"But why?" I say. "Proof of what?"

Shannon sighs; then she pulls the neck of her T-shirt down to reveal the chain around her neck. She walks right over to me as she takes off the chain and hands me the locket that hangs at the end.

I prize it gently open. The photo booth pic of Julia and Kara, smiling, their eighteen-year-old faces cheek-to-cheek, stares back at me. I hold it tightly, a tiny piece of Kara back in my hands after all these years.

"This was my sister's," I say, barely able to breathe. "This belonged to Kara."

I flip the locket over. There is the minute scratch, just to the left of the hinge, where Kara dropped it in a pub parking lot one cold day in January, the month before she was killed. It was Dad's birthday, and he and Mum had driven to Exeter to spend the day with us. It was the last time the four of us were together.

I look up, into Shannon's eyes. Her expression is sympathetic. She takes the locket back from me and sighs.

"Where did you get this?" I ask, my voice barely a whisper.

Shannon's expression grows more fearful. Instinctively I can tell she feels she's said enough.

"Please," I realize I'm holding my breath and take a gulp of air. Wild thoughts run through my head. Shannon can't have been more than six or seven years old when Kara was murdered. "What do you know? Were you there? Did you see my sister? What about Julia?"

"Where did you get the locket?" Damian urges. He drops his pack of cigarettes on the coffee table. His voice is strained.

"I was given the locket," Shannon says. She backs away from us. The patch of wall behind her is freshly painted, just like the furniture. "The person who gave it to me owed me money. I got a couple of the guys at Aces High to put some pressure on—"

She catches the look in my eye and frowns. "Don't get me wrong, they're pussycats, those guys, but they *look* tough. Anyway, it worked. The loser who owed me eventually coughed up some cash and a few bits and pieces, like the locket, to sell."

"Who?" I ask. "*Who* owed you money, who gave you the locket?"

Shannon ignores me. "I tried to sell it on eBay. That's when Julia saw it. She contacted me, but . . . but her message sounded weird. She was offering way more than it's worth and she wanted to meet me. In person. I thought it was a trap, like maybe the locket was hot . . . so I made her meet me at Aces High, where I know people, so I'd be safe and I didn't take the actual locket with me, so—"

"Wait. Slow down." I'm still completely bewildered. "What about Honey Hearts? How does that fit in? You said that Julia hiring you to talk to Will was a cover. What did you mean? Cover for what?"

"Who gave you the locket?" Damian persists. He turns to me. "Don't you see? *This* is what Julia found out. She worked out that whoever gave Shannon the locket was Kara's killer." He turns back to Shannon. "That's right, isn't it?"

"Sort of," Shannon admits. "Julia knew there was a link between the locket and the killer. That's why she told me to come here if anything happened to her—or if anyone threatened me."

"We were threatened earlier too," I say. An image of the *STOP* letters stuck to their piece of paper flashes before my mind's eye.

"*You* were threatened?" The color drains from Shannon's cheeks. "*Where? When?*"

I look away, not wanting to admit to breaking into her flat. "This morning," I explain. "A guy was sent to give us a message to back off."

"Was someone *following* you?" Shannon's voice rises.

"Er, yes." My heart drums against my ribs.

"Did he see where you went?" I can hear the panic in Shannon's voice. "Could he have followed you *here*?"

"We got away in Damian's car," I say. "I don't think—"

"Which is *here*?" She turns to Damian. "Your car is *here*? *Now*?"

"Yes," I say. "Please, Shannon—"

"Oh my God." Shannon blinks. "I have to go. Right now. *God,* I can't believe you've risked—" She turns and runs up the stairs.

"Wait." Damian charges after her. I follow.

The cottage upstairs is even smaller than I remember. Just two tiny bedrooms and an even smaller bathroom. The woodwork here is far shabbier than downstairs, though a couple of cans of paint stand ready to use. Shannon rushes into the bedroom on the right. She pulls a Louis Vuitton suitcase out from under the bed, hurls it on top of the comforter, then pushes past me to the chest of drawers.

"Please, Shannon, you *have* to talk to us," I insist. "Who do you think might have followed us? Who's threatening me? Did *he* give you the locket?"

"*Tell* us," Damian demands.

Shannon ignores us, just carries on hurling clothes into her suitcase.

"Please." I'm almost in tears.

"Enough." Damian strides to the bed and slams the suitcase lid shut. "I'll take you wherever you want to go, but you have to tell us where you got the locket."

There's a pause. The silence drums in my ears.

"Okay," Shannon says at last. "But we have to get out of here first. You could have been followed." She points to the case. "I'm done."

"Fine." Damian clicks the locks and hauls the case off the bed. "Let's go."

I follow him and Shannon back downstairs. The photo of Julia and Kara is on the sofa, where Damian dropped it earlier. I pick it up and place it carefully into my handbag. The three of us leave the cottage.

Shannon pulls the front door shut, locking it with trembling fingers. Damian's already halfway to his car. I follow, impatient to get away.

"Oh, shit," Shannon mutters. "I forgot something." She unlocks the door again. "I'll just be a sec."

She disappears inside. I wait, halfway along the sidewalk, tapping my foot. Damian is loading the suitcase in the trunk. There's something in the way, a bottle. I stare as he pushes it aside and the label rolls forward: it's whisky, Talisker.

I gasp. What's a recovering alcoholic doing with a full bottle of whisky in his trunk? Damian straightens up and looks around. He clocks me along the sidewalk and heads over.

"Where's Shannon?"

I point to the cottage, still thinking about the whisky. "She forgot something."

Damian frowns.

I have to ask him.

"Why do you have whisky in your car if you don't drink?" I ask.

Damian's face flushes. "It helps to know it's there and I'm not touching it."

I stare at him.

"Seriously," he says. "If I have it, then I'm in control of whether I drink it or not. I keep it in the car, out of sight, because it's not actually in my face that way, but I know it's there."

"Right." I don't know what to say, whether or not to trust what he is telling me, so I say nothing. We watch Shannon's front door, waiting for her to reemerge. And we wait.

A minute passes. Two.

"Something's happened." Damian strides to the front door. He hammers on it. "Shannon!" he yells.

No reply. We exchange a worried glance. I press the doorbell, leaving my finger pressing down hard. The bell inside rings on, high-pitched and insistent.

"Fuck!" Damian pushes at the front door. It's locked. *Fuck.* He hurls himself at it. Again. Harder. Again. The door snaps and flies open. I follow him inside, a sense of déjà vu washing over me. Another break-in. It feels surreal.

The cottage is still. Silent.

"Shannon!" Damian yells. He rushes up the stairs.

I stand by the tray of gloss paint cans and mineral spirits bottles in the living room, listening to Damian pounding across the small landing, into Shannon's bedroom. The door to the kitchen is closed. I cross the room and open it. A carton of milk from one of Shannon's shopping bags has been upended over the floor. Shannon's high-heeled sandals rest on their sides beside it. The running shoes that were lying here before are gone. The back door out to the beach is open. A breeze bangs it against its frame. I rush over and peer outside. The stony beach beyond is deserted. I look up and down, past the breakers on both sides. All I can see is an elderly couple in the far distance, both walking slowly, with sticks.

There is no sign of Shannon.

A moment later, Damian rushes outside. He skids to a stop and peers up and down the beach, as I have just done.

I point to the sandals. "She changed into shoes she could run in." The realization settles on me like a deadweight. "She's gone."

"No." Damian pounds along the path that separates the backyard from the pebbles of the long beach. He runs hard, fast. After a few seconds he swerves left and disappears through what must be a gap between the houses. I can't see from where I'm standing. I look up and down the beach again. A group of mums with strollers are walking along the path, laughing over some shared joke.

I go back into the cottage. Shannon is gone. Our only lead to the

191

truth about Julia's—and Kara's—death has vanished. Despair seeps through me.

I try to take comfort in the fact that Shannon said Will had nothing to do with any of it. Then I remember what Martha told me. Julia's Honey Hearts visit may have been a red herring, but Will still slept with Catrina. I put down my handbag and sit on the sofa, my head in my hands. The pain of his betrayal is unbearable.

A minute later Damian is back. He's out of breath, a sheen of sweat on his forehead.

"Couldn't—see—her," he pants.

I step back to let him in. He knocks over a bottle of mineral spirits as he collapses on the sofa with a groan. I absently set the bottle upright and look around the room.

"Why did she run away? We've got her suitcase, all her things are here. . . ." Damian looks up at me. He takes a cigarette out from the pack he dropped earlier on the coffee table and rolls it between his palms.

"She must have been really frightened," I say. "You heard her. She thinks we were followed here."

"By Julia's killer," Damian says.

"Maybe Kara's killer too."

We're silent for a moment. Suppose Shannon is right? Suppose he *has* followed us.

"If Shannon was scared, maybe we should be."

Damian raises his eyebrows. "You think we should leave? Surely Shannon's got to come back at some point for her stuff."

"I don't know." I look around the room. "I can't see her handbag, so she probably took that with her, which means she's got money." I sigh, feeling defeated. "I can't see why she *would* come back. Not soon, anyway."

Damian springs to his feet. "Then we need to see what we can find here."

"Okay." I hesitate. "But suppose someone *did* follow us?"

He runs his hand through his hair with a frown. "Let's give ourselves ten, fifteen minutes max to search the place, see if we can find anything that might help us work out where Shannon got your sister's locket. We can take it away and look through it properly later."

We work systematically rifling through the drawers and cupboards in the kitchen. There's nothing remotely relevant here. I deposit the groceries from Shannon's shopping onto the countertop and we each take a plastic bag. Damian hurtles upstairs while I grab anything I can find that might be worth a second look from the living room. There isn't much, just a bunch of receipts on the dresser and a shoe box of photos under the coffee table.

After a couple of minutes I head up the stairs. Damian is busy rifling through the chest of drawers in Shannon's bedroom, his own plastic bag bulging. Again, I have a sense of déjà vu.

"Anything useful?" I ask.

He shrugs. "Not really." As he speaks, his phone rings.

It's Gaz, Damian's friend who's been looking at the hard drive from Julia's computer. He tells Damian that he's retrieved some fragments, and is going to e-mail them over.

I head next door. It's a spare room. Just a bed and two side tables, with a shelf of books next to the wardrobe.

"I don't think there's much in here," I call out. "Two more minutes, then let's take what we've got and go."

Damian agrees. I open the wardrobe. It's full of more designer clothes. I move to the bookshelf. These are Julia's, I'd bet money on it. She was studying psychology at uni, like Kara, and I remember years ago her being in awe of my own degree in history—and of all the books she thought I had read.

My taste in books makes your average airport novel look highbrow, she once told me. *I just want to escape when I read, not have to think.*

I run my fingers over the paperback spines. They feel old and dusty. I don't recognize any of the author names, but the covers are all in lurid golds and pinks.

The firm smack of a door closing downstairs makes me turn.

"Damian?" I walk to the door.

He's still visible in Shannon's bedroom, now on his hands and knees looking under her bed.

I catch a whiff of cigarette smoke, then the sharp scent of mineral spirits.

As I turn to face the stairs, I hear the crackle of flames. My guts clench as thick black smoke curls up onto the landing. I take a step toward it. Time slows down. My mouth opens.

"Fire!" I hear myself say. "Damian! *Fire!*"

CHAPTER FOURTEEN

"Damian! Fire!"

In an instant he's beside me. "Fuck!" He looks wildly around.

I am transfixed by the smoke. Flames crackle and writhe on the stairs below us. The smell is acrid, stifling. There's absolutely no way past the fire to the ground floor.

I glance back through to the spare room. There's a window opposite.

"Come on." I rush over, all my focus on opening the window and getting out.

I yank at the sash. It's locked. My fingers fumble with the catch. Damian pushes my hand away and flips it in a single movement. He hauls the sash up. Peers out.

"Shit. Shit. Shit." I'm moaning with fear.

"We're going to have to climb onto the roof," Damian says. "We can't jump down."

I push past him to look out of the window myself. There's a deep ledge and a sheer drop to the paving stone below. My stomach lurches as I peer down. Damian's right. It's too far to jump. He's already easing himself out onto the ledge. I look out, up and down the beach. Where is everyone? The mums with strollers are distant specks. There's a man walking his dog in the opposite direction. I yell out, but he doesn't hear.

"Come on." Damian gets to his feet on the ledge. It's just deep enough for him to stand on. He's holding on to the tiles above the top of the window with his fingers.

"Oh, God." I look over my shoulder. Smoke is filling the room behind me.

Outside, Damian is clawing his way up, onto the roof. I watch his legs go past, then creep out onto the ledge myself. I'm trembling all over, my heart beating furiously against my ribs.

"Please, help us, *please*," I mutter under my breath. I don't know whom I'm praying to. When Kara died, my parents lost their faith. I never had any in the first place.

I edge a little farther out so I'm sideways onto the ledge, one leg still left inside the bedroom. I peer up. The sky is clear blue against the red tiles. Damian's feet disappear over the gutter just above. He is prostrate on the roof. Turning, his face is red with effort. He reaches his hand down to me.

"Livy, here."

I look inside the bedroom again. I can't see the door. Smoke fills the air, thick and acrid against my throat. Another minute and the fumes will get me. I have to move.

I grip the frame above my head and ease myself up. Now I am standing on the window ledge. I will myself not to look down. One sweating palm grips the gutter above. I have the strange sense of being out of my own body, watching myself cling to the roof.

Careful, Livy, don't break a nail. Julia's ironic voice is so clear inside my head, I almost turn to see where she is.

"Livy." Damian's voice cuts across my imagined conversation. "Hold my hand. Reach for the tiles. The gutter won't take your weight.

It takes a second to register what he's said.

"Cheers," I mutter, snapping back to full reality.

Damian gives up a bitter laugh. "Now you're reminding me of *her*."

I take a deep breath and shift my hand onto the edge of the tiles. Damian grabs my other wrist.

"Got you," he says. "Now push yourself up."

I flex my legs and push up. One hand clutches the tiles. The pain in my fingers is agonizing. Damian holds my wrist so tightly, it's sore. There's a ripping sound as my pants tear. I can feel the material flap against my ankle as I rise up, my body against the tiles. I'm clawing for a better purchase. Damian hauls me higher. Another rip, this time my shirt. My cheek grazes against the hot tile. The sun burning, blood pulsing at my temples.

With a groan, Damian heaves me up again. I find the gutter with my feet and push against the metal. My knee stings. Another claw at the tiles. A final heave. And I'm up, lying flat on the roof just below Damian.

I gasp for breath. Damian releases my hand.

"Are you okay?"

"Yes," I rasp. I'm still trembling and my whole body feels sore and bruised, but I'm on the roof. Smoke is filtering out of the window, curling in wisps around us. We are on the beach side of the roof. There are people in the distance. I can't tell if any of them have noticed the smoke yet. But surely they will. Surely someone will call for the fire brigade. I reach for my own phone, but the movement sets me off balance. I slip, dangerously, down the tiles, just as a series of small explosions erupt from the cottage. I look up, terrified. Damian hasn't seen me slip. He is inching forward, commando style. He's right. It's dangerous to stay put. Pushing thoughts of my 999 call away for now, I follow him. Every muscle in my body is tensed. The roof slopes and it's hard to keep balance. The sun beats down on my head as the rough edges of the tiles scrape against my elbows and knees.

I creep along. Damian is gaining on me. I try to speed up. Smoke pours out of the cottage windows, rising into the air above me. I think of the dresser—then of my handbag, somewhere still inside the house and of the two plastic bags we had filled with Shannon's things, our clues—all going up in smoke. Damian is crawling, inching forward. He reaches the edge of the roof. Shaking, I arrive beside him. There's a series of iron steps down the side wall between one set of cottages and the next, into a narrow alley way that leads between the beach and the main road. This must be where Shannon ran.

It's another treacherous balancing act to swing my legs off the side of the roof. I clamber after Damian, down the iron steps as a fire engine alarm sounds in the distance. Less than five minutes can have passed since I saw the smoke on the stairs. It feels like a lifetime. I look down as I reach the ground. My shirt is filthy and the pocket is ripped. There's a long tear on the right side of my pants. I can feel my cheek and arms are bruised and grazed. Damian has survived the climb better. His clothes are intact and, being black, his shirt just looks a little dusty.

"Let's get back to my car," he says.

"Do you think it's safe?" My hands are still shaking. "The man from earlier, he must have followed us after all."

"I know, but we need to get out of here." Damian puts his arm across my shoulders and leads me along the alleyway, toward the road.

His car is parked just a few meters away. A crowd has gathered outside Magalan Cottage. Everyone is watching the flames, unaware of our presence behind them. The fire truck is getting closer, it's siren blaring into the air. Damian ushers me into his car. As a getaway vehicle, it leaves a lot to be desired, being both attention-grabbing and relatively slow, compared to more modern engines. I don't point out either of these drawbacks to Damian, who looks tense with fear. He drives away. I pull down the passenger seat mirror. The damage—to my face at least—is not so bad as I feared, just a graze on my left cheek. I feel lost without my bag.

"In there." Damian points to the glove compartment. Inside, I find a pack of tissues. I peel one, spit and dab at the dirt on my face.

My hands are still shaking.

I glance over my shoulder as we turn the corner. Julia's cottage is going to be burned to the ground, a ruin. Everything inside it, from Shannon's designer clothes to that photo of Julia and Kara, is gone. Forever.

A tear bubbles up behind my eye and trickles down my cheek. I turn my face away, so Damian can't see.

"Don't hold back on my account," he says, and I can hear he's grimacing as he speaks. "I've never been so scared in my life."

"What are we going to do?" It comes out as a whisper. "If he followed your car here, he's going to notice it's gone.

"We'll have to leave the car somewhere. I just . . . Jesus, I don't know. . . ."

"We have to go to the police. Tell them everything."

Damian shrugs. "Tell them what? That we just escaped from a fire?"

"That someone deliberately tried to kill us," I say, my voice rising. How can Damian *not* see that this is the obvious course of action. "I smelled cigarette smoke just before the fire started. The man must have followed us, from Shannon's place in Torquay. He must have been downstairs, using a cigarette and the mineral spirits, maybe."

"But cigarettes and mineral spirits don't prove anything happened deliberately. If it comes to that they were probably *my* cigarettes down there. I even spilled mineral spirits on the floor. Plus *we* broke the door down when we went back inside."

"You mean if we tell the police someone set the fire deliberately, it will just look like we're trying to shift the blame from *ourselves*?"

"Exactly." Damian shakes his head, a despairing gesture. "If we go to the police, we have to explain why we were in the cottage at all and once we tell them that, it'll be hard not to explain about breaking into Shannon's flat in Torquay too."

"But we can explain all of that, if we just tell them about—"

"No." Damian's voice is angrier than I've ever heard it. "No fucking way."

I sit back as we drive on, a riot of emotions racing through my head. Damian's hands grip the wheel, a furious expression on his face.

Damian is hiding something, *has* been hiding something from the beginning. It's to do with the police and with the lock-picking—something criminal, I'm certain. I pull my phone out of my pocket, open the browser, and put his real name, Damian Chambers, in the search box. Then I add in the words "arrested," "charged," and "convicted" in turn.

Seconds later, I'm staring openmouthed at what I've found. I turn to Damian. "You have a suspended sentence for domestic burglary."

He says nothing.

"Damian?" I persist.

"Okay." He hesitates. "I didn't lie to you, Livy."

"And that makes it okay?" I glare at him. "Anyway, what about lock-picking being something you 'picked up' in college?"

"It was," he says quietly. "Another addict showed me. We were off our heads most of the time, thought we were something out of *Natural Born Killers*."

He catches the horrified look in my eye.

"We *never* hurt anyone," he says quickly. "We stole stuff to sell, for money."

"For drugs?"

He nods. There's a long pause. "It all feels like it happened to another person now."

"Tell me," I say. "Please."

"Okay," Damian says. "It was years ago, when I was at art school. I'd only done some E and a bit of spliff before that." He hesitates. "Then I started using coke to get me going in the morning and I was still partying at night and . . . and my drinking was . . . well, I was getting through a bottle of whisky a day at one point. It wasn't long before I couldn't afford the half of it, so me and this girl, we ended up housebreaking. We took whatever we could carry: jewelry, laptops, cameras." He glances at me and his eyes are filled with shame. "Looking back, I can't believe I wasn't caught sooner. In the end, I almost went to prison for it. But my sentence was suspended, I did some rehab. It didn't really work so . . . after a couple of relapses Mum and Dad found a private clinic. They put their home on the market to pay for me to dry out. And that time, it was different. I stopped doing drugs. Went back to college. Turned things around. Like I told you before, it's been five years plus since I used anything. I still go to meetings, do the whole AA thing."

"Right." I try to take in what he's said. "So you have a record as a burglar. *That's* why you don't want to talk to the police, why you said ages back that they wouldn't believe anything you said?"

"Yes," Damian says. His eyes are fixed on the road ahead, a deserted stretch of dual carriageway lined with trees on either side.

"Did Julia know?"

"Of course." Damian flashes a look at me. "I told her straightaway. She was brilliant about it, said everyone deserved a second chance. She used to turn to me sometimes, in the middle of a row and say, 'How's that searching and fearless moral inventory of yourself coming, Crime Boy?'" He smiles sadly at the memory. "She insisted that that I could still make up to my parents for what I'd put them through, whereas she could never give Kara her life back. She said I should work hard 'to make direct amends.'"

I look down at my lap.

"Look, Livy, it's not just my past that's stopping me going to the police," Damian adds with a sigh. "Think about where we broke into."

"The cottage?" I say. "Why would anyone think we wanted to damage that?"

"Don't Julia's family already think you stole her ring? Maybe they'll suspect you of wanting the cottage too, and getting angry about not having it."

He's right. I feel disoriented, as if the world has shifted on its axis and everything now looks slightly different than it did a few days ago.

"Let's go, then," I say. "There's bound to be a car park at the train station. We can leave your car. It'll be safe. And we can catch a train. I . . . I don't have any money now, but—"

"Shit, your handbag." Damian glances at me, horrified. "I was only thinking about us losing those plastic bags with all Shannon's stuff in them." He pulls off the two-lane road and slows the car as we reach the lights.

I turn my head away so that Damian can't see the tear that trickles down my face.

"Hey." His voice is soft.

I feel his fingers on my cheek, turning my face toward his. We gaze into each other's eyes, and for a single, terrifying moment I think he is about to kiss me. Then he clears his throat and his hand drops from my face.

"I'll pay for the tickets, for whatever you need until you can get back home," he offers gruffly.

"Thank you." I wipe my eyes as the lights ahead change. Damian shifts gears and we drive on in silence. My thoughts jump about. I can't settle. When I close my eyes I see the fire burning and then the messenger from earlier, then Damian looking at me, his finger trailing down my cheek. My hands are still shaking.

More than anything, I want Will. A lump lodges in my throat. I so want to call him, to turn to him for help and reassurance. And yet, how can I trust him? Shannon might have said Julia only used his name as a "cover" for whatever she was really doing, but he has still lied to me. He has still been unfaithful. And I still found Julia's ring in his toolbox, which I simply can't explain at all.

The car stops and I open my eyes. We're at Honiton station. Damian and I get out. After a short discussion we decide to buy tickets for London but get off the train well beforehand, at Salisbury. I had been planning to go back to Bath, back to Mum and the kids. But now that idea seems like too big a risk, possibly even putting them in danger. We might have dumped the car, but we could still be being followed. Anyway, Salisbury is only an hour's drive from Bath. I can get a taxi there if I need to.

Damian lugs his laptop and Shannon's suitcase out of the trunk and over to the ticket office, then steps up to the counter to buy us two singles to London. The guy in the ticket office frowns as he catches sight of me, my shirt all ripped.

I rummage in Shannon's case and find a blue T-shirt than looks a little larger than the others. I disappear into the ladies' room to change and wash. There's not much I can do about my pants. I can just about squeeze into one of Shannon's tops, but her designer jeans are at least two sizes too small. In the end, I rip both my own trouser legs off just below the knee and roll them up. The effect is better than I was expecting. The cut-offs look good with my sandals and against my legs, tanned from the past few sunny weekends. In fact, as I look at myself in the mirror, it occurs to me that the trousers are looser than they were a few weeks ago, that I've lost weight since Julia's death.

Glad something good came out of it, honeypie, I hear her chuckle.

202

I peer closer. Apart from the anxious lines around my eyes, I look better than I have for ages. My hair could do with a brush, for sure, but my features are more sharply defined than they have been for a while, and my face has a healthy glow. Noticing this makes me feel calmer. I scrub my face and tie my dirty hair back with one of Shannon's black bands.

Damian raises his eyebrows as I come out of the restroom. "You look great," he says. His directness makes me blush. How long has it been since Will complimented me on how I looked? Apart from that guilt-induced attempt at flattery at Leo and Martha's party, I can't remember him saying anything unprompted about my appearance for a long time. Still, maybe I look different in some way. I glance down. Shannon's T-shirt is every bit as tight on me as it would have been on her, though my breasts are definitely smaller. The top emphasizes all my curves. I place my hand over my stomach self-consciously.

The next London train arrives within ten minutes and we get on board. I fish my phone out of my pants pocket—it's survived the escape from the cottage remarkably intact—and call Mum. She's on her mobile and sounds distracted. I can hear carnival noises in the background—music and metallic clanking sounds and lots of excited chatter. I hurriedly explain that I've bumped into my friend Mandy and we're going to make a night of it, so if she doesn't mind, I won't be back until tomorrow. Mum sounds surprised, but takes the news in stride. She's used to having the kids, after all. Last summer they spent a long weekend on their own with her while Will and I had a getaway to Madrid.

I ask to speak to them. Zack comes on immediately, full of the ride he's just been on. "It went up and down and up and down reee-ally fast, Mummy." I smile and tell him I miss him. He accepts my impending absence with the same trusting ease with which he approaches virtually everything.

Then Mum offers Hannah the phone. I can hear her urging Hannah to take it, but Hannah says nothing.

Mum comes back on the line. "Sorry, love, she's busy eating some cotton candy."

"It's fine," I interrupt. I'm tired of fighting with my daughter. Right now, it feels like I've got way bigger things to worry about. "I'll call again tonight." I get off the phone.

Damian is watching me, a curious expression on his face. "It must change everything, having kids," he muses.

"It does," I say.

He hesitates a second, then starts asking questions about Zack and Hannah: basic stuff, like how old they are and what subjects they enjoy most at school. I'm amused—and touched—by his interest.

"Do you see yourself becoming a father one day?" I ask.

He nods. "I guess. It was something Julia and I talked about . . . that we both wanted."

My jaw drops. Is he kidding? "I . . . I didn't . . . *Julia*?"

"I know." He grins. "She used to make out that she had no interest in being a mum, but like I told you before, that was because she was scared. I saw it straightaway." There's a pause as he stares out the window. I follow his gaze. Fields and trees pass by in a blur against a hazy blue sky. "The week before she died, when we got engaged, she said she wanted kids in the next couple of years."

"Wow." Again, I'm at a loss for words. I thought I knew Julia better than anyone in the world. How can she still be surprising me like this even after her death?

We get off the train at Salisbury, find a small pub hotel, and book in. Despite my self-conscious request at the desk for separate rooms, there's an illicit thrill about the whole thing. I wonder, with a stab of misery, if this is what Will feels like when he sleeps with Catrina, Damian pays in advance in cash, explaining that we'll be moving on tomorrow, and we head upstairs.

My room is basic but clean, with simple white linen on the bed and pine furniture. Damian says he's going to get straight online to check out what his friend Gaz found on the fragment of Julia's hard drive. In all the trauma of the past few hours, I had almost forgotten Gaz called him, that we have this extra lead.

I take a shower, then wander along the corridor to his room. Damian looks perturbed as he lets me in.

"What is it?" I say.

He points to his open laptop on the dressing table. "It's an e-mail from Julia's computer. There were hundreds of fragments. Gaz filtered them, looking for key words. I've had a look at what he found, and this is the only e-mail that looks like it might be relevant. It's just a series of scraps, but . . . well, take a look yourself."

I walk over and peer down at the screen. The date—three days before her death—and sender's name—Julia Dryden—are clear, but the name and e-mail address of the person she was writing to are not there, and the message itself is only partial, just a few words.

. . . HOW DARE YOU THREATEN ME? THIS IS MY . . .

I freeze.

"Who's she writing to, d'you think?" Damian asks. "She never mentioned anyone threatening her."

"I don't know, and I don't see how we can tell from just this." I look at the send date again. "D'you think it could be something to do with what she found out about Kara?"

"There's a bit more of the e-mail here. I only had a quick look before you came in. See?" Damian scrolls down the page. None of the other fragments sound as angry as the first one, but the word "money" comes up several times.

"Maybe there was some kind of blackmail element?" Damian muses.

I shake my head. It's so frustrating, all hints and possibilities—with nothing holding the whole e-mail together. And then I see the final few words extracted from it. I gasp and point to the screen.

Damian follows my gaze. He reads the line out loud: "'. . . so typical of you, Dickweasel. . . .'" He turns to me, and I see in his eyes the same light of recognition that burns inside me.

"Dickweasel," I say slowly. "That's Julia's brother, Robbie. She always called him that. I never heard her say it about anyone else."

Damian nods.

I stare at him, aghast. "Do you really think Robbie could have hurt her?"

"I don't know," he says.

205

It suddenly occurs to me that we are both jumping to almighty conclusions here. The "threat" Julia refers to could be about anything. And apart from the word "dickweasel," there is no indication that Julia sent the e-mail to Robbie. She might just as well have sent it to Damian himself.

I don't say this.

"Could Robbie have had something to do with Kara's death?" Damian frowns. "He and Julia were twins, so he's the same age as she is . . . as Kara was. Was he at the same college? Julia never said."

"No, he didn't do a degree. He lived at home with Joanie in Bridport, where they grew up. But he was always coming over to Exeter and going out with us. He actually had a bit of a crush on me—Will thinks he still does. Julia thought that was hilarious." My mind reels. I'm suddenly exhausted. I sink down onto the bed. Could Julia's brother have taken his own sister's life? Could he really have killed Kara all those years ago? He was certainly unpleasant about Julia at the funeral, but that doesn't make him capable of murder.

"Another suspect," I say flatly. "And still no proof of anything."

Damian sits down beside me on the bed. He's completely wrapped up in his thoughts.

I take the opportunity to look at him for several long seconds. He is particularly handsome in profile. His nose is broad, his chin square and strong. And there's just a hint of arrogance around his lips and eyes. I can see why Julia fell for him. He's strong and masculine enough to challenge her, yet there's something soft and unformed about him too. Nonthreatening and, ultimately, controllable.

He senses me staring and turns to meet my gaze. His expression is one of profound misery. A wave of compassion washes through me. Damian is hurting over Julia in the same way that I hurt over Kara: He didn't protect her. He doesn't know if he *could* have protected her. He doesn't know what happened. And without understanding, there can be no closure.

I see no guilt in his eyes, no hidden agenda. He truly loved her and is consumed by his grief for her. It's almost unbearable to look at his face and see so much of my own pain reflected, and in that moment I'm transported back to that day, years ago, when I saw my loss for my sister echoed in Julia's eyes.

"I miss her so much." His voice is broken. His eyes glisten.

My own fill with tears, and I take his hand and squeeze his fingers.

Damian reaches over and we hold each other. His body is warm. I can feel the muscles of his arms, pressing against my sides. Desire fills me and I have to fight the urge to tilt my head toward his, to find his mouth. I stop myself, of course. Tell myself it's not lust. Not really. It's just a deep longing to be held, safe, in another person's arms. Because I can't remember the last time Will and I properly hugged.

The thought of Will brings with it a shard of jealousy, piercing through me to the core. Where is Will? Could he be with someone else right now?

Damian pulls away and wipes furiously at his eyes. "Sorry, Jesus, I didn't mean to . . . God . . . sorry."

"Don't apologize. . . ." I clear my throat as an unbidden image of Will kissing Catrina flashes horribly before my eyes. "Okay, so . . . so far we've got a lot of bits of information, but nothing that adds up. It looks as if someone—possibly Julia's brother, Robbie—was threatening her." I pause. "And there's Kara's locket, which someone gave Shannon to pay off a debt."

"And there's Honey Hearts," Damian adds, sitting up straighter on the bed.

I get up and wander over to the window. The sun is still high in the sky, bright against the blue. "Julia must have talked to Alexa Carling, just like I did, then picked and hired Shannon—but why, when she'd already contacted Shannon through eBay? And Shannon said entrapping Will was a cover. But what for? I don't get it."

Damian frowns. "Wait a sec, we're assuming Julia went to Honey Hearts *before* she met Shannon at Aces High, but what if she went *afterwards*? What if her meeting with Shannon *led* her to Honey Hearts?"

207

I stare at him. "But we know she saw Shannon for the first time on Thursday evening, just two days before she died. How would there have been time to go to a honey trap agency before she died on Saturday? You have to make an appointment, and Julia wouldn't have been able to call until Friday morning at the earliest."

"That wouldn't have stopped Julia." Damian is on his feet, cheeks flushed.

Adrenaline floods through me. We're on to something. I can feel it. I rack my brains, trying to remember what Shannon said. "Okay, so Julia contacts Shannon through eBay, pretending to buy the locket that Shannon was selling, Kara's locket."

"Right." Damian paces across the room to the window, then back again to the bed. He sits down, brow furrowed.

"Okay," I say slowly. "Suppose Julia meets Shannon and finds out whom she got the locket from. She's going to try to track *them* down too, isn't she? "

Damian looks up. "You think that person worked at the *honey trap* agency?"

"It fits with what we know," I say. "Julia finds out where Shannon got the locket on Thursday. On Friday she goes to the agency. By Saturday evening she's telling you she knows who the killer is, straight after which, she tries to tell me."

Damian blinks rapidly. "Yes. Which means Julia was just doing what *you* did, pretending to hire Shannon from the agency as a cover in order to get information." His voice rises with excitement.

I nod. "Information about Kara's killer."

"Yes."

I hug my arms to my chest. We're getting close to the truth; I can feel it. "We have to find Shannon again. Force her to explain."

"And fast," Damian adds grimly. "Before whoever set that fire finds her—or us."

We talk for another hour, trying to work out where Shannon might have gone. She said she had friends at Aces High. Perhaps it will be worth going back there and asking around. "She knew the bartender. She might have other friends who work there," Damian points out. "Maybe there'll be someone who'll have some idea where she might have gone."

After a while, I'm so tired, I'm finding it hard to think clearly anymore. Damian yawns, which sets me off.

"Hey, we're both exhausted," I say, yawning again. "Let's get some sleep, then have something to eat downstairs. We can talk about all this later.

Damian agrees and I go back to my room. I lie on the bed and pull the comforter over me. The window is open a fraction, but all I can hear is the soothing swish of wind in trees. I can't believe I'm here in this strange room, with Damian, whom I barely know, just down the hall. I turn onto my side, watching the door. My heart is still thudding with fear, and yet for all my anxiety, I feel alive. I have a sense of purpose, something to drive me. I realize how much I have lost that over the past few years.

And how much I miss it all.

I mean to lie awake for a while and try to plan our next step. But I'm asleep almost before I've closed my eyes.

When I wake up, it's almost dark. I blink. The room is cooler, but I'm warm under the comforter. I sit up and check the time. *Jesus,* it's quarter to nine. I must have slept for hours. My whole body feels stiff and sore, and my cheek is smarting from the graze on the roof. I shiver, remembering the fire.

There's a knock at the door. Feeling groggy, I stumble over.

It's Damian. His face is pink from his shower, and his black shirt looks sponged and pressed. He smiles as I stifle a yawn. "You too?"

I nod. "I just woke up."

"They're still open for dinner," he says. "Shall we go down? I'm starving."

"Sure." I automatically turn back for my makeup, then remember it's in my handbag, which is gone in the fire. I shiver again. "I don't have any of my normal things with me." My voice comes out all fragile and forlorn, far more pathetic-sounding than I mean it to.

"Hey." Damian squeezes my arm. The touch of his hand sends a different kind of shiver through me. "We'll get you some new stuff tomorrow, okay?"

"Thanks." I follow him down to dinner. At first I don't think I'm hungry, but as soon as the bread arrives, I realize I'm ravenous.

Damian and I eat two courses without stopping for breath, washing our pan-fried cod and treacle tart down with water for Damian and a glass of red wine for me. I ask for just the house wine, but Damian takes the drinks menu and upgrades my request, picking a delicious rioja with a surprising level of wine knowledge.

"I thought when you drank, you drank whiskey?" I say.

"When I drank, I drank whatever I could get my hands on."

"I still wouldn't have figured you for a wine buff. Where d'you learn about Spanish reds?"

He laughs. "My dad taught me. He said being able to navigate a wine menu would impress women. Kind of old-fashioned, but there you are. "

"Was . . . is he fierce too? Like you said your mum was? They sound amazing, all the support they've given you."

"They are. Nah, Dad's a big softie. Henpecked a bit, but I reckon he loves getting pushed around at home a bit, after being a captain of industry all day."

I think about my own parents. Bath seemed very dull to me growing up. It makes me laugh to think that Exeter once seemed edgy—even dangerous—in comparison and that I couldn't wait to leave home to go to university there. The day I discovered, two years later, that Kara had chosen to follow me to the same place, I'd felt angry, as if she were trying to steal my freedom . . . muscle in on my choices. I didn't stop to think that she might have been scared of going away, picking the same uni as me because my presence made the whole experience feel less daunting, because I would be there to look after her. To show her the ropes. To protect her.

The old guilt rears up inside me. I try to ignore it, focusing on what Damian is suggesting—a return to Exeter in the morning and a fresh visit to Aces High.

"You could try to speak to Robbie, too?" Damian suggests. "Sound him out about that 'dickweasel' e-mail Julia sent."

I agree, then look up train times on my phone. After we've eaten, Damian suggests a stroll along the road, away from the hotel. The night sky has clouded over and the air is still and sultry, building up to a storm.

I check the time and am shocked to realize it's almost 11 P.M. It's far too late now to call the kids; Mum will be going to bed too. I feel guilty. Then it occurs to me that I haven't heard from Will all day either. I wonder if he phoned Mum and discovered I'm not there.

Why hasn't he called me?

Is he with Catrina?

Damian gestures toward a small patch of private parkland that backs onto a row of high houses. I'm still preoccupied with thoughts of Will when, to my surprise, Damian leaps over the gate.

"We shouldn't," I say.

He grins at me. "Go on, Livy, live a little."

I smile at such a Julia-esque phrase coming from his lips and clamber over the gate after him.

Damian holds my hand as I jump down. He keeps holding it as we walk across the grass. I flush, grateful for the dark night. My heart is beating faster—and not because we're trespassing. I tell myself Damian can't really be interested in me. He's just being friendly.

We wander into the trees and he lets my hand go. Music is playing from one of the flats in the houses opposite. The air is sweet and humid as we stroll along. I think of Will again and how he hasn't checked in to find out how I am. Still, I rationalize, I haven't rung him either. I am too churned up to call; I'm hurt and jealous and angry. More than *anything,* I'm angry. Will has lied to me, made a fool of me. *Again.* And I have let him.

"You aren't like I thought you would be, you know." Damian's voice breaks our silence.

I glance at him, curious. "How d'you mean?"

"Julia said you were the sensible one: classic mum, salt-of-the-earth, heart-of-the-house kind of thing." He hesitates. "I guess I

211

assumed, before I met you, that you'd be a bit, I dunno, *dull,* maybe. With a small life."

I offer up a wry laugh. "Small by name, small by nature. That definitely sounds like me. Compared to Julia, anyway."

"No." Damian frowns. "That's not it, Livy. I can see why you and Julia worked. She did all the glamorous things and you lived them through her and she felt grounded through you. But that didn't . . . doesn't . . . make your life small."

"No?"

The trees grow thicker as we walk closer to the houses. The music is louder here.

"Your life isn't small," Damian says . "You've just got too used to living at the edges of it."

I stare at him. The song playing finishes and a DJ introduces the next track, but I'm not really listening. I'm thinking about what Damian has just said, instinctively feeling the truth of it. Then, as the floaty sound of a guitar drifts toward us, Damian gives a gasp of recognition.

"Julia loved this," he says.

I turn my attention to the song. The mournful guitar has been joined by a man singing. The sound of his voice is vaguely familiar, but I can't quite place either him or the track. It's yet another way in which my life has diminished. I can't remember when I stopped listening to music; sometime after the kids arrived, I guess.

"What is this?" I ask.

" 'Why Worry.' Dire Straits," Damian says. "One of Julia's guilty pleasures."

I stare at him. "Julia hated this kind of '80s music."

Damian grins. "In public, she did. Hey, come here." He reaches for my hand again and pulls me toward him.

I let him hold me and sway me. He puts one strong hand on my back. The other is still holding my hand. And we are dancing. The night is so dark and quiet. The music is haunting. We move together, slowly, and I close my eyes as the song floats around us. Desire fills me again and I let my cheek rest against Damian's. I feel ridiculously excited, my pulse racing. I have no idea what I'm doing—the world and the rest of my life feel a million miles away.

The music fades away and a new tune starts up. The beat is stronger, rhythmic. Again it sounds familiar, but I don't recognize the song.

"Oh yes." Damian's grip on my hand tightens. He presses his other palm more firmly against my back and moves me faster.

I open my mouth to ask what we're dancing to now, when the vocals start and the unmistakable sound of Elvis Presley growls around us. I recognize the song, with its infectious tune and chirpy rhythm. I've no time to feel self-conscious as Damian moves me in time with the music.

It's fun. I'd forgotten how much fun dancing could be. I haven't danced in years.

I let Damian lead me as we spin through the trees. He's a great dancer, his movements flexible and rhythmic. I'm breathless, laughing, all the terrors of the day forgotten as we glide over the soft grass,

And then the music fades again, to radio ads. And the world comes crashing back. A car passes in the street beyond. Another honks in the distance. Farther away, two men are shouting. Damian and I stop moving and stand, still holding each other. Seconds pass. The radio is still blaring out. The ad finishes and the station jingle sounds. I don't catch the name of the station, but suddenly the music is over and a male voice announces:

"This is the news at eleven o'clock."

I step back, away from Damian. He lets me go, but keeps his gaze on my face. There's an expression I can't read in his eyes: part longing, part misery. He moves, a slight inflection of the head. It's barely there, but clear as the voice in the background: an invitation to kiss.

I move back farther, suddenly terrified. I bow my head, avoiding his gaze. And then I focus back on the radio, and I hear what the news announcer is saying.

213

"...has been identified as former escort, Shannon Walker, twenty-five. The body was washed ashore on the beach at Lympstone. Walker was under the influence of a cocktail of recreational drugs when she drowned. . . ."

"Oh, Jesus." I turn back to Damian. He is listening too, horror in his eyes.

"He found her," Damian says. Fear fills me to my bones. "He found her after all."

SANDRA

I think that God in creating Man somewhat overestimated his ability.
— Oscar Wilde

And so we come to Sandra. I waited a long time to find her. There were other distractions in the meantime: simple affairs, disappointments at work, the onslaught of Amis's time passing with its "ropes of steam" and "hoarse roar of power or terror." But none of this really touched me at my core. There I slept, waiting, trusting my instincts and my belief that when the killer is ready, the victim will appear, to paraphrase one of my earlier entries.

It wasn't a promising start. Unlike Annalise, Sandra had no veneer of intelligence or professional ability. In fact, she did not possess any obvious qualities at all. And yet . . . other than with Kara, of course, I have never felt such a desire to take a person in my life. It was overwhelming. Perhaps my ultimate challenge. You see, I could have killed Sandra within minutes of meeting her. And yet I waited. I waited to test myself. To see how far I could triumph over my own impatience. It was then I realized that I, myself, was the rival I had been waiting for. In that moment things fell apart and the center could not hold. As I dissolved, so I was reborn. Sandra was nothing in herself, but she represents my own second coming.

We met on Dartmoor one hot day a few summers ago. I was driving home from seeing a client, reminding myself that I needed to pick up some flowers as a present for my wife, and that I should probably buy some milk while I was at it, when I passed Sandra on a deserted road. She was with her two small children (both girls, born to different fathers) and I could see, as I passed her, the slouch in her walk that told me everything. I don't really know why I

215

pulled over. I was just suddenly sure that Sandra was next. My destiny. I got out of my car and waited for them to walk by.

"Hello." I said.

Sandra looked at me suspiciously. Her hair was a mess of unspeakable highlights in dire need of a cut, and her clothes were desperate. The two little girls had grubby smears on their arms and legs. She was carrying one; the other was whining at her legs. All three of them looked exhausted.

"Might I offer you a lift?" I smiled disarmingly and indicated the cool interior of my car.

Sandra frowned.

I glanced at the picture I had placed on the dashboard, hoping her gaze would follow mine.

"Is that your family?" she asked.

"That's right," I said. "Quite the handful."

Sandra hesitated. The older girl whined. "Please, Mummy." Sandra still hesitated.

"It's fine. I just stopped because you all looked so tired and hot and I wanted to help," I said with a rueful shrug. "But I totally understand. You can't be too careful these days."

I headed for the car. I got inside. I took hold of the door handle, ready to pull the door shut.

"Okay, er, thanks." Sandra blushed.

And in they came. Easy as pie.

I put on my best face as I drove them to their little home on the moor. Sandra was clearly lonely and miserable. I gradually drew her out, complimenting her on the children and commiserating about the challenge of single parenting. I used my old favorite, the dead daughter leukemia story. I thought it would be just the ticket for Sandra. It was. By the time I dropped her at the end of her road, she was very open to another meeting. We didn't even swap numbers—I just arranged to pick her up the following Saturday afternoon, when the girls would be with Sandra's mother.

We met and walked across the moor, to the River Dart. We were seen by several couples, which helped my resolution not to take things further too fast. Sandra, yawn, was eager to tell me her story, which predictably featured a series of brutal ex-boyfriends. She was delighted to inform me that leaving

216

the last bully who had humiliated her had been a huge step, that she was turning her life around . . . blah, blah . . . I told her, in faltering tones, that my wife didn't understand me, that our marriage was a sham. And then I kissed her—ever so gently—near where the Dart pooled into a mini-lake, surrounded by rocks. As I stared into the cool dark depths, my plan resolved itself inside my head.

And so I waited. I held myself back the following Friday, when Sandra and I met again for a couple of hours. And the weekend after that, when she brought her daughters with her to introduce me to them properly, as she said with a silly, shy smile. Both times I could have killed her in any number of ways. God knows I was bored enough to do it. My view of Sandra's personality had in no way been enhanced since our first meeting. Often, I thought of Kara as I watched her. Like so many others I've been drawn to, Sandra had one tiny echo of my angel girl: her fine blond hair. Though Sandra's came out of a bottle. And yet the differences were overwhelming. Kara had been sacred ground. Sandra was an ugly scrap of wasteland: soiled and littered. Still, it was such sweet agony to delay the gratification, to resist myself.

I had only a few hours the Friday after, but I knew it was time. I determined to make this count, even when Sandra turned up to our meeting with fresh highlights in her hair and the younger of her daughters who, she said, had not been well and hadn't wanted to stay with her grandmother that day. I should explain that Sandra, knowing I was married, had not told her mother she was meeting me. This was the beauty of our country walks. Few witnesses. No explanations. Limited risk.

It was a hot, sticky day, the third in row where the temperatures were in the low thirties. Sandra was on tenterhooks from the start of our walk, fishing for compliments about her new hairdo—she had pinned those blond locks back with an execrable butterfly-shaped hair grip. I knew she was expecting me to seduce her. I kissed her while her little girl played behind a rock.

"Wait," she giggled, all simpering and irritating.

"I can't wait," I groaned, shamming sexual desire for her. "I want you, I need you." Or some such. Whatever. My words worked. Sandra let me peel off her clothes; then I led her into the water, slightly warmer than normal from days of fierce sunshine. "So we can be private," I whispered. She blushed and murmured her appreciation of my consideration. I took her into the *water, then drew back. She looked at me hesitantly. We were both naked now, up to the neck in the cool lake. Our clothes were on the dry grass, the trees beyond. The little girl out of sight behind the rock with her coloring book or her doll. I told Sandra I wanted to swim with her under the water. She nodded, and I drew her down into the deep. The sun sparkled on the surface above as I held her hand and swam her closer to the rock I had found on an earlier, solo visit. The stones I'd left in place were still there. On we swam. Sandra was running out of breath, tugging at my hand to pull me up to the surface.*

I pointed to the rock, holding up one finger from my free hand. Just a moment, I was signaling. Look here. And the stupid woman did as she was told. I slid my hand along her leg, with a slick movement pushing her foot into the hole in the rocks. I picked up the rock I had gotten ready in advance off the bottom of the pool and shoved it into position so her leg was trapped. Then, holding the rock firmly in position, I turned to see her face. My exertions had left me short of breath myself, but I still watched, fascinated, as Sandra's body jerked then slowed then finally slumped. I took my hands away from the rock. It held. Unable to last any longer without breath, I shot to the surface.

I burst, glorious, into the fresh, warm air. Eyes open, I blinked away the water. I turned. And saw a pair of feet in little pink sneakers.

Sandra's daughter was standing on the rocks, beside our pile of clothes, her mouth a shocked O. She was staring into the pool. I followed her gaze. Sandra was clearly visible underwater, the outline of her naked body smudged and pink and floating up from its prison. The little girl turned to me. I realized with a thrill she was the first-ever witness to a kill of mine. I felt a throb of pride. Then the little girl let out a thin, high scream. Instantly I was out of the water. I swept her into my arms, my hand over her mouth. I jumped in, under the surface again. This had not been planned, of course, but my whole killing life so far had led me to this, this ease under pressure, this sure touch decision-making. The girl crumpled in my arms. Niamh, her name was, not yet three. I left her floating facedown, just above her mother; then I got out of the water.

I was cool and calm as I dragged on my clothes and removed all traces of my footprints. Not hard to do, the grass by the water was soft and lush but already considerably trampled upon by previous passersby. I looked around once more. I was pretty sure how the police would interpret the scene. Sandra went skinny-dipping, got trapped underwater, panicked, and drowned in a freak accident. Her tiny daughter fell in—or jumped in to rouse her mother—and died too. I had left no marks on the bodies and no trace of myself at the scene. I checked everything of Sandra's for telltale signs. It was fine: no hair, no fabric, no prints. I took her butterfly-shaped hair clip and went back to the car. Then I changed into different clothes—just to be sure—and drove off, dumping my original outfit in a trash barrel a couple of miles away..

I was home within the hour, full of the latest tales from work. I pretended to show an interest in my wife's day, but inside I was bursting with a new pride. I had delayed gratification. I had improvised to deal with collateral damage. And I had triumphed. Again.

CHAPTER FIFTEEN

The sunshine glints off the glass-walled office buildings as our train zooms past. Fields and trees, soft green and brown open up to the right. It's another beautiful day, but Damian and I are traveling in a tense, anxious silence.

Once we'd heard the news of Shannon's death, we made our way back to our hotel, feeling stunned. We sat in the deserted bar for a while, trying to calm our nerves. Then we went to bed.

Separately.

Shannon's murder—and I'm as sure as Damian that she was killed deliberately—kept me awake much of the night. I felt sick with fear, shoving a chair under the handle of my hotel room door and getting up several times to check that it was properly locked.

Even now, hours later, I'm still on edge. Damian clearly is too, his hands fiddling nervously with a cigarette, refraining from smoking only because it's forbidden on the train. There's a new awkwardness between us since last night, but I'm not letting myself think about that.

I desperately want to call Will. But I am too hurt and too angry to speak to him. It doesn't matter if he slept with Catrina once, or one hundred times; it doesn't matter if there were lots of other women over the years, or only her. It still changes everything. I can't hold my feelings back any longer. There are things here I must face. Most important, that our life together has been shattered. Will's affair the first time around tore at the heart of our marriage. But at least back then, I believed there *was* a heart, something that we could, together, heal and mend. But now everything is ripped to shreds, broken beyond mending. Will has destroyed our marriage, and I cannot see a way back for us. I think this; then I think of Hannah, grappling with early adolescence, and I think of sweet, loving Zack. I think of the pain that our breaking up will cause them.

I cannot bear it.

Damian and I barely speak on the journey home. I don't know what to make of how he looked at me last night, how close we came to kissing, how easily that could have led to everything else. In the state I'm in, it's hard to see anything clearly. Paranoia fogs my brain. My fears run riot. I suspect everyone and everybody of Julia's death. Maybe Will has a dark side I've never seen. Maybe Damian has set up everything we have experienced—from the messenger in Shannon's flat to the fire at Julia's cottage—as some kind of elaborate double bluff. Maybe Julia's brother, Robbie, is a psychopath whose constrained, ordinary life masks a whole series of sick desires and evil actions.

Our train draws close to Exeter, and I rouse myself from my horrific musings to give Mum a ring. She says that Zack has been up for hours but that Hannah is still in bed. I glance at my watch. It's almost ten. I tell Mum to wake Hannah if she's not up in half an hour and that I'll be with them later—though I don't know exactly when. Then I have a chat with Zack, who is full of the "bug paradise" he's been making in Granny's garden, "with a home for beetles under a stone and some flowers for the bees to visit and some earth for worms."

We arrive in Exeter as I finish my phone call. Outside the cool of the air-conditioned car, the air feels hot and humid.

As we pass through the turnstile, Damian clears his throat. "So do you still want to go to Aces High?" he asks.

I'm jolted back to the reality of the plan we made last night, before we knew about Shannon's death. "What's the point of going there?" I ask. "We were only going to try to find Shannon again. And now . . ."

Damian's shoulders sag. "I know, but I can't give up," he says. "I

221

need to know who killed Julia." He pauses. "Whoever it is probably killed Shannon too. *And* your sister."

I nod. I owe it to Kara and Julia to find out as well.

As we emerge into the sunshine, Damian sighs. "How about if we go to Aces High to try to find out if anyone knows who Shannon got that locket from? She said she got one of the guys there to put pressure on the person who owed her. Maybe we can find him."

"Okay, but whoever it is, is hardly going to admit to threatening anyone." I think it through. "Maybe *you* should go to Aces High, and I'll see if Robbie will meet me later. The more I think about it, the more I'm sure he's involved. He got Joanie to destroy Julia's computer—"

"I agree," Damian says. "But I don't like the idea of you meeting him alone."

"I'll be fine. I'll try to arrange to meet him for lunch in Exeter, then we'll be in a public place."

"All right, but be careful."

We head toward a taxi stand, where Damian hands me money for a cab. I'm going to have to replace virtually the entire contents of my handbag, from house keys to bank cards. The thought fills me with exhaustion.

"So, you promise you'll be careful when you talk to Julia's brother?" Damian looks at me with real concern in his eyes.

"I promise."

"Okay, then." Damian hesitates. "Don't forget to use the fact that he liked you once, maybe still does."

His words echo in my ear as I watch him head off to Aces High. I take a steadying breath, then call Robbie.

He answers straightaway, sounding delighted to hear from me. "I was so hoping you'd call back."

"Call back?" For a moment I'm thrown. Then I remember the phone call he made just before I found Julia's ring a few days ago. "Right." I'm about to suggest meeting up later, but before I can formulate the sentence, Robbie asks me to meet him right now for coffee.

"I have to be at the hotel for work in an hour, but I could slip out now if you fancy it? Could you meet me in ten minutes? Wendy won't notice."

He's speaking so fast, with such enthusiasm, that I can barely follow what he's saying, but that reference to his wife at the end makes it sound, worryingly, as if he is proposing some kind of secret rendezvous.

"Shall I come to the hotel?" I say, determined to make it clear my own intentions are entirely aboveboard.

"God no," Robbie says with feeling. "Don't want to get to work before I have to. There's bound to be some problem to sort out. I'll get roped in straightaway. How about Top Tiffin?"

"What's that?" I ask.

"Great little café about five minutes from the cathedral. Could you meet me there now?"

I reluctantly agree. I'd wanted to go home to Heavitree first to change—plus I seriously don't like the idea that Robbie is sneaking out to see me behind his wife's back. However, I don't want to put the meeting off, so I head straight for the café he's suggested.

He's already there when I arrive, his head buried in a book, his fingers tapping nervously on the table. I glance at the cover—Julian Barnes's *The Sense of an Ending*. I stand, watching him for a moment. After a few seconds, Robbie looks up with an anxious glance at the door. He spots me and beams.

I head over, feeling decidedly unsettled. Robbie makes a show of switching off his cell phone before asking what I want. I say I'd like a cappuccino and switch my own mobile off too.

Robbie goes over to the counter and orders our drinks. He smiles at me again as he comes back and sits down. "It's *so* great to see you, Livy. You look gorgeous. I thought so when you turned up at Mum's the other day. I can't tell you how pleased I am you called me. I was scared that, after Mum accused you of taking that ring—"

I flush, suddenly remembering where the ring turned up. I stare at Robbie's open face. Does he know? Is this somehow a trick? I'd completely forgotten until this minute that when Will took the ring

223

from me, he *definitely* said he was going to return it to Robbie the next day. Has he done so?

"What's the matter?" Robbie asks. He self-consciously smooths down the hair that curls over the back of his neck. "I'm sorry, I didn't mean to upset you by—"

"You haven't." I touch his arm.

Robbie blushes. I glance outside. Despite the heat, the sky is overcast. A dark cloud looms in the distance.

"I'm sorry if I've disturbed, er, your plans." I pause.

"Don't be sorry." Robbie is still smiling at me. "I'm not sorry."

The atmosphere shifts and tightens. I'm suddenly very aware of the lustful glint in Robbie's eyes. I draw away, feeling uncomfortable. Better to get straight to the point. "Actually, I wanted to ask you about something," I say. "I found . . . an e-mail Julia wrote. I think she sent it to you just before she died. She's angry. It's about, well, I'm not sure, but—" I stop, unwilling to come right out and say that the e-mail implies Robbie was threatening his sister.

His face tenses, a tiny involuntary movement of the muscles. "I'm sorry, Livy, but Julia hadn't e-mailed me for years." And it's there, in the way his voice rises slightly at the end of the sentence: He's lying.

I keep my gaze on his face, trying to work out what to say, how to draw him out. "Well, she sent an e-mail, and she sounded furious in it."

Robbie looks uncomfortable. "Livy, I have no idea what outrageous, angry, manipulative things Julia might have written down in a random e-mail, but I wouldn't pay it too much attention." He frowns. "How come *you've* seen it?"

I sit back in my chair, unsure what to say. The waiter comes over with our coffees. He sets them both down on the table. Two black coffees with a jug of hot milk.

I'm about to point out that I'd asked for a cappuccino when Robbie leans across the table and takes my hand. "I ordered Americanos with hot milk. That's what we drank on our first, our only date, remember?" He smiles.

I stare at him. Is he serious? "Blimey, Robbie, that was eighteen years ago."

"I know, but I remember as if it were yesterday."

His hand is still on mine, his palm heavy and damp on my fingers. It takes all I've got not to pull away, but somehow I resist. The café hums about us as I stare at the steam rising off our coffees.

Julia's cutting words from years ago echo in my head: *My dickweasel of a brother worships you big-time. Couldn't you talk to him, Liv? Get him to swap rooms with me at home? Mum let him have the big room and I got rammed into this fucking broom closet. Go on, he'd do anything for you.*

I wonder. Damian's suggestion that I should use the fact that Robbie likes me flits through my head. I look up. Robbie is gazing at me, his expression barely short of adoring. I gulp, then gaze back, trying to make my eyes soft and interested. "Actually, I remember too," I say, "I just can't believe that you . . ." I look down at our hands. Robbie squeezes my fingers, encouraging me to say more. "I can't believe that you feel the same way I do, that is . . . if you do?" My face is burning. I'm useless at this. I'm acting like a bloody honey trap agent, and I feel awkward and guilty. Do the women at Honey Hearts ever feel like this, I wonder? Or do they see what they do as a job?

Robbie grips my hand tighter and I make myself look up, into his eyes.

"I often think about that time," he says with feeling.

I squeeze his hand gently back. I'm playing with fire here, but I can't stop. I have to get him to trust me, to open up, to tell me what he knows.

"Sometimes I wonder if we didn't take what we had back then for granted," Robbie goes on in a low voice. "I feel that . . . maybe I let you go too easily. Sometimes we don't realize what we've lost until it's too late. Do you know what I mean?"

I glance away. "Yes," I whisper.

Oh, Jesus.

"Sometimes I wish we could turn back the clock . . . before Wendy, before Will," Robbie says. I can feel him gazing at me, waiting for my response.

I take a deep breath and squeeze his hand again. "I know," I say softly. "Of course, however far we go back, there's always Julia."

Robbie sighs. "Yeah, Julia. Everyone loved Julia, but honestly, Livy, if you knew her like I did . . . she was *such* a bitch."

My mouth drops open. Even though I heard him at the funeral, I'm not prepared for this.

"A bitch?" My voice sounds hollow.

"Said things for effect most of the time. Nothing behind them at all," Robbie says bitterly. "She liked to taunt me. She was hateful to me and Mum, so manipulative, *always*."

I stare at him. It's true that Julia was dismissive of her family, right from when I first met her. She hardly ever went home, even when her dad died and even though Joanie only lived an hour's drive away. But surely she wasn't as bad as Robbie says. Okay, so she used to call her mother "an emotional vampire" and refer to her brother as "dickweasel," but Julia was often harsh in the way she expressed herself. And it wasn't as if Joanie and Robbie were angels themselves. Julia was always full of stories about how they had sneered at her. *It's everything, Livy,* she once told me, *how I look, how I dress, my work, my love life. Mum and Robbie act like I'm a total loser.*

I draw my hand from Robbie's at last and sip at my coffee. "I didn't realize you felt like that."

"Well, it's the truth." He looks at me anxiously. "I know you were her friend and I know she was good at making out like she was a nice, normal person, but she wasn't. She was mean and cruel, and she never let people get close to her. She didn't really care about anyone."

I shake my head. That isn't true. *I* was close to Julia. She told me all the things that mattered.

A little voice mutters in my head: *Yeah, except that she'd been looking for Kara's killer for years, that she had hired a honey trap agent using Will as part of some cover story, and that she'd fallen in love with Damian despite claiming he was just another fling.*

"Julia was a good friend," I insist.

"Really? If she was such a good friend, why didn't she tell you she was planning to leave all her money to her boyfriend, Damian something or other?"

"What?" I stare at him. "How do *you* know she was?" My pulse quickens.

Robbie's voice is terse. "Look, I'm going to tell you the truth, Livy, because I don't want to start anything with any dishonesty between us. I *did* get an e-mail from Julia a few days before she died, and she *was* angry with me."

"Why . . . what was it about?"

Robbie rolled his eyes. "I'd just told her she was being a bitch."

I frown. "I don't—"

"Mum needs money," Robbie says. "The house she lives in costs far more than her pension. I help out as much as I can, but Wendy and I are stretched with our mortgage and the kids. . . . Mum has been struggling ever since Dad died, and in the last year, with the cutbacks and interest rates being garbage and everything, things have got worse. She's desperate to stay in that house, but she's got no money. So a month or so ago, I suggested to Julia that she might consider selling that cottage she was left in Lympstone and using what she made to buy part of Mum's house."

My mind flashes to the cottage. And to the fire. Robbie leans forward, intent on his explanation.

"It wasn't unreasonable. Julia would get her money back when Mum died, so it's not like we were asking for handouts, but Julia went berserk."

"Did she?" My chest feels tight. Julia didn't mention *any* of this to me.

"She shouted at me. Said I was a bully. Called me names. *Horrible* names. Honestly, Livy, she was like a woman possessed. And afterwards, she sent the most vicious e-mail, accusing me of threatening her, saying not only would she not consider helping Mum out, but that she was going to write a new will and leave everything to her damn boyfriend. She actually said that she *hoped* Mum lost her house. And that she was going to make sure Mum and me and my kids— her *nephews,* Livy—that *none* of us ever got a penny from her."

My heart thunders in my ears. I don't know what to think. Or say. "Julia often—her bark was worse than—"

"Don't defend her." Robbie takes a gulp of coffee, then sets the cup down in the saucer with an angry clatter. "She'd known this Damian only a few months. She'd never have stuck with him. She was incapable of loving anyone properly. She was a *psycho,* Livy. A fucking *psycho.*"

I draw back, my breath catching in my throat. "So you burned her computer and her papers in case she had made a new will?"

"Oh, she'd done it, all right. I found the file straightaway. It was written, but she hadn't gotten around to registering it anywhere, so we were in time. I was just trying to help Mum. Why should some boy toy she barely knew get that money? Mum and Dad worked hard for me and my sister all their lives, but to hear Julia talk about them, you'd think they'd spent our entire childhood abusing her."

"She never said anything like that," I insist, my mind still racing. Did Damian know Julia had wanted to leave him everything? If he did, it puts his desire to search through her files in a completely different light, not to mention giving him a motive for killing her.

"She did to me. Look, please understand—I loved my sister no matter what vile nonsense came out of her mouth." Robbie takes my hand again. His eyes bore into me, beseeching me. "I'm not being vindictive, but like I said, I don't want to lie to you. I want . . . I'd like to see you again. Like this. Or dinner, maybe? . . ."

"What about Wendy?" I take my hand away.

"Wendy and I . . . that's just for show. We have an understanding, together for the kids and all that. But it's not, it hasn't been a proper relationship for a long time."

The words slip off his tongue so easily. In fact, he exudes sincerity and purpose. He wants me. He is making it clear. Is this what Will sounds like when he seduces someone? Is this what he said when he first flirted with Catrina?

Robbie gulps at his coffee. I take another sip of mine. It's cold.

"Plus there's Will," I say.

Robbie tilts his head to one side. "You don't trust him," he says. "And for good reason."

My mouth falls open.

"Julia told me about his affair a few years ago," Robbie goes on. "I'm sorry to tell you this, but it was another one of her rants."

I close my mouth. I feel numb. "What do you mean?"

"Julia told me as a taunt. You know . . . 'Your wife is such a bitch, Dickweasel. You only stay with her because you're a pathetic coward and you'd never be able to persuade anyone else to sleep with you anyway. . . .' That kind of thing." He sighs. "She actually said: 'At least Will is man enough to go after what he wants.'"

"No." I feel sick. Robbie is making this up. Julia was always fond of Will—but totally on my side over the affair. "That's not what Julia really thought."

"Who knows what she really thought," Robbie says. "That's my point. You know, when we were younger, she used to tell people I was gay. I mean there's nothing *wrong* with being gay, but I *wasn't,* so it hurt." He runs his hand over his hair. "She probably told you I was, didn't she?"

I sit back in my chair, a long-forgotten memory surging to the front of my mind. Before I met Robbie, Julia *did* tell me he was gay. I'd thought I came to that conclusion on my own, but now I remember Julia said it first. And she reinforced the idea a few weeks later, after it was obvious that he liked me, insisting his big crush on me was some kind of displacement activity:

"He totally adores you, but for him, it's like you're a goddess . . . untouchable. Underneath, he's totally gay. Seriously, Liv, I've seen what he looks at online."

"You mean he's in the closet." I'd made a face, wondering why anyone our age felt the need to hide their sexual orientation.

"Honeypie, Robbie is so far inside the closet, he's practically reached Narnia."

It didn't occur to me that she was lying. I wonder whether her words had an impact on me. Did the fact that I believed he was gay influence me when Robbie asked me out? I don't remember now.

"She did tell you that, didn't she?" Robbie says bitterly. "Just think, Livy—Julia kept us apart."

"No." I drain my cold coffee. It's time to put a stop to this litany of accusations. "Julia did say stuff that maybe she shouldn't have, but I don't believe she meant to be cruel. And I don't think I would have gone out with you back then anyway." I catch my breath, worrying I've sounded unkind.

Robbie gives me a small, unhappy look. "But what about what you said before . . . just now?"

I gulp. "It wasn't you that was the problem," I say, knowing this is only half true. "I was in no state to go out with anyone at that point, just after Kara had died."

"Of course." He falls silent.

We've both finished our coffees. My head is aching. I want to get out of here and think about everything he's told me. Have I really been so wrong about Julia? And if Robbie is right about the terms of her will, does that put Damian's interest in finding out what happened to her into a different light? Can I trust Damian—or his motives? He's already admitted he's an ex-thief. Of course, if Damian had wanted to kill Julia, then surely he would have waited until she'd made her will official. Still, my nagging doubts remain.

"I have to go," I say.

"When will I see you again, Livy?" Robbie stands as I do. There's a bright smile on his face, but his voice is low and almost threatening to my ears. I shiver, despite the heat of the day and the warmth of the café.

"I don't know," I say, feeling awkward. I try to think of a formal function that we both might attend as a way of putting our relationship back on its proper footing. "Maybe when your mother decides what to do with Julia's ashes?"

Robbie's face falls. "Oh, Livy, I'm so sorry, but Mum already sorted them. Well, she left them, actually . . . in an urn at the crematorium." He leans forward with a look of concern. "I could go with you to visit if you like, though it's not much of a date." He laughs.

I gulp, my head spinning with the news that Julia's final remains have been so unceremoniously dealt with.

"Er, no, that's okay. Well, I'm sure I'll see you soon, anyway."

"Absolutely." Robbie smiles with relief. "Don't worry about the coffees—I'll pay," he says.

"Thank you." I hold my hand up in a sort of wave, but before I can stop him, Robbie has lurched forward and planted a clumsy kiss on my cheek.

"Bye." I'm flushing, embarrassed as I turn and rush out of the café.

I switch my phone on as I walk along the street. The sky is heavy with dark, low clouds, and central Exeter full of Saturday-morning shoppers and sightseers. My clothes feel sticky against my skin.

I have a terse text from Will—CALL ME IT'S URGENT—and a voice message from Damian, saying he hasn't found anything out at Aces High and that he's waiting for me at the cathedral. I'm only a few minutes away, so I send a quick text saying I'm on my way and scurry along the sidewalk. Perhaps Damian will be able to make sense of what Robbie has told me. I still don't know if I can really trust him, but Damian was as much a victim of the cottage fire as I was. That has to count in his defense, no matter how heavily his past weighs against him.

The street leading to the cathedral is heaving with tourists. I battle my way past a group of Italian teenagers laughing and shrieking at each other. I'm psyching myself up to call Will, when he rings me himself. I hesitate. I'm dreading talking to him.

On the other hand, avoiding him isn't going to solve anything.

I wipe a bead of sweat from my forehead with the back of my sleeve and press the phone to my ear. "Will?" I feel numb.

"Livy." Will's voice is tight-lipped. "Where the fuck are you?"

I gasp, shocked by how angry he sounds. "I'm in Exeter. Why?"

There's silence on the other end of the phone. I reach the cathedral. The green is spread out in front of me.

"Will?"

"Mandy with you?" His tone is sarcastic.

My heart sinks. He knows I told Mum I was with my friend Mandy. And somehow, he also knows that I haven't been with her at all.

"Er, no . . . ," I stammer. "Not now, I—"

"Cut the crap," Will snaps. "I *know* you haven't even *seen* Mandy. You lied to your mum. To our kids." He stops, his breathing ragged. "So where are you, Liv? What are you doing?"

The cathedral green is packed with people: tourists clicking away at their cameras; office workers chatting on the grass, enjoying a break from their jobs; lovers lying entwined in each other's arms.

"I'm not the only one who's lied," I say, looking around for Damian.

He's about twenty meters away, leaning against the cathedral wall, smoking. He senses me watching him and looks up. A group of girls ogle him as they walk past. He doesn't notice; he's just looking at me.

Will snorts. "Don't start that again. Anyway"—his voice darkens— "that isn't why I've been calling you every two minutes."

"What d'you mean?" A shiver runs down my spine. He sounds so menacing.

There's a long silence on the other end of the phone.

Damian mouths *Are you okay?* at me as I walk over to him.

"Will?" I ask. "What do you mean? What's the matter?"

"It's our daughter," Will says. "She's missing."

232

CHAPTER SIXTEEN

"What do you mean, Hannah's missing?" My heart is pumping violently. Beside me, in the shade of the cathedral, Damian watches me, intent.

"I mean," Will snarls, "that she ran away from your mother's house very early this morning to catch the train to Exeter. And I can't reach her on her mobile."

I gasp. "But I spoke to Mum earlier—she said Hannah was still in bed."

"That's what she thought until about twenty minutes ago. Then she went to wake her up, as per your suggestion, and found she was gone."

"No." I can't believe what he's telling me.

"Yes, Liv. Your mother tried to call you but your phone was switched off. I'm at work. Leo called me in for a bloody meeting at the office with Werner Heine and the Düsseldorf clients. I've been coming out of the meeting every two minutes to call you too, but your phone"—his voice rises as he repeats himself—"has been switched off."

I groan, thinking back to the past half hour in the café with Robbie. "Wait," I say. "You said Hannah had gone to Exeter. How do you—?"

"She sent your mother a text that she didn't notice until after she realized Hannah was gone. It was sent about an hour ago. Shall I read it? It says: '*just got to Exeter going shops if Mum can do it, why can't i?*'" He almost spits the last few words.

"Oh God." My legs threaten to give way. I sag against the cool stone of the cathedral wall. Damian reaches out to stroke my arm. I let him. My head is spinning with fear.

"So there you have it, Liv. Our twelve-year-old daughter, whom you claim is perfectly well-adjusted, has run away and is presently fuck knows where, with fuck knows who, doing fuck knows what." Will sucks in his breath.

"No." Tears prick at my eyes. I'm terrified to the core at the thought of Hannah on her own. What if she gets mugged? Or worse? A chill snakes down my spine. What if the man who followed us yesterday is tracking Hannah now? She may be in terrible danger. And it's all my fault.

"Hannah's a sensible girl," I say, trying to calm Will—and myself—down. "She says she's going to the shops. Exeter's not exactly South Central L.A., is it? She knows the area. I'm sure she'll be okay."

"Then why isn't she answering her phone?" Will shouts.

"She often puts it on silent—or ignores it."

"Not when *I* call her."

"But you *don't* call her," I say. "At least hardly ever. I speak to her every day, when she's forgotten something for school, when she's on her way home."

"Oh, God." Will's voice cracks. The anger drops away from his voice. "God, Livy, I'm scared."

"Me too." Tears well in my eyes, and for a moment, everything else dissolves into this shared bond of love and fear for our daughter.

Damian's frown deepens. He pulls me toward him, his arm round my shoulder, and I lean against his chest. I don't care if it's inappropriate or if Damian is untrustworthy or if he's really grieving for Julia and using me as a substitute. This is my fault. I have handled Hannah so badly that she is now running away . . . possibly into the arms of a killer.

"If anything happens . . ." Will pauses and I can hear the words he is not saying: *because you've been so preoccupied with this nonsense about Julia . . . and imagining I'm having an affair . . .*

"I know." I'm crying now, my voice muffled against Damian's shirt.

Damian strokes my hair. "Hey," he says softly. "Hey."

There's a sharp intake of breath on the other end of the line. Oh, God, did Will just hear that?

"Are you with that boyfriend of Julia's?" Will asks, his voice terse and bitter. "Did you spend the night with him? Is that why your phone was off?"

"*No,*" I insist. I pull away from Damian. "I'll try calling Hannah now. I'll keep calling. She'll *have* to answer in the end."

"I fucking hope so," Will says. "I have to go back into this meeting. I'll ring again in a few minutes."

He hangs up. I turn to Damian and explain what has happened. A soft rumble of thunder growls in the distance.

"Shit. What are you going to do?"

"I'm going to try to call her. Hopefully she's got fed up of shopping—she can't have very much money with her—and is on her way home now." I trail off, my head full of other possibilities. If Julia's killer *hasn't* gotten her, there are still a million other terrible fates that could befall her: being kidnapped by men on street corners or lured into passing cars. No, I'm overreacting. Such things hardly ever happen. And Hannah is not stupid. She wouldn't let herself be tricked. Would she?

"Okay." Damian nods.

He waits while I call Hannah and leave a message on her voice mail saying I'm going home and she should either go there immediately if she is nearby or call me so I can pick her up. I try not to sound cross. I'm sure Will's voice mail will have been much angrier, and if Hannah is okay—and I force myself to recognize I have no evidence to suggest that she isn't—I don't want her to worry she's in so much trouble that she stays away. I ring home too, just in case Hannah is already there, but there is no reply.

It starts to rain as we leave the cathedral grounds and walk up the road. The tourists and office workers are heading away too, mostly looking for shelter in shop doorways. Raindrops trickle down my face as I glance sideways at Damian. He is still frowning. It feels like he's been constantly frowning since we got the news of Shannon's death.

I think about calling for a cab, but the bus stop for Heavitree is only around the corner. It will probably be quicker to use that. I reach the end of the road. The bus shelter is just a few meters away now. There's no sign of a bus, but it's worth checking the timetable to see when the next one is due.

I turn to Damian and breathe out slowly, trying to focus. "I'm going to go home now," I say.

"Sure, would you like me to go with you?" As Damian speaks, the rain starts falling more heavily. He puts his arm around my shoulders and steers me under the bus shelter. There's no one else here, but plenty of people are passing by on the other side of the street. I feel a sudden flush of shame. What if someone I know sees me with Damian? Then I think about Julia dying and Will's betrayal and Hannah being missing—and the thought of someone seeing me with Damian seems so unimportant as to be laughable.

We stand under the shelter. I check the schedule and discover there's a bus due in three minutes. Damian smiles at me with such kindness that I lean against him and cry properly. Damian pulls me close, so my head rests on his chest again. I can't remember the last time Will held me like this—for comfort, with affection. It makes me cry harder.

I have no idea how much time passes. Only a minute or two. When I look up, the rain has slowed to a drizzle. Cars and vans speed past. Pedestrians bustle on either side. Damian looks down at me, full of compassion and concern. And suddenly I'm caught up in his eyes, my stomach flipping over. In that moment, all I want is for him to kiss me. And even as I'm thinking this makes no sense, he dips his face and presses his lips against mine.

I open my mouth, letting in his kiss. I'm lost in the heat of it, the lust of it. I forget where I am. I forget everything.

For about ten seconds.

Then I pull away. Damian is gazing down at me, hungry for more, his beautiful face slightly flushed and his strong hands still holding me tight. With a thrill, it strikes me I could take him home, we could make love. It feels like a fantasy.

I sigh. Of course it does. It *is* a bloody fantasy. The longing in Damian's eyes is not, really, for me. It's just an attempt to stop feeling the pain for a few minutes. He loved—still loves—Julia. He is vulnerable and grief-stricken and angry that she has been taken from him. As for me . . . I am drawn to him, sure. He's easy to like . . . desire, even. But the truth is, I'm confused and unsure of myself because of everything that's been happening. When it comes down to it, this moment between us is no more real for me than it is for him.

I take a breath and step away. "Sorry," I say.

"Don't be." He shakes his head.

"I need to go home," I say, my voice not entirely steady. "I need to keep trying my daughter. And I need to be there when she comes back."

Damian nods. The gleam fades from his eyes. He steps back, releasing my arms. "Call me later, yeah?"

I nod. Then he walks off. I try Hannah. No reply. A bus comes a few minutes later and I'm home in a quarter of an hour. My own keys have perished in the cottage fire, so I root around for the spare key that we leave under the maple tree—planted in memory of Kara—in the front garden. Hannah clearly hasn't been here, or she would have used the key herself. I let myself in and call her again. Still no reply. I send Will and my mum texts telling them where I am and that there's no news. Then I try Hannah yet again. I tell her to call me, to come straight home and that I'm worried about her, that I want to talk and that I love her.

Another ten minutes pass. Still no phone call. Will rings on the house phone so both our mobile lines are still free. He sounds frantic. We discuss whether or not to call the police and agree there is no point at this stage.

"They won't do anything yet," Will reasons. "She hasn't been gone long enough. Technically, she's not even missing, just not answering our calls."

He's right, of course. Hannah's last communication was that text to her grandmother an hour and a half ago, when she said she had just arrived in Exeter. Between us, Will and I have been calling her for only about fifty minutes.

"How much longer will your meeting go on? I ask.

Will sighs. "Another half hour or so. Forty minutes, max."

I blow out my breath. "Let's call the police after, then. That will be two hours since Hannah's text to Mum."

"Okay." Will sounds slightly calmer now that we have a plan. "If it wasn't for this meeting, I'd start driving around Exeter looking for her, but—"

"But some random street patrol makes no sense," I say. "Anyway, Hannah might not even *be* in Exeter. She could have changed her mind."

"I guess so." He sounds close to tears. "God, Liv, call me if you hear anything."

I promise I will and get off the phone. Fear consumes me. I couldn't bring myself to tell Will just now, but I'm haunted by the possibility that the man who followed me and Damian has taken her. He knew us. He tried to kill us, I am almost certain, by setting Julia's cottage on fire. And he must have murdered Shannon too. Perhaps he's taken Hannah as a threat, a signal to me that I must keep quiet about him.

My mobile rings. I snatch it up. It's Paul. Before I can speak, he is talking.

"Hi, Livy, I'm sorry to call on this line—I know you're probably leaving it clear for Hannah. I'm at work with Will—Dad roped me in to sort some files—but I'm done now, and I wondered if you'd like me to come over until Will's finished. I know he's upset and I'm sure you're the same." He pauses. "What do you say? I could just sit with you for a bit."

A sob rises in my guts. "Yes," I say. "Thank you, Paul."

He hangs up and I try Hannah yet again. I leave another message for her, this time in tears, begging her to call me if she can. I pace up and down the living room. Then a thought occurs to me and I run up to the chest of drawers in my bedroom. I go straight to the bottom drawer, where I shoved Hannah's revolting leopard-skin bra-and-thong set after confiscating it from her.

The underwear is gone.

A new panic clutches me. Did Hannah take the clothes away with her? Has someone been talking to her? Trying to persuade her to wear them?

Chaotic, terrifying thoughts career around my head. I rush into Hannah's own bedroom and start turning out her wardrobe and her drawers. To my relief, I find the leopard-skin lingerie almost immediately. At least she hasn't smuggled it away to wear for some secret meeting. And then it hits me that there could be other bits of underwear, things I don't know about, maybe even things that someone else has bought for her.

More agonized fears speed through my mind. Hannah looks so like Kara. Has the man who attacked us realized this? Has he somehow managed to groom her? Kidnap her? I can't believe it's possible—after all, he saw us in Shannon's Torquay flat only yesterday. But my mind is in free fall, my fears infinite.

A few minutes later, Paul arrives on his bike. He must have broken the speed limit the whole way here to have completed the journey so fast. I collapse into his arms on the doorstep, weeping uncontrollably. He ushers me indoors and pours us both a glass of Will's whisky. I take a sip, then wipe my fingers under my eyes and blow my nose.

Paul pats my hand. "She'll be fine, Livy. You know what kids are like."

I hesitate. The urge to tell Paul about the man who has tried to kill me is almost overwhelming. It's just hard to know where to begin.

"Thanks so much for coming over," I start.

"Please, Liv." Paul shrugs. "How long have we known each other? It's the least I can do. I mean, I know I'm not Julia, but you're still one of my oldest friends. How many other people can remember you when you had a perm and a riot grrrl T-shirt?"

I squeeze his hand, laughing in spite of myself.

"Not to mention that Hasselblad of yours." Paul sighs. "You were always taking pictures with that thing? Whatever happened to it?"

I shrug. Somehow not knowing where that camera has gotten to seems to sum up everything that's gone wrong with my life.

"Anyway." Paul clears his throat. "I know things are difficult here too. I mean with you and Will—that you're having . . . er, problems. That's why you called me earlier in the week, asking about Will, wasn't it?"

I look up. "Did Will say something?"

"No, it was Dad." Paul shakes his head wearily. "I mentioned the pair of you to him last night and he told me what happened in Geneva, what he saw. It was a big shock. I mean I wasn't there in Geneva myself, so I had no idea. You know I don't go on as many work trips as Mr. Polyglot."

A slight edge creeps into his voice as he makes this reference to Will, and it flits through my mind that maybe Paul resents the way Leo recently promoted Will to deputy managing director.

"Not that I'm complaining," he goes on quickly. "I love working directly with clients. Dad knows I'm not cut out for all that management and admin shit. Will's great at it—he's a born bureaucrat."

"Right," I say.

"Hey." Paul pats my arm. "I *introduced* you, remember? He's been an idiot, but if anyone can find a way through all this, the two of you can."

I nod, thinking back to that evening in the bar when Will and I met and how young we were then, all our lives ahead of us. I glance at my phone, willing it to ring. Will should be out of his meeting soon. Another twenty minutes, and we will definitely call the police.

"I don't remember . . . how long was Kara missing before they found her?" Paul asks, his voice low and sympathetic.

"Only a couple of hours," I say. "Julia realized she wasn't home as soon as she got back from the party. When Kara didn't answer her phone, Julia dialed 999 immediately. A jogger found Kara by the canal soon after that."

"Poor Julia." There's a faraway look in Paul's eye and I wonder if he is remembering their one night together all those years ago.

I think of Robbie's ugly version of Julia, then Damian's idealized one, and I'm gripped with a sudden desire to hear someone without an agenda give their verdict on my best friend.

"You did like her, didn't you?" I ask. "I mean I know you and she . . . that one time, but . . ."

Paul turns to me. "Julia was fun," he says firmly. "And she loved you and the kids very much." He pauses. "Having said that, she was *deeply* fucked up, all that sleeping around." For a second, a judgmental look flashes into his eyes; then his expression softens and he sighs. "Like I said, poor Julia. And poor you, I'm sure it's even worse to be worrying when it's a child."

I bite my lip. Again, I'm on the verge of telling Paul everything.

My phone rings. I grab it, heart thudding.

Please be Hannah.

But no name flashes up on the screen. Just the words NUMBER WITHHELD.

I snatch the cell to my ear.

"Hello?" I say. "Who is this?"

JULIA

I cannot believe in a God who wants to be praised all the time.
—Friedrich Nietzsche

I admit it, I didn't see Julia coming. See, I can do humble! I knew her well, of course, but I had no idea that she had persisted in trying to track down her best friend's killer for eighteen years. Unbelievable tenacity. Still, that was Julia: a strange creature—as warped as she was clever, as ugly inside as she was beautiful outside, as unhappy as she was full of zest for life.

My first warning came when I discovered, several days after the event, that my box had been tampered with and Kara's locket was gone. I knew straightaway who had taken it—and why—for money, of course. I confronted the thief, comforted only slightly by the knowledge that I had previously told them the box belonged to someone else—someone the thief disliked and mistrusted. I demanded to know where the locket was now. I was told it had been sold anonymously on eBay, though not that it was that slut, Shannon, who had done the selling. The thief, fearing reprisals, was careful not to mention her name. However, the lowlife did confess to having been found and interrogated by Julia just a couple of hours before. My fury grew as I realized that the thief had passed on the name of the person who supposedly owned both box and locket, that Julia therefore almost certainly thought she knew the identity of Kara's killer, and that she was, in consequence, only a heartbeat away from discovering my own identity.

I acted immediately. Julia was not the victim I would have chosen, but fate had placed her in my path and I made a challenge for myself out of her murder: I had faked accidents before, and driven girls to suicide. But this time I would fake the suicide itself. I knew Julia had been researching fashion industry suicides—we'd even talked about it a few months before—how she'd researched the different methods, how certain drugs were actually quite easy to find on the Internet.

Armed with both the brochure and the Nembutal itself, I went to her flat. Avoiding the security camera at the end of the road, I crept in through the main front door, up to where she lived. She didn't really want to let me in, but when I told her I had just found out about Kara's murderer too and wanted her advice about what to do next, she relented. This was a cunning move on my part because, of course, I knew Julia was facing exactly the same dilemma herself. If Livy had only answered her phone that evening, the news would have been out. A thrill shuddered through me as I realized how nearly too late I was.

Julia was deeply agitated. We sat down. I asked for a Jack Daniel's. Disgusting drink. As I've mentioned before, I prefer a single malt. But I knew Julia would have a bottle of Jack on the go. She always did. And of course, once I told her my own "discovery" regarding that darn locket, she explained, with evident relief, what she knew too (though leaving out any mention of Shannon). Our stories matched up. Well, of course they did. I was the source of all the information! Poor Julia. She was so nearly there, so right in so many respects. And yet, in the end, she had arrived at the wrong conclusion.

She still lied to me about where the locket was. Perhaps by that point, she was starting to suspect me, or perhaps deceiving people was simply second nature to her, but she strongly implied the locket was buried in a safe place and that no one except her would ever find it. Of course, in reality Shannon— who had been too suspicious to bring the trinket to their meeting two days before—still had it.

I had already slipped the odorless Nembutal into her drink, and soon after she died where she sat, on the sofa. I wiped surfaces, checking for hairs and fibers. But I hadn't touched her. I was clean. I deleted all the Kara files on her computer and added the suicide note, placed the brochure on Nembutal on her desk; then I left as carefully as I'd arrived, taking all the Kara papers and—as usual—a small memento.

And that, I thought, was that. Done. Over.

I didn't have the locket, but I was certain that no one would be looking for *it. I was also certain no one would question Julia's "suicide." However, on both those counts, I miscalculated.*

Never mind. I have already retrieved the locket.

And, soon, I will deal with those who persist in searching for it.

CHAPTER SEVENTEEN

"Hello, Livy?" It's a woman's voice.

"Yes?" I'm thrown. All my thoughts are with Hannah. I need to get whoever this is off the phone as fast as possible. Paul is watching me across the kitchen table, his eyes wide with concern. "Who is this?"

"It's Sally Collins, Romayne's mum. Er, Hannah asked me to call you."

I jump to my feet. "Is Hannah with you? Is she okay?"

"Yes, yes, she's fine. We've been out shopping. I understand you've left a few messages on her phone. I'm terribly sorry that she didn't let you know what she was doing. Both girls swore blind to me that you knew exactly where we were."

Relief shudders through me, my limbs turning to rubber. I sink into the chair. Across the table, Paul catches my eye. He points to his phone and I nod, knowing he is going to call Will and give him the news.

"Please can you put Hannah on the phone?" I ask.

There's a short pause, the sound of muffled voices. I brace myself, ready to insist on Hannah talking to me if she refuses, as she did yesterday. She is clearly scared of my reaction—hence her persuading poor Sally to make this call.

But moments later, Hannah herself comes on the line. "Mum?" She sounds weepy.

"Oh, Hannah, sweetheart, thank God you're all right. You had us both so, so worried."

There's a silence on the other end of the phone. Then Hannah says in a tiny voice: "Daddy's really angry with me, isn't he?"

"We both are, sweetie," I say, trying to put some steel in my voice. Paul has left the room now. I can hear him talking to Will in the hall. "But you know what we are *most* of all . . . what we have been since we started calling you . . . is *scared.*"

"But I didn't pick up your messages. We were in Top Shop and—"

"It's not about not answering, Hannah—it's about going off in the first place. Think about it from our point of view. You're our little girl and you ran off and—"

"But I'm *twelve,*" she interrupts, sounding more like her usual truculent self.

"I know," I say, trying to sound soothing. "I know you're more grown-up than either of us realize, but it's still a big deal to catch the train and go all that way on your own, and anyway, you didn't have our permission to do it."

"I sent Granny a text."

"Leaving a note and asking permission are not the same thing." I make my voice as conciliatory as possible. "You know that. You're a smart girl. Come on, you know this was unacceptable, don't you?"

"Yes, Mum." Hannah's voice is tiny. She sounds very fragile. "I'm sorry."

I pause. "So where are you?"

Hannah sniffs. "Princesshay," she says. "At a pizza place."

"Well, I want you home now," I say gently but firmly. "I'll come and get you."

"Can't Romayne's mum bring me home? We'll be leaving as soon as we've had lunch. We've already ordered the pizzas."

I hesitate, weighing up the pros and cons of this. On the one hand, I want Hannah back as soon as humanly possible. Partly because I've been so worried, but also because she needs to know she can't just run away without there being some consequences. Plus, it's what Will will want. On the other hand, she will get home faster if someone brings her than if I have to drive to Princesshay.

"Let me speak to Romayne's mum again," I say.

I can hear the clank of plates and scrape of chairs as she walks to her table and hands the phone over. Sally comes on the line.

She immediately offers to bring Hannah home as soon as their meal is over, apologizing again for not having realized Hannah hadn't cleared the outing with me. I thank her, then get off the phone and let out a relieved sigh as Paul walks back into the kitchen.

"Will asks if you'll call him," he says. "He says his meeting's just ended."

"Okay, thanks."

Paul picks up his jacket off the back of his chair. "She's all right, then?"

I nod.

"Good." He hesitates.

"You don't have to rush off," I say. "Really."

Paul gives me a rueful smile. "I have some work to do," he says. "Then I'm heading over to Dad's. Martha's still away. And . . . so is Becky, as you know, so . . . but call me if there's anything I can do, or if you just need a shoulder to cry on." He pauses. "I know Will and I are in the office together, but he hasn't said anything and, well, you were my friend first, Liv. I hope it doesn't come to that, but if you two can't sort things out, then I'm here for *you*. Anytime. Understand?"

"Thanks, Paul." I give him a hug, then walk him to the door. "Say hi to Leo."

Paul drives off on his bike and I call Will. He is still angry, though I can hear the relief in his voice as I relate my phone conversation with Hannah.

"I have to take *another* bloody conference call with yet more Germans in ten minutes, but I'll come home straight after." He pauses. "We need to talk, Liv."

"About Hannah?"

"And about us."

"Okay," I say. "Later. Tonight."

I feel sick to my stomach at the prospect of the conversation we are likely to have.

I call Mum next, reassuring her that Hannah is fine. She sounds a bit shaky, but she holds back from crying though I can hear she's close to it. Her tone becomes more distant as she talks. I know she's thinking about Kara, but she doesn't say so out loud and neither do I. As we skirt around the memories that fill both our minds, I think of Damian's phrase again:

Your life isn't small—you've just got too used to living at the edges of it.

Maybe that's a way of life I learned from Mum. It's certainly how the two of us behave when we're together.

After a minute or two, Zack takes the phone. He, unlike Mum, is openly weepy and saying he wants to come home. I speak to Mum again, apologizing for disrupting our time together with the kids. Mum brushes this off as unimportant under the circumstances. I tell her that either Will or I will drive over soon to pick up Zack, then phone Will.

He offers to go for Zack immediately after his conference call. I agree, saying I'll wait in for Hannah.

"We'll all be at home for supper," I say, trying to sound cheerful.

"Yeah, happy bloody families," Will says with a sigh.

He sounds so miserable. A sob rises inside me. Maybe it's good Will and I are falling apart like this. Maybe we need things to come to a head so that they can be resolved once and for all. Because—and I have to face this—it's impossible for me to trust him, ever again.

My thoughts stray to Damian. I wonder how he's doing. I think about calling him, just to try to put all the pieces we've discovered in some kind of context. But before I do, I want a cup of tea—Paul pouring me that scotch was a nice idea, for a couple of sips, but I can't take hard liquor at this time of day—and the only milk in the fridge is going bad. Plus, there's no food for supper. I don't have my purse and cards, of course, and I can find very little cash in the house, so I rummage around for an old bank card from a sole account in my maiden name that I hardly ever use. Then I get dressed quickly in jeans and a long-sleeved top. It's much cooler than it was earlier; the rain that fell when Damian and I left the cathedral seems to have cleared the air.

I drive to Sainsbury's. I have only another twenty minutes before Hannah will be back, so I'm scuttling past the stacks of pet food, heading to the dairy section, when a familiar figure turns the corner just in front of me.

"Leo, hi." Will's boss is the last person I am expecting—or wanting—to see, but I force a smile on my face as I greet him. "What are you doing here? I thought you were in the office with Will?"

"Just left!" he booms. "Popped in here on the way home." Leo's eyes express genuine warmth. He's dressed in corduroy slacks and an open-neck shirt. Tufts of gray chest hair poke out from the carefully ironed cotton. "Will told me about Hannah. Thank *God* she's okay." He shakes his head. "Kids . . . honestly. Poor Will, I couldn't believe he managed to remember any of his German this afternoon, but he did. He's an asset, a brilliant asset."

I can feel my cheeks burning at this show of admiration for Will. Desperate to change the subject, I find myself saying that it seems weird to have bumped into Leo in a supermarket. Leo looks slightly confused, but points out that I shouldn't be *that* surprised to see him, as he and Martha live just ten minutes away, albeit in the opposite direction from my own house.

"It's not that," I confess, blushing slightly. "It's more that I've never imagined you doing any food shopping."

Leo laughs, a rich belly laugh. "Well, Martha's still away, so I'm fending for myself this weekend. I was out last night." He lowers his voice, his tone confiding, though he is still speaking much more loudly than I am. "Had *far* too much to drink. Paul's coming over later to watch the football and grab some takeout." He holds up his basket in which nestles some tins of cat food, a box of tea, and a bag of salad. He points to the lettuce leaves. "Health kick."

"Right, yes, Paul said he was going to see you later." I explain how Paul came round to give me some moral support.

"Good lad," Leo says approvingly. "He's very loyal to his friends. Always has been."

Loyal, unlike Will.

I can see Leo clocking the shadow that must pass over my

expression. At once, his own face falls. "Sod it, Livy, I can't leave without talking about this," he says suddenly. "I'm sorry Martha told you about . . . about what happened in Geneva."

I stare at him. He knows? Martha was adamant she wasn't going to tell him she'd spoken to me.

"I guessed she told you," Leo says with a grimace. "You can't be married to someone for fifteen years without knowing when they're keeping something from you."

"Right." I smile at the irony of this remark. "I hope you weren't too hard on Martha—she was just trying to be a friend."

"To be honest, I'm more concerned about you." Leo pauses. "When my first wife and I broke up, my world fell apart. I was devastated. Didn't see Paul for ages." He shakes his head. "I know there's no comparison, but I do understand the hurt."

Tears spring to my eyes at his kindness. I turn away, humiliated and touched. "Don't be nice to me," I whisper. "You'll make me cry."

"Oh, Livy." Leo shakes his head sadly. "Will's a fool. I wish I hadn't seen what I saw. . . ." He trails off, and I remember what Martha told me again: Will and Catrina, kissing good-bye as Will left her hotel room.

I close my eyes against the image. I feel so stupid. So unbearably stupid. And in that moment, I know that I have to leave Will. I can't give him another chance and retain any self-respect. It won't be good for the children, but neither will a browbeaten, desperately unhappy mother. Maybe I *have* gotten too used to living at the edges of my life. Well, as of today, I'm walking right back into the center of it, changing the way I look at everything, including my family.

You go, girl, I can hear Julia drawl. *Just remember you can't teach an old dogma new tricks.*

"What are you going to do?" Leo's forehead is creased with a deep frown. His expression is so kind and fatherly that a tear escapes my eye and trickles down my cheek. If only Dad were here. It's years since he died, but at times like this, when I really need his solid, common-sense affection, I miss him as much as ever. Across the aisle, a man struts self-consciously toward a stack of speciality teas. As I watch

250

him, I think of Will's easy, laidback stroll, and my heart seems to shrivel in my chest.

"I don't know," I whisper. "I just don't know."

Suddenly everything Damian and I have been doing, trying to find out what really happened to Julia, seems utterly pointless. Nothing we find out will bring her back. Nothing can turn back the clock.

Nothing can make Will and me whole again.

Leo pats my arm; his hand is large and heavy. "Give me and Martha a call if there's anything we can do." He leans over, pecks me on the cheek, then leaves.

His kindness is touching—yet my overwhelming feeling is one of humiliation.

And loss.

I make it to the dairy counter before I break down. I stand, pretending to examine the ice cream boxes in the freezer. Tears stream down my face. The pain fills my entire body. I hold myself together, resisting the desire to collapse onto the floor and wail and howl. How can Will have done this? Images of him and Catrina fill my head. I can't bear it. I see them kissing, her taking her clothes off for him, his eyes full of hunger and lust. I feel like I'm going mad. That I *will* go mad.

"Stop it." I say the words out loud, willing the images away. I force myself to focus on the ice cream tubs below me. Zack likes strawberry. Hannah prefers chocolate. I'm about to take one of each when I spot the Neapolitan. That's good. Will and I can eat the vanilla section.

One last supper, I think, before I tell him to leave the house for good.

Hannah puts her knife and fork together and pushes her plate away. For once, she has eaten everything—I made stew and mashed potatoes—and sat meekly throughout the meal. However, despite the peace, I'm not at all sure her behavior is a good sign. She didn't talk back when Will arrived home with Zack and told her, stern and unsmiling, that she was grounded for a week and must never run off without telling us where she is going again. I think he handled her well, not coming down too hard but setting solid boundaries. Hannah kept her head bowed throughout, then scuttled off to her room. She looks preoccupied and miserable now. I resolve that when Will and I talk later, we must do so in the garage, where neither child will overhear us.

Zack is still eating, sauce stains all around his mouth. I reach over and wipe his lips with a piece of kitchen towel. He glances at me and beams, his eyes shining with happiness from under long, black lashes. I gaze at his round, fresh face and wish that I could keep him like this forever. The knowledge that, in a few more years, he will be a grunting, lanky, pimpled teenager is almost impossible to accept.

I look up. Will is watching me, his expression one of frustration. I frown, not understanding. Then Will picks up his plate and Hannah's and takes them to the counter above the dishwasher.

"I bought ice cream for dessert," I say.

"No thanks," Hannah says, getting up.

"Not for me." Will turns and leaves the room.

I glance back at Zack. He swallows his stew in a huge gulp.

"Is it strawberry?" he asks hopefully.

I fetch his ice cream and make myself a cup of tea. I can hear Hannah padding upstairs to her room. Will has switched on the TV in the living room. So much for our family dinner. Ten minutes of a shared meal, then we each fall back into our default groove. I chew on my lip. Maybe Will and me splitting up will have some positive—as well as negative—effects. It should certainly change these ruts and routines.

I load the dishwasher, wondering resentfully how I have let a situation build where I both cook and wash up. Is it really my own fault? Sure, Will and I agreed when I gave up work that I would run the home while he focused on his career, but why does that mean he doesn't even help clean up? Yes, of course, I could always ask him to help—Hannah and Zack too—but why should I have to? Will should *see* I need a hand in the kitchen. He should *offer*.

I resentfully shove a plate into the dishwasher. Zack is swallowing his final spoonful of ice cream, the mess around his mouth now various shades of pink.

"Bathtime in twenty minutes," I say.

"Can I play *Temple Run*?"

"Sure."

He scampers off and I scrape the leftover stew into a Tupperware container and leave it on the counter, ready to put in the freezer.

The next hour creeps by. Will doesn't emerge from the living room, while I maneuver Zack into first his bath and then his pajamas. He falls asleep within seconds of me turning off the light.

I wander next door into Hannah's room and stand in the doorway. Hannah looks up from her bed, where she's sitting cross-legged and listening to music on her headphones. She switches off the music.

"Everything okay, Hanabana?" I ask.

This is Will's name for her, and as I speak, I'm braced, ready for Hannah to tell me not to call her that or to scowl and demand for the thousandth time that I leave her room. But Hannah does neither of those things. She simply nods and goes back to her music.

As I hear the faint hiss and slap of the beat behind me, I know that it's time for Will and me to talk. I go into the living room.

"Shall we?" I say.

Will looks at me, then switches off the TV without a word.

My heart thuds as he follows me out to the garage. It is cool, but bright under the artificial light out here. There's a smell of wood and gasoline. I stare at Will's stash of old bike mags, then down at the place where I found Julia's ring. It feels like my life, as I know it, is over. That after this conversation, everything will change forever.

CHAPTER EIGHTEEN

Will and I stand in the middle of the garage, facing each other. There's nowhere to sit, but that is a good thing. We shouldn't be too comfortable for this.

"So?" Will says.

"Catrina." The one word, hard and bright as glass. It sticks in my throat.

Will looks at me, his expression both angry and wary. "I already told you, Liv, I didn't sleep with her," Will says.

I stare at him, hate and humiliation welling in my guts. How can he look me in the eye and lie like that? "You were seen," I say. "In Geneva."

"What?" Will frowns. "What are you talking about? Seen where? Doing what? We *weren't* doing anything!"

"You left her hotel room in the middle of the night. You . . . you kissed her at the door." The image of Will and Catrina, locked together in the afterglow of their adultery cuts through me.

"Who told you that?" Will's frown deepens.

I say nothing, still reluctant to give up Martha and Leo as my sources.

Will shakes his head. "You're not making any sense. The first night, I only saw Catrina on the airplane and in the car to the hotel. She checked in before me and went up to her room. I don't even know *which* room. The second night, she was still in the bar when I went to bed. That was the night after Julia died. I was worried about you.

254

About the kids having, you know, seen her. I was upset I wasn't home, for God's sake. I wasn't even—"

"Leo saw you." My voice shakes as I speak. "Outside Catrina's room at about five A.M."

Will's eyes open wide. "*Leo* said that?"

I give him a brisk nod. "Martha did first—she told me what he told her. But I've spoken to Leo since. He confirmed it."

Silence. Will looks dumbstruck. "I don't . . . I can't imagine . . . what Leo thinks he saw, but whatever it is, he's wrong."

"He saw you kissing."

"No." Will's voice rises. "No, I *swear*. That didn't happen."

I breathe out, a long, slow sigh. So he can't even give me this. He can't even admit his guilt.

Will is shaking his head, pulling his phone out of his pocket. "Leo can tell *me* what he thinks he saw. I don't believe this."

"No," I say, "that's not fair on Leo. Or Martha."

"Not fair on—?" Will glares at me as he clutches his mobile. "What about what's fair on *me* . . . on *us*? They're lying, Liv, or . . . or you've misunderstood . . . or—"

"I *haven't*." A poisonous cocktail of emotions swirls in my stomach, making me feel sick. I feel utterly humiliated, guilty that Leo will be put in such a horribly awkward position, furious with him for bringing me this terrible news, beyond furious with Will for cheating and then lying. And through it all, the agony of betrayal. The toolbox catches my eye. I remember Julia's ring. And in that moment, I'm certain Will's crime goes way beyond his betrayal of me.

"Julia found out too, didn't she?" I ask. "Did she know about Catrina? Or was it someone else?"

"No." Will raises his phone to his ear. "Julia didn't know *anything*. There was . . . *is* . . . nothing to know."

"Why did you take her ring, then?"

"I *didn't*—"

"So why haven't you sent it back to Robbie like you said you would?"

255

"I FedEx-ed it to Joanie in Bridport. *Jesus.*" Will lowers his phone. "Leo's mobile is switched off. I'm calling the house." He scrolls down, making the new call.

I chew on my lip. I don't think I have ever felt worse in my life.

"Hi, Paul, it's Will. . . . Yes, I'm fine. . . . Is Leo there?"

I hold my breath, waiting for Paul to pass the phone to Leo. They should both be there. When I saw them earlier, Leo said they were staying in with takeout for dinner.

"When will Leo be back? Right." Will nods at whatever Paul is saying. "Fine, I'll try him later." He snaps his phone off. "Leo's out until late. Paul doesn't know where."

I let out my breath. I can't decide whether I'm relieved or not that Leo either has changed his plans or, more likely, isn't prepared to take Will's call.

"Never mind Leo, you're making everything ten times worse by not admit—"

"How could it be ten times worse, Livy?" Will's voice rises again. "Tell me how this situation could be *any* fucking worse?"

I swallow hard. "I just—"

"I know we're in a bad place, that things have been difficult for a while," Will says. "I know you don't . . . *haven't* . . . trusted me for a long time." He rubs his forehead.

"I did." Emotion swells inside me. "I *did* trust you, and you've made an idiot of me." My voice cracks.

"Why don't you believe me?" Will asks, his voice almost as broken as mine.

"Because . . . how can I?"

"So you'll take Leo's word over mine?"

"Leo has no reason to lie to me."

"Unlike me, you mean?" Will says. "Liv, I'm *not* lying."

We stare at each other.

"You lied before," I say. "You lied six years ago."

"But that was different," Will insists. "You *know* that was different. Back then, it was just after Zack and . . . *God,* Livy, you were so

256

obsessed with him. It was like I didn't matter. Like you fell in love with being his mother, and all I was . . . was a walking wallet."

I turn away. I remember clearly Will's complaints at the time about existing in the family only to fund it. It was never true—not for me, anyway. And it's not relevant. Not to what we're talking about now.

"Don't make this about me," I say. "You *love* being at work. You *enjoy* what you do. You always have."

"It's not that black-and-white." Will sighs. "Come on, Liv. Do you really think I *want* to be at work all the time? I'd love to be able to spend more time here. I look at you and I *envy* the fact that after the kids and the house, you can snatch yourself an hour here and there if you want. You could even get back into photography—or do that master's you used to talk about."

I stare down at the dusty floor. "It's not that easy."

"It's not easy for me either," Will goes on. "It's horrible not to be trusted."

Irritation roils inside me. I look up. "Well, whose fault is that?"

"Don't you think I *know* it's my fault? Don't you think I haven't regretted what happened for the past six years? I thought things were getting better, but now . . . now . . ."

I have the sense of us both, teetering on a cliff edge, held back only by the magnitude of the jump ahead.

"It's not working," I say.

"I know."

We look at each other.

"Do you still love me?" Will asks. "Because I still love you."

A lump lodges itself in my throat. "I don't know," I admit.

Will nods, the fire of his anger dying in his eyes. Another long silence stretches between us. I feel hollow inside, as if all the hope and life of our relationship have burned to ashes. Everything I touch dies. Kara. Julia. My marriage.

"I want you to move out," I say.

"No, Livy, for God's sake. I haven't even had a chance to talk to Leo yet. Find out what he's playing at. You can't—"

"You can't tell me what to do, Will. You've thrown it away. You've fucking thrown everything we had away." I spit out the last words. My stomach is churning, my guts a sea of acid. Everything is poison.

Will stares at me, his mouth trembling with hurt and anger.

"We need a break, at least," I say.

"What about the kids?" Will glares at me. "I don't want to do this, Liv. Surely we—"

"We need to see how we feel apart. I'm not saying you can't come around. See the kids whenever you—"

"Jesus Christ!" Will explodes. "Don't start talking about when I can see the kids. It's—"

"It's the only way." I stare at him, knowing my eyes are hard even as my insides are crumbling. He won't admit it. He won't give us a way of working through things. I don't trust him. Can't ever trust him now.

"Fine," Will snarls. "I'm going to a hotel. I'll tell the kids it's work. But I want them tomorrow. And I want them *here*. You can stay in the hotel tomorrow. Or with that boy toy of Julia's. Or wherever you fucking want."

I open my mouth to protest, but before I can speak, Will storms out. I stand in the middle of the garage, numb. For a moment it feels like the room, the house, the world is turning circles inside my head. Will has left the door to the kitchen open. I can hear him cross the hall, his feet on the stairs. Two . . . three minutes pass. Then he's stomping down the stairs. Across the hall. The front door shuts. A firm click. He's gone.

I sink to the floor. The little Thomas the Tank Engine boot is on its side in front of the toolbox where I found Julia's ring. It reminds me of Zack. And Hannah. And how Will—how Will and I together—are about to shatter their lives. I haven't told him anything that Damian and I found out about Julia. I haven't told him about the fire or Shannon's death. And it is remembering how much I wanted him at my side earlier, when I felt so vulnerable, that brings me, finally, to a bawling mess, my cheek cold against the dirty floor, my heart shattering into a million tiny pieces.

The next morning passes in a daze. Both kids sleep late, though in Zack's case, this only means until eight o'clock. I barely sleep at all, partly because of everything that's happening with Will and partly out of fear for my and the kids' safety. I get up several times to check that every door and window is properly locked.

At eleven, Zack is picked up for an outing to Paignton Zoo with his friends Noah and Barney and Barney's parents. I let him go with severe misgivings. Yesterday's scare with Hannah may have had nothing to do with Julia's murderer, but the man who followed Damian and me is still out there. I'm certain, though I have no proof, that he killed Shannon and my sister as well as Julia. And he set fire to the cottage while Damian and I were still inside it.

He knows who I am; he could know everything about me. I'm not safe, which means my children aren't either. Yet, in the sunny light of this summer's day, I can find no logical reason to stop Zack from going out. After all, the fire was now two days ago, and there has been no further threat to me since then. Damian calls to make sure I am all right. He is still preoccupied with everything we have found out about Julia's last days and points out that in all the drama over Hannah, I never told him what I'd learned from Robbie.

I hesitate. I have given that conversation—and what it revealed—little thought since yesterday morning.

"What is it, Livy?"

I take a deep breath and tell him about Julia's will, the one Robbie claims to have destroyed.

"He says she left you everything, but the will was never registered with a solicitor, so—"

Damian gasps. "I had no idea she did that," he says, his voice swelling with emotion.

I believe him. After all, if he'd known about the will, he would surely have told the police to look for it. He certainly wouldn't have killed Julia for her money before making sure he was definitely going to inherit it. Anyway, right now, I have to trust someone.

I don't tell Damian about Will and me, however. I haven't told anyone about that. It's far too early to upset Mum with the news, and I don't want the pity I know I'll get from any of my other friends. I would have confided in Julia at this point. Partly because she would have told me, straight off, that she was on my side, whatever I chose to do. And partly just because I always told her everything. Yesterday, Robbie almost spoiled the memories I have of Julia. I'm going to try to forget everything he said about her, and today I make a point of telling Damian how much I miss Julia's sharp wit and practical, hardheaded outlook on life.

He responds with his own stories of Julia's humor and support. How she kept him going when he lost three projects in a row and was starting to doubt his own abilities, how she made him laugh, how soft she was "on the inside, where nobody saw, Livy." It's hard to reconcile Damian's version of Julia with Robbie's. The truth is that I don't recognize my best friend in either of their portraits. And that knowledge leaves me more depressed than ever.

Our conversation turns to what we should do next. Damian has at last come round to the idea that I should talk to the police, though he is still reluctant to go himself.

"I know we've got no evidence, but everything we've found out *must* add up," he says. "Shannon's death. The fire. The guy who followed us. You're going to have to tell the police everything. Let them take over." He hesitates. "You're going to have to tell them about Will taking Julia's ring."

Despair crawls through my veins again at the thought of Will's angry face. I don't want to talk to the police about Julia. I don't want to talk to anyone. However, I agree to meet Damian later—after all, if Will was serious about having the kids here tonight, then I will have to find somewhere else to go anyway. I'm aware Will and I can't keep such a situation going for very long, but right now I can't think beyond tonight.

I end my call with Damian, only to have my cell ring again almost immediately. It's Robbie.

"Hi, Livy." His voice is breathy and expectant. It turns my stomach.

"Hi . . . sorry, Robbie, it's not a good time."

"Okay, sure, sure. I can call later. I just . . . I wanted to tell you how wonderful it was to see you yesterday. I wondered if you wanted to meet later on. Perhaps a drink?"

I shake my head, amazed at his confidence. "Thanks, Robbie, but I'll have to call you back."

"Sure, sure." He lets me go.

I sit on the sofa, put down my phone, and rest my head in my hands. I can't think straight. My head is full of fog. Robbie is the last thing I need. Hannah drifts in to the living room. To my surprise, she comes over and curls up beside me. I put my arm around her tentatively. We sit in silence for a minute; then Hannah uncurls, stretching out like a cat.

"Can I go over to Romayne's?" she asks.

So that was what her show of affection was about. Cupboard love, as my mother would say. I feel irritated. "No, Hannah. You're grounded for the rest of the week. Dad explained all that yesterday."

Hannah sits upright, a mutinous downturn to her mouth. "That's not fair," she pouts.

I shake my head. "That's how it is." I walk off, into the kitchen.

Hannah trails after me, complaining. We end up shouting. Hannah flees the room in hysterical tears. The next thing I hear is her bedroom door slamming upstairs. I spend the next hour sitting at the kitchen table. I don't seem to be able to move. In the end I register that I am hungry, that I haven't eaten anything since yesterday's dinner, so I make a slice of toast for lunch. I manage only half of it. Hannah still hasn't reappeared.

The doorbell rings. I drag myself to the door in a fog of misery. Paul is standing on the doorstep. The sun is shining, though the sidewalk outside glistens wetly. I hadn't even been aware it rained earlier. Paul smiles. His teeth are very white, his trousers pressed, and his shirt crisp. He looks fresh and rested. I, on the other hand, am wearing a loose top over sweatpants and no makeup. My hair feels lank about my face. I shield my eyes from the sun, now embarrassed by the state of my appearance on top of everything else.

"Are you all right?" Paul says gently.

"Yeah, just haven't got my 'It Girl' look together yet."

Paul chuckles. "You sound like Julia. Um, but you look like shit."

"Cheers. No, seriously, I'm fine."

He tilts his head to one side. "I'm not sure I believe you." He smiles again. A warm smile, full of concern.

It completely undoes me, and before I know where I am, the tears are streaming down my face again. Paul frowns, then puts his arm lightly across my shoulders and steers me across the hall and back into the kitchen. I'm hiccupping, desperate to stop crying, hideously embarrassed. And yet relieved to be letting out some of the pain that I feel. Paul sets me in a chair and fetches a piece of kitchen towel from the counter. He passes it to me, then walks over to the sink and fills the kettle.

"Tea or coffee?" he asks.

"Tea, thanks." I sniff, then blow my nose. "God, Paul, I'm so sorry."

"Don't." Paul turns from the fridge, a carton of milk in his hand. "Don't apologize. I know how awful this is, what's happening with you and Will."

It's not just my marriage.

As Paul fetches mugs and makes a pot of tea, I try to work out how on earth to begin telling him what I know: that Julia was almost certainly murdered because she found out who Kara's killer was, that the killer knows I am on his trail, that he is almost certainly someone I know.

Paul sits down opposite me. He places the steaming teapot on the table between us.

"Will called last night. Dad wouldn't speak to him—I pretended he was out."

"I know. Paul, listen."

"Then Will came round. He was furious."

"What?" Images of a fight spring into my mind's eye: Will's face screwed up in anger, blood on his knuckles. "Will went to Leo's house? What happened?"

"He stood on the doorstep, yelling his head off, hammering on the door."

My eyes widen. "Oh my God, did Leo talk to him? Did you?"

"No." Paul shakes his head. "We didn't even go to the door, just sat in the living room until he gave up and went away."

I let my head sink into my hands. What a mess.

Paul clears his throat. "Liv?" he says. "Can I tell you something?"

"Sure." I blow my nose again and look up.

"Becky and I are having problems too," he says. "So I know what it's like. I wanted to tell you yesterday, but it seemed . . . I dunno, inappropriate with everything over Hannah."

He's joking, surely. I stare at him, remembering the way he and Becky had their arms around each other at Leo's party.

"You two?" I say. "It didn't look like you had problems the last time I saw you."

"Becky and I are good at putting on a show for everyone else, but the truth is she hasn't gone to Spain to be with her parents. She's there to get away from me, a . . . a trial separation. I talked to her yesterday. She said she was even thinking about divorce."

"No." My mouth drops open.

"I'm afraid so," Paul says, a rueful note to his voice. "We didn't want to spoil Dad's party by letting the cracks show, but . . ."

"You're kidding."

"Nope."

My mouth is still gaping. I can't believe I didn't see any sign of problems in their relationship. "But how . . . *Why?* What *happened*?"

"I don't know." Paul shrugs. "I still love her, but she says I don't listen to her, don't notice her . . . that she's tired of being the one making all the effort. Usual old clichés." He pauses. "Personally, I think it's more about Becky's life feeling empty, though she'd never admit it. She was always adamant she didn't want kids, but I think it's hard when so many of her friends have become mums in the past few years." He looks at me. "I often wondered why you two were friends, you're so different. Becky's all dynamic, no soft edges. . . . She goes straight after what she wants."

263

"Whereas I skirt around the edges of life?" It's hard to keep the bitter tone from my voice. Have I really lived this vicariously since Kara died? Experiencing my life through Julia's adventures—or Will's status at work—or the kids?

"No." Paul's face reddens. "I didn't mean it as a diss. You're fantastic, Livy. A brilliant wife. A wonderful mother . . ."

"Right."

Silence falls between us. I don't want to think about the implications of what Paul has said; his words echo Damian's too strongly. Instead, I turn my mind back to that party at Leo and Martha's just a few weeks ago, and how envious then I'd felt of Paul and Becky. You really can't understand other people's relationships.

"I'd never have guessed about you two in a million years," I say.

"Yeah, well . . ." Paul pours the tea. His phone beeps. "I just thought it might help to know that all marriages go through bad patches."

"Our situation is different." I sniff. "It isn't the first time Will's done this. And we have two children whose lives will be devastated. . . ."

"I know." Paul checks his phone. "All the more reason to hang in there, wouldn't you say?" He stands up. "Sorry, Liv, I've got to go. I'm staying in one of my mum's houses while the builders are doing up ours. Mum wants me to check on some damp or something." He pauses. "Actually, Becky and I are doing up the house to sell it on. We talked about that last night too."

"Paul, I'm so sorry." The words seem entirely inadequate.

"Thank you," he says with a sigh. "Er, I really do have to go."

I stare at the mugs on the table between us. "What about your tea?"

Paul makes a face. "Rain check. Take care." He swoops down, planting a kiss on the side of my head. "Don't get up, I'll see myself out. Call you soon. And don't forget, I'm here for you. Anytime."

He leaves. I take a sip of tea. It's perfect, just the right strength. Will always pours it too fast, while I tend to forget I've made it and end up drinking it cold. As I put my mug down, my engagement ring clinks against the china. It feels loose on my finger, just as my pants

264

feel loose against my hips. An image of Julia's diamond and emerald ring flashes into my head. I still don't know how that ended up in Will's possession. I still don't know what Julia found out about Kara's killer. Or who killed her.

A few minutes later, Hannah reappears from her room with her phone held triumphantly aloft. "Dad says I can go to Romayne's," she says.

"What?" I take the phone. Will confirms he has relented on Hannah's punishment. This is so unlike him that I can only believe he is doing it to set himself up as the "good cop" parent and to defy me. I'm itching to accuse him of undermining me—as well as to ask what the hell he thought he was doing, going round to Leo's and banging on his front door last night—but Hannah is standing here, all excited. "Fine," I say. "I'll drop you off in an hour or so." Hannah skips around the room, delighted. I turn to Will, still on the phone. "You can pick her up later," I say, my voice tight. "Zack will be home at six or so. D'you want me to wait in for him, or will you be here by then?"

"I'll be there," Will says quietly. "You don't need to be."

"Right," I say. "There's food in the fridge, so I'm sure you'll manage tonight without me. If it's what you want."

"None of this is what I want," he says coldly.

We say good-bye and ring off. My guts twist as I hand Hannah back her phone. I almost call Will again to tell him I don't want this either. Then I remember Catrina and how he can't even admit to the resumption of their affair. There's no point in speaking.

I put on a brave face while I drop off Hannah, but tears stream down my face as I drive home. I feel like such a failure. I check the time as I park in the road outside the house. It's just after 5 P.M., and the temperature has dropped sharply, all traces of yesterday's humidity gone. I get out of the car but hesitate instead of walking straight up the path to the front door. The air is cool against my hot cheeks. The house is going to feel so alone. *Jesus,* how can my world be disintegrating like this? I lean against the gate that leads onto the front path. My limbs feel heavy; my head feels light. I haven't eaten anything today except half a slice of toast. The thought of food makes me feel nauseated.

I stand up, taking a deep breath. Whatever happens, I'm going to have to be strong for the kids.

But now I know the things I know, and do the things I do. And if you do not like me so, to hell my love, with you.

Julia's sharp tongue sounds in my ear with one of her favorite Dorothy Parker quotes. I almost manage a smile. Somehow, I will survive this.

I turn, ready to open the gate. From nowhere, a chill prickles down my spine. I have the strong sense I'm being watched. I whip around, peering up and down the road. I catch a shadow, a shape, moving quickly, ducking behind a van across the road.

I stare for a second, holding my breath; then a young woman in a T-shirt and shorts emerges from behind the van. Very skinny, with lank, straggly brown hair. She fixes her gaze on me as she crosses the road.

I'm rooted to the spot. I don't feel threatened—she's shorter and slighter than I am and there's something cowed, defeated about the way she holds herself. A low rumble of thunder sounds in the far distance as the girl reaches the sidewalk and walks up to me.

Close up, I can see she is in her late twenties or early thirties, with terrible skin, all acne and pockmarks.

"You're Livy, aren't you?" she says. Her voice is surprisingly middle-class. Her face is puffy and pasty, and she is definitely way, way too thin.

"How do you know my name?"

"I've got something you want," she says, scratching her arm as she speaks.

I glance down. Track marks run up and down the inside of her arm. I take a step away. She's a junkie.

"Don't go," she says. It's a plea, not an order.

I look into her eyes. They're haunted. Miserable. There's a tarnished chain around her neck. The letter *P* dangles from the end.

"What's your name?" I ask.

She stares at me, blinking.

"Does it begin with *P*?"

She says nothing.

"*P* for what?" I persist. "Penny? Patsy? Pippa?"

She shakes her head. Another rumble of thunder sounds in the distance. "It was me gave Shannon that locket you've been looking for," she says. "I came here to tell you where I got it. I was just waiting to ring on your door."

My head spins. Conflicting emotions fight in my head. She could be lying about the locket. Except, if she is, how the hell does she know about Shannon having it? Dammit, she's a drug addict. She's *got* to be lying. Still, I can't let it go. If she knows something, anything, I have to find out.

"Who are you? How do you know where I live?"

"It doesn't matter."

Could she be Kara's killer? She could be older than she looks. Still, surely she wouldn't be here, making claims, selling information, if she were a murderer.

"Tell me about the locket?" I ask. "What did it look like?"

"Silver," she says straightaway "With a picture of two girls inside."

"Okay, so where did you get it from?"

The girl scratches her arm again. "I'll tell you if you pay me," she says.

I hesitate. Money. Of course. She wants money.

"How do I know any of what you're saying is true?"

The girl shakes her head. Backs away.

"Wait." I reach out, grab her arm. She's all skin and bone. She winces. Then she twists out of my reach. "I just want money," she says. "Five hundred pounds."

I glance along the road, back toward our house. Panic surges through me. This girl is a drug addict, connected in some way to a killer. She knows who I am. Where I live. Where my children live. My throat is dry. The girl backs away again.

"Well?" she says.

"Wait, okay." I pull the bank card for my old, sole account from my pocket. "I don't have five hundred pounds on me, but I can go with you to an ATM."

The girl hesitates, then gives a quick, sharp nod. "Okay."

I head for my car, but she holds back. "I'm not getting in there with you."

"But . . ." My heart thuds painfully. A voice in my head is telling me I should walk away, not trust her, that she can't possibly really know anything. Still, she had Shannon's name, she described the locket. . . .

"Fine, we'll go to Fore Street, there's a cash machine there."

She nods. We walk off together. The girl says nothing. Her breathing is labored and I realize I'm going too fast for her. I try to slow down, but my body is jumping with anxiety, the same questions tumbling over and over in my mind: *What do you know? Where did you get the locket?* I contemplate calling Damian, but I don't want to frighten her away.

In a few minutes, we've reached the bank with the cash machine. I slide in my card. The girl stands beside me, and I cover the keypad with my hand as I put in the numbers—Kara's birth date. The money is issued and I grab it quickly. The girl draws closer.

"Please tell me who you are and where you got the locket."

She stares at me mutinously.

"Okay," I try again. "You don't want to tell me who you are, so tell me how you know Shannon."

She shakes her head again.

"You have to tell me something before I can give you any cash," I insist. "How did you get the locket? Why did you give it to Shannon?"

"I owed her money and she was getting heavy about it," the girl says reluctantly. "She got these big guys from a club to threaten me if I didn't pay her back."

I nod. This ties in with what Shannon herself told us. "What about the locket?"

"I found it."

"Where?"

"Where I've been staying."

"Which is *where*?" I demand.

"Money first," she says.

I count out one hundred pounds in twenties and hand them over.

"More," she says.

I give her another hundred. "Now tell me *where* you got the locket. Then I'll give you the rest."

The girl nods. She pockets the money carefully. I watch and wait, the gray sky pressing down, traffic fumes filling my nostrils, the air heavy and damp.

The girl takes a step away from me. Her lips curl into a snarl. I sense she's going to dart away and reach out to stop her.

"Fuck you." She kicks out, her foot making contact with my shin.

I clutch it, consumed by the pain for a couple of seconds. Then I force myself up. The girl is flying down the road. I take a step forward. Pain shoots through my shin. Gritting my teeth, I push myself on. The girl is heading for the bus stop.

She slows as I speed up. A bus is pulling up.

I have to catch her before she gets on board. I have to find out what she knows. I chase after her, running hard. Harder.

SHANNON

The wrath of God lies sleeping. It was hid a million years before men were and only men have the power to wake it.
                                        —Cormac McCarthy, *Blood Meridian*

When I found out that Shannon had my locket, I was very angry.

Angry with everyone.

Shannon herself, of course, but also Poppy for stealing it in the first place. And most of all with Julia, the sneaky, self-righteous little bitch.

I didn't find out Shannon had the locket for a long time. Poppy claimed that she had sold it anonymously on eBay. In fact, she had given it to Shannon as payment for one of her junkie debts, and it was Shannon who had put it online. Julia just told me she had seen the locket on eBay, and that it had taken her several days to track Poppy down .

As neither of them mentioned Shannon—who was in possession of the wretched thing all along—I assumed the transaction had been a direct trade between the two of them. I discovered the truth only when Livy started sniffing around. Between the three of them, they caused Shannon's death.

After following Livy into Shannon's Torquay flat, it was easy to trail her to that cottage of Julia's in Lympstone. I was furious I hadn't thought before that Shannon might be hiding out there.

Of course, the fire failed to kill any of them, but at least it destroyed all trace of Julia's belongings. Finding Shannon afterwards wasn't hard either. I'd been on her trail for over a week by that time, so I knew who her friends were. Shannon, predictably, turned for help to the nearest person. I was already watching out for her. Stupid whore.

That's how she made the money she spent on her fancy clothes and jewelry. . . . She was a highly paid prostitute. Alexa Carling fixed it up for her— she's a whore too. Still, I don't think Shannon liked the life despite all the money she made. I think she preferred her job at Honey Hearts, where she was free to entrap men, to take from them with nothing given in return.

Anyway, I followed Shannon when she slipped out to the shops. Told her I had a knife. Forced her into my car. Took her to the beach.

In the darkness, I did what had to be done, retrieved Kara's locket and took one of Shannon's Chanel earrings as a keepsake. Blah, blah . . . another easy kill, dressed up to look like an accident thanks to drink and drugs.

So Shannon is over. An unplanned event born out of necessity. I don't like being pushed or challenged.

Those responsible will pay.

Julia has already paid with her life.

For Livy, the price is going to be much higher.

CHAPTER NINETEEN

I pound along the sidewalk. The bus is already at the bus stop. The number 57 to Brixington. The girl jostles through the queue of elderly ladies easing themselves on board. Angry heads turn. I rush toward her. Almost there. The doors wheeze to a close and the bus pulls away.

The girl is on board. I race up to the stop, seconds too late. I slam my hand against the side of the shelter and bend over, panting.

"Shit."

All the other people standing here stare at me as if I'm a lunatic. But it's my life that's insane right now. So insane, in fact, that chasing after a drug addict demanding money for information seems an entirely logical thing to do. If that skinny, greasy-haired girl up ahead gave Shannon Kara's locket, then she must know something about who killed her. And, therefore, who killed Julia.

I can't let her get away. It starts to rain. The road is packed: shoppers bustling and weaving around each other. I peer along the road. The bus is right at the other end of it, but I'm certain I can see the girl peering out at me through the back window, her lank hair framing her anxious face. I watch, defeated, as the bus vanishes around the corner.

"In a hurry, my love?" An old man with a cane and a cheery, red face smiles at me.

I nod, grimacing.

"Never mind, eh."

But I do mind. My best chance to find out what really happened to Julia and Kara is vanishing before my eyes. I can't let this be it. I dash along the sidewalk to the little mini cab office. I hurtle inside.

"I need a cab. *Now,*" I say.

The young guy behind the counter eyes me nervously. "Ben!" he calls out. A middle-aged man with close-cropped gray hair saunters out from the back office.

"Where to?" he says cheerily.

"I just saw an old friend get on a bus," I say, the lie sliding off my tongue with frightening ease. "We lost touch, but we used to be really close. I have to try to find her. Please, hurry."

The two men look at each other; then the older man grins. "Car's outside, love. Let's go."

I explain which bus I saw the girl on. My driver knows its local route, and a few tense minutes later we see it up ahead.

"D'you want me to drop you so you can get on board?" he asks.

"Er, no," I say, blushing at how odd I sound. "I think I'd rather wait to see when she gets off."

"Okeydokey." The driver glances at his meter and drives on.

I strain my eyes, looking for a glimpse of the girl. She's still standing at the back of the bus, staring out of the side windows. I shrink back against my seat. I don't want the girl to see me, to know I'm following her.

On we drive. It turns out the bus goes to Topsham, then Lympstone—where Julia's cottage is. I keep my eyes focused on the girl. At every stop, my cabdriver slows. He must think I'm mad. I smooth down my hair, feeling self-conscious. We reach Lympstone, but the girl doesn't get off the bus. Past Lympstone, we zoom alongside fields, their flowers shiny yellow in the lowering light, and turn onto the main road into Exmouth.

I watch. And watch. Bus stops come and go. A drizzle sets in, the passing sidewalks gleam for a few seconds as the clouds part to allow sunshine through, then deaden again. The scrawny girl with the lank hair and the track-marked arms stays on the bus, though as it fills, I lose sight of her from my taxi.

Minute after minute passes, and I'm just starting to think I must have missed her somehow when the bus stops close to the center of Exmouth and the girl gets off. She looks around, her gaze shifty, then scuttles away, hunched over against the rain.

My phone rings as I shove some cash at my cabdriver and scramble out. It's Robbie.

For goodness' sake.

"Hi, Livy." His voice is warm and intimate. Far too intimate. "Can you talk? I was a bit worried about how we left things earlier. I—"

"I can't talk, Robbie," I snap. I'm beyond irritated, wound up like a spring and tired of being nice. "I explained earlier that I would call you when I could."

"I know, it's just—"

"You're not listening," I interrupt. "Please don't call me again." I flick the phone off.

The girl takes the right turn at the roundabout at the top of the road. I follow her, keeping my head down. I'm aware that if she turns around, she will see me immediately, but she doesn't. She takes a right, then a left. She's walking purposefully, like she's got a definite goal in mind. Or maybe she's just hurrying to a place where she can get out of the rain. It's still drizzling, a fine mist settling on my hair and my clothes.

The girl makes a sharp right turn. I peer around the corner after her. My heart thuds as I realize where we are: the building containing the Honey Hearts office is halfway down this road, and the girl is heading straight for it. A moment later she stops outside and jams her finger on the intercom buzzer. A voice answers. Male. I can't hear what he's saying, but the girl is speaking loudly.

"*Yes,* Honey Hearts on the second floor . . ."

I stiffen, remembering how Damian and I wondered if Shannon had originally been given Kara's locket from someone at the honey trap agency and if discovering this connection was what had brought Julia here. The scrawny girl doesn't look much like the other agents I've seen, but if she's not an agent, then what is she doing at Honey Hearts?

"There's no one on reception up there, but I know Mrs. Carling

274

is in." The girl is shouting now. "She *always* comes in on a Sunday afternoon to catch up on paperwork. Please let me in, she's my *mother*, for fuck's sake."

Alexa Carling is this girl's mother? My heartbeat quickens.

I edge closer. If the girl looks around, she'll see me, but she's pushing at the door, as if expecting it to be buzzed open. It stays firmly shut.

I reach the office block next to Honey Hearts. I duck behind the far wall, then peer carefully around it. The rain is getting heavier. I wipe a strand of damp hair out of my eyes.

The girl is hammering the door now with her fist. She swears out loud, then pulls a phone from the small plastic bag that swings from her hand. She presses at the buttons, making a call, then holds the mobile to her ear.

A second or two pass. The girl is huddled under the doorway. She makes a pathetic figure, white-faced, rocking slightly back and forth.

"Mum?" The girl's voice is harsh: hurt, trying not to cry. "I'm outside. That bastard security guard won't let me in."

There's a pause while whoever is on the other end of the line speaks.

"*Please,* Mum. I'm not going to—" The girl stops abruptly as the door opens.

A second later and she disappears inside.

I lean against the wall behind me and let out my breath in a slow, shaky sigh. I am close now, to answers. Everything comes back to that locket. And the locket keeps bringing me here. Honey Hearts is the connection between all the disparate elements that Damian and I have been struggling to make sense of since Julia died.

And yet I still don't understand how.

The rain falls harder, driving into my face like tiny knives. Water trickles down the back of my neck. Without stopping to think through what I'm doing, I march over to the front door of the office building. I press on the buzzer for the Honey Hearts office on the second floor. There's no reply, so I press the button marked MAIN RECEPTION.

"Yes?" It's the security guard who spoke to the girl.

275

"Hello." I give my maiden name, Small, as I did before. "I'm one of Mrs. Carling's, er, clients at Honey Hearts. I'm sorry to bother everyone on a Sunday, but I really need to speak to her. Please let me in so I can pop up to see her. It won't take long, but I have to see her now. It's an emergency."

I wait. A drop of rain threads its way down my cheek. There's a long pause. And then the door buzzes. I push at it, my chest tight with anticipation.

I'm in.

The security guard does a slight double take when he sees the state of me: wet through with bedraggled hair.

"I spoke to Mrs. Carling," he explains. "She's with someone right now, but she says she can see you in just a minute if you want to wait up in their reception."

"Thank you." I take the flight of stairs to the second floor. Was it really only a week since I was here? It feels like I've lived several lifetimes.

I reach the deserted reception area, wood-floored and beige, and remember how struck I was before by how respectable and dull the place seemed. I look around, but there's no sign of either the girl or Alexa Carling.

I'm too wound up to sit down and wait. I pace backwards and forward. How is Alexa Carling mixed up in all this? I peer along the corridor to her office. She must be inside. I head towards the room, slowing as I reach the door. I glance up and down. There's no one else here. I stop and press my ear to the door.

I hear Alexa Carling immediately. "I don't want to hear it, Poppy." She sounds so full of contempt that I shiver.

"I'm sorry, Mummy." It's the girl, Poppy, her voice all wheedling and babyish. She's clearly hoping to come across as endearing, but from the sound of Alexa Carling's voice, she's falling way short of the mark.

I take another look along the corridor. No one is coming. I bend down and peer in through the keyhole. I can see the pair of them facing each other in the middle of the room.

Alexa takes her daughter by the wrist and wrenches her arm away from her body. She stares down at the track marks I know are there, then shakes her head. "Give me back the keys," she says.

"No." Poppy tries to back away, but Alexa keeps a tight grip of her wrist.

"This was your last chance. I told you, if you started using again . . ." Alexa's voice is like steel, but I can hear the pain behind her words. For a second I forget why I'm here and imagine how I would feel if my own daughter were a drug addict.

"Please, Mummy." Poppy is weeping now, her head hanging. "I've got some money, I—"

"It's not about the money." Even from where I'm standing, I can see the agony etched on Alexa's face. "I just can't do this anymore. *Keys*."

Poppy holds up the plastic bag. Alexa takes it, finally letting her daughter go. Poppy slumps against the wall. "Where will I go? You can't kick me out."

Alexa fishes in the plastic bag and pulls out the keys. I hear the clink of metal as she shoves them inside the drawer behind her and slams it shut.

"What you have to understand is there's only so much help other people can give you," Alexa snaps, coming into view again. "I have given you chance after chance. I know you've been stealing from Crowdale. How could you do that, Poppy?"

"I didn't," Poppy protests, but she can't meet her mother's eyes. "It wasn't my fault," she says, more quietly.

"It never is, is it?" Alexa sighs. "You need to leave now."

"No," Poppy sobs.

"Now."

I back away from the door as footsteps approach. Turning, I scurry along to the bathroom, darting inside just as Alexa's office door opens. I rush into a cubicle, my heart pounding.

I'm getting closer and closer. Poppy told me earlier she got the locket from the place she was staying. It sounds like she stole it from somewhere called Crowdale, the keys to which are now in a drawer in Alexa Carling's office.

277

I emerge from the cubicle and check my face in the mirror. I look terrible, my damp hair plastered against my flushed cheeks, no makeup and a wild, unhinged look in my eye. No wonder the security guard did a double take.

I push myself away from the sink and head outside. Alexa Carling is waiting for me. She looks up as I appear, giving me a smooth, professional smile. There's no trace of emotion in her face.

"Dear me, Olivia, you're soaked," she says.

"I'm fine," I say as she lets me into her office. My eyes dart immediately to the drawer where I saw her put the keys.

Alexa gestures for me to sit. As I do, I'm suddenly and uncomfortably aware of just how damp I am. My palms are clammy with sweat. Now that I'm here, I have no idea what to say.

"Olivia, has something happened?" Alexa leans forward, a picture of concern. "What are you doing here on a Sunday?"

For a moment I doubt everything I've assumed. How can this woman have anything to do with Julia's death? I take a deep breath. "I heard you just now," I say, plunging recklessly in. "Was that your daughter."

Alexa looks away but not before I see the pain behind her eyes. I imagine for a second just how terrible she must feel, cutting her daughter off as she's just done. It's unthinkable. Except . . . look how nuts Hannah drives me right now, aged twelve, when I can make all manner of excuses for her bad behavior. For all I know, Alexa has been supporting Poppy for years and this is the last straw.

"I heard you say she stole from you? Was it from your home?" I'm on terrifyingly dangerous ground with these questions, but I have to know.

Alexa frowns. "Just one of my vacation properties," she says. "But we're here for *you*, Olivia. I'm sorry if you overheard anything unpleasant."

I run my hands through my damp hair, confused. What was Kara's locket doing in a rented holiday house?

"It's not that," I say quickly. "It's just things are worse, aren't they, when your home is violated. It's kind of like a rape."

Alexa's frown deepens. "Olivia, please tell me why you're here."

I force my eyes to focus on her face, keeping them away from the drawer with the keys. I take a quick look around the rest of the office. The case files are still neatly stowed on the shelves, the desk still cluttered with papers.

"It's my husband." I heave a huge sigh. "I'm more sure than ever he's seeing someone else." The truth of these words brings real tears to my eyes. I swallow them down.

It all pours out of me. My heart cracks; there's no need to lie. I don't give anyone's names, just explain that since I was last here, I've got more proof that Will has been unfaithful. "You see, my husband's boss actually *saw* him leaving her hotel bedroom—it's the same woman he slept with before."

Alexa nods sympathetically.

"The problem is, my husband is still refusing to admit what has happened. I need him to confess so I can move on. I need to know for sure what he's capable of."

"Oh, my love," Alexa says soothingly. "I'm so sorry, this all sounds very painful for you."

"It is." I look around the room with a sniff. No sign of any tissues. "Do you have a handkerchief?"

"Of course." Alexa reaches behind the couch where we're sitting and retrieves a box of tissues from the low table that I hadn't even noticed.

I take one. "Thanks."

I glance at the drawer with the keys again, a plan forming in my mind. Maybe I could take a look at this holiday rental myself, see if there are any clues that might lead me closer to the truth about what happened to Julia. Now that Alexa has kicked Poppy out, the place should be empty. I'm not going to take anything. I won't even be breaking in. I'm just going to have a look.

But first I need the keys. Which means getting Alexa out of this room.

"Now, let me check my notes." Alexa flicks through a file as I blow my nose. "Ah, now, what about Brooke? She's here right now. I was just briefing her on another client so she's right next door. Would you like to meet her? It sounds like you need closure on all this as soon as possible."

"Yes, please," I say, hoping Alexa will leave the room. Instead she heads for the desk and picks up the phone.

"Could you come into my office, please, Brooke, dear?" Alexa replaces the receiver and stands in front of the desk, leaning against it. My eyes light on the water jug and two glasses beside her. They give me an idea.

Before I can even think how to execute it, the door opens and a tall, curvy blonde walks in. Apart from her height, she's got the same looks as Shannon—a sort of coy, baby doll prettiness dressed up in a tight, cropped T-shirt and red silk pants that hang from her slim hips. She's gorgeous, late twenties, I'd say, and with a sleepy sexiness about her dark, slightly slanted eyes.

She comes straight over and shakes my hand.

"Olivia. Brooke." Alexa's manner is suddenly brisk and professional. "Now, Olivia, perhaps you would explain your situation to Brooke."

I do as I'm told. Brooke nods throughout. She's not stupid, this girl. I can see it in her eyes. When I've finished, she glances at Alexa, who gives her an approving nod, encouraging her to speak.

"So the way it works . . . ," Brooke says. "You tell me where I'm likely to find your husband—maybe a bar he goes to after work—then I'll approach him there one evening in the next few weeks. I'll make eye contact, tell him he looks good in his suit, or that his aftershave smells great . . . something small. Then I'll get chatting, flirt a bit, sound him out, really. Usually I tell the guys that I manage a hotel around the corner, lead the conversation to how people check in for flings, especially married men. That's often all it takes to get them talking about sexual encounters they've heard of. We swap stories for a bit, then if there's anything to confess, that's usually confession time."

I stare at her, forgetting the keys in Alexa's drawer for a moment. "You mean the guys you seduce *tell* you what they've done, just like that?"

Brooke smiles and her slant eyes narrow like a cats. "Firstly, I *don't* seduce. We *never* go that far. Not even a kiss. The conversation is all recorded, so you can hear that for yourself. Secondly, sure they tell me. To be honest, by the time we've talked a bit, maybe had a couple of drinks and I'm laughing at everything they say, they're, like, boasting about what they've got away with in order to impress me."

Beside us, Alexa smiles. My jaw drops. Is it really that simple to flatter a man into revealing himself?

"Are men that stupid?" The words blurt out of me in a hollow whisper.

Brooke and Alexa laugh. Alexa's chuckle is a light tinkle, but Brooke's is earthy, as sexy as her eyes. Suddenly I'm not so surprised that men give up their secrets to her. For a second I waver. Then I think of Will and his refusal to admit to reigniting his affair with Catrina. I grit my teeth. Will deserves this. I deserve the truth. And if I say no now, then I will leave here without any way of knowing the truth. And without those keys.

"Let's just say men aren't as smart as they sometimes think they are," Alexa says with another wry chuckle.

I nod, determined to see this through. "Show me where to sign," I say.

Alexa leaves and Brooke takes notes on a form just like the others I saw in the case files. I hesitate before giving Will's details. Not because I'm having second thoughts, but because I'm aware it's the same name as on Julia's form. Still, it's perfectly possible for there to be two Will Jacksons in Exeter. Neither part of his full name is unusual. We finish filling out the form. I send Brooke a picture of Will from my phone, tell her where he usually goes for a drink on a Friday after work, then I sign the form at the bottom and look up, expectant.

"Thanks, Brooke." Alexa returns as the girl leaves. She sits beside me. "You won't regret this, Olivia. Brooke is one of our best girls. She'll get the truth from your husband, then you'll know exactly what you're dealing with."

"How, er, how long will it take?" I ask.

"It's in Brooke's hands now," Alexa says smoothly. "She'll contact you in a week or two, I expect, to set up a feedback meeting." She produces a portable credit card machine, and I pay using the card from my old bank account—the one that's still in my maiden name. Alexa stamps my form with the letter *P*.

P for "paid."

I have a sudden flashback to Julia's unstamped form. So Julia never actually paid for Shannon to approach Will. That ties in with what Shannon said about the whole thing being a cover.

I chew on my lip, feeling anxious. It's time. I get up and pace across the room. Not to the desk at first, just to the end of the couch. I pace back, wringing my hands together.

"There's no chance my husband will find out, is there?" I glance over at the desk where Alexa's papers are spread out between the computer and the water jug.

"No," Alexa says firmly. "Our Honeys are discreet above everything. Our business depends on it."

She has clearly forgotten about Damian bursting in to the reception area last time I was here—or, at least, is hoping I've forgotten.

I turn and pace again. This time I walk right over to the desk and indicate the water jug. "May I have some?" I ask.

"Of course." Alexa starts to rise, but I'm much closer to the jug.

I reach for it. And send it flying. Water splashes across the phone and the pages on the desk and onto the beige carpet. "Oh," I say, dropping to my hands and knees and patting, ineffectually, at the spillage. "Oh, I'm so sorry."

"Not a problem," Alexa says. For a moment I think she's going to try to use the waterlogged phone to call for help, but instead she walks to the door. "I'll get a towel."

As soon as she's left the room, I scramble to my feet. In a flash I'm across the room to the drawer, opening it, grabbing at the keys. There are two of them on the key ring, together with a simple plastic label spelling out: CROWDALE.

Footsteps sound outside. There's no time to think. I shove the keys into my jeans pocket, shut the drawer, and scuttle back to the front of the desk. I drop to my knees as Alexa reenters, a towel in one hand and a glass of water in the other.

She walks over to me. "Oh, there's no need," she says.

I stand up and take the glass of water she offers. I take a few sips, but the water almost chokes me. The keys in my pocket feel like they are giving off some flashing neon sign. *Stay calm*, I tell myself.

"So . . ." I force a wan smile onto my face. "We're all set?"

Alexa looks up from the floor, where she's laying out the towel to soak up the water and gives a brisk nod. "Absolutely." She gets to her feet. "Like I told you, Brooke will take it from here. She'll be in touch soon."

I make myself walk down the stairs rather than run, though I can't resist jogging down the final set of steps. Outside, the rain has stopped though the sky is still overcast, the steel gray clouds lowering and heavy.

I scurry away from the Honey Hearts office. My heart is thumping. I'm a thief. I've stolen a set of keys. I've never robbed anything before, not even as a little girl. Kara did. A memory flashes into my head, sharp and true. It's hard to square with the image I have of Kara now, but when she was thirteen or so she stole sweets from under the nose of our local, elderly newsdealer. Kara would smile her angelic smile, and the Asian man who ran the shop would smile back, oblivious of the fact that as soon as his back was turned, checking on newspaper returns or dealing with another customer, Kara's slim fingers would filch a couple of chocolate bars and slip them into her pocket.

She never panicked either, just strolled out of the shop like a hardened criminal. I would be watching from the doorway, half-impressed and half-appalled. I always gave her a hard time about it, telling her she was evil and stupid, but the truth was I was envious of her cool and her ability to feel no guilt whatsoever. I liked the Asian man with his stooped back and graying beard. My cheeks burned at the thought we had robbed him.

But I never told on Kara. And it wasn't just because she always took an extra chocolate bar for me. I didn't want to expose her because, on some level, her guilt felt shameful. Maybe, even then, I wanted to protect the family version of my little sister—the one that Mum and Dad and I had built up over the years: Kara the dreamer, Kara the naïve, Kara the meek.

But perhaps our version of Kara was an illusion, a construct that we simply *wanted* to believe in. After she died, Innocent Kara became the only possible version of the person she had been: the victim who was too good for this world, taken from us too young. Everyone who knew her believed in Innocent Kara.

Everyone except Julia, I think wistfully. Perhaps that was why Kara adored her so much, because Julia let her be herself.

I reach the end of the road and break into a jog as I turn the corner. I try not to run too fast and draw attention to myself, but the keys are now burning a hole in my jeans pocket and I'm imagining Alexa noticing they're gone and calling the police immediately. My imagination is so fixed on this outcome, I can almost hear the sirens as I duck into a coffee bar. It's a bit of a dive—with stained plastic tables and the smell of stale coffee wafting across the dirty linoleum floor. I head for a table at the back and ask for a cappuccino from the sallow-skinned waitress. She retreats behind the counter. I look around. There are only three other customers in the café, a man reading a newspaper in the corner and two women intent on their conversation by the window.

No one is watching me. I put my hand in my pocket and take out the keys to Alexa's vacation house. I hold out the plastic label attached. CROWDALE.

I whip out my phone and Google the word. Less than a second later the details flash up on screen. Crowdale, in Princetown, Dartmoor. There's even a postal code. I click through to Zoopla. The house last changed hands three years ago.

I shake my head. I still don't see how anything significant could be stored in a vacation rental. Even if Alexa—a groomed, middle-aged businesswoman, albeit with a rather seedy business—is somehow connected to a rape and murder from eighteen years ago, why would she keep part of the evidence somewhere so public?

I look at the keys again. Princetown is about an hour's drive away, in a fairly desolate part of Dartmoor. My cappuccino arrives. I take a sip. The coffee tastes both weak and burnt. Disgusting.

I call Damian, explaining where I am and that I have news, but I can't speak. He tells me he is at Honiton staion, picking up his car, and that I should wait while he drives over. I can't finish my coffee, so I order an orange juice, then use the dryer in the ladies' to get the worst of the damp out of my hair. My clothes still feel uncomfortable against my skin. I sip my juice and think about calling Will. He should have both Zack and Hannah with him by now. I send him a text, asking if the kids enjoyed their day, but he doesn't reply.

An hour passes. Damian is stuck in traffic. I order another juice and wait. The sun is setting and the café is about to close by the time Damian arrives. He leaps out of his Mercedes and rushes into the café before I can even get up from the table. We head outside, into the rain, and walk over to his car.

"What did you find out?" he asks, his whole body tensed.

We sit in his car and I explain how Poppy sought me out and tried to sell me information. "I don't think she was ever really going to tell me where she got the locket—or who from—she just wanted my cash. Anyway, I followed her to Honey Hearts. . . ."

Damian's eyes widen at this, getting bigger still as I explain how I overheard Poppy's conversation with her mother and, then, how I stole the keys to the holiday rental where she's been staying.

"It's called Crowdale, on Dartmoor."

"What about the police, Livy?" Damian interrupts, looking shocked. "I thought we agreed earlier you were going to take everything to the police?"

I stare at him. I'd completely forgotten our earlier plan for me to go to the authorities.

"I can still do that." Rain drums on the car roof. "I can give the police the keys. They can look in the the rental."

"But . . . but . . ." Damian shakes his head. "Don't you see that if Alexa is involved with Julia's death, then she'll know the locket that

Poppy stole is significant—and the house where she stole it from is a significant place."

"Okay, then—"

"So if she realizes you took her keys, she's going to try to cover her tracks straightaway."

"Why does that stop me taking the keys to the police?" I look at him, bemused. "Like I said, *they* can go there and investigate."

Damian stares at me as if I'm mad. "The police won't go anywhere without a warrant, which there's no reason to grant, other than you saying the locket was once there."

"But it *was*. Poppy said she found it where she'd been staying. Which was her mother's vacation house."

Damian shakes his head again. "The word of a drug addict won't count for much, believe me, that's if you can even find her again or if Alexa backs up her story, neither of which seems very likely." He sighs and rests his head on the steering wheel.

"So what do we do?"

Damian looks up. "Well, we don't have much choice now. Alexa Carling said this Crowdale place is a vacation home, right?"

I nod.

"So . . . if her daughter has been using it, but she's just had to give Alexa back the keys, the chances are high that the place is empty. We need to take a look at it as soon as possible, before Alexa works out what you've done."

We drive in silence toward Dartmoor. The sky darkens as we travel. I check my phone, but Will still hasn't replied to my text. He will definitely be with Zack and Hannah now. My heart twists at the thought of the three of them together, in our home, without me. I glance across at Damian. He suddenly seems very young and far less attractive than he did yesterday.

The rain grows heavier, bringing with it a soft gray mist that makes it hard to read the passing signposts. In the end, we get lost only once on the way to Princetown, but it's still not easy to find Crowdale once we're there. The houses are spread out across the moors and set back from the narrow lanes with their dry stone walls. Our task is made harder by the driving rain and the mist that swirls creepily around us.

We crawl along as the light fades completely from the sky and the rain slows to a pattering. The darkness and drizzle make it feel later than it really is.

"Here." Damian looks up from the map he's consulting and points to a turnoff on the left. We drive along the unpaved road—not much more than a muddy track—stopping when we reach a low gate that crosses the path. A sign by the gate reads CROWDALE. The house it-self is fifty yards or so beyond—a squat stone cottage on two floors. I pull the hood of my jacket up as I get out of the car. Damian turns up his collar. Silently, we climb the gate and trudge along the path to the house. Against the charcoal and silver sky, it looks bleak. De-serted. Spooky. Dark curtains hang at the closed windows. No lights are on.

We reach the front door. There are two locks. Ivy crawls up the wall on either side. A sign hung over the door flaps against the stone: CROWDALE. Damian looks at me.

"You're up," he says.

I take Alexa's keys out of my pocket and fit the first of the two into the top lock. It turns with a click. I take the dead bolt key and twist that inside the lower lock. It sticks at first. I give it a wrench. The door, stiff and old and heavy, swings open. The house inside is in darkness. I step in, the stone flags on the floor are cold underfoot, even through my shoes.

Behind me, Damian fumbles for the light switch.

With a flick, the corridor fills with bright light. There are two doors, one on either side and a flight of stairs leading up to the first floor. Both doors are open. I peer around the first door, into a living room. It's anally neat.

A memory from Kara's murder investigation years ago flashes into my head: *Our profilers say the guy who did this is obsessive about covering his tracks. He has left no clue, no hint of his presence.*

I shiver as I follow Damian into the living room. There is hardly any furniture. Just two low couches and a large-screen TV.

A built-in cupboard on the far wall opens easily to reveal a shelf of DVDs. I pick a couple at random. They are all art films, mostly foreign.

"These are odd films for a vacation rental," I whisper. "You'd expect stuff for kids, not this."

Damian nods.

I look around for evidence of Poppy's stay. Surely the stragglyhaired addict I met would make more mess? I cross the hall into the room opposite: a kitchen. A large bottle of Pepsi stands open on the table, along with the detritus from a meal—bread, a slab of butter, some cheese.

We head upstairs. The landing at the top of the stairs is tiny. A small bathroom with the door open is opposite; a closed door on either side. I peer inside the bathroom. A sink, with a small cupboard above and a bath. No ornaments. No decoration. Just like the rest of the house. Not even a mirror.

I open the cupboard. It contains a bottle of mouthwash, a toothbrush, and toothpaste on one shelf. Shaving foam and a shaving brush and razor on the other. This is, literally, all. I stare down at the sink. A large bar of orange soap. A threadbare towel hangs to one side.

"I don't understand. It looks like a *man* lives here," I say, coming out of the bathroom. "A *monk*."

"Really?" Damian gestures into the room on the right. He is standing in the doorway. I go over and peer in. It's a tiny bedroom in a phenomenal mess. Clothes and magazines scatter the floor. A small wooden wardrobe is empty, the doors hanging open. A low bed stands in the center of the room. A single blanket is strewn over a dirty mattress. No sheets. Two grubby cushions appear to serve as pillows. A toiletries bag is open on the mattress. Two tubes of lipstick, an apparently unused toothbrush and a box of tampons spill out, onto the blanket.

"Christ, I don't know." I turn away and head to the other room, opposite this one. I open the door.

We're back to Mr. Anal. The iron bedstead is covered with a tightly drawn white duvet. The walls, floor and fitted cupboards are painted white. Damian strides over and pulls open the doors. Inside rows of shirts and a couple of suits and slacks hang neatly, each item spaced separately from the next, so none of the hangers touch. A row of men's shoes—mostly smart and brown or black—line up underneath the clothes. As Damian heads for the chest of drawers under the window, I look around. There is absolutely nothing to give any indication of the personality of the owner of this room. No books—in fact, there's not a single book in the house. No computer. No photos. No pictures. No ornaments. Even the top of the chest of drawers is completely empty. I check under the pillows. No sleepwear lurking anywhere. All I can find is a long, old-fashioned key, tucked under the mattress.

The room is eerily sterile. I shiver. Damian puts his hand on my shoulder.

"I don't get it," he says.

We head back downstairs. I'm about to tell him that the whole house—apart from the messy bedroom—fits the profile of Kara's killer, when I catch sight of a small door under the stairs. I turn to Damian. "What about in there?"

Damian strides over. The door is locked. He steps back with a groan. "If I break it down, it'll be obvious we've been here."

I open my palm, revealing the key I found under the mattress upstairs.

"Try this."

It fits the lock. Damian turns it with a click. The door opens onto stairs. Narrow and concrete, they lead down into darkness. Damian feels for the light switch. Turns it on. I follow him down the stairs. It's a small, square cellar. No doors, no windows, just bare brick walls and a concrete floor. Two cardboard boxes stand against one window. I peer inside and see only books: crime novels, dog-eared paperbacks, a few ancient encylopedias. Nothing personal, nothing to indicate who the books' owner might be. A naked lightbulb hangs from the ceiling.

"This is hopeless." Damian's voice sounds hollow.

I peer around the room, searching for something, anything, that might explain how Alexa Carling's daughter found Kara's locket in this strange house. I run my hands over the wall at the far end of the cellar. My fingers glide over the bricks, then hit a ridge. I stop. Peer closer. The gap between these two bricks and the two below is looser than the rest, the bricks not flush against the wall. I pick at the cement. It crumbles in my hand.

"Look," I say.

Damian rushes over and kneels beside me. We slide our fingers between the bricks. All four come away easily, revealing a dark hole behind. There's no sound in the room. All I can hear is my own, jagged breathing.

"Go on," Damian urges.

I reach my hand inside. My sweating fingers meet cool metal. It's a box. I grip the sides and pull it out. It's beautiful—about the size of a large shoe box and hammered out of some kind of silver. Very simple and very unusual.

"I've never seen anything like this before," I whisper.

"Let's open it." Damian crouches down and reaches for the lid. It's locked, and this time, there's no sign of a key.

I glance at Damian, chills creeping down my spine.

"There's something bad about this box," I say, my voice hoarse.

I put my hand on the metal. It's cold to the touch. I don't believe in ghosts or evil spirits but, if I did, I would be certain that one lurks inside this box, right now.

"I don't want to open it," I say. The silence around us—from the house and the moor beyond—weighs down on me like a physical presence. The evil is here, in this room, coming from this box. "If we open it, we let the evil out."

"That's ridiculous." Damian takes the box from me. "We need to see what's inside this."

I look up, frozen with fear. Damian peers at the lock.

"Don't you feel it?" I ask.

He shakes his head, intent on examining the box. He disappears, returning a minute later with a knife from the kitchen. He levers the blade between the lid and the main part of the box, then prizes it open with a snap.

I gasp.

"We have to, Livy—he was hiding it." Damian sets the box on the floor between us. "Ready?"

I nod, my eyes intent on the box, as Damian slowly raises the lid.

I look inside. It's a random collection: a small exercise book, a plastic button, a tiny gilt brooch, a bottle of nail varnish, a belt buckle in the shape of a snake, an butterfly-shaped hair grip, and a single double-C Chanel earring.

"What are all these?" I ask.

Damian points to the earring. "Shannon was wearing that when we met her."

He's right. I look more closely at the little exercise book. It says *scientiffik experiment* on the cover. I lift it up. My heart jumps into my throat. Kara's locket lies underneath. Pulse beating wildly, I take it out. It's definitely Kara's locket, complete with the little nick on the back and the picture of her and Julia inside. I stare down at it, sick to my stomach.

This is it. This box belongs to the killer.

We have found him.

CHAPTER TWENTY

"Oh Jesus, look at this," Damian breathes. He holds up the nail polish. "I think this was Julia's."

He's right. I recognize the silvery color from Julia's toes the night she died. I back away, my skin crawling, unable to bear the thought that her killer, *Kara's* killer, touched this box.

"Okay, that's it." Damian slams the box shut. "We're out of here. Take all this to the police. Hand everything over."

I nod, then stumble after him up the stairs. Damian holds the box with one hand. He's fishing for his phone with the other. A moment later he curses. "No signal."

I check my own cell. Same story. It isn't surprising. We're in the middle of Dartmoor. Outside, the air is cold and the sky dark. Rain is falling again, a light drizzle. I still can't make any connection between Alexa Carling and the masculine interior of much of the house, but right now it isn't important. What matters is to get out of here, to take what we've found to the police.

We race along the path and over the gate. It's gloomier than ever, dark and still drizzling, with the muddy track shrouded in mist. Still feeling spooked, I hurry into Damian's car. He gets in beside me and hands me the silver box. I don't want to touch it, so I keep my hands on the dashboard. Damian starts the engine, then switches on the high beam. Light floods the track as Damian turns the car around and we move off slowly.

Mist swirls around us, glowing eerily in the car's bright headlamps. Almost as soon as we start driving I catch movement up ahead: a shadow crossing the track.

"What was that?"

"Probably just a fox," Damian says, but he doesn't sound sure.

I glance down at the box on my lap and feel spooked again. Stupid, I know, but I can't get the thought of the evil spirits out of my head.

"What's *that*?" Damian leans forward, peering through the windshield.

I follow his gaze. There's a shape lying on the track up ahead. A shiver snakes down my spine as Damian slows the car to a crawl.

A child—no more than seven or eight—is lying on the track in jeans and an outsize hoodie that bunches around the waist. Damian stops the car. My heart pumps furiously in my ears.

Has a child been run over? I can't see any blood. Thanks to the large hood, pulled down over the face, it's impossible to tell whether a boy or a girl is lying there. The car is just a meter in front of the body. The child isn't moving. Fear clutches at my throat.

"Oh, Christ." Damian is frozen beside me.

He turns off the engine but leaves the high beam on. The child is wearing yellow sneakers. I lean forward, peering more closely. Zack has a pair just like them.

Reality swerves around me, and the truth crashes into me like a fist.

"Zack." I breathe his name, and already I'm pushing the box to one side and flying out of the car. I drop to my knees, by his body, barely aware of the cold, wet mud beneath me. Everything is Zack. My beautiful boy.

I reach for his face. Turn it to mine. His eyes are closed. No blood. Is he gone? He *can't* be. I wet my finger and place it under his nose, just as I did when he was a tiny baby. Every cell in my body releases as I feel the shallow breath cool my finger.

"Zack? Zack?" I call his name, shake his shoulder, but he lies motionless. Panic swirls inside me. I feel his arms and legs, his stomach. Nothing feels wrong. No broken bones. I touch his head. No swelling, no lumps, no bruises.

I don't understand. I don't understand.

"Damian!" Why isn't he here? I fumble for my phone. Still no signal. "Damian!" Where is he? I need his help to get Zack back to the car.

As I turn to face him, the car lights go off. The track is plunged into total darkness.

"Damian!" I yell. The rain is falling harder now. I hug Zack to me. He's a deadweight, too heavy to pick up off the ground, so I drag him back toward the car. I can barely see it in the misty gloom. "Damian!" I shout out again. What the hell is going on? My heart is in my mouth, my head about to explode with fear.

"Help!" Zack's legs bump over the mud. I'm breathing heavily as I reach the car. I set Zack down at my feet and feel for the car door. Locked.

"Damian?" I try the car door again. Why is it locked? "Damian!"

Fear crawls like ants over my skin. I am shaking, rain running down my face, into my mouth. Zack lies slumped against my trembling legs as I draw my phone from my pocket. It lights up as I touch it. Still no signal. I hold the phone up to the car window. There's just enough light for me to make out Damian's outline. He is sitting where I left him, in the driver's seat, upright, his eyes glazed but open.

"Damian?" My voice quavers. I bang on the window, shouting his name again. What is the matter with him? Why doesn't he hear me? Then the light catches the dark red pool, gleaming on the dashboard, dripping onto the floor of the car. I peer in through the window, wiping the rain from my eyes, trying to force my brain to make sense of what I'm seeing.

Blood. It streams from Damian's throat, staining his shirt, a slick sea around him. A terrible second passes; then his head lolls to the side. I stare, unable to take it in. His throat is cut. With a click, the car unlocks. I spin around.

"Who's there?"

The only sound is the rain, falling steadily around me.

I'm shaking uncontrollably. Zack is still lying slumped at my feet. The sight of him spurs me to action. I drag him away from the door, then open it. The car interior lights up. Oh God, the whole inside of the car is red with blood. Everywhere, the seats, the ceiling, the dashboard.

I reach inside and touch Damian's face. His eyes are wide and staring. I bring my trembling fingers to his arm. It hangs limp and heavy. I press, hard, against his wrist. I move my fingers. There's no pulse.

"Damian?" I let out a low moan. My fingers move to his neck, wet with blood. I feel around the side of his throat. Nothing.

"Oh, Damian." It's a whisper. I stagger back from the car, bile rising in my stomach. The stench of blood fills my nostrils: a sharp metallic tang. I take a deep breath of the cool, dark air. Who has done this? Where are they?

I look all around me. I can't see whoever it is, but they must be here, nearby.

Zack is still out cold. I try to focus, to force my scrambled brain to think. I have to get Zack out of here. I have to get away.

Which means moving Damian so I can drive the car.

The blood is wet on his neck. I grit my teeth and try to push him across the car. He's too heavy. I rush around the other side, open the passenger-side door and try to pull him toward me. I can't. Sobbing, I run back around and tug at his arm, desperate now just to get him out of the car.

And then I hear footsteps behind me. I look around. Someone holding a flashlight is walking toward me.

"Hello?"

The person doesn't speak. I can't see his face, because of the bright beam from the flashlight. I shield my eyes. It's a man. I'm sure of that. He's wearing plastic overalls, the kind forensic scientists use.

It's him. The killer.

I reel back, reaching for Zack. The man steps forward. He stands over Zack's legs.

"Drink this." He sets a water bottle on the ground. His hand is gloved. His voice is a low whisper. I can't place it, but I'm sure I know it.

"No." I back away, pulling Zack with me along the track. "Who are you?"

The man steps forward again. He holds out a knife. "Stop."

I freeze. The man crouches down beside Zack. I still can't see his face. The plastic overalls are white. He has plastic boot covers too, like the pathologists in Julia's flat.

"Drink or I'll kill him." The long blade of the knife glints in the torchlight. He holds it out so the tip rests against Zack's throat.

"Oh God, no, please." I rush forward and grab the water bottle. I pick it up. "Please don't hurt him."

"Drink," the voice says in a soothing whisper. I *know* I've heard it before. "Drink and I promise you'll see your son again."

I place the bottle to my lips and take a sip. The liquid tastes salty.

"More," the man orders.

"What is it?" I ask.

"It won't kill you," the voice says.

I hesitate again, my eyes on the knife at Zack's neck. One tiny slip and his fair skin would be ripped open, just like Damian's.

I take two big gulps of the drink. Then two more. I've drunk about half the bottle.

"Good, now, get in the trunk and I'll put Zack in there with you."

I experience a throb of terror that the man knows Zack's name. "Why? What are you going to do to us?"

"Do you want your son in the trunk with you? Or shall I slit his throat here?"

"Okay." I have no choice but to trust what he says. I edge around the car, still blinded by the flash beam. The man reaches the trunk before me. He flicks it open. I crawl in, then look back out. All I can see is the glare of the light, a white hole in the dark night sky. "Zack," I say. My mind whirrs. If Zack is with us here, then where is Hannah, where is Will?

"Phone."

I reach into my pocket and hand him my mobile. "What have—?"

The lid slams shut. Panic rises inside me. What about Zack? I thump on the metal above my head. There's no room. I can't move. Claustrophobia closes in. I open my mouth to scream, but before any sound can come out, the trunk lid lifts again. No flashlight, just the outline of the man. I still can't see his face properly; he's wearing a surgical mask. Zack is in his arms. I reach up as Zack is lowered in beside me. The gloved hand brushes my cheek. It smells of rubber and chemicals.

"What are—?"

"Quiet or I kill your daughter."

I gasp. The lid slams shut. I hug Zack to me, my heart beating wildly.

He has Hannah too.

I hold my breath as thuds and bangs echo through the car toward me. The darkness in the trunk presses in on me. Is Hannah in the car somewhere? What about Will?

I touch Zack's face. He is still out cold.

The car engine starts. We are driving away.

I try to steady my breathing. To work out what on earth I can do to get away. The trunk is tightly shut. Where is Hannah? Where is Will?

I lie still, trying to focus. Time passes. Zack stays unconscious. I recognized the man's voice. But where? How? I can't make sense of what is happening. The darkness swirls around me. I grip Zack tightly, afraid I will fall. Fall from what? I suddenly realize I can't feel Zack anymore. I can't feel anything. I can't move, not even my fingers. I can't speak.

It all feels like a dream. Zack is my only reality. I strain my eyes open, trying to see into the darkness.

The world dances inside my head. I am clammy with sweat.

Suppose I died now?

Suppose this was death?

The man said I wouldn't die.

You can't trust him.

He said you'd have Zack and you do.

297

You can't trust him.

You can't trust anything.

I close my eyes, letting the vibrations of the moving car throb through me as the darkness swallows me up.

My head feels tight and sore. My throat is so dry, it hurts. My muscles ache. I can't move. There's darkness all around, pressing in on me. For a second I think I'm in a coffin. Then I remember. I am in the trunk of Damian's car.

Zack.

The memory of his unconscious body obliterates all other thoughts. We were crammed in before, our bodies right next to each other. I try to reach out, my eyes straining to see in the darkness. Where is he?"

Gone.

I want to yell out, to thump my fists against the roof of the trunk, but I'm paralyzed. Terror rises inside me. I register that the car is still, the engine no longer running. Long minutes pass. Then the trunk lid opens. Cold air slaps against my face. I smell the sea. I hear waves crashing against rocks. The man from before is here, still head to toe in his plastic coveralls, the surgical mask still over his face. I try to shrink away, but he hauls me out with a grunt.

He carries me away from the car. I can see only the thin plastic of his overalls in front of my face. I can't turn my head. It is dark. How much time has passed? Where is Zack? I try to speak but I make no sound. We are walking downhill. The wind is getting stronger. My hair blows in front of my eyes.

And then there's a click. Lights flash. I hear a thump. A trunk opens in front of me. I am laid inside. How can we be back at the car? We have just walked away from it, downhill? I don't understand.

This trunk contains things. I can feel shapes pressing against me. It smells different from the other trunk. I'm certain it's bigger too. A different trunk. A different car. I don't understand.

I lie there, my eyes straining into the darkness.

Hours pass. The car doesn't move. I lose all sense of time. Fear ransacks my brain. I can't think, can't move, can't speak.

More time passes. The car stays stationary. In a daze, I move my hand. Realize that I *can* move. I stretch out. My leg connects with something T-shaped and plastic. I feel down its length. It's the arm of a scooter. I reach the broad, flat metal of the base.

I yell out. "Help!" My voice is hoarse, but at least I can speak now.

Gradually I regain more movement. More sound. I yell and I thump and I kick. No one comes.

And then, without warning, the trunk opens. A figure looms over me. It's the man again. He stares down at me, only his eyes visible over that mask.

"Where is Zack?"

The man ignores me. He reaches in, grabs my arm. "Out!"

I force my aching, cramped muscles to move. I bang my leg and my head scrambling out of the car. I don't recognize where I am, but it's a cliff by the sea. The night sky is lighter than before. How much time has passed. To the left I can see the crests of the waves, far below. To my right is only sky and the outline of trees in the distance. No lights. No buildings.

No people.

In my mind's eye I see Damian: his unfocused stare, the blood dripping down his neck. Nausea rolls through me, up into my throat.

I turn to face the man who has brought me here.

"Where's Zack?" I ask again.

The man grips my wrist. I pull away. My head is still groggy, but I'm stronger than he expects. I dig in my heels, letting the fierce salt wind chill through me, waking me fully. Then I wrench the mask off his face.

Horror slams into me.

I know who he is. But I can't believe it.

And then he smiles. "Calm down, Livy. I'm taking you to the children. Trust me."

LIVY

God pours out love upon all with a lavish hand, but He reserves vengeance for His very own.

—Mark Twain

Livy found my place. My home from home, for goodness' sake. Trust Alexa bloody Carling to be right in the middle of that mess. The woman's not just a whore, she's a black hole.

Livy found my box too. Just like Poppy did. Except that stupid Poppy only took the locket to sell to pay her debts. Livy and that idiot boyfriend of Julia's took the whole box, to expose me.

How dare they?

I am white hot with fury. Never have I taken more pleasure in slicing skin and seeing blood spurt and sluice.

Damian's death calmed me. Yet it was rushed, a hurried, inelegant kind of murder. Likewise the disposal of the body. With Livy, I will regain my equilibrium, then exceed all former achievements.

I have a plan. Sheer bliss, this moment of anticipation. And such sweet irony that I will bring the full might of my vengeance down on the sister of the only woman I have ever truly loved.

If Kara was an angel, then Livy is the devil herself. And, like the devil, she shall be brought face-to-face with her own deepest, darkest shame. Yes. Now . . . here . . . through Livy . . . I will create a new, dark poetry.

I will not write more. Not yet. Not until it is done. Ah, now . . . "if it were done when 'tis done, then 'twere well. It were done quickly . . ."
My thoughts exactly.
Back I go.

CHAPTER TWENTY-ONE

It's *Paul*. Paul, one of my oldest friends who, only a few hours ago, sat with me in my kitchen, sympathizing over the state of my marriage, sharing his own pain, his own story.

I'm so shocked, I can hardly believe it. "You killed Julia? You killed *Kara*?"

Paul looks me in the eye. In the light from the open trunk, I can see the strong curve of his cheek, the fierce press of his lips.

"I did." He sounds proud, almost arrogant.

My legs buckle beneath me. He's a killer. *The* killer. "And Damian? And Shannon?"

"Yes." Paul takes me by the wrist.

"How? *Why?* I don't understand. Paul, please, this is *me*. This is *us*."

Paul says nothing. I look around, desperate. The car he's just pulled me out of is parked at the top of the cliff. With a jolt I realize it is Will's Rover. Paul must have transferred me here from Damian's car, so that I've just been lying inside my own trunk, with Zack's scooter digging into my legs. I turn back to Paul in disbelief. "Where are Zack and Hannah?"

He still says nothing. I yell out: "Zack! Hannah!"

I expect Paul to tell me to shut up, but he just smiles. "There's no one to help you here, Livy," Paul says.

The cliff edge is just a few meters away. I'm certain I know where we are now: about thirty or so miles from the vacation house where Damian and I found the box, where poor Damian was killed.

We are close to Julia's favorite spot, Bolt Head. It's dark as pitch out to sea. What is Paul going to do?

"Where are the kids? You said you'd take me to the kids?" I can't take this in, can't make sense of any of it. Beyond the cliff edge, the rocks slope sharply downhill. Paul gives my wrist a yank. I stumble after him, past the car. Will is inside, his head slumped against the window, eyes closed.

"Will!" I shout. *"Will!"*

Will doesn't wake. Is he drugged? Is he dead?

Paul gives my arm a jerk. "Do be quiet," he says, his voice sharp with irritation. "Will's had the same drug you did. He can't hear you."

"Will!" Paul drags me beyond the car. *"Will!"*

"Enough." Paul slaps my face. I gasp—more at the shock that Paul has hit me than at the pain. My cheek stings as Paul pulls me a few more meters along the side of the cliff. I'm trying to twist around, to look back at the car. I don't notice the small hut, part set into the cliff face, until we reach the door. A huge boulder stands outside it. Still holding me by the wrist, Paul reaches for the crowbar propped against the boulder.

I pull away, straining against his grip, kicking out.

Paul wrenches my arm painfully back. "Hannah and Zack are in here," he hisses. "Don't you want to see them?"

I stop moving, frozen at the menace in his voice. Paul takes the crowbar and levers the boulder from in front of the door. He pushes me inside. It's dark. Cold. The only light a paraffin lamp in the corner. Two small figures are on the ground beside it.

Paul lets go of my wrist. I stumble forward. As the door slams behind me, one of the figures hurtles toward me. I see a flash of blond hair and then she's on me, burying her head into my chest, clinging to me like her life depends on it.

"Hannah."

"Oh, Mummy, Mummy." She is sobbing, loud, hysterical.

I hold her. "Hannah." My voice is croaky. I turn. Paul has gone. I push at the door, putting all my weight into opening it. It won't budge.

Hannah's sobs slowly subside. I lead her across the room, to the lamp. Zack is lying curled up beside it. His eyes are shut. I bend over him, holding Hannah tight. I shake his shoulder. "Zack?" He's still unconscious. My head throbs as I wrap my arms around Hannah again and slump to the ground. After a moment, my eyes adjust to the lamp's dim glow. The hut has a low ceiling, less than six feet off the ground. Apart from the lamp, it is empty—bare concrete walls and floor. A draft whips in under the locked door. There are dried bloodstains on my top and my hands from Damian. I rock my daughter back and forth as she sobs. "What happened, Hannah?"

"Paul brought us here, he made Zack sick, he tied Daddy up." Her voice is tiny and terrified, her words tumbling over each other.

I hug her to me. "Hey, slow down. I'm here. Tell me what happened."

Hannah shakes in my arms. "Daddy picked me up from Romayne's. He already had Zack. He was in a bad mood and he had already let Zack sit in the front, which meant I couldn't, so I had to get in the back."

"Go on."

"So we get home and Paul comes over before we've even got out of the car and he and Daddy talk about a motorcycle, then Paul gets in the back next to me, which was weird. Then he got out a knife and . . . and he was going to kill me unless Daddy drives." She dissolves into tears.

"Oh, my God." I hold her tighter, stroking her arms. She is shivering. I pull her closer. "What happened next?"

"So Zack starts screaming. And Paul says to him to stop but he doesn't, so Daddy tells him. Then the man gets out a water bottle and makes Zack drink some. Then he makes me drink some but it's salty but he makes me. And we drive along. And then I don't remember anymore."

I nod. The image of Damian with his throat cut fills my head again. I almost vomit. I glance down at Zack. If all three of us have been drugged, why is Zack the only one still unconscious?

"Why is this happening, Mummy?" Hannah curls herself into a ball at my side. She seems so young, almost as little as Zack suddenly.

"I don't know." I lean against the wall behind me, letting my head clear. Unbelievable though it is, Paul killed Damian and Julia and Shannon—and my baby sister. I think of how Kara was brutalized before she died and my blood runs cold at the thought of what Paul is capable of.

"Mummy, there's something else." I open my eyes and Hannah looks up at me, her expression full of fear and pain. There's a dirty smudge on her cheek. I smooth it away.

"What, sweetheart?"

"I took something . . ." Hannah's voice shakes. "A while ago."

I frown. "I don't—"

"It was the day we found Julia."

I stare at her. "What do you mean?"

Hannah clasps her hands together. She is trembling.

"It's okay," I say, trying to reassure her. "Just tell me."

"It was Julia's ring," Hannah confesses with a sob. "I took it from her bedroom while you were outside with Zack. I'm sorry, Mummy, I know it was wrong. I just saw it there and . . ." Her words dissolve into tears.

"Hey, Hannah, it's okay, it's all right." I hug my daughter to me, rocking her to and fro again. "It doesn't matter." I thought it was Will. I accused Will.

"I hid it in Daddy's toolbox, 'cause you're always saying he never uses it, so I knew no one would think to look there!" she wails.

"It's okay. It doesn't matter now." I chew on my lip. So Will didn't take the ring. He had nothing to do with Julia's death. And now he is tied up in our car, outside.

What is Paul going to do to him? Why isn't he in here with the rest of us? A cold chill creeps through me. I don't care what Will has done, the affair with Catrina . . . I still love my husband. I didn't know how much until this moment. I can't lose him. I can't lose my children.

These thoughts circle me like an animal as Hannah's sobs

subside again. I stroke her cheek, wiping the tears away. She looks younger than ever, and so beautiful, her eyes bright blue and shining, her skin pale and clear.

"It really doesn't matter about the ring, Hannah. I found it and I was just talking to Daddy about—"

"I know." Hannah's mouth trembles. "I heard you arguing. You thought he took it, didn't you? That was why you got angry. That was why he left, wasn't it?" Her whole face crumples.

I stare at her, horrified that she has understood—and yet misunderstood—so much.

"No," I start, eager to reassure her. "Daddy and I were having problems nothing to do with—"

The sound of a key turning, then the door slams open. Hannah and I jump. Turn. I scramble to my feet as Paul walks in. He is still dressed from head to toe in his white plastic suit and tight rubber gloves, though without the mask over his face.

He's making sure he leaves no trace.

Hannah scrambles behind my back. I shield her, glancing to check Zack, still unconscious on the floor.

Paul stares at us.

"Why are we here? What are you going to do?"

He says nothing.

For a second I consider grabbing Hannah's hand and trying to rush past him. I can't see his knife, and the door is wide open, the cold sea air whipping in and sending goose bumps up my arms. Then I remember Zack. There is no way I could make it through the door with both children. I doubt I could even pick up Zack. And what about Will?

Paul just stares. His eyes are bright, glinting in the lamplight.

"What do you want?" My voice falters.

No response.

"Hannah, come here." Paul holds out his hand.

Hannah shrinks away, clutching me, whimpering.

"No," I say, panic rising.

Paul strides toward us, hand still outstretched. I shove Hannah behind me. "No," I repeat. "*Please*, no."

Paul smiles and his eyes crinkle. For a sick second it strikes me that he thinks he is being charming. "She's so like Kara," he says. "I didn't really see it before, but tonight . . ."

I gasp. He grabs Hannah by the wrist. She goes limp, releasing me, surrendering to him.

"No." Instinct takes me forward. I put my arm up to force his away. But with his free hand, Paul pushes me back. Hard. I fall to the ground beside Zack.

Hannah screams. "Mummy! Mummy!"

Paul has her halfway across the room now. "Quiet!"

"Hannah!" I scramble to my feet, but he's dragging her through the door. Slamming it shut in my face. Hannah's cry fades into silence.

"Come back!" I yell. "Bring her back!"

But they are gone. I press my ear against the cold stone door, but all I can hear is the faint whoosh of the waves outside.

I thump on the door. "Help! Come back!" It's useless. I turn away, too shocked, too scared to cry. I can barely breathe. Zack is still unconscious. I go over, bend down and touch his face, smoothing his hair back. He still doesn't wake. For the first time I'm glad. I don't want him to see me like this, so utterly terrified.

I pace up and down. The room is only ten paces long and five paces wide. Solid concrete. No windows. No way out apart from the door. I check Zack again. I can't find anything physically wrong; he's just not waking up. What is Paul doing with Hannah? I think about what the killer did—what *Paul* did—to Kara before he killed her.

Oh, Jesus. Bile rises into my throat; my breath is jagged. I can't keep still.

Think, Livy. I force myself to sit. To breathe. I have to try to work out what to do.

I count ten slow breaths, but jerky images fill my head. Damian covered in blood. Will in our car, unconscious. And now Hannah, her mouth open in a scream as the man who has taken her presses one hand against her throat, forcing her down. I make myself stare at Zack, trying to follow his own, steady breathing.

"Help me," I pray into the void. "Help me."

My mind won't keep still. Ten minutes pass. Fifteen. I realize I have absolutely no idea what time it is. From the way the sky looked outside, I'd say somewhere between 3 and 4 A.M., but I can't be sure.

The door opens again, and Paul comes in. He's alone. I stand over Zack. "Where's Hannah?" I demand. "What have you done with her? Where's Will?"

Paul tilts his head to one side, watching me. It's unnerving. A beat passes. A new resolution forms in my guts. I will not let this man harm my family. I will die before I will let that happen.

"I need Zack," Paul says.

I glance down at my boy. Agonizing tears roil up inside me. "No, you're not taking him." I clench my fists, ready to fight. "You'll have to kill me first."

Paul chuckles as if I've missed the point entirely. "No, Livy. You're coming too. Pick him up."

I try to haul Zack into my arms, but he's too heavy. I end up half carrying, half dragging him across the room. Outside, I look around for the car. It's still there, but I can't make out whether or not Will is still inside. It's lighter now, almost dawn. Paul directs me down the cliff edge, to a small, rocky ledge high above the sea. Hannah is already lying there.

I gasp.

"She's just unconscious," Paul explains. "I gave her some more GHB, same as everyone else has had."

"GHB?" I turn to him. "What's that?"

"A date rape drug," he says. "Like Rohypnol, but it acts faster. No trace after a few hours."

"Date rape?" I stare at him. "Have you—? Are you—?" I can't bring myself to ask the question.

Paul shoots me a contemptuous look. "For goodness' sake, Livy," he says. "She's a *child*."

He directs me to lie Zack down beside Hannah. His dark head nestles next to her blond one. They look like they are sleeping.

"What *are* you going to do to them, then?" My whole body is trembling, but I am hyperalert, seeing everything sharp and clear.

Paul smiles, and I remember the many evenings he and Becky and Will and I have spent together and how kind he was when he came to the house earlier. My head spins. How can someone so normal, a person I have been friends with for almost twenty years be *doing* this?

"Aren't you concerned about your husband?" Paul asks dryly.

"Yes, of course." I look over toward the car again. I can just make out its shape in the light that seeps out from the hut door. I turn back to my captor.

Paul smiles again, sensing my confusion. "My mother called and told me that she was almost certain one of her clients—an Olivia Small—had taken the set of keys Poppy was using—"

"Your mother? You mean Alexa Carling?"

Paul nods. "Remember I told you I've been staying in one of my mother's properties while our house is remodeled and Becky is away? We talked about it at Leo and Martha's party. I mentioned it earlier today as well."

Memories of these conversations filter through my brain. So Alexa was the link, the reason why everything kept coming back to Honey Hearts.

"Poppy's my half sister," Paul says. "I told you about her too—years ago."

I shake my head. I have no recollection of Paul ever talking about a sister. I vaguely remember his contempt for his mother back when we met as students. Paul was angry she had remarried. I definitely recall him saying he hated his stepfather, but did he mention a little sister? I can't be sure.

"Poppy got into drugs years ago. Not surprising, considering what a bastard her dad was. She hasn't kicked it, though from time to time she persuades our mother she has." Paul sighs. He doesn't sound angry now, just sorrowful. I can't make him out. It's like we're having a normal conversation. "Poppy got chucked out of her last place, so

Mum insisted she stay in the rental with me for a few weeks. Then when she stole that locket . . . I couldn't explain why it mattered so much. Mum was all about giving Poppy a second chance. And Poppy was trying. But I couldn't have her stay after the locket, so I made it easy for Poppy to start using." He sighs again. "It didn't take much."

"You took that locket from my sister." My head can't process what I know to be true. "You took it when you killed her. She was only eighteen."

"I know," he says. "She was beautiful, wasn't she? An angel."

He seems genuinely moved by Kara's memory. I don't understand him. I don't understand any of this. "How *could* you?"

Paul rolls his eye. "Such predictable questions. Don't you want to ask me about my father? It's his fault Poppy found you earlier."

"What do you mean?"

"Poppy overheard me talking about you on the phone to Dad . . . Leo . . . this morning. That's how she worked out you were looking for the locket."

I frown. "What's Leo got to do with this?"

Paul smirks. "Poor Julia thought Leo was your sister's murderer."

"What? *Why?*"

"I told Poppy the box containing the locket belonged to my dad, that I was storing it for him. Poppy told Shannon. Shannon told Julia."

"Does Leo know you said that? Does he know what . . . who you really are? Does *anyone* . . . Martha? Becky?"

"No, no, and no. But Dad did find my bottle of Nembutal the day after Julia died. He challenged me about it. At first I blamed it on Poppy. Then, when we heard the postmortem on Julia, he couldn't help but make the connection. He came to me again, *furious.*" Paul sighs. "I told him Julia had asked for the Nembutal as part of some article she was doing into fashion industry suicides. That I'd had no idea she wanted to kill herself. Dad believed me. He *wanted* to believe me. But he could see straightaway that there would be a huge scandal if people found out I'd supplied her an illegal drug, whatever I thought she was going to do with it." Another smile twists around

310

Paul's lips. "The whole suicide story worked very well, actually. Almost *everyone* believed she was secretly depressed and suicidal."

"I didn't. Damian didn't."

"That's right," Paul says softly. "And when Dad knew you were suspicious about Julia's death, he got scared that you would find out what I'd done. Scared for me, of course. But also terrified of the scandal. I could have gone down for fourteen years. I'm Paul Harbury, the boss's son. Harbury Media would never have survived me going to jail. Dad would have lost his business. We had to distract you, stop you investigating, so I came up with a lie for him to tell you."

"A lie?"

"About Will. To preoccupy you, so you'd forget about Julia. It was sadly easy to convince you he'd gone with that whore Catrina again," Paul says with contempt. "No trust."

What's he saying? That Will didn't sleep with Catrina? That, all along, Will was telling the truth?

"I can't promise Will is faithful, but my father didn't see anything in the hotel in Geneva. I know that."

"Leo *lied* to me about that?"

"And to his own wife," Paul says with relish. "And you believed them both."

Shame fills me. I look back at the car where Will lies unconscious, and my guts twist into a tight knot. "If you hurt me and my family, your father will work that out too," I say, trying to sound convincing.

Paul's eyes widen. "Who's being hurt?"

"You killed Damian." Another image of the blood in the car, the throat oozing red, flashes in front of my mind's eye.

"That's right," Paul says smoothly. He points across the cove to a pinprick of red that glows in the darkness. "D'you see that fire?"

I nod.

"That's Damian's car with Damian inside it. After I transferred you to the trunk of your own car, I took his and torched it on a field just outside Salcombe. It'll look like a bunch of drunken vagrants got carried away." He sounds smug. "The police won't find anything of me in there."

311

Oh, God. Poor Damian. "So what are you going to do with us?" I glance from Zack to Hannah, then look up at Paul again.

"We're going to play a game," Paul says, his eyes gleaming.

My heart thunders against my ribs. "What game?" I keep my gaze fixed on Paul's dark, mean eyes.

"A choosing game," Paul says. "Kind of like musical chairs." He chuckles and looks down at the children.

My heart skips a beat. "Choose?" I say, my voice a whisper. "You mean you want me to choose which one you kill?"

"No." Paul shakes his head contemptuously. The easy smile has gone. Suddenly he looks furious. "Credit me with a little original-ity, you stupid bitch."

I stare at him, my stomach falling away. "What do you mean, then?"

He watches me. I get the sense he's waiting to see if I can work it out.

My head spins. I can't think. I try to work out what he must mean. He is a murderer, but he's saying he doesn't want to kill my children. "Choose. Choose." I repeat the word, hoping it will help me under-stand. "Choose what then, if no one dies?"

Paul shakes his head. "Oh, *one* of them *will* die," he says slowly. "And you *are* going to decide which one."

Panic spirals up into my throat. I can barely speak. "But you said you *weren't* going to kill them. *Either* of them."

"That's right, Livy," he says. "*You* are."

CHAPTER TWENTY-TWO

"Kill one?" I stare down at my children, unconscious in the damp, cold night. The wind plasters my blouse to my body. Spray mists my face. I'm frozen, yet I barely feel the cold. A single tear leaks out of my eye.

Paul watches as my entire world spins on its axis. I gaze from my beautiful boy to my angel girl, curled up on the bare rock.

Kill Zack to save Hannah. Kill Hannah to save Zack.

No.

The tear dries on my face. I will not let this man take my children. Seconds tick away. I breathe in, then out, trying to slow myself down. My fear transforms to rage. How dare he take us and threaten us?

"Have you chosen, Livy?"

I turn on him. "How can you expect me to do that?"

"Because the alternative is me killing them both. This way you save one. Livy's choice." He laughs, his dark eyes like bullets. How could I ever have thought he was kind?

My fury sharpens like the point of a knife. I meet his gaze. I will not tremble. I will not show fear.

"How do I know they're both still even alive?" I demand. "Zack's been unconscious for hours."

"He's smaller than the rest of you," Paul says in a bored, matter-of-fact voice. "The GHB will take longer to work itself out of his system. But check them both, if you like."

I drop to my knees and feel for Zack's pulse. It's steady and strong.

313

I shake his shoulder and he moans in his sleep. I turn to Hannah. She is more deeply unconscious, but her breathing is warm on my finger.

A muffled yell sounds from the car, then a series of thuds. I scramble to my feet, looking round. I can't see Will from here, but I can hear him. He must be hurling his body against the door.

"Ah, you see? Will has come round." Paul rubs his gloved hands together. "Perfect timing. He can watch."

He walks away, toward the car. I crouch down again, willing the kids to wake up.

"Zack! Hannah!" I hiss their names and shake their arms. I try to lift them, to drag them away, but they are heavy. I have barely moved them an inch before Paul is back, Will at his side. His hands are tied behind his back, but the gag has been removed.

Will's eyes search my face. "Are you all right? The kids?"

"They're all fine," Paul says impatiently.

I nod. "I'm okay." I look down at the children. "They've been drugged, so—"

"We're waiting, Livy," Paul interrupts. He folds his arms. "Who's it to be?"

"What are you talking about?" Will's voice rises. "Paul, please, it's *us*. We're *friends*. You can't—"

He stops abruptly as Paul produces a sheathed knife from his pocket. He draws the blade out of the leather. It's at least six inches of gleaming steel. The same knife that killed Damian, that I last saw held to my son's throat. Now he places the tip against Will's shirt, just under his ribs.

"Quiet," he orders.

Will looks down at the knife, but Paul is watching me. His black eyes glint as he searches my face. He's expecting me to be frightened. But I'm not. I am only one emotion. I am only one idea. One ambition.

"So which child will you sacrifice?" he asks.

Will gasps.

"You promise you'll let the other one live?" I know Paul will not keep this promise, but still there's a voice in my head arguing that he told the truth about putting Zack in the trunk of the car with me, that maybe I can bargain with him.

The same idea clearly occurs to Will.

"Kill me instead," he says. "Take me. Save the children. Save Livy. Please, for God's sake." Will glances at the knife again. "God, Livy, he was talking about his bike as he got in the car. I had no—"

"Be quiet." Paul presses the edge of the knife harder against Will's side.

"He's lying about this choice," Will says. "He's going to kill *all* of us, make it look like you went off the rails, just like he did with Julia."

"Quiet," Paul says again.

Will falls silent.

"Livy. *Now,*" Paul urges.

"I'll make a choice," I say, keeping my voice steady. I have to keep him talking. Buy myself time to think. "Just tell me *why* you're doing all this? *Why* did you kill Julia? And my sister? She was only eighteen, her whole life ahead of her and you took it away."

Paul tilts his head to one side. He seems to be seriously considering my question. "You wouldn't understand, Livy *Small.*" He sneers as he speaks my old surname. "I didn't want a limited life. I wanted to fulfill my potential."

I stare at him. What is he talking about?

"You can't make Livy do this," Will says through gritted teeth. "What d'you expect her to do? Kill them with that?" He looks down at the knife.

"Her hands," Paul says. "Her bare hands."

I shiver, looking at my hands. They are cold, numb. "Come on, Livy."

I kneel down on the rock and gaze at Hannah. I put my palm over her face, letting my fingers trail onto her throat. Her skin is soft and pale, her pulse throbbing under my touch.

"She looks *so* like Kara, doesn't she?" Paul says.

Beside him, Will stiffens. I look up. What on earth am I going to do?

"You want me to make it her . . . Hannah?"

315

Paul's face darkens. "I want you to *choose*, you stupid bitch. Now, get on with it."

I press my hands against Hannah's throat. For a moment I imagine what it would feel like to squeeze the life out of her. The thought is unbearable.

Impossible.

Please, help me. I flash back to Kara's funeral. I prayed then, but stopped halfway through what I was saying: a request to some vague notion of a higher power. *Please, give me strength.*

A new energy fills me. I stand up and look Paul in the eye.

"I can't," I say. "I *won't.*"

We stand in silence for a moment. Then Paul sighs. He holds up his knife. "Say good-bye to your husband, Livy."

"No!" In a second I'm across the rock, hurling myself at Will, trying to get between him and Paul to push the knife away. Taken by surprise, Paul staggers back. I fling my arms around Will. He bends his head, whispers in my ear:

"Get the knife."

A split second later, Paul is dragging me off him, pushing Will away. He is angry now, his breathing fast and furious. He yanks me over to Zack, who is nearest. He forces me down, to my knees, then kneels beside me. He shoves the knife into my hand, keeping his own, gloved hand on top of mine.

"When the teacher is ready, the student will appear," he murmurs.

I'm barely listening. My throat is dry.

"It's quickest if you cut the jugular," Paul instructs. "Tip the head back, then side to side. He won't feel a thing."

My fingers curl around the metal handle. It's warm from being in his hand. I can't stop shaking. I shuffle closer to Zack. His skin is so smooth and clear. The thought that I have the power to slice it open sends terrifying shivers through my whole body. I glance at Paul. He is tense with anticipation, those dark eyes fixed on me. Will is several meters away, on his knees, watching.

"I'm ready," I say. Rain begins to fall. The sound fills the air.

"Good."

I tighten my grip on the knife and reach for Zack's head. I tip it back and he moans gently. His hair is soft in my hands, already damp from the rain. I hold the knife in position over his throat. One slip now . . . Oh God, I'm so close. Paul loosens his grip just a little. He wants me to choose this, to take responsibility, to make the cut.

My hand trembles. I fill with hate and fury. It's now. It has to be now.

Paul crouches right next to me. I am looking down at Zack, but I still can feel the heat from Paul's body, his air of expectation.

Fast, I pull my arm across my body, away from Paul. He loses his hold on the knife. Lunges for it. I whip it out of the way and it flashes, bright, before my eyes. With a roar I bring it down, all my body weight behind it. I plunge it through Paul's plastic overalls, into his belly.

He yells with pain. Shock fills his eyes. He reels back. I cling on to the knife. It slides out of him. In a split second I take in the blood that oozes out onto the white of his plastic suit. He doubles over and I whip round.

Will is right there. He turns, holding out his bound wrists. I fumble with the knife, trying to slice through the rope. Rain patters on my face. Hands grab me from behind. I turn. The knife falls from my hand, clattering onto the rock. Paul looms over me. He raises his hand. A second later he hits me across the side of the head. I crash to the ground, lights flashing before my eyes.

Paul staggers over me, holding his belly with one hand. He falls to the ground beside me. He is panting, bleeding, furious.

"You bitch," he says. "You fucking bitch."

I try to rise up, but he is stronger. He pushes me down, flat on my back. And suddenly he is on top of me, his weight bearing down, his knee heavy into my belly, his free hand forcing my shoulder back. Pain sears through me.

I scream.

His hands are around my throat, squeezing the air out of me. The scream dies on my lips. He's going to kill me. And then he will kill my family. Images flash through my mind. Zack wrapping his small arms about my neck, his breath smelling of chocolate, Hannah's fingers trailing over her makeup bag on the kitchen table. I see Will on the day she was born, his smile of love and pride and relief that the long labor is over and we are safe. I see Dad's mouth tremble as he walks away from Kara's body. I see Mum's gentle eyes. I see Julia, her hair falling over her face as she laughs. And I see Kara, my little sister, running after me as I walk to school, her blond hair tied neatly in plaits, her soft eyes full of an adoration I didn't want or understand until it was too late.

"You can't kill that," I whisper. But my words make no sound. Blackness flickers around my vision. I am desperate to breathe.

From the distance comes a roar. Paul moves. Is moved. His weight is suddenly off me. Will has the knife. He is fighting Paul. They roll across the rock. I get to my knees. Will holds the knife, forcing it toward Paul's chest. Paul's hand scrabbles at the knife. Seizes it.

"No!" I lurch toward them. Paul swipes with the knife. Misses. Again, he brings the blade down. He's aiming for Will's face, but Will catches his arm. Twists it. I reach them and throw my weight against Paul's arm too. He struggles. But together we're too strong. The knife plunges down, into Paul's chest. The force of the movement pushes him over the cliff.

With a roar, he tumbles down, down.

Then silence.

Less than an hour later, and everything I have been through already feels like a dream. Even more so when the police sirens signal the arrival of cars and an ambulance and a kind paramedic who reassures me the children are unconscious but breathing and wraps me in a foil blanket and tends to the cut on the side of my head. Nothing feels real.

After Paul fell, Will scrambled a little way down the cliff to see where he was, but there was no sign of him. Logically we know he must have fallen into the sea. He was badly injured in the chest, and if the knife wound and the fall didn't kill him, the rocks or the current probably did. And yet . . . I can't stop thinking about the silver box and the way it felt. I can't stop thinking about Paul's dark eyes.

318

We moved the children into the little hut to provide some shelter from the wind. As dawn split the sky with pink light, Will searched our car for the keys, but they were gone. As Will said, they were probably in Paul's pocket, but again, the fact that he has not been found leaves me fearful that he is planning on coming back, that if he still has means to take our car, he still has power over us. I know that's illogical, but I can't help it, just as I can't stop shivering.

At least Will found our phones in the car, along with a bag containing several disposable plastic suits, and a bottle of a clear liquid that I'm certain will prove to be more GHB, the drug Paul gave us all earlier. Will called for the police and an ambulance. Together we stood over our children, waiting.

Now, in the hospital, we have been examined by doctors and interviewed separately by the police and, two hours after we arrived, we have been allowed back into the room where our children lie sleeping. The medical staff say both of them will wake up properly soon. And so Will and I watch and wait.

We haven't touched since I flung myself at him and he told me to get Paul's knife. You would think after everything we have just been through, that we would hold each other and not let go, but our shared purpose, survival, has gone, and I do not know what to say to him.

Part of this is Will himself. He is angry, and trying not to show just how furious in front of me. So angry, that I suspect he is scaring himself. He paces up and down the hospital room, glancing at the kids, then looking up at the clock. After ten or so minutes, he goes to fetch coffee.

"Will?" I say, following him outside into the corridor.

He turns to me, his eyes blazing.

"You did what you could," I say.

He nods. "It's just, when I think about how close he came . . ." Will shudders.

"I know." I hesitate. This is not the time for us to talk, but I can't leave these words unsaid any longer. "Paul told me Leo lied about you being with Catrina," I say.

Will looks at me.

319

"They wanted to distract me from looking into Julia's death, they knew you'd been unfaithful before. . . ." I turn away, feeling my cheeks burn. "I'm sorry I didn't trust you." My voice is a whisper. "I'm sorry you've had to live with me not trusting you for so long."

There's a long pause. A nurse passes, her cart of drugs rattling against the linoleum floor.

Will takes my hand. "You have to trust me now," he says, his voice low and sad. "It's . . . I know I made a mistake six years ago, and I understand why it's hard to move on, but if we can't do that, then we don't have anything."

"We have them." I point to the room where Hannah and Zack are sleeping.

"You know what I mean."

I nod. "Then we have to be honest," I say.

"Okay." Will pauses. "If you want the truth, here it is: When I went to Geneva, Catrina did flirt with me. She made it clear we could start things up again. I made it clear I didn't want that."

I swallow hard. "Were you tempted?"

Will meets my gaze. "For a few seconds. Were you tempted with Damian?"

I pause, remembering our bus stop kiss. "For a few seconds," I say.

We look at each other. "There are always going to be those times," Will says.

"I know."

And in that moment, I accept the past.

Another hour passes. Zack wakes, groggy and with a headache, but also hungry. Remarkably he seems largely untraumatized by the whole experience, but then, as the doctors point out, he was drugged for most of the night and has no memory of what he went through. Once we have reassured him that Paul has gone, he regains his equilibrium, polishing off two rounds of toast and a glass of milk and charming all the nurses who pass his way.

Hannah takes longer to awaken and, when she does, shakes with fear at her memories of the past night. Paul didn't rape her physically, but he whispered filth into her ear, terrorizing her. I fill with a new hatred for this man who has betrayed our friendship and violated my family in the worst ways possible. But my fury does Hannah no good. I try to hide it, just as Will tries to conceal his own anger, and we comfort our daughter as best we can.

We have each been interviewed by the police again. Piecing the information I have together, I learn that Leo has confessed to his lie about Will's affair but claims complete ignorance over Paul's true nature and actions. The same is true of Alexa Carling. Since being interviewed by the police, she has fled to the other end of the country, far away from Devon gossip.

I look at my own children and wonder how anyone could survive knowing that their own flesh and blood was capable of so much cruelty and violence.

I tell my mother that Paul was Kara's killer, that he confessed it to me before he fell from the cliff. She takes the news with her usual stoicism. After all, as she says, the knowledge won't bring Kara back. Paul didn't kill only Kara. The police have found that silver box—and his diary—and are currently tracing the contents to other victims.

In contrast to my own mother, Joanie has taken the news that Julia was murdered—and by someone actually present at the funeral—very badly. At least this is what I hear from Robbie. Joanie won't speak to me herself, having apparently decided that Will's return of Julia's ring is absolute confirmation that I must have stolen it—and that we're using Hannah as a smoke screen.

Robbie himself calls me on a daily basis for three days until I finally get so furious with his refusal to listen to my own requests for space that I pass the phone to Will, who tells him to fuck off and leave me alone.

It works. Not just with Robbie. In some way, it brings Will and me closer together again. He goes with me to Damian's funeral the following week, a sad affair featuring a large, weeping family and many ex-girlfriends. I take Julia's picture and leave it beside his grave. It's hard to understand other people and their relationships, but I believe they did love each other and in some romantic part of my mind, I allow myself to believe that they are together now.

That night Paul's body is washed up along the coast and my fears about evil spirits begin to ease. The following day Will officially resigns from Harbury Media. He hasn't spoken to Leo. Nobody has. He and Martha have gone to ground in their designer home; by all accounts Leo is a broken man. He has been arrested—though not charged—by the police for his part in shielding Paul and hasn't been seen in the office since the night Paul died. Becky is avoiding everyone too. She has stayed out in Spain, claiming no knowledge of Paul's hidden life. According to her, there weren't any problems in their marriage. So Paul even lied about that. I can't bring myself to call her, and she doesn't contact me either. Whatever she says, and the police are clearly convinced, I can't believe she can possibly have lived with Paul for all those years and not at least suspected what he was up to.

His parents are a different story. Like his friends, they would have been easier to fool. I try to imagine how Leo and Alexa must feel: Paul not only dead but also revealed as a vicious killer. At first I am angry with Leo for lying to me. Then I start wondering how far I would go to protect Zack or Hannah. I was prepared to kill for them that night on the cliff. Without question or hesitation. So, in spite of my anger, I pity Leo. There's a lot of speculation about what will happen to Harbury Media. Some of the senior guys are contemplating a management buyout, but Will wants to do something new, to move on.

I am thrilled with his decision and we spend hours talking about the future, contemplating every possible avenue, from traveling around South America for six months to moving to London, where the opportunities for jobs are greater. Will is veering toward setting up on his own. To be honest, I don't mind what he does, I just love the fact that he is talking to me like never before, that we are happier than we have been for years. We make love, late at night or first thing in the morning, as we did before the kids. We say how much we love each other.

Most of all, I tell him I trust him. And I do.

Another few days pass. We receive confirmation there will be no charges brought against us, no trial. And although neither of us really thought we would be prosecuted over Paul's death, the news is still a huge relief.

My thoughts turn more and more to Julia. I am proud that I kept faith with her, refusing to accept that she killed herself. And yet the thought nags away at me that, if I hadn't tried to find out the truth, Damian would still be alive and my children wouldn't have been put through the horror of that night on the cliff.

And it will have lasting consequences. Not, perhaps, with Zack. After the first few days, he stopped talking about "scary Paul," and, since then, Will has spent a lot of time playing football with him out in the park, giving him time and attention that Zack has soaked up. Hannah, on the other hand, has turned into an anxious shadow of her former self. She can't bear to be alone, trailing me around the house and insisting that I sit with her until she falls asleep every night.

Be careful what you wish for, the saying goes. Well, my desire to have my little girl back has been granted, but at a terrible cost. I never thought I would miss Hannah being rude and difficult, but now, as she trembles with fear when the door bangs or waits anxiously outside the bathroom for me to come out, I can't help but wish for her old self to reappear. The doctors say that with consistent care and support, she will be all right, but I can't help but fret that what she went through will scar her forever.

At least she doesn't have to worry about Will and me.

Another week passes and the weather grows hotter. We have booked a last-minute beach vacation to Portugal and leave later this morning. I wake early and finish off the last bits of packing, then wander into Will's office to find him poring over his laptop, researching limited company tax law. Zack putters around him, playing with a couple of action figures, content just to be near his dad. I peer into Hannah's room. She is still asleep, her blond hair strewn over her pillow, her body starfished on the bed. She will wake in an hour or two, I know, and immediately seek me out.

I take advantage of my free time to clear out the fridge, then I go around the house, gathering up dirty laundry. I have bought a new camera. A good model. And I'm planning on taking pictures throughout our trip, so I need a variety of lenses and some other bits and pieces. I'm so busy checking on all of these that I don't see the missed call on my cell phone for nearly an hour. I don't recognize the number, but they've left a voice message:

"Hi, Olivia, it's Brooke. Sorry it's taken a bit longer than I expected—we've had a few, er, technical problems here—but I have the 'report' you ordered and I'd love to meet up to discuss. If I don't hear back, I'll try again a bit later. I wanted to catch you, as I know you're going on holiday this morning, so . . . anyway . . . speak then, bye."

I frown, for a second I have no idea who Brooke is, or what on earth she's talking about. Then in a flash I remember my meeting at Honey Hearts, how I told Alexa Carling about Will, how I hired Brooke to entrap him. *Oh, shit.* I'd completely forgotten about it. I listen to the message again. Brooke's voice is low and gravelly but there's a lightness—something arch—in her tone. I remember how I looked at her and wondered how any man could resist her. She's talking about the "report," which presumably means she must have engineered a meeting with Will at some point in the past week or so. . . . I can't imagine when, he certainly hasn't said anything. And yet she knows about our holiday, that we're leaving this morning. . . .

My heart pounds as I pace up and down the kitchen. How could I have forgotten about this? For a moment I'm staggered that Alexa Carling didn't realize who I was and query me turning up at Honey Hearts. Then I remember the reports I've read about Paul's mother fleeing Exeter. Alexa Carling has been in hiding in another part of the country since the day after I met Brooke at the Honey Hearts office. There's no reason why Brooke should connect the Olivia Small who hired her with the Livy Jackson who was nearly killed by Alexa's son. That's if she even knows the name Livy Jackson. Thanks to the children being minors, all our names and pictures have, mercifully, been kept out of the press.

Upstairs I can hear Will and Zack laughing about something. The

324

bathroom door creaks open, then shuts. That will be Hannah. She'll be down here looking for me as soon as she's finished.

I don't have much time to decide what to do. I listen to the voice mail again: "I have the report you ordered."

I don't need a report. I just need to know if my husband flirted, asked for her number, boasted about any affairs, agreed to meet her again.

As I lay my cell phone on the counter it rings. It's her. It's Brooke.

My finger hovers over the accept button. *Shit. Shit. Shit.*

I trust Will, I do. But I *have* to know.

Then you don't trust him at all, honeypie, Julia's voice sounds in my head.

Another ring.

Footsteps pad across the landing. I pick up the phone. I need to know.

I put it down. No, I don't. I trust my husband—and if I speak to Brooke, then I break that trust, because if she tells me something good, I can't let Will know I tested him, and if it's bad news, I will have to confront him. Either way, *I'll* know I wasn't honest.

The phone rings a third time.

And yet how can I not know at all?

"Mum?" Hannah calls out, her voice quavering and full of fear. And my head clears. There's only one possible choice.

Only one future.

"Down here, sweetheart."

I pick up the phone. "Hello."

"Olivia?" Brooke's tone professional and confiding. "I saw your husband last night. I thought you'd want to know."

My mind reels. Last night? How? Will was home all day. He went out for only an hour or two yesterday evening. A drink with Mike from work, he'd said.

"Olivia, if now isn't a good time, we can meet in person. I'm just aware you're heading off on holiday in a couple of hours, so—"

"*Will* told you that?"

"Yes, I approached him in the pub where he was drinking. I—"

"Stop." I take a deep breath. "You see, the thing is, Brooke, I'm very sorry to have wasted your time, but I don't want to take things any further."

Silence.

"You mean you don't even want to know what your husband said to me?" Brooke sounds bewildered. "What he did when I approached him?"

I hesitate. The truth is that I *do* want to know. Very much. But what good will it do?

I couldn't leave Will right now, even if he proved to have a string of lovers. Hannah needs us to be together for the foreseeable future. Zack too.

Anyway, if Will wants to have an affair, a Honey Hearts investigation won't stop him. And if he doesn't, then an investigation isn't needed in the first place.

"Are you still there?" Brooke says, a note of impatience creeping into her voice.

"Yes." I try to work out what to say to her, how to express my feelings. The truth is that Will's affair with Catrina six years ago probably means I won't ever feel completely certain that he will always be faithful. But so what? People you think are friends can betray you. And people you love can die, long before their time. There is no certainty in life.

Except that's not quite right either. I know Will loves me. I know he loves us, his family. I see him in my mind's eye, kneeling on the cliff top, offering his own life if Paul would spare the rest of us.

"Trust that," I murmur under my breath.

"Sorry?" Brooke says. "What did you say?"

"Actually, Brooke, I was just saying good-bye."

I smile as Hannah wanders into the room. Her face is pale and there are dark shadows under her eyes. And I put down the phone so that my arms are free to wrap around my daughter, keeping her safe, chasing the darkness away.